PENGUIN BOOKS

THE PORTABLE ARTHUR MILLER

Each volume in The Viking Portable Library either presents a representative selection from the works of a single outstanding writer or offers a comprehensive anthology on a special subject. Averaging 700 pages in length and designed for compactness and readability, these books fill a need not met by other compilations. All are edited by distinguished authorities, who have written introductory essays and included much other helpful material.

"The Viking Portables have done more for good reading and good writers than anything that has come along since I can remember."
—Arthur Mizener

Harold Clurman, an internationally known stage director and former executive consultant for the Repertory Theater of Lincoln Center for the Performing Arts, has previously published *Lies Like Truth: Theatre Essays and Reviews.*

Other volumes in
THE VIKING PORTABLE LIBRARY

THE PORTABLE

Arthur Miller

Edited, and with an Introduction, by

HAROLD CLURMAN

PENGUIN BOOKS

Penguin Books Ltd, Harmondsworth,
Middlesex, England
Penguin Books, 40 West 23rd Street,
New York, New York 10010, U.S.A.
Penguin Books Australia Ltd, Ringwood,
Victoria, Australia
Penguin Books Canada Limited, 2801 John Street,
Markham, Ontario, Canada L3R 1B4
Penguin Books (N.Z.) Ltd, 182–190 Wairau Road
Auckland 10, New Zealand

First published in the United States of America
by The Viking Press 1971
Reprinted 1971, 1972, 1973, 1974, 1975, 1976
Published in Penguin Books 1977
Reprinted 1980, 1982, 1983, 1984, 1985

LIBRARY OF CONGRESS CATALOGING IN PUBLICATION DATA
Miller, Arthur, 1915–
The portable Arthur Miller.
I. Title.
[PS3525.I5156A6 1977]   812'.5'2   76–47606
ISBN 0 14 015.071 4 (pbk.)

Printed in the United States of America by
Kingsport Press, Inc., Kingsport, Tennessee
Set in Linotype Times Roman

Contents

Biographical Notes

There can be no doubt at this point in our literary and theatrical history as to Arthur Miller's position in it. Among the playwrights since the emergence of Eugene O'Neill only Lillian Hellman, Clifford Odets, and Tennessee Williams are at all comparable to him. Hellman's and Odets's writing does not possess so wide a formal range, nor has it extended over so long a period. Only Williams has been more prolific. Miller is the author of nine plays, a screenplay, numerous short stories and essays, a novel, occasional poems, reportage, and, most recently, commentary on a trip to the Soviet Union which accompanies Inge Morath's photographs assembled under the title *In Russia. Death of a Salesman,* which won the Pulitzer Prize in drama in 1949, has been produced in virtually every one of the world's capitals and has been read in book form by several million people who have never seen it performed—unusual for a contemporary play.

When he was asked recently in what way his plays were related to the events of his life, Miller replied, "In a sense all my plays are autobiographical." The artist creates his biography through his work even as the events of his life serve to shape him.

He was born on 112th Street in Manhattan on October 17, 1915. He is one of three children. He has an elder brother in business, a sister on the stage. The Millers were unequivocally middle-class and Jewish. His mother, no longer living, was born in the United States; his father, a manufacturer of women's coats, was born in what before the First World War was part of the Austro-Hungarian empire. Until the Depression of the 1930s the Millers were a moderately well-to-do family. Arthur attended grammar school in Harlem and went to high school in Brooklyn.

By the time he finished high school, his parents could no longer afford to send him to college. His grades were not sufficiently high to qualify him for entry into the school of his choice, the University of Michigan. He found two ways out of this dilemma. He got himself a job in a warehouse on Tenth Avenue and 60th Street as a "loader" and shipping clerk, and saved a sum sufficient to pay his tuition. He also wrote a letter to the president of the university and asked for a chance to prove his merit within the first year of his studies. If he failed to distinguish himself he would quit. He did very well and stayed on to take his degree of Bachelor of Arts in 1938.

In his boyhood Arthur was neither particularly bright nor very well read. He was a baseball fan. He began to read while working at the warehouse. He is probably the only man who ever read through *War and Peace* entirely on the subway, standing up. At college he also began to write—plays. Several of them were awarded the University of Michigan's Jule and Avery Hopwood prizes. One of them won a prize of $1250 given by the Theatre Guild's Bureau of New Plays. With money from these prizes and $22.77 a week from the Federal Theatre Project, Miller was able to support himself during the early years of his career. He was living at Patchogue, Long Island, at the time and had to check in every day at the project office in Manhattan, fifty-seven miles away, to collect his wage. He wrote a play about Montezuma which was submitted to the Group Theatre, as well as to others, no doubt, and which the editor of the present volume, then the Group

Theatre's Managing Director, found several years later in his files—unread!

In 1944, a diary Miller had kept while visiting Army camps in the United States, researching for a film, *The Story of G.I. Joe* (the war life of the journalist Ernie Pyle), was published under the title *Situation Normal.* In 1945, as a reaction to the activities of a fascist organization known as the Christian Front, Miller wrote his only novel, *Focus,* which attracted considerable attention. Its subject was anti-Semitism.

Also in 1944 came the production of Miller's first play in the professional theatre, *The Man Who Had All the Luck,* which had no luck at all: there were only four performances. Still, Miller was launched! One critic, Burton Rascoe, recognized a potentially powerful playwright. More important, several producers, including myself, got in touch with Miller, requesting him to submit his next play. That was *All My Sons,* which was produced by Harold Clurman, Elia Kazan, and Walter Fried on January 29, 1947. It was a box-office success and was voted the Best Play of the Season by the Drama Critics' Circle. The dates and circumstances of his other plays will be found in the Introduction.

Along with his life as a playwright, Miller has been an engaged public figure. He has lectured widely, written articles on the theatre and its relation to world affairs, and participated in liberal movements of the day. In 1956, when he appeared before the House Un-American Activities Committee, he refused to name people who had attended a meeting to which he had been invited as a guest, some of whom he surmised were members of the Communist Party. On this account he was convicted of contempt of Congress in 1957, a conviction which was reversed by the Supreme Court in 1958. In 1965 Miller was elected international president of P.E.N., the worldwide society of poets and playwrights, essayists and editors, novelists and nonfiction writers. Though nonpolitical by its charter, P.E.N. was momentarily torn by conflicting national interests. His presidency was so successful in the causes of international understanding through literature and of freedom for writers everywhere that he was unanimously elected to a second term.

Arthur Miller has been married three times. His first marriage—to Mary Slattery, a sometime social worker—took place in 1940. Two children, a boy and a girl, were born of this marriage, which ended in divorce in 1956. His second marriage took place the same year, to Marilyn Monroe, the actress. They were divorced in 1960. In 1962 he married the photographer Inge Morath, Austrian-born and educated in France and Germany, where she had lived through the Hitler regime and the war. A daughter was born of this union. The Millers now live in a country place in Connecticut.

—H.C.

June 1970

Editor's Introduction

Reading Arthur Miller's plays and stories in sequence reminded me of an anecdote I heard told about Einstein. A reporter interviewing him asked if any "new ideas" had occurred to him lately. "You know," Einstein answered, "one has only one or two ideas in a lifetime."

There is considerable variety in Miller's work but, viewing it as a body, we soon come to discern its essential unity. All his ideas are parts of one Idea. This does not make his writing "ideological," nor does it render it monotonous. One test of an artist's excellence is the degree to which he is capable of giving his idea constantly renewed or enriched embodiment.

If we follow Miller's career from the reportage of *Situation Normal,* written in 1944 when he was twenty-eight, and his only novel, *Focus,* written a year later, to his most recently produced full-length play, *The Price* (1968), we are struck by the wide range in subject matter which his idea assumes. We may also observe how the theme in one play or book becomes the seed of still another. Each new work may be likened to a function or an organ of the growing corpus.

The incident which opens *Focus* resembles the point of departure in Camus' *The Fall,* written eleven years after Miller's book. In *The Fall* a respected lawyer hears the splash of a body as it strikes the Seine. He does not turn back to find out if a woman he has just seen as he was crossing the bridge has attempted suicide and what he might do about it.

This momentary lapse of conscience causes a crisis of self-examination which turns to self-accusation. In the Miller novel a humdrum citizen asleep in bed one night is awakened by the agonized cry of a woman in the street calling, "Police! Police!" He rationalizes his failure in responsive action and goes back to sleep, apparently forgetting all about the momentary disturbance. But later, under very different circumstances, when his own safety is threatened, the woman's wild appeal for help resounds in his consciousness and prods him into an awareness of his connection with it.

We are all part of one another; all responsible to one another. The responsibility originates on the simplest, almost animal level: our immediate kin. But this vital attachment to the family—father, mother, children, brothers and sisters—is germinal and with the maturing of the person extends beyond its initial source.

In *Situation Normal* (Miller's first published book) there is the "story" of Watson, a soldier who is under close observation while a candidate in officers' training after a period of efficient and brave service in Japan. What troubles him is that his backwardness in the required mathematics may lead to his rejection for a commission as an officer. This would seem to him like a betrayal of his company companions, to whom he has become deeply attached. (The expression of this bond among "brother" combatants in the Army is echoed in a speech in *All My Sons*.)

On reflection about Watson's "case," Miller asks himself to what sort of folk Watson will feel similarly devoted when he returns to civilian life. Will that interdependence, that strength which comes from helping to sustain and being sustained by a group such as the Army company, be found again in the postwar world? Miller hopes that this may be so, but his fear that the contrary may be true is apparent in the quasi-patriotic concluding pages of his report.

Basic elements of Miller's feeling may be deduced from these two instances: a sense of responsibility for our fellow creatures, and belief in the need for a common goal which validates the act of responsibility. Irresponsibility, in Miller's view, is the root of sin. Without profoundly nurtured belief, the concept of responsibility becomes null and void.

I speak of "sin." It is an unfashionable word nowadays and Miller rarely uses it. He is, as we shall see, sufficiently imbued with the skepticism of modern thought to shy away from the presumptions implicit in it. But that Miller is willy-nilly a moralist—one who believes he knows what sin and evil are—is inescapable.

Along with the moral conflict—one of the attributes that give Miller's work its dramatic tension—we find, too, an ever-increasing awareness that there is arrogance and even menace inherent in the moralist's posture. Sue Bayliss, the doctor's wife in *All My Sons* (Miller's first successful play), says of its "hero," "Chris makes people want to be better than it's possible to be." When asked, "Is that bad?" she flashes back with "I resent living next door to the Holy Family. It makes me look like a bum." Sue's quite understandable challenge is keenly felt by Miller himself. Even though in *All My Sons* he brings wrath to bear on the sinner, it is mitigated by the fact that the sinner in this case may possibly have recognized his misdeed and punished himself for it. But I venture to suggest that it is the moral stance in Miller, with its seemingly punitive bent, which causes a certain resistance to his work in some quarters.

More often than not the moralist posits a god. God is the father. The father in Miller's work is a recurrent figure regarded with awe, devotion, love, even when he is proved lamentably fallible and when submission to him becomes painfully questionable. The father is a godhead because he is the giver and support of life; he is expected to serve as an example of proper conduct, of *good*. He therefore inspires and confirms *belief*, informing all our most significant actions, and fosters our reason for living. He gives identity and coherence to our being, creates value.

"A father is a father," the hard-pressed and culpable Joe

Keller shouts in *All My Sons* and defends his malfeasance perpetrated on behalf of his family. To which his wife replies, referring to their son, Chris, "It doesn't excuse it that you did it for the family." Keller counters with, "It's got to excuse it." Then the mother says, "There's something bigger than the family' to him." Keller retorts, "Nothing is bigger." The mother again: "There is to him." And we gather that Miller believes this too.

In the crucial confrontation with his father, Chris reveals himself (and Miller) by exclaiming, "I know you're no worse than most men but I thought you were better. I never saw you as a man. I saw you as a father." In this he has moved beyond the realm of common sense and speaks of fatherhood in a religious sense.

The family is pivotal, but beyond the family is the family of mankind. The family has its extension in the community, the social body—the *polis,* as it was once named. Here, then, is where Miller locates the focus of responsibility. This may become an evasion where "society" is so generalized a concept as to be dehumanized, faceless. God, whether it be the head of the family or the *polis,* cannot be reified. Miller does not write what in the 1930s we dubbed "social plays." Our relation to society is particularized in immediate and close contact with neighboring individuals.

Connection with others—the need to feel others as part of ourselves and ourselves as part of them—is not an intellectual matter. It is an impulse native to all of us, an almost universally recognized intuition, indeed a fact. We call people without it "sick." Yet we see this prime impulse constantly being impeded and crippled. Miller's work is largely devoted to the dramatization and depiction of the forces that induce impediments to responsibility—which is based on mutuality. Like all moralists, he seeks to expose the sin.

Everywhere today, and most glaringly in America, what diverts us from our responsibilities is the heartless functionalism of the marketplace, of *practicality.* "The cats in the alley are practical," Chris protests. "This is a zoo, a zoo!"

Practicality too has its god: it is success. In Miller's first and now out-of-print play, *The Man Who Had All the Luck* (produced in 1944), the central figure is a boy who fears success when it is not founded on work or merit. In that play there is a father who presses his son toward success, regardless of its origins. Five years later the destructive role played by the consecration of or fixation on success (shall we call it *Dementia Americana?*) was to be given its amplest and most affecting expression in *Death of a Salesman.*

Willy Loman believes wholeheartedly in the operative ideal of his fellow countrymen. Being a kindly man, he speaks not of success so much as of being "well liked." The crass vibrations implied in the more general term take on an aspect of smiling benevolence. He has forsworn his modest gift for carpentry to become a salesman because it promises a brighter future of ease and affluence. By turning away from himself he becomes an utterly confused person. He is now only half a man, a blind man, always in contradiction to himself, even to the smallest details of his existence. He dreams the American legend—the brother who walked into the jungle and when he was twenty-one came out of it rich. He sees everything in its light: the boss's good will, the business contacts, advertisements, publicity, bigness, gladhanding, being "impressive." He has misplaced and can no longer recognize his own reality.

So Willy Loman wreaks havoc on his own life and on that of his sons. The blight of his own confusion is visited upon them. Unaware of what warped his mind and behavior, he commits suicide in the conviction that a legacy of twenty thousand dollars is all that is needed to save his beloved but almost equally damaged offspring. This may not be "tragic," but such distorted thinking maims a very great number of folk in the world today.

Dramatically absorbing in itself, *The Crucible* may be viewed as a transitional piece if we consider it in the context of Miller's later development. Using a historical subject, the play shows how a materialistically instigated social trauma may fester into a sadistic fever to which an entire community suc-cumbs. It leads it to superstitious hysteria and to the abandon-ment of all moral scruple and intelligence. (A similar theme stimulated Miller to undertake the adaptation of Ibsen's *An Enemy of the People.*) The fear and frenzy of the McCarthy era is plainly the fire which ignited *The Crucible.* "Is the accuser always holy?" is its key line. But there is something more to the play than "propaganda."

It contains two features which time and further experience magnified. One of them has to do with marital relationships. There is a certain Puritan coldness in Elizabeth, *The Crucible*'s heroine. She forgets nothing, and forgiveness comes hard to her. Her husband, Proctor, admonishes, "Learn charity, woman." Perhaps it is this forbidding quality in her which has betrayed him into a momentary adultery. It is a fall from grace in his eyes. Despite his plea for compassion, he finds it difficult to forgive himself. "The magistrate sits in your heart that judges you," she says. "I never thought you but a good man, only somewhat bewildered." She is right, and the web of their intimate struggle with each other anticipates some of the marital complexities in the thematic material of *After the Fall.*

A note first struck in *All My Sons* is developed in *The Cruci-ble,* and in another vein in *Incident at Vichy* and again in *The Price,* where it leads to a sort of impasse. It may be isolated in a phrase from *All My Sons* in which a character refers to "the star of one's honesty." But something more than "honesty" is involved. Proctor chooses to die in *The Crucible* rather than live and besmirch his "name." Von Berg in *Vichy* chooses to face punishment (possibly death) to save a man he hardly knows. Victor Franz chooses to give up his education to aid his fault-ridden father. Apelike Tony Calabrese in the short story "Fitter's Night" decides to risk his neck doing a job for which there is neither obligation nor recompense. What is manifest in all these instances is a sort of gratuitous heroism—determinations without "rational" imperative. Even the "mixed-up" and not at all admirable Eddie Carbone in *A*

View from the Bridge pleads to preserve his "name" (or honor) and virtually commits suicide because this is not granted to him. It is just this sort of drive in men, almost as integral to them as the sheer animal impulse to self-preservation, in which Miller finds the glory as much as the mystery of life.

A moralist stops at nothing in his pursuit of virtue. If he is honest he is driven to sit in judgment upon himself. Pressed by this self-induced compulsion, he can hardly forbear from self-accusation and self-condemnation. To recover from what must surely prove a debilitating or destructive sense of guilt, he gropes toward self-rehabilitation. This process is most vividly traced in *After the Fall.*

That there is an autobiographical base to this drama is undeniable, but to enlarge upon it is to miss the play itself. What anyone who carefully studies *After the Fall* must recognize is that Miller does not exculpate his *alter ego,* Quentin. "I don't know if I have lived in good faith," he confesses. He examines the evidence that has aroused his suspicion.

His mother planted in him the notion that he would be a bright star, "a light in the world." His successful career as a liberal lawyer seemed to substantiate the prophecy. He became convinced of being in the right and of his ability to help the less favored, even to guide them. His failures in marriage undermined the foundations of his self-esteem. He begins to doubt the subjective authenticity of all his former benefactions. His first wife, whom he reproaches for being hard, may simply be a reflection of his own moral rigor. But after his second wife accuses him of not knowing how to relate to a woman, he remembers that this is exactly what his first wife had said.

Quentin's conceit has led him to believe he could shape Maggie's (the second wife's) innocent, trusting, tormented soul and transform it to splendor. The girl is a victim both of her unwholesome background and of the image of herself created by the gaudy environment into which she has been promoted. Torn and wounded by the enormousness of his ambition in regard to her, Quentin comes to realize that his noble design may have been little more than the mask of his sensual desire and, much worse, a bent toward power. The stern humanist he believed himself to be, the judge and scold of others, the apostle of justice, lacks the gift of love. And where love is missing, the urge to power always steps in.

There was a flaw, he now burningly suspects, in all his attitudes. His principles so stanchly maintained, so haughtily proclaimed, were not altogether sound—that is, organic to his nature. Abstract principles are delusive. That is why he turns for sustenance to the German woman, whose knowledge of the Nazi horror is personal. She understands its complexity, its relevance to all our blindness and failures. It is her "uncertainty," the absence of spiritual arrogance, he now blesses. She doesn't seem to be looking, he says, for some "goddamned moral victory." Recognizing that the lofty posture of his earlier days was a species of hypocrisy, he is impelled to seek a new direction. "To admit what you see," he muses, "endangers principles."

Yet he cannot live without them. "I can't be a separate person!" he exclaims, still another formulation of Miller's root idea. This very need for connection makes him understand his tie with the evil he abhors. The Nazis were killers, but we are all, to some degree, killers. All of us, through lack of self-knowledge, have contributed to the building of concentration camps and the gas chambers, those monuments of human depravity.

How may we resolve this appalling contradiction? We must recognize the quotient of the murderous within ourselves, the base egotism which lingers in all but the saintly; it is imperative that we strive with all our forces to master it, no matter how difficult this may be. This in the end can be accomplished only through the fortitude of love, which is also innate in us. Thus Quentin has reason to hope that he will cast off the garment of a spurious sanctity, to go forward again with a consciousness of his own all too human fallibility

Surviving this test of conscience without nihilistic bitterness, achieving skepticism without its becoming the excuse for a pretentious or cynical passivity, Miller writes a stark morality play, *Incident at Vichy*. The play is not just another dramatization of the Hitler holocaust; it is a fresh statement of the main theme in nearly all his previous plays, whether they deal with the crime of delation, as in *A View from the Bridge,* or with co-operation among poor folk, as in *A Memory of Two Mondays.*

The spokesman in *A View* decries the demand for "absolute justice" by saying that "one settles for half and I like it better," which Miller at the time of its writing (1955) was hardly able to do, for then he thought of the "squealer" Eddie Carbone as largely villainous. In *A Memory,* the gentlest of Miller's plays, all the warehouse fellows sense their kinship with their alcoholic comrade broken by the conditions that obtain there, and they try to protect him.

What *Incident at Vichy* reiterates is our proclivity to evade troublesome facts so that confrontation with evil and hence our responsibility for it are avoided. Miller sees in the emergence of Hitler not simply a historical calamity but evidence of the absence of operative ideals, of a truly binding faith everywhere in our time. In such a period "what we used to conceive a human being to be will have no room on this earth'

In this play the ones who stand fast against the prevailing brutalization are the orthodox Jew; the Communist worker (who is mistaken in his interpretation of the situation); the adolescent boy made stanch by his devotion to his mother; the embittered doctor, who finds no alleviation through what we ordinarily term "human nature"; and the Catholic aristocrat, who has few ideas and acts mindlessly, that is, without a reason he might be able to explain or "sensibly" defend. The others are to die abjectly.

A choice is made; and that is freedom. When, as previously noted, Calabrese is asked by the naval captain to undertake the perilous job described in "Fitter's Night," he feels that "for the first time . . it was entirely up to him with no punishment if he said no, nor even a reward if he said yes, gain and loss had collapsed, and whatever was left standing was a favor asked that would profit nobody"—and Calabrese chooses to do it. Here again I am reminded of a character in Camus: in *The Plague,* the doctor who stoically chooses to remain in an infected city and tend to the sick, though he hardly expects to save them by his efforts. There is an inner compulsion in the making of such decisions which is no less real for not having an honored name.

Choice entails a price. It does not come easily where there is no identifiable measure, cash value, or public blessing. There are two brothers in *The Price,* as in several of Miller's plays (emblematic of the tensions within him): one aggressive and lucky, the other loyal and obscure. The first is the more "realistic," the second the somewhat foolish and perhaps defeated. Miller is no longer prone to plead for one against the other. Nowhere else in his work are these opposites so evenly matched or so closely studied as in *The Price.* Both are justified. One has given up "golden" opportunities which might have led to a success equal to that of his more resolutely practical brother. He did so on behalf of a father who was hardly worth the sacrifice. The son speaks of love within the family. But his brother challenges him to ascertain whether there really has been so much love in their home. Who, then, was the "winner"?

Some critics have gone so far as to suggest that in this ambiguity, given the futility of the idealistic brother's choice, we may read a retreat from radical struggle against the "establishment" of Miller's beginnings, a surrender. But if we look closely we see that the failure, the presumably defeated brother, is the play's Victor.

In the final reckoning it is perhaps Solomon, the almost ninety-year-old Jewish furniture dealer, who possesses something like wisdom. His is the existential conclusion that life is enough, provoking laughter as well as tears. Yet even he takes a stand and calls the contestants to account, demands moral

commitment: "What is the matter with you people! . . .
Nothing in the world you believe, nothing you respect—how
can you live? You think that's such a smart thing? That's so
hard, what you're doing? Let me give you a piece advice— it's
not that you can't believe nothing, that's not so hard—it's that
you still got to believe it. *That's* hard. And if you can't do that,
my friend—you're a dead man!"

It is hardly necessary at this point to expatiate on the
fluency and rhythm of Miller's dialogue, coupled with his su-
perb sense of play structure. But there is another aspect of his
writing, less often noted, that bears consideration here.

In describing the setting for *Death of a Salesman*, Miller
speaks of it as "a dream rising out of reality." This may be
equated with his aesthetic aim. His plays are always firmly
planted in specifically rendered environments. (The very color
of the walls in the improvised police station is noted in *Incident at Vichy*.) Yet it would be hasty to set these plays down—
with the possible exception of *All My Sons* and *A Memory of
Two Mondays*—as wholly naturalistic.

"I prize the poetic above all else in the theatre," Miller
writes. An artist's declared intention is not always proof of its
accomplishment. But I believe Miller's plays move toward poetry. I refer not to language but to conception and intensity.
The poetry in Miller's plays and in several of his stories is that
of the impassioned moralist who, as in a parable, seeks to convey not so much a thought as an emotion which goes beyond
the factual material employed. Virtually all the artists who
have devised settings for the Miller plays have been aware of
their transcendence of the naturalistic and have expressed this
awareness through designs of a semi-abstract or symbolic
character.

What is unmistakably convincing and makes Miller's theatre writing hold is its authenticity in respect to the minutiae of
American life. He is a first-rate reporter; he makes the details
of his observation palpable. The description of the Calabrese

assignment in "Fitter's Night" is an admirable instance. There is also excellent descriptive writing in "The Misfits," the story that provided the basis for the screenplay in which Marilyn Monroe and Clark Gable starred. Miller knows our lower middle class as very few other dramatists do. In this he does not strain, as so many other writers do, for comic stage effect. He understands people through his sympathy for them.

Willy Loman is his supreme character creation. Loman is a pathetic fool, but so is Gaev in *The Cherry Orchard.* It does not make the Russian a more notable figure that he apostrophizes a bookcase while Loman extols (or curses) his car. Willy Loman is more recognizable as well as more generally meaningful—to laugh at, commiserate with, or deplore—than Babbitt.

Moralists are usually humorless. There is an abundance of humor in the portrayal of Solomon in *The Price,* both charming and hilarious. In fact, a vein of humor runs through most of Miller's work.

Miller's women are usually shadowy characters, rarely as fully realized as even some of the secondary men. The exceptions are the women in *After the Fall:* the mother, Elsie, Holga. Here too we find the helpless Maggie, one of the most perceptively delineated women in all of American drama. (When she hurls the epithet "Judgey" at Quentin, she delivers the *coup de grâce* to all his pretensions.) Miller values her far more than he does his mouthpiece, Quentin. Maggie is woman, redemptively sensual, intuitive, captivating, tormented and tormenting, the glamour girl as victim, of which our society offers too many examples.

Surprisingly in a dramatist of the urban middle class, there is a remarkable feeling for the outdoors in Miller's writing. This is not merely a yearning, as in various passages of *Salesman,* but something both fresh and eloquent as in "The Misfits." Even the battered car in that story takes on a poetic aura as it rarely does for drivers in the big cities: it is made to seem part of nature. It is alive with the impulse toward movement in the restless American who seeks a home, not just a house. The men in this story, once pioneers, are now "misfits." They don't like to work for wages.

The writer of plays, unlike the novelist, has a medium other than merely the printed word between himself and his audience. His understanding of that medium is obviously a part of his effectiveness. I feel impelled to add a note about Miller's contribution through his presence prior to and during the rehearsal periods of his plays. As the director of national companies of both *All My Sons* and *Death of a Salesman* and as the director of the original production of *Incident at Vichy* at the Repertory Theatre of Lincoln Center—and adviser in the production there of *After the Fall*—I have first-hand evidence.

He is a most meticulous craftsman. Hardly any revisions are demanded of him by his producers because, except for occasional cutting, as in the case of *After the Fall,* his plays are virtually complete in every detail by the time he submits his scripts to them. I remember that some clarifications were requested for *Death of a Salesman.* Miller consented to make them. But when these clarifications were written, the producers acknowledged that they were redundant. No "fixing" had been needed.

Miller is extremely respectful of his producers and directors and, though he is sometimes uncertain or hesitant in the matter of casting actors, he is usually glad to abide by his theatre collaborators' final choice. He likes to read his plays to the acting company, which he does convincingly. He leaves the actual staging—placement and movement of characters, or what in theatre parlance is called "business"—almost entirely to the director. His reflections on the acting and direction are in the main judiciously helpful.

If there is a fault in Miller's theatrical habit, it is his impulse to expatiate to the acting company too elaborately, sometimes too intellectually, on the motivations of his writing. Actors are seldom stimulated as actors by this sort of exegesis. Their insights in performance rarely arise from critical verbalization.

Their intuitions have to be set in motion by indirect sugges-
tions, a process which is a bit of a "mystery" and best left to
the skills of the director.

There can be no question that Miller has a sure sense of
what he has written and what he would like to see conveyed in
the productions of his plays. Still, he always stands ready to be
gratifyingly astonished. Both these attributes are highly appreciated by all who take part in the creation of the completed
stage event.

Of Miller's stories, I have dealt with "Fitter's Night" along
with his plays because I regard it as the most salient and the
one to which no parallel appears in any of the plays. But I
have omitted comment on "I Don't Need You Any More"
(written in 1959) because, while it is in itself an absorbing nar-
rative, its relevance to the meaning of Miller's work as a whole
and to the early years of his life's history is suggested in several of the plays. I am thinking especially of the "strength of
ministry" and a premonition that "he would astonish the
world" inspired by the recurrent mother figure. These are sen-
timents, as we have seen, which haunted him in his mature
days and which he at times felt the need to resist and, in some
measure, came to fear.

The conflict too between a man's moral self-esteem and the
sensual pressures of the old Adam within him, which manifests itself almost covertly in *The Crucible* and pronouncedly
in *After the Fall,* is spelled out in a short story written in 1961,
"The Prophecy." The satisfaction an Italo-American finds in
discovering his roots or generic traditions in Italy, and which
awakens in his companion a sense of his own connection with
his Hebraic ancestry, is the core of "Monte Sant' Angelo"
(1951). "A Search for a Future" reveals still another person
drawing strength from the example of an old man (the narra-
tor's father) who persists, against all reasonable expectation,
to live, to count, to go forward, to be free.

Miller has written extensively about drama. But when an

artist sets down speculations on the art he practices they usually tend to be apologies, defenses, or explications of work which requires none. Miller's work is not in the least recondite: it speaks for itself. To the degree that elucidation may be helpful to readers less well acquainted with Miller's writing, I have attempted to supply it, chiefly in regard to his plays, in this Introduction. But I have purposely omitted his own critical articles from this *Portable Arthur Miller*.

Let me conclude with a word about Miller's role in the world of the theatre today. Europeans prefer Miller to any other American playwright. His plays always register ("get across") in New York, Paris, Berlin, London, Vienna, Rome, Tel Aviv, and almost everywhere that modern drama is performed. He is popular and respected among us, but he means something special to the European.

We are enveloped in a mood of chaotic rage and negation. We are apparently so disappointed in ourselves, so distraught and disgusted by the shortcomings of our civilization, so frustrated by the fact that our "know-how" has left us bereft of a knowledge of how to live, that we seem to resent any affirmative counter-statement. Anything which remotely resembles a generalization, a panacea, an encouraging word, has virtually become taboo, a sop for suckers. Europeans have for a long time now given voice to this mood, with considerable artistic ingenuity and poignancy. (We imitate this with less skill and genuineness.) Now they are sick of their own sickness, because, sick or not, they must live. The basic health of Miller's plays, not to be categorized as "edifying," is something Europeans crave as much as a man in the desert craves water. While they appreciate and applaud Miller's criticism of America, what stirs them subliminally is precisely the vigorous, courageous, optimistic moral concern which is one of the most enduring contributions of our American heritage.

Harold Clurman

May 1970

◧ I ◨

PLAYS

Death of a Salesman

Certain Private Conversations in Two Acts and a Requiem

THE CAST

(in order of appearance)

WILLY LOMAN	Lee J. Cobb
LINDA	Mildred Dunnock
BIFF	Arthur Kennedy
HAPPY	Cameron Mitchell
BERNARD	Don Keefer
THE WOMAN	Winnifred Cushing
CHARLEY	Howard Smith
UNCLE BEN	Thomas Chalmers
HOWARD WAGNER	Alan Hewitt
JENNY	Ann Driscoll
STANLEY	Tom Pedi
MISS FORSYTHE	Constance Ford
LETTA	Hope Cameron

Directed by Elia Kazan; produced by Kermit Bloomgarden and Walter Fried. Opened February 10, 1949, Morosco Theatre, New York City.

The action takes place in Willy Loman's house and yard and in various places he visits in the New York and Boston of today.

Throughout the play, in the stage directions, left and right mean stage left and stage right.

Act One

(AN OVERTURE)

A melody is heard, played upon a flute. It is small and fine, telling of grass and trees and the horizon. The curtain rises.

Before us is the Salesman's house. We are aware of towering, *angular shapes behind it, surrounding it on all sides. Only the blue light of the sky falls upon the house and forestage; the surrounding area shows an angry glow of orange. As more light appears, we see a solid vault of apartment houses around the small, fragile-seeming home. An air of the dream clings to the place, a dream rising out of reality. The kitchen at center seems actual enough, for there is a kitchen table with three chairs, and a refrigerator. But no other fixtures are seen. At the back of the kitchen there is a draped entrance, which leads to the living room. To the right of the kitchen, on a level raised two feet, is a bedroom furnished only with a brass bedstead and a straight chair. On a shelf over the bed a silver athletic trophy stands. A window opens onto the apartment house at the side.*

Behind the kitchen, on a level raised six and a half feet, is the boys' bedroom, at present barely visible. Two beds are dimly seen, and at the back of the room a dormer window. (This bedroom is above the unseen living room.) At the left a stairway curves up to it from the kitchen.

The entire setting is wholly or, in some places, partially transparent. The roof-line of the house is one-dimensional; under and over it we see the apartment buildings. Before the house lies an

apron, curving beyond the forestage into the orchestra. This for-
ward area serves as the back yard as well as the locale of all Wil-
ly's imaginings and of his city scenes. Whenever the action is in
the present the actors observe the imaginary wall-lines, entering
the house only through its door at the left. But in the scenes of the
past these boundaries are broken, and characters enter or leave a
room by stepping "through" a wall onto the forestage.

From the right, Willy Loman, the Salesman, enters, carrying
two large sample cases. The flute plays on. He hears but is not
aware of it. He is past sixty years of age, dressed quietly. Even as
he crosses the stage to the doorway of the house, his exhaustion is
apparent. He unlocks the door, comes into the kitchen, and
thankfully lets his burden down, feeling the soreness of his palms.
A word-sigh escapes his lips—it might be "Oh, boy, oh, boy." He
closes the door, then carries his cases out into the living room,
through the draped kitchen doorway.

Linda, his wife, has stirred in her bed at the right. She gets out
and puts on a robe, listening. Most often jovial, she has developed
an iron repression of her exceptions to Willy's behavior—she
more than loves him, she admires him, as though his mercurial
nature, his temper, his massive dreams and little cruelties, served
her only as sharp reminders of the turbulent longings within him,
longings which she shares but lacks the temperament to utter and
follow to their end.

LINDA, *hearing Willy outside the bedroom, calls with some trep-*
idation: Willy!

WILLY: It's all right. I came back.

LINDA: Why? What happened? *Slight pause.* Did something
happen, Willy?

WILLY: No, nothing happened.

LINDA: You didn't smash the car, did you?

WILLY, *with casual irritation:* I said nothing happened. Didn't
you hear me?

LINDA: Don't you feel well?

WILLY: I'm tired to the death. *The flute has faded away. He sits on the bed beside her, a little numb.* I couldn't make it. I just couldn't make it, Linda.

LINDA, *very carefully, delicately:* Where were you all day? You look terrible.

WILLY: I got as far as a little above Yonkers. I stopped for a cup of coffee. Maybe it was the coffee.

LINDA: What?

WILLY, *after a pause:* I suddenly couldn't drive any more. The car kept going off onto the shoulder, y'know?

LINDA, *helpfully:* Oh. Maybe it was the steering again. I don't think Angelo knows the Studebaker.

WILLY: No, it's me, it's me. Suddenly I realize I'm goin' sixty miles an hour and I don't remember the last five minutes. I'm —I can't seem to—keep my mind to it.

LINDA: Maybe it's your glasses. You never went for your new glasses.

WILLY: No, I see everything. I came back ten miles an hour. It took me nearly four hours from Yonkers.

LINDA, *resigned:* Well, you'll just have to take a rest, Willy, you can't continue this way.

WILLY: I just got back from Florida.

LINDA: But you didn't rest your mind. Your mind is overactive, and the mind is what counts, dear.

WILLY: I'll start out in the morning. Maybe I'll feel better in the morning. *She is taking off his shoes.* These goddam arch supports are killing me.

LINDA: Take an aspirin. Should I get you an aspirin? It'll soothe you.

WILLY, *with wonder:* I was driving along, you understand? And I was fine. I was even observing the scenery. You can imagine, me looking at scenery, on the road every week of my life. But it's so beautiful up there, Linda, the trees are so thick, and the sun is warm. I opened the windshield and just let the warm air bathe over me. And then all of a sudden I'm goin' off the road! I'm tellin' ya, I absolutely forgot I was driving. If I'd've gone the other way over the white line I might've killed somebody. So I went on again—and five minutes later I'm dreamin' again, and I nearly— *He presses two fingers against his eyes.* I have such thoughts, I have such strange thoughts.

LINDA: Willy, dear. Talk to them again. There's no reason why you can't work in New York.

WILLY: They don't need me in New York. I'm the New England man. I'm vital in New England.

LINDA: But you're sixty years old. They can't expect you to keep traveling every week.

WILLY: I'll have to send a wire to Portland. I'm supposed to see Brown and Morrison tomorrow morning at ten o'clock to show the line. Goddammit, I could sell them! *He starts putting on his jacket.*

LINDA, *taking the jacket from him:* Why don't you go down to the place tomorrow and tell Howard you've simply got to work in New York? You're too accommodating, dear.

WILLY: If old man Wagner was alive I'd a been in charge of New York now! That man was a prince, he was a masterful man. But that boy of his, that Howard, he don't appreciate. When I went north the first time, the Wagner Company didn't know where New England was!

LINDA: Why don't you tell those things to Howard, dear?

WILLY, *encouraged:* I will, I definitely will. Is there any cheese?

LINDA: I'll make you a sandwich.

WILLY: No, go to sleep. I'll take some milk. I'll be up right away. The boys in?

LINDA: They're sleeping. Happy took Biff on a date tonight.

WILLY, *interested:* That so?

LINDA: It was so nice to see them shaving together, one behind the other, in the bathroom. And going out together. You notice? The whole house smells of shaving lotion.

WILLY: Figure it out. Work a lifetime to pay off a house. You finally own it, and there's nobody to live in it.

LINDA: Well, dear, life is a casting off. It's always that way.

WILLY: No, no, some people—some people accomplish something. Did Biff say anything after I went this morning?

LINDA: You shouldn't have criticized him, Willy, especially after he just got off the train. You mustn't lose your temper with him.

WILLY: When the hell did I lose my temper? I simply asked him if he was making any money. Is that a criticism?

LINDA: But, dear, how could he make any money?

WILLY, *worried and angered:* There's such an undercurrent in him. He became a moody man. Did he apologize when I left this morning?

LINDA: He was crestfallen, Willy. You know how he admires you. I think if he finds himself, then you'll both be happier and not fight any more.

WILLY: How can he find himself on a farm? Is that a life? A farmhand? In the beginning, when he was young, I thought, well, a young man, it's good for him to tramp around, take a lot of different jobs. But it's more than ten years now and he has yet to make thirty-five dollars a week!

LINDA: He's finding himself, Willy.

WILLY: Not finding yourself at the age of thirty-four is a disgrace!

LINDA: Shh!

WILLY: The trouble is he's lazy, goddammit!

LINDA: Willy, please!

WILLY: Biff is a lazy bum!

LINDA: They're sleeping. Get something to eat. Go on down.

WILLY: Why did he come home? I would like to know what brought him home.

LINDA: I don't know. I think he's still lost, Willy. I think he's very lost.

WILLY: Biff Loman is lost. In the greatest country in the world a young man with such—personal attractiveness, gets lost. And such a hard worker. There's one thing about Biff—he's not lazy.

LINDA: Never.

WILLY, *with pity and resolve:* I'll see him in the morning; I'll have a nice talk with him. I'll get him a job selling. He could be big in no time. My God! Remember how they used to follow him around in high school? When he smiled at one of them their faces lit up. When he walked down the street . . . *He loses himself in reminiscences.*

LINDA, *trying to bring him out of it:* Willy, dear, I got a new kind of American-type cheese today. It's whipped.

WILLY: Why do you get American when I like Swiss?

LINDA: I just thought you'd like a change—

WILLY: I don't want a change! I want Swiss cheese. Why am I always being contradicted?

LINDA, *with a covering laugh:* I thought it would be a surprise.

WILLY: Why don't you open a window in here, for God's sake?

LINDA, *with infinite patience:* They're all open, dear.

WILLY: The way they boxed us in here. Bricks and windows, windows and bricks.

LINDA: We should've bought the land next door.

WILLY: The street is lined with cars. There's not a breath of fresh air in the neighborhood. The grass don't grow any more, you can't raise a carrot in the back yard. They should've had a law against apartment houses. Remember those two beautiful elm trees out there? When I and Biff hung the swing between them?

LINDA: Yeah, like being a million miles from the city.

WILLY: They should've arrested the builder for cutting those down. They massacred the neighborhood. *Lost:* More and more I think of those days, Linda. This time of year it was lilac and wisteria. And then the peonies would come out, and the daffodils. What fragrance in this room!

LINDA: Well, after all, people had to move somewhere.

WILLY: No, there's more people now.

LINDA: I don't think there's more people. I think—

WILLY: There's more people! That's what's ruining this country! Population is getting out of control. The competition is maddening! Smell the stink from that apartment house! And another one on the other side . . . How can they whip cheese?

On Willy's last line, Biff and Happy raise themselves up in their beds, listening.

LINDA: Go down, try it. And be quiet.

WILLY, *turning to Linda, guiltily:* You're not worried about me, are you, sweetheart?

BIFF: What's the matter?

HAPPY: Listen!

LINDA: You've got too much on the ball to worry about.

WILLY: You're my foundation and my support, Linda.

LINDA: Just try to relax, dear. You make mountains out of molehills.

WILLY: I won't fight with him any more. If he wants to go back to Texas, let him go.

LINDA: He'll find his way.

WILLY: Sure. Certain men just don't get started till later in life. Like Thomas Edison, I think. Or B. F. Goodrich. One of them was deaf. *He starts for the bedroom doorway.* I'll put my money on Biff.

LINDA: And Willy—if it's warm Sunday we'll drive in the country. And we'll open the windshield, and take lunch.

WILLY: No, the windshields don't open on the new cars.

LINDA: But you opened it today.

WILLY: Me? I didn't. *He stops.* Now isn't that peculiar! Isn't that a remarkable— *He breaks off in amazement and fright as the flute is heard distantly.*

LINDA: What, darling?

WILLY: That is the most remarkable thing.

LINDA: What, dear?

WILLY: I was thinking of the Chevvy. *Slight pause.* Nineteen twenty-eight . . . when I had that red Chevvy— *Breaks off.* That funny? I coulda sworn I was driving that Chevvy today.

LINDA: Well, that's nothing. Something must've reminded you.

WILLY: Remarkable. Ts. Remember those days? The way Biff used to simonize that car? The dealer refused to believe there was eighty thousand miles on it. *He shakes his head.* Heh! *To Linda:* Close your eyes, I'll be right up. *He walks out of the bedroom.*

HAPPY, *to Biff:* Jesus, maybe he smashed up the car again!

LINDA, *calling after Willy:* Be careful on the stairs, dear! The cheese is on the middle shelf! *She turns, goes over to the bed, takes his jacket, and goes out of the bedroom.*

Light has risen on the boys' room. Unseen, Willy is heard talking to himself, "Eighty thousand miles," and a little laugh. Biff gets out of bed, comes downstage a bit, and stands attentively. Biff is two years older than his brother Happy, well built, but in these days bears a worn air and seems less self-assured. He has succeeded less, and his dreams are stronger and less acceptable than Happy's. Happy is tall, powerfully made. Sexuality is like a visible color on him, or a scent that many women have discovered. He, like his brother, is lost, but in a different way, for he has never allowed himself to turn his face toward defeat and is thus more confused and hard-skinned, although seemingly more content.

HAPPY, *getting out of bed:* He's going to get his license taken away if he keeps that up. I'm getting nervous about him, y'know, Biff?

BIFF: His eyes are going.

HAPPY: No, I've driven with him. He sees all right. He just doesn't keep his mind on it. I drove into the city with him last week. He stops at a green light and then it turns red and he goes. *He laughs.*

BIFF: Maybe he's color-blind.

HAPPY: Pop? Why he's got the finest eye for color in the business. You know that.

BIFF, *sitting down on his bed:* I'm going to sleep.

HAPPY: You're not still sour on Dad, are you, Biff?

BIFF: He's all right, I guess.

WILLY, *underneath them, in the living room:* Yes, sir, eighty thousand miles—eighty-two thousand!

BIFF: You smoking?

HAPPY, *holding out a pack of cigarettes:* Want one?

BIFF, *taking a cigarette:* I can never sleep when I smell it.

WILLY: What a simonizing job, heh!

HAPPY, *with deep sentiment:* Funny, Biff, y'know? Us sleeping in here again? The old beds. *He pats his bed affectionately.* All the talk that went across those two beds, huh? Our whole lives.

BIFF: Yeah. Lotta dreams and plans.

HAPPY, *with a deep and masculine laugh:* About five hundred women would like to know what was said in this room.

They share a soft laugh.

BIFF: Remember that big Betsy something—what the hell was her name—over on Bushwick Avenue?

HAPPY, *combing his hair:* With the collie dog!

BIFF: That's the one. I got you in there, remember?

HAPPY: Yeah, that was my first time—I think. Boy, there was a pig! *They laugh, almost crudely.* You taught me everything I know about women. Don't forget that.

BIFF: I bet you forgot how bashful you used to be. Especially with girls.

HAPPY: Oh, I still am, Biff.

BIFF: Oh, go on.

HAPPY: I just control it, that's all. I think I got less bashful and you got more so. What happened, Biff? Where's the old humor, the old confidence? *He shakes Biff's knee. Biff gets up and moves restlessly about the room.* What's the matter?

BIFF: Why does Dad mock me all the time?

HAPPY: He's not mocking you, he—

BIFF: Everything I say there's a twist of mockery on his face. I can't get near him.

HAPPY: He just wants you to make good, that's all. I wanted to talk to you about Dad for a long time, Biff. Something's—happening to him. He—talks to himself.

BIFF: I noticed that this morning. But he always mumbled.

HAPPY: But not so noticeable. It got so embarrassing I sent him to Florida. And you know something? Most of the time he's talking to you.

BIFF: What's he say about me?

HAPPY: I can't make it out.

BIFF: What's he say about me?

HAPPY: I think the fact that you're not settled, that you're still kind of up in the air . . .

BIFF: There's one or two other things depressing him, Happy.

HAPPY: What do you mean?

BIFF: Never mind. Just don't lay it all to me.

HAPPY: But I think if you just got started—I mean—is there any future for you out there?

BIFF: I tell ya, Hap, I don't know what the future is. I don't know—what I'm supposed to want.

HAPPY: What do you mean?

BIFF: Well, I spent six or seven years after high school trying to work myself up. Shipping clerk, salesman, business of one kind or another. And it's a measly manner of existence. To get on that subway on the hot mornings in summer. To devote your whole life to keeping stock, or making phone calls, or selling or buying. To suffer fifty weeks of the year for the sake of a two-week vacation, when all you really desire is to be outdoors, with your shirt off. And always to have to get ahead of the next fella. And still—that's how you build a future.

HAPPY: Well, you really enjoy it on a farm? Are you content out there?

BIFF, *with rising agitation:* Hap, I've had twenty or thirty different kinds of jobs since I left home before the war, and it always turns out the same. I just realized it lately. In Nebraska when I herded cattle, and the Dakotas, and Arizona, and now in Texas. It's why I came home now, I guess, because I realized it. This farm I work on, it's spring there now, see? And they've got about fifteen new colts. There's nothing more inspiring or—beautiful than the sight of a mare and a new colt. And it's cool there now, see? Texas is cool now, and it's spring. And whenever spring comes to where I am, I suddenly get the feeling, my God, I'm not gettin' anywhere! What the hell am I doing, playing around with horses, twenty-eight dollars a week! I'm thirty-four years old, I oughta be makin' my future. That's when I come running home. And now, I get here, and I don't know what to do with myself. *After a pause:* I've always made a point of not wasting my life, and every time I come back here I know that all I've done is to waste my life.

HAPPY: You're a poet, you know that, Biff? You're a—you're an idealist!

BIFF: No, I'm mixed up very bad. Maybe I oughta get married. Maybe I oughta get stuck into something. Maybe that's my trouble. I'm like a boy. I'm not married, I'm not in business, I just—I'm like a boy. Are you content, Hap? You're a success, aren't you? Are you content?

HAPPY: Hell, no!

BIFF: Why? You're making money, aren't you?

HAPPY, *moving about with energy, expressiveness:* All I can do now is wait for the merchandise manager to die. And suppose I get to be merchandise manager? He's a good friend of mine, and he just built a terrific estate on Long Island. And he lived there about two months and sold it, and now he's building another one. He can't enjoy it once it's finished. And I know that's just what I would do. I don't know what the hell I'm workin' for. Sometimes I sit in my apartment—all alone. And I think of the rent I'm paying. And it's crazy. But then, it's what I always wanted. My own apartment, a car, and plenty of women. And still, goddammit, I'm lonely.

BIFF, *with enthusiasm:* Listen, why don't you come out West with me?

HAPPY: You and I, heh?

BIFF: Sure, maybe we could buy a ranch. Raise cattle, use our muscles. Men built like we are should be working out in the open.

HAPPY, *avidly:* The Loman Brothers, heh?

BIFF, *with vast affection:* Sure, we'd be known all over the counties!

HAPPY, *enthralled:* That's what I dream about, Biff. Sometimes I want to just rip my clothes off in the middle of the store and outbox that goddam merchandise manager. I mean I can outbox, outrun, and outlift anybody in that store, and I have to take orders from those common, petty sons-of-bitches till I can't stand it any more.

BIFF: I'm tellin' you, kid, if you were with me I'd be happy out there.

HAPPY, *enthused:* See, Biff, everybody around me is so false that I'm constantly lowering my ideals . . .

BIFF: Baby, together we'd stand up for one another, we'd have someone to trust.

HAPPY: If I were around you—

BIFF: Hap, the trouble is we weren't brought up to grub for money. I don't know how to do it.

HAPPY: Neither can I!

BIFF: Then let's go!

HAPPY: The only thing is—what can you make out there?

BIFF: But look at your friend. Builds an estate and then hasn't the peace of mind to live in it.

HAPPY: Yeah, but when he walks into the store the waves part in front of him. That's fifty-two thousand dollars a year coming through the revolving door, and I got more in my pinky finger than he's got in his head.

BIFF: Yeah, but you just said—

HAPPY: I gotta show some of those pompous, self-important executives over there that Hap Loman can make the grade. I want to walk into the store the way he walks in. Then I'll go with you, Biff. We'll be together yet, I swear. But take those two we had tonight. Now weren't they gorgeous creatures?

BIFF: Yeah, yeah, most gorgeous I've had in years.

HAPPY: I get that any time I want, Biff. Whenever I feel disgusted. The only trouble is, it gets like bowling or something. I just keep knockin' them over and it doesn't mean anything. You still run around a lot?

BIFF: Naa. I'd like to find a girl—steady, somebody with substance.

HAPPY: That's what I long for.

BIFF: Go on! You'd never come home.

HAPPY: I would! Somebody with character, with resistance! Like Mom, y'know? You're gonna call me a bastard when I tell you this. That girl Charlotte I was with tonight is engaged to be married in five weeks. *He tries on his new hat.*

BIFF: No kiddin'!

HAPPY: Sure, the guy's in line for the vice-presidency of the store. I don't know what gets into me, maybe I just have an overdeveloped sense of competition or something, but I went and ruined her, and furthermore I can't get rid of her. And he's the third executive I've done that to. Isn't that a crummy characteristic? And to top it all, I go to their weddings! *Indignantly, but laughing:* Like I'm not supposed to take bribes. Manufacturers offer me a hundred-dollar bill now and then to throw an order their way. You know how honest I am, but it's like this girl, see. I hate myself for it. Because I don't want the girl, and, still, I take it and—I love it!

BIFF: Let's go to sleep.

HAPPY: I guess we didn't settle anything, heh?

BIFF: I just got one idea that I think I'm going to try.

HAPPY: What's that?

BIFF: Remember Bill Oliver?

HAPPY: Sure, Oliver is very big now. You want to work for him again?

BIFF: No, but when I quit he said something to me. He put his arm on my shoulder, and he said, "Biff, if you ever need anything, come to me."

HAPPY: I remember that. That sounds good.

BIFF: I think I'll go to see him. If I could get ten thousand or even seven or eight thousand dollars I could buy a beautiful ranch.

HAPPY: I bet he'd back you. 'Cause he thought highly of you, Biff. I mean, they all do. You're well liked, Biff. That's why I say to come back here, and we both have the apartment. And I'm tellin' you, Biff, any babe you want . . .

BIFF: No, with a ranch I could do the work I like and still be something. I just wonder though. I wonder if Oliver still thinks I stole that carton of basketballs.

HAPPY: Oh, he probably forgot that long ago. It's almost ten years. You're too sensitive. Anyway, he didn't really fire you.

BIFF: Well, I think he was going to. I think that's why I quit. I was never sure whether he knew or not. I know he thought the world of me, though. I was the only one he'd let lock up the place.

WILLY, *below:* You gonna wash the engine, Biff?

HAPPY: Shh!

Biff looks at Happy, who is gazing down, listening. Willy is mumbling in the parlor.

HAPPY: You hear that?

They listen. Willy laughs warmly.

BIFF, *growing angry:* Doesn't he know Mom can hear that?

WILLY: Don't get your sweater dirty, Biff!

A look of pain crosses Biff's face.

HAPPY: Isn't that terrible? Don't leave again, will you? You'll find a job here. You gotta stick around. I don't know what to do about him, it's getting embarrassing.

WILLY: What a simonizing job!

BIFF: Mom's hearing that!

WILLY: No kiddin', Biff, you got a date? Wonderful!

HAPPY: Go on to sleep. But talk to him in the morning, will you?

BIFF, *reluctantly getting into bed:* With her in the house. Brother!

HAPPY, *getting into bed:* I wish you'd have a good talk with him.

The light on their room begins to fade.

BIFF, *to himself in bed:* That selfish, stupid . . .

HAPPY: Sh . . . Sleep, Biff.

Their light is out. Well before they have finished speaking, Willy's form is dimly seen below in the darkened kitchen. He opens the refrigerator, searches in there, and takes out a bottle of milk. The apartment houses are fading out, and the entire house and surroundings become covered with leaves. Music insinuates itself as the leaves appear.

WILLY: Just wanna be careful with those girls, Biff, that's all. Don't make any promises. No promises of any kind. Because a girl, y'know, they always believe what you tell 'em, and you're very young, Biff, you're too young to be talking seriously to girls.

Light rises on the kitchen. Willy, talking, shuts the refrigerator door and comes downstage to the kitchen table. He pours milk into a glass. He is totally immersed in himself, smiling faintly.

WILLY: Too young entirely, Biff. You want to watch your schooling first. Then when you're all set, there'll be plenty of girls for a boy like you. *He smiles broadly at a kitchen chair.* That so? The girls pay for you? *He laughs.* Boy, you must really be makin' a hit.

Willy is gradually addressing—physically—a point offstage, speaking through the wall of the kitchen, and his voice has been rising in volume to that of a normal conversation.

WILLY: I been wondering why you polish the car so careful. Ha! Don't leave the hubcaps, boys. Get the chamois to the hubcaps. Happy, use newspaper on the windows, it's the easiest thing. Show him how to do it, Biff! You see, Happy? Pad it up, use it like a pad. That's it, that's it, good work. You're doin' all right, Hap. *He pauses, then nods in approbation for a few seconds, then looks upward.* Biff, first thing we gotta do when we get time is clip that big branch over the house. Afraid it's gonna fall in a storm and hit the roof. Tell you what. We get a rope and sling her around, and then we climb up there with a couple of saws and take her down. Soon as you finish the car, boys, I wanna see ya. I got a surprise for you, boys.

BIFF, *offstage:* Whatta ya got, Dad?

WILLY: No, you finish first. Never leave a job till you're finished—remember that. *Looking toward the "big trees":* Biff, up in Albany I saw a beautiful hammock. I think I'll buy it next trip, and we'll hang it right between those two elms. Wouldn't that be something? Just swingin' there under those branches. Boy, that would be . . .

Young Biff and Young Happy appear from the direction Willy was addressing. Happy carries rags and a pail of water. Biff, wearing a sweater with a block "S," carries a football.

BIFF, *pointing in the direction of the car offstage:* How's that, Pop, professional?

WILLY: Terrific. Terrific job, boys. Good work, Biff.

HAPPY: Where's the surprise, Pop?

WILLY: In the back seat of the car.

HAPPY: Boy! *He runs off.*

BIFF: What is it, Dad? Tell me, what'd you buy?

WILLY, *laughing, cuffs him:* Never mind, something I want you to have.

BIFF, *turns and starts off:* What is it, Hap?

HAPPY, *offstage:* It's a punching bag!

BIFF: Oh, Pop!

WILLY: It's got Gene Tunney's signature on it!

Happy runs onstage with a punching bag.

BIFF: Gee, how'd you know we wanted a punching bag?

WILLY: Well, it's the finest thing for the timing.

HAPPY, *lying down on his back and pedaling with his feet:* I'm losing weight, you notice, Pop?

WILLY, *to Happy:* Jumping rope is good too.

BIFF: Did you see the new football I got?

WILLY, *examining the ball:* Where'd you get a new ball?

BIFF: The coach told me to practice my passing.

WILLY: That so? And he gave you the ball, heh?

BIFF: Well, I borrowed it from the locker room. *He laughs confidentially.*

WILLY, *laughing with him at the theft:* I want you to return that.

HAPPY: I told you he wouldn't like it!

BIFF, *angrily:* Well, I'm bringing it back!

WILLY, *stopping the incipient argument, to Happy:* Sure, he's gotta practice with a regulation ball, doesn't he? *To Biff:* Coach'll probably congratulate you on your initiative!

BIFF: Oh, he keeps congratulating my initiative all the time, Pop.

WILLY: That's because he likes you. If somebody else took that ball there'd be an uproar. So what's the report, boys, what's the report?

BIFF: Where'd you go this time, Dad? Gee we were lonesome for you.

WILLY, *pleased, puts an arm around each boy and they come down to the apron:* Lonesome, heh?

BIFF: Missed you every minute.

WILLY: Don't say? Tell you a secret, boys. Don't breathe it to a soul. Someday I'll have my own business, and I'll never have to leave home any more.

HAPPY: Like Uncle Charley, heh?

WILLY: Bigger than Uncle Charley! Because Charley is not— liked. He's liked, but he's not—well liked.

BIFF: Where'd you go this time, Dad?

WILLY: Well, I got on the road, and I went north to Providence. Met the Mayor.

BIFF: The Mayor of Providence!

WILLY: He was sitting in the hotel lobby.

BIFF: What'd he say?

WILLY: He said, "Morning!" And I said, "You got a fine city here, Mayor." And then he had coffee with me. And then I went to Waterbury. Waterbury is a fine city. Big clock city, the famous Waterbury clock. Sold a nice bill there. And then Boston—Boston is the cradle of the Revolution. A fine city. And a couple of other towns in Mass., and on to Portland and Bangor and straight home!

BIFF: Gee, I'd love to go with you sometime, Dad.

WILLY: Soon as summer comes.

HAPPY: Promise?

WILLY: You and Hap and I, and I'll show you all the towns. America is full of beautiful towns and fine, upstanding people. And they know me, boys, they know me up and down New England. The finest people. And when I bring you fellas up, there'll be open sesame for all of us, 'cause one thing, boys: I have friends. I can park my car in any street in New England, and the cops protect it like their own. This summer, heh?

BIFF and HAPPY, *together:* Yeah! You bet!

WILLY: We'll take our bathing suits.

HAPPY: We'll carry your bags, Pop!

WILLY: Oh, won't that be something! Me comin' into the Boston stores with you boys carryin' my bags. What a sensation!

Biff is prancing around, practicing passing the ball.

WILLY: You nervous, Biff, about the game?

BIFF: Not if you're gonna be there.

WILLY: What do they say about you in school, now that they made you captain?

HAPPY: There's a crowd of girls behind him every time the classes change.

BIFF, *taking Willy's hand:* This Saturday, Pop, this Saturday— just for you, I'm going to break through for a touchdown.

HAPPY: You're supposed to pass.

BIFF: I'm takin' one play for Pop. You watch me, Pop, and when I take off my helmet, that means I'm breakin' out. Then you watch me crash through that line!

WILLY, *kissing Biff:* Oh, wait'll I tell this in Boston!

Bernard enters in knickers. He is younger than Biff, earnest and loyal, a worried boy.

BERNARD: Biff, where are you? You're supposed to study with me today.

WILLY: Hey, looka Bernard. What're you lookin' so anemic about, Bernard?

BERNARD: He's gotta study, Uncle Willy. He's got Regents next week.

HAPPY, *tauntingly, spinning Bernard around:* Let's box, Bernard!

BERNARD: Biff! *He gets away from Happy.* Listen, Biff, I heard Mr. Birnbaum say that if you don't start studyin' math he's gonna flunk you, and you won't graduate. I heard him!

WILLY: You better study with him, Biff. Go ahead now.

BERNARD: I heard him!

BIFF: Oh, Pop, you didn't see my sneakers! *He holds up a foot for Willy to look at.*

WILLY: Hey, that's a beautiful job of printing!

BERNARD, *wiping his glasses:* Just because he printed University of Virginia on his sneakers doesn't mean they've got to graduate him, Uncle Willy!

WILLY, *angrily:* What're you talking about? With scholarships to three universities they're gonna flunk him?

BERNARD: But I heard Mr. Birnbaum say—

WILLY: Don't be a pest, Bernard! *To his boys:* What an anemic!

BERNARD: Okay, I'm waiting for you in my house, Biff.

Bernard goes off. The Lomans laugh.

WILLY: Bernard is not well liked, is he?

BIFF: He's liked, but he's not well liked.

HAPPY: That's right, Pop.

WILLY: That's just what I mean. Bernard can get the best marks in school, y'understand, but when he gets out in the business world, y'understand, you are going to be five times ahead of him. That's why I thank Almighty God you're both built like Adonises. Because the man who makes an appearance in the business world, the man who creates personal interest, is the man who gets ahead. Be liked and you will never want. You take me, for instance. I never have to wait in line to see a buyer. "Willy Loman is here!" That's all they have to know, and I go right through.

BIFF: Did you knock them dead, Pop?

WILLY: Knocked 'em cold in Providence, slaughtered 'em in Boston.

HAPPY, *on his back, pedaling again:* I'm losing weight, you notice, Pop?

Linda enters, as of old, a ribbon in her hair, carrying a basket of washing.

LINDA, *with youthful energy:* Hello, dear!

WILLY: Sweetheart!

LINDA: How'd the Chevvy run?

WILLY: Chevrolet, Linda, is the greatest car ever built. *To the boys:* Since when do you let your mother carry wash up the stairs?

BIFF: Grab hold there, boy!

HAPPY: Where to, Mom?

LINDA: Hang them up on the line. And you better go down to your friends, Biff. The cellar is full of boys. They don't know what to do with themselves.

BIFF: Ah, when Pop comes home they can wait!

WILLY, *laughing appreciatively:* You better go down and tell them what to do, Biff.

BIFF: I think I'll have them sweep out the furnace room.

WILLY: Good work, Biff.

BIFF—*he goes through wall-line of kitchen to doorway at back and calls down:* Fellas! Everybody sweep out the furnace room! I'll be right down!

VOICES: All right! Okay, Biff.

BIFF: George and Sam and Frank, come out back! We're hangin' up the wash! Come on, Hap, on the double! *He and Happy carry out the basket.*

LINDA: The way they obey him!

WILLY: Well, that's training, the training. I'm tellin' you, I was sellin' thousands and thousands, but I had to come home.

LINDA: Oh, the whole block'll be at that game. Did you sell anything?

WILLY: I did five hundred gross in Providence and seven hundred gross in Boston.

LINDA: No! Wait a minute, I've got a pencil. *She pulls pencil and paper out of her apron pocket.* That makes your commission . . . Two hundred—my God! Two hundred and twelve dollars!

WILLY: Well, I didn't figure it yet, but . . .

LINDA: How much did you do?

WILLY: Well, I—I did—about a hundred and eighty gross in Providence. Well, no—it came to—roughly two hundred gross on the whole trip.

LINDA, *without hesitation:* Two hundred gross. That's . . . *She figures.*

WILLY: The trouble was that three of the stores were half closed for inventory in Boston. Otherwise I woulda broke records.

LINDA: Well, it makes seventy dollars and some pennies. That's very good.

WILLY: What do we owe?

LINDA: Well, on the first there's sixteen dollars on the refrigerator—

WILLY: Why sixteen?

LINDA: Well, the fan belt broke, so it was a dollar eighty.

WILLY: But it's brand new.

LINDA: Well, the man said that's the way it is. Till they work themselves in, y'know.

They move through the wall-line into the kitchen.

WILLY: I hope we didn't get stuck on that machine.

LINDA: They got the biggest ads of any of them!

WILLY: I know, it's a fine machine. What else?

LINDA: Well, there's nine-sixty for the washing machine. And for the vacuum cleaner there's three and a half due on the fifteenth. Then the roof, you got twenty-one dollars remaining.

WILLY: It don't leak, does it?

LINDA: No, they did a wonderful job. Then you owe Frank for the carburetor.

WILLY: I'm not going to pay that man! That goddam Chevrolet, they ought to prohibit the manufacture of that car!

LINDA: Well, you owe him three and a half. And odds and ends, comes to around a hundred and twenty dollars by the fifteenth.

WILLY: A hundred and twenty dollars! My God, if business don't pick up I don't know what I'm gonna do!

LINDA: Well, next week you'll do better.

WILLY: Oh, I'll knock 'em dead next week. I'll go to Hartford. I'm very well liked in Hartford. You know, the trouble is, Linda, people don't seem to take to me.

They move onto the forestage.

LINDA: Oh, don't be foolish.

WILLY: I know it when I walk in. They seem to laugh at me.

LINDA: Why? Why would they laugh at you? Don't talk that way, Willy.

Willy moves to the edge of the stage. Linda goes into the kitchen and starts to darn stockings.

WILLY: I don't know the reason for it, but they just pass me by. I'm not noticed.

LINDA: But you're doing wonderful, dear. You're making seventy to a hundred dollars a week.

WILLY: But I gotta be at it ten, twelve hours a day. Other men—I don't know—they do it easier. I don't know why—I can't stop myself—I talk too much. A man oughta come in with a few words. One thing about Charley. He's a man of few words, and they respect him.

LINDA: You don't talk too much, you're just lively.

WILLY, *smiling:* Well, I figure, what the hell, life is short, a couple of jokes. *To himself:* I joke too much! *The smile goes.*

LINDA: Why? You're—

WILLY: I'm fat. I'm very—foolish to look at, Linda. I didn't tell you, but Christmas time I happened to be calling on F. H. Stewarts, and a salesman I know, as I was going in to see the buyer I heard him say something about—walrus. And I—I cracked him right across the face. I won't take that. I simply will not take that. But they do laugh at me. I know that.

LINDA: Darling . . .

WILLY: I gotta overcome it. I know I gotta overcome it. I'm not dressing to advantage, maybe.

LINDA: Willy, darling, you're the handsomest man in the world—

WILLY: Oh, no, Linda.

LINDA: To me you are. *Slight pause.* The handsomest.

From the darkness is heard the laughter of a woman. Willy doesn't turn to it, but it continues through Linda's lines.

LINDA: And the boys, Willy. Few men are idolized by their children the way you are.

Music is heard as behind a scrim, to the left of the house, The Woman, dimly seen, is dressing.

WILLY, *with great feeling:* You're the best there is, Linda, you're a pal, you know that? On the road—on the road I want to grab you sometimes and just kiss the life outa you.

The laughter is loud now, and he moves into a brightening area at the left, where The Woman has come from behind the scrim and is standing, putting on her hat, looking into a "mirror" and laughing.

WILLY: 'Cause I get so lonely—especially when business is

bad and there's nobody to talk to. I get the feeling that I'll never sell anything again, that I won't make a living for you, or a business, a business for the boys. *He talks through The Woman's subsiding laughter; The Woman primps at the "mirror."* There's so much I want to make for—

THE WOMAN: Me? You didn't make me, Willy. I picked you.

WILLY, *pleased:* You picked me?

THE WOMAN, *who is quite proper-looking, Willy's age:* I did. I've been sitting at that desk watching all the salesmen go by, day in, day out. But you've got such a sense of humor, and we do have such a good time together, don't we?

WILLY: Sure, sure. *He takes her in his arms.* Why do you have to go now?

THE WOMAN: It's two o'clock . . .

WILLY: No, come on in! *He pulls her.*

THE WOMAN: . . . my sisters'll be scandalized. When'll you be back?

WILLY: Oh, two weeks about. Will you come up again?

THE WOMAN: Sure thing. You do make me laugh. It's good for me. *She squeezes his arm, kisses him.* And I think you're a wonderful man.

WILLY: You picked me, heh?

THE WOMAN: Sure. Because you're so sweet. And such a kidder.

WILLY: Well, I'll see you next time I'm in Boston.

THE WOMAN: I'll put you right through to the buyers.

WILLY, *slapping her bottom:* Right. Well, bottoms up!

THE WOMAN—*she slaps him gently and laughs:* You just kill

me, Willy. *He suddenly grabs her and kisses her roughly.* You kill me. And thanks for the stockings. I love a lot of stockings. Well, good night.

WILLY: Good night. And keep your pores open!

THE WOMAN: Oh, Willy!

The Woman bursts out laughing, and Linda's laughter blends in. The Woman disappears into the dark. Now the area at the kitchen table brightens. Linda is sitting where she was at the kitchen table, but now is mending a pair of her silk stockings.

LINDA: You are, Willy. The handsomest man. You've got no reason to feel that—

WILLY, *coming out of The Woman's dimming area and going over to Linda.* I'll make it all up to you, Linda, I'll—

LINDA: There's nothing to make up, dear. You're doing fine, better than—

WILLY, *noticing her mending:* What's that?

LINDA: Just mending my stockings. They're so expensive—

WILLY, *angrily, taking them from her:* I won't have you mending stockings in this house! Now throw them out!

Linda puts the stockings in her pocket.

BERNARD, *entering on the run:* Where is he? If he doesn't study!

WILLY, *moving to the forestage, with great agitation:* You'll give him the answers!

BERNARD: I do, but I can't on a Regents! That's a state exam! They're liable to arrest me!

WILLY: Where is he? I'll whip him, I'll whip him!

LINDA: And he'd better give back that football, Willy, it's not nice.

WILLY: Biff! Where is he? Why is he taking everything?

LINDA: He's too rough with the girls, Willy. All the mothers are afraid of him!

WILLY: I'll whip him!

BERNARD: He's driving the car without a license!

The Woman's laugh is heard.

WILLY: Shut up!

LINDA: All the mothers—

WILLY: Shut up!

BERNARD, *backing quietly away and out:* Mr. Birnbaum says he's stuck up.

WILLY: Get outa here!

BERNARD: If he doesn't buckle down he'll flunk math! *He goes off.*

LINDA: He's right, Willy, you've gotta—

WILLY, *exploding at her:* There's nothing the matter with him! You want him to be a worm like Bernard? He's got spirit, personality . . .

As he speaks, Linda, almost in tears, exits into the living room. Willy is alone in the kitchen, wilting and staring. The leaves are gone. It is night again, and the apartment houses look down from behind.

WILLY: Loaded with it. Loaded! What is he stealing? He's giving it back, isn't he? Why is he stealing? What did I tell him? I never in my life told him anything but decent things.

Happy in pajamas has come down the stairs; Willy suddenly becomes aware of Happy's presence.

HAPPY: Let's go now, come on.

WILLY, *sitting down at the kitchen table:* Huh! Why did she have to wax the floors herself? Everytime she waxes the floors she keels over. She knows that!

HAPPY: Shh! Take it easy. What brought you back tonight?

WILLY: I got an awful scare. Nearly hit a kid in Yonkers. God! Why didn't I go to Alaska with my brother Ben that time! Ben! That man was a genius, that man was success incarnate! What a mistake! He begged me to go.

HAPPY: Well, there's no use in—

WILLY: You guys! There was a man started with the clothes on his back and ended up with diamond mines!

HAPPY: Boy, someday I'd like to know how he did it.

WILLY: What's the mystery? The man knew what he wanted and went out and got it! Walked into a jungle, and comes out, the age of twenty-one, and he's rich! The world is an oyster, but you don't crack it open on a mattress!

HAPPY: Pop, I told you I'm gonna retire you for life.

WILLY: You'll retire me for life on seventy goddam dollars a week? And your women and your car and your apartment, and you'll retire me for life! Christ's sake, I couldn't get past Yonkers today! Where are you guys, where are you? The woods are burning! I can't drive a car!

Charley has appeared in the doorway. He is a large man, slow of speech, laconic, immovable. In all he says, despite what he says, there is pity, and, now, trepidation. He has a robe over pajamas, slippers on his feet. He enters the kitchen.

CHARLEY: Everything all right?

HAPPY: Yeah, Charley, everything's . . .

WILLY: What's the matter?

CHARLEY: I heard some noise. I thought something happened. Can't we do something about the walls? You sneeze in here, and in my house hats blow off.

HAPPY: Let's go to bed, Dad. Come on.

Charley signals to Happy to go.

WILLY: You go ahead, I'm not tired at the moment.

HAPPY, *to Willy:* Take it easy, huh? *He exits.*

WILLY: What're you doin' up?

CHARLEY, *sitting down at the kitchen table opposite Willy.* Couldn't sleep good. I had a heartburn.

WILLY: Well, you don't know how to eat.

CHARLEY: I eat with my mouth.

WILLY: No, you're ignorant. You gotta know about vitamins and things like that.

CHARLEY: Come on, let's shoot. Tire you out a little.

WILLY, *hesitantly:* All right. You got cards?

CHARLEY, *taking a deck from his pocket:* Yeah, I got them. Some place. What is it with those vitamins?

WILLY, *dealing:* They build up your bones. Chemistry.

CHARLEY: Yeah, but there's no bones in a heartburn.

WILLY: What are you talkin' about? Do you know the first thing about it?

CHARLEY: Don't get insulted.

WILLY: Don't talk about something you don't know anything about.

They are playing. Pause.

CHARLEY: What're you doin' home?

WILLY: A little trouble with the car.

CHARLEY: Oh. *Pause.* I'd like to take a trip to California.

WILLY: Don't say.

CHARLEY: You want a job?

WILLY: I got a job, I told you that. *After a slight pause:* What the hell are you offering me a job for?

CHARLEY: Don't get insulted.

WILLY: Don't insult me.

CHARLEY: I don't see no sense in it. You don't have to go on this way.

WILLY: I got a good job. *Slight pause.* What do you keep comin' in here for?

CHARLEY: You want me to go?

WILLY, *after a pause, withering:* I can't understand it. He's going back to Texas again. What the hell is that?

CHARLEY: Let him go.

WILLY: I got nothin' to give him, Charley, I'm clean, I'm clean.

CHARLEY: He won't starve. None a them starve. Forget about him.

WILLY: Then what have I got to remember?

CHARLEY: You take it too hard. To hell with it. When a deposit bottle is broken you don't get your nickel back.

WILLY: That's easy enough for you to say.

CHARLEY: That ain't easy for me to say.

WILLY: Did you see the ceiling I put up in the living room?

CHARLEY: Yeah, that's a piece of work. To put up a ceiling is a mystery to me. How do you do it?

WILLY: What's the difference?

CHARLEY: Well, talk about it.

WILLY: You gonna put up a ceiling?

CHARLEY: How could I put up a ceiling?

WILLY: Then what the hell are you bothering me for?

CHARLEY: You're insulted again.

WILLY: A man who can't handle tools is not a man. You're disgusting.

CHARLEY: Don't call me disgusting, Willy.

Uncle Ben, carrying a valise and an umbrella, enters the fore-stage from around the right corner of the house. He is a stolid man, in his sixties, with a mustache and an authoritative air. He is utterly certain of his destiny, and there is an aura of far places about him. He enters exactly as Willy speaks.

WILLY: I'm getting awfully tired, Ben.

Ben's music is heard. Ben looks around at everything.

CHARLEY: Good, keep playing; you'll sleep better. Did you call me Ben?

Ben looks at his watch.

WILLY: That's funny. For a second there you reminded me of my brother Ben.

BEN: I only have a few minutes. *He strolls, inspecting the place. Willy and Charley continue playing.*

CHARLEY: You never heard from him again, heh? Since that time?

WILLY: Didn't Linda tell you? Couple of weeks ago we got a letter from his wife in Africa. He died.

CHARLEY: That so.

BEN, *chuckling:* So this is Brooklyn, eh?

CHARLEY: Maybe you're in for some of his money.

WILLY: Naa, he had seven sons. There's just one opportunity I had with that man . . .

BEN: I must make a train, William. There are several properties I'm looking at in Alaska.

WILLY: Sure, sure! If I'd gone with him to Alaska that time, everything would've been totally different.

CHARLEY: Go on, you'd froze to death up there.

WILLY: What're you talking about?

BEN: Opportunity is tremendous in Alaska, William. Surprised you're not up there.

WILLY: Sure, tremendous.

CHARLEY: Heh?

WILLY: There was the only man I ever met who knew the answers.

CHARLEY: Who?

BEN: How are you all?

WILLY, *taking a pot, smiling:* Fine, fine.

CHARLEY: Pretty sharp tonight.

BEN: Is Mother living with you?

WILLY: No, she died a long time ago.

CHARLEY: Who?

BEN: That's too bad. Fine specimen of a lady, Mother.

WILLY, *to Charley:* Heh?

BEN: I'd hoped to see the old girl.

CHARLEY: Who died?

BEN: Heard anything from Father, have you?

WILLY, *unnerved:* What do you mean, who died?

CHARLEY, *taking a pot:* What're you talkin' about?

BEN, *looking at his watch:* William, it's half-past eight!

WILLY—*as though to dispel his confusion he angrily stops Charley's hand:* That's my build!

CHARLEY: I put the ace—

WILLY: If you don't know how to play the game I'm not gonna throw my money away on you!

CHARLEY, *rising:* It was my ace, for God's sake!

WILLY: I'm through, I'm through!

BEN: When did Mother die?

WILLY: Long ago. Since the beginning you never knew how to play cards.

CHARLEY, *picks up the cards and goes to the door:* All right! Next time I'll bring a deck with five aces.

WILLY: I don't play that kind of game!

CHARLEY, *turning to him:* You ought to be ashamed of yourself!

WILLY: Yeah?

CHARLEY: Yeah! *He goes out.*

WILLY, *slamming the door after him:* Ignoramus!

BEN, *as Willy comes toward him through the wall-line of the kitchen:* So you're William.

WILLY, *shaking Ben's hand:* Ben! I've been waiting for you so long! What's the answer? How did you do it?

BEN: Oh, there's a story in that.

Linda enters the forestage, as of old, carrying the wash basket.

LINDA: Is this Ben?

BEN, *gallantly:* How do you do, my dear.

LINDA: Where've you been all these years? Willy's always wondered why you—

WILLY, *pulling Ben away from her impatiently:* Where is Dad? Didn't you follow him? How did you get started?

BEN: Well, I don't know how much you remember.

WILLY: Well, I was just a baby, of course, only three or four years old—

BEN: Three years and eleven months.

WILLY: What a memory, Ben!

BEN: I have many enterprises, William, and I have never kept books.

WILLY: I remember I was sitting under the wagon in—was it Nebraska?

BEN: It was South Dakota, and I gave you a bunch of wild flowers.

WILLY: I remember you walking away down some open road.

BEN, *laughing:* I was going to find Father in Alaska.

WILLY: Where is he?

BEN: At that age I had a very faulty view of geography, William. I discovered after a few days that I was heading due south, so instead of Alaska, I ended up in Africa.

LINDA: Africa!

WILLY: The Gold Coast!

BEN: Principally diamond mines.

LINDA: Diamond mines!

BEN: Yes, my dear. But I've only a few minutes—

WILLY: No! Boys! Boys! *Young Biff and Happy appear.* Listen to this. This is your Uncle Ben, a great man! Tell my boys, Ben!

BEN: Why, boys, when I was seventeen I walked into the jungle, and when I was twenty-one I walked out. *He laughs.* And by God I was rich.

WILLY, *to the boys:* You see what I been talking about? The greatest things can happen!

BEN, *glancing at his watch*: I have an appointment in Ketchikan Tuesday week.

WILLY: No, Ben! Please tell about Dad. I want my boys to hear. I want them to know the kind of stock they spring from. All I remember is a man with a big beard, and I was in Mamma's lap, sitting around a fire, and some kind of high music.

BEN: His flute. He played the flute.

WILLY: Sure, the flute, that's right!

New music is heard, a high, rollicking tune.

BEN: Father was a very great and a very wild-hearted man. We would start in Boston, and he'd toss the whole family into the wagon, and then he'd drive the team right across the country; through Ohio, and Indiana, Michigan, Illinois, and all the Western states. And we'd stop in the towns and sell the flutes that he'd made on the way. Great inventor, Father. With one gadget he made more in a week than a man like you could make in a lifetime.

WILLY: That's just the way I'm bringing them up, Ben—rugged, well liked, all-around.

BEN: Yeah? *To Biff:* Hit that, boy—hard as you can. *He pounds his stomach.*

BIFF: Oh, no, sir!

BEN, *taking boxing stance:* Come on, get to me! *He laughs.*

WILLY: Go to it, Biff! Go ahead, show him!

BIFF: Okay! *He cocks his fists and starts in.*

LINDA, *to Willy:* Why must he fight, dear?

BEN, *sparring with Biff:* Good boy! Good boy!

WILLY: How's that, Ben, heh?

HAPPY: Give him the left, Biff!

LINDA: Why are you fighting?

BEN: Good boy! *Suddenly he comes in, trips Biff, and stands over him, the point of his umbrella poised over Biff's eye.*

LINDA: Look out, Biff!

BIFF: Gee!

BEN, *patting Biff's knee:* Never fight fair with a stranger, boy. You'll never get out of the jungle that way. *Taking Linda's hand and bowing:* It was an honor and a pleasure to meet you, Linda.

LINDA, *withdrawing her hand coldly, frightened:* Have a nice—trip.

BEN, *to Willy:* And good luck with your—what do you do?

WILLY: Selling.

BEN: Yes. Well . . . *He raises his hand in farewell to all.*

WILLY: No, Ben, I don't want you to think . . . *He takes Ben's arm to show him.* It's Brooklyn, I know, but we hunt too.

BEN: Really, now.

WILLY: Oh, sure, there's snakes and rabbits and—that's why I moved out here. Why, Biff can fell any one of these trees in no time! Boys! Go right over to where they're building the apartment house and get some sand. We're gonna rebuild the entire front stoop right now! Watch this, Ben!

BIFF: Yes, sir! On the double, Hap!

HAPPY, *as he and Biff run off:* I lost weight, Pop, you notice?

Charley enters in knickers, even before the boys are gone.

CHARLEY: Listen, if they steal any more from that building the watchman'll put the cops on them!

LINDA, *to Willy:* Don't let Biff . . .

Ben laughs lustily.

WILLY: You shoulda seen the lumber they brought home last week. At least a dozen six-by-tens worth all kinds a money.

CHARLEY: Listen, if that watchman—

WILLY: I gave them hell, understand. But I got a couple of fearless characters there.

CHARLEY: Willy, the jails are full of fearless characters.

BEN, *clapping Willy on the back, with a laugh at Charley:* And the stock exchange, friend!

WILLY, *joining in Ben's laughter:* Where are the rest of your pants?

CHARLEY: My wife bought them.

WILLY: Now all you need is a golf club and you can go up-stairs and go to sleep. *To Ben:* Great athlete! Between him and his son Bernard they can't hammer a nail!

BERNARD, *rushing in:* The watchman's chasing Biff!

WILLY, *angrily:* Shut up! He's not stealing anything!

LINDA, *alarmed, hurrying off left:* Where is he? Biff, dear! *She exits.*

WILLY, *moving toward the left, away from Ben:* There's nothing wrong. What's the matter with you?

BEN: Nervy boy. Good!

WILLY, *laughing:* Oh, nerves of iron, that Biff!

CHARLEY: Don't know what it is. My New England man comes back and he's bleedin', they murdered him up there.

WILLY: It's contacts, Charley, I got important contacts!

CHARLEY, *sarcastically:* Glad to hear it, Willy. Come in later, we'll shoot a little casino. I'll take some of your Portland money. *He laughs at Willy and exits.*

WILLY, *turning to Ben:* Business is bad, it's murderous. But not for me, of course.

BEN: I'll stop by on my way back to Africa.

WILLY, *longingly:* Can't you stay a few days? You're just what I need, Ben, because I—I have a fine position here, but I—well, Dad left when I was such a baby and I never had a chance to talk to him and I still feel—kind of temporary about myself.

BEN: I'll be late for my train.

They are at opposite ends of the stage.

WILLY: Ben, my boys—can't we talk? They'd go into the jaws of hell for me, see, but I—

BEN: William, you're being first-rate with your boys. Outstanding, manly chaps!

WILLY, *hanging on to his words:* Oh, Ben, that's good to hear! Because sometimes I'm afraid that I'm not teaching them the right kind of— Ben, how should I teach them?

BEN, *giving great weight to each word, and with a certain vicious audacity:* William, when I walked into the jungle, I was seventeen. When I walked out I was twenty-one. And, by God, I was rich! *He goes off into darkness around the right corner of the house.*

WILLY: . . . was rich! That's just the spirit I want to imbue them with! To walk into a jungle! I was right! I was right! I was right!

Ben is gone, but Willy is still speaking to him as Linda, in nightgown and robe, enters the kitchen, glances around for Willy, then goes to the door of the house, looks out and sees him. Comes down to his left. He looks at her.

LINDA: Willy, dear? Willy?

WILLY: I was right!

LINDA: Did you have some cheese? *He can't answer.* It's very late, darling. Come to bed, heh?

WILLY, *looking straight up:* Gotta break your neck to see a star in this yard.

LINDA: You coming in?

WILLY: Whatever happened to that diamond watch fob? Remember? When Ben came from Africa that time? Didn't he give me a watch fob with a diamond in it?

LINDA: You pawned it, dear. Twelve, thirteen years ago. For Biff's radio correspondence course.

WILLY: Gee, that was a beautiful thing. I'll take a walk.

LINDA: But you're in your slippers.

WILLY, *starting to go around the house at the left:* I was right! I was! *Half to Linda, as he goes, shaking his head:* What a man! There was a man worth talking to. I was right!

LINDA, *calling after Willy:* But in your slippers, Willy!

Willy is almost gone when Biff, in his pajamas, comes down the stairs and enters the kitchen.

BIFF: What is he doing out there?

LINDA: Sh!

BIFF: God Almighty, Mom, how long has he been doing this?

LINDA: Don't, he'll hear you.

BIFF: What the hell is the matter with him?

LINDA: It'll pass by morning.

BIFF: Shouldn't we do anything?

LINDA: Oh, my dear, you should do a lot of things, but there's nothing to do, so go to sleep.

Happy comes down the stairs and sits on the steps.

HAPPY: I never heard him so loud, Mom.

LINDA: Well, come around more often; you'll hear him. *She sits down at the table and mends the lining of Willy's jacket.*

BIFF: Why didn't you ever write me about this, Mom?

LINDA: How would I write to you? For over three months you had no address.

BIFF: I was on the move. But you know I thought of you all the time. You know that, don't you, pal?

LINDA: I know, dear, I know. But he likes to have a letter. Just to know that there's still a possibility for better things.

BIFF: He's not like this all the time, is he?

LINDA: It's when you come home he's always the worst.

BIFF: When I come home?

LINDA: When you write you're coming, he's all smiles, and talks about the future, and—he's just wonderful. And then the closer you seem to come, the more shaky he gets, and then, by the time you get here, he's arguing, and he seems angry at you. I think it's just that maybe he can't bring himself to—to open up to you. Why are you so hateful to each other? Why is that?

BIFF, *evasively:* I'm not hateful, Mom.

LINDA: But you no sooner come in the door than you're fighting!

BIFF: I don't know why. I mean to change. I'm tryin', Mom, you understand?

LINDA: Are you home to stay now?

BIFF: I don't know. I want to look around, see what's doin'.

LINDA: Biff, you can't look around all your life, can you?

BIFF: I just can't take hold, Mom. I can't take hold of some kind of a life.

LINDA: Biff, a man is not a bird, to come and go with the springtime.

BIFF: Your hair . . . *He touches her hair.* Your hair got so gray.

LINDA: Oh, it's been gray since you were in high school. I just stopped dyeing it, that's all.

BIFF: Dye it again, will ya? I don't want my pal looking old. *He smiles.*

LINDA: You're such a boy! You think you can go away for a

year and . . . You've got to get it into your head now that one day you'll knock on this door and there'll be strange people here—

BIFF: What are you talking about? You're not even sixty, Mom.

LINDA: But what about your father?

BIFF, *lamely:* Well, I meant him too.

HAPPY: He admires Pop.

LINDA: Biff, dear, if you don't have any feeling for him, then you can't have any feeling for me.

BIFF: Sure I can, Mom.

LINDA: No. You can't just come to see me, because I love him. *With a threat, but only a threat, of tears:* He's the dearest man in the world to me, and I won't have anyone making him feel unwanted and low and blue. You've got to make up your mind now, darling, there's no leeway any more. Either he's your father and you pay him that respect, or else you're not to come here. I know he's not easy to get along with—nobody knows that better than me—but . . .

WILLY, *from the left, with a laugh:* Hey, hey, Biffo!

BIFF, *starting to go out after Willy:* What the hell is the matter with him? *Happy stops him.*

LINDA: Don't—don't go near him!

BIFF: Stop making excuses for him! He always, always wiped the floor with you. Never had an ounce of respect for you.

HAPPY: He's always had respect for—

BIFF: What the hell do you know about it?

HAPPY, *surlily:* Just don't call him crazy!

BIFF: He's got no character— Charley wouldn't do this. Not in his own house—spewing out that vomit from his mind.

HAPPY: Charley never had to cope with what he's got to.

BIFF: People are worse off than Willy Loman. Believe me, I've seen them!

LINDA: Then make Charley your father, Biff. You can't do that, can you? I don't say he's a great man. Willy Loman never made a lot of money. His name was never in the paper. He's not the finest character that ever lived. But he's a human being, and a terrible thing is happening to him. So attention must be paid. He's not to be allowed to fall into his grave like an old dog. Attention, attention must be finally paid to such a person. You called him crazy—

BIFF: I didn't mean—

LINDA: No, a lot of people think he's lost his—balance. But you don't have to be very smart to know what his trouble is. The man is exhausted.

HAPPY: Sure!

LINDA: A small man can be just as exhausted as a great man. He works for a company thirty-six years this March, opens up unheard-of territories to their trademark, and now in his old age they take his salary away.

HAPPY, *indignantly:* I didn't know that, Mom.

LINDA: You never asked, my dear! Now that you get your spending money someplace else you don't trouble your mind with him.

HAPPY: But I gave you money last—

LINDA: Christmas time, fifty dollars! To fix the hot water it cost ninety-seven fifty! For five weeks he's been on straight commission, like a beginner, an unknown!

BIFF: Those ungrateful bastards!

LINDA: Are they any worse than his sons? When he brought them business, when he was young, they were glad to see him. But now his old friends, the old buyers that loved him so and always found some order to hand him in a pinch—they're all dead, retired. He used to be able to make six, seven calls a day in Boston. Now he takes his valises out of the car and puts them back and takes them out again and he's exhausted. Instead of walking he talks now. He drives seven hundred miles, and when he gets there no one knows him any more, no one welcomes him. And what goes through a man's mind, driving seven hundred miles home without having earned a cent? Why shouldn't he talk to himself? Why? When he has to go to Charley and borrow fifty dollars a week and pretend to me that it's his pay? How long can that go on? How long? You see what I'm sitting here and waiting for? And you tell me he has no character? The man who never worked a day but for your benefit? When does he get the medal for that? Is this his reward—to turn around at the age of sixty-three and find his sons, who he loved better than his life, one a philandering bum—

HAPPY: Mom!

LINDA: That's all you are, my baby! *To Biff:* And you! What happened to the love you had for him? You were such pals! How you used to talk to him on the phone every night! How lonely he was till he could come home to you!

BIFF: All right, Mom. I'll live here in my room, and I'll get a job. I'll keep away from him, that's all.

LINDA: No, Biff. You can't stay here and fight all the time.

BIFF: He threw me out of this house, remember that.

LINDA: Why did he do that? I never knew why.

BIFF: Because I know he's a fake and he doesn't like anybody around who knows!

LINDA: Why a fake? In what way? What do you mean?

BIFF: Just don't lay it all at my feet. It's between me and him —that's all I have to say. I'll chip in from now on. He'll settle for half my pay check. He'll be all right. I'm going to bed. *He starts for the stairs.*

LINDA: He won't be all right.

BIFF, *turning on the stairs, furiously:* I hate this city and I'll stay here. Now what do you want?

LINDA: He's dying, Biff.

Happy turns quickly to her, shocked.

BIFF, *after a pause:* Why is he dying?

LINDA: He's been trying to kill himself.

BIFF, *with great horror:* How?

LINDA: I live from day to day.

BIFF: What're you talking about?

LINDA: Remember I wrote you that he smashed up the car again? In February?

BIFF: Well?

LINDA: The insurance inspector came. He said that they have evidence. That all these accidents in the last year—weren't— weren't—accidents.

HAPPY: How can they tell that? That's a lie.

LINDA: It seems there's a woman . . . *She takes a breath as*

⎰ BIFF, *sharply but contained:* What woman?

⎱ LINDA, *simultaneously:* . . . and this woman . . .

LINDA: What?

BIFF: Nothing. Go ahead.

LINDA: What did you say?

BIFF: Nothing. I just said what woman?

HAPPY: What about her?

LINDA: Well, it seems she was walking down the road and saw his car. She says that he wasn't driving fast at all, and that he didn't skid. She says he came to that little bridge, and then deliberately smashed into the railing, and it was only the shallowness of the water that saved him.

BIFF: Oh, no, he probably just fell asleep again.

LINDA: I don't think he fell asleep.

BIFF: Why not?

LINDA: Last month . . . *With great difficulty.* Oh, boys, it's so hard to say a thing like this! He's just a big stupid man to you, but I tell you there's more good in him than in many other people. *She chokes, wipes her eyes.* I was looking for a fuse. The lights blew out, and I went down the cellar. And behind the fuse box—it happened to fall out—was a length of rubber pipe—just short.

HAPPY: No kidding?

LINDA: There's a little attachment on the end of it. I knew right away. And sure enough, on the bottom of the water heater there's a new little nipple on the gas pipe.

HAPPY, *angrily:* That—jerk.

BIFF: Did you have it taken off?

LINDA: I'm—I'm ashamed to. How can I mention it to him? Every day I go down and take away that little rubber pipe. But, when he comes home, I put it back where it was. How can I insult him that way? I don't know what to do. I live from day to day, boys. I tell you, I know every thought in his mind. It sounds so old-fashioned and silly, but I tell you he put his whole life into you and you've turned your backs on him. *She is bent over in the chair, weeping, her face in her hands.* Biff, I swear to God! Biff, his life is in your hands!

HAPPY, *to Biff:* How do you like that damned fool!

BIFF, *kissing her:* All right, pal, all right. It's all settled now. I've been remiss. I know that, Mom. But now I'll stay, and I swear to you, I'll apply myself. *Kneeling in front of her, in a fever of self-reproach:* It's just—you see, Mom, I don't fit in business. Not that I won't try. I'll try, and I'll make good.

HAPPY: Sure you will. The trouble with you in business was you never tried to please people.

BIFF: I know, I—

HAPPY: Like when you worked for Harrison's. Bob Harrison said you were tops, and then you go and do some damn fool thing like whistling whole songs in the elevator like a comedian.

BIFF, *against Happy:* So what? I like to whistle sometimes.

HAPPY: You don't raise a guy to a responsible job who whistles in the elevator!

LINDA: Well, don't argue about it now.

HAPPY: Like when you'd go off and swim in the middle of the day instead of taking the line around.

BIFF, *his resentment rising:* Well, don't you run off? You take off sometimes, don't you? On a nice summer day?

HAPPY: Yeah, but I cover myself!

LINDA: Boys!

HAPPY: If I'm going to take a fade the boss can call any number where I'm supposed to be and they'll swear to him that I just left. I'll tell you something that I hate to say, Biff, but in the business world some of them think you're crazy.

BIFF, *angered:* Screw the business world!

HAPPY: All right, screw it! Great, but cover yourself!

LINDA: Hap, Hap!

BIFF: I don't care what they think! They've laughed at Dad for years, and you know why? Because we don't belong in this nuthouse of a city! We should be mixing cement on some open plain, or—or carpenters. A carpenter is allowed to whistle!

Willy walks in from the entrance of the house, at left.

WILLY: Even your grandfather was better than a carpenter. *Pause. They watch him.* You never grew up. Bernard does not whistle in the elevator, I assure you.

BIFF, *as though to laugh Willy out of it:* Yeah, but you do, Pop.

WILLY: I never in my life whistled in an elevator! And who in the business world thinks I'm crazy?

BIFF: I didn't mean it like that, Pop. Now don't make a whole thing out of it, will ya?

WILLY: Go back to the West! Be a carpenter, a cowboy, enjoy yourself!

LINDA: Willy, he was just saying—

WILLY: I heard what he said!

HAPPY, *trying to quiet Willy:* Hey, Pop, come on now . . .

WILLY, *continuing over Happy's line:* They laugh at me, heh? Go to Filene's, go to the Hub, go to Slattery's, Boston. Call out the name Willy Loman and see what happens! Big shot!

BIFF: All right, Pop.

WILLY: Big!

BIFF: All right!

WILLY: Why do you always insult me?

BIFF: I didn't say a word. *To Linda:* Did I say a word?

LINDA: He didn't say anything, Willy.

WILLY, *going to the doorway of the living room:* All right, good night, good night.

LINDA: Willy, dear, he just decided . . .

WILLY, *to Biff:* If you get tired hanging around tomorrow, paint the ceiling I put up in the living room.

BIFF: I'm leaving early tomorrow.

HAPPY: He's going to see Bill Oliver, Pop.

WILLY, *interestedly:* Oliver? For what?

BIFF, *with reserve, but trying, trying:* He always said he'd stake me. I'd like to go into business, so maybe I can take him up on it.

LINDA: Isn't that wonderful?

WILLY: Don't interrupt. What's wonderful about it? There's fifty men in the City of New York who'd stake him. *To Biff:* Sporting goods?

BIFF: I guess so. I know something about it and—

WILLY: He knows something about it! You know sporting goods better than Spalding, for God's sake! How much is he giving you?

BIFF: I don't know, I didn't even see him yet, but—

WILLY: Then what're you talkin' about?

BIFF, *getting angry:* Well, all I said was I'm gonna see him, that's all!

WILLY, *turning away:* Ah, you're counting your chickens again.

BIFF, *starting left for the stairs:* Oh, Jesus, I'm going to sleep!

WILLY, *calling after him:* Don't curse in this house!

BIFF, *turning:* Since when did you get so clean?

HAPPY, *trying to stop them:* Wait a . . .

WILLY: Don't use that language to me! I won't have it!

HAPPY, *grabbing Biff, shouts:* Wait a minute! I got an idea. I got a feasible idea. Come here, Biff, let's talk this over now, let's talk some sense here. When I was down in Florida last time, I thought of a great idea to sell sporting goods. It just came back to me. You and I, Biff—we have a line, the Loman Line. We train a couple of weeks, and put on a couple of exhibitions, see?

WILLY: That's an idea!

HAPPY: Wait! We form two basketball teams, see? Two water-polo teams. We play each other. It's a million dollars' worth of publicity. Two brothers, see? The Loman Brothers. Displays in the Royal Palms—all the hotels. And banners over the ring and the basketball court: "Loman Brothers." Baby, we could sell sporting goods!

WILLY: That is a one-million-dollar idea!

LINDA: Marvelous!

BIFF: I'm in great shape as far as that's concerned.

HAPPY: And the beauty of it is, Biff, it wouldn't be like a business. We'd be out playin' ball again . . .

BIFF, *enthused:* Yeah, that's . . .

WILLY: Million-dollar . . .

HAPPY: And you wouldn't get fed up with it, Biff. It'd be the family again. There'd be the old honor, and comradeship, and if you wanted to go off for a swim or somethin'—well, you'd do it! Without some smart cooky gettin' up ahead of you!

WILLY: Lick the world! You guys together could absolutely lick the civilized world.

BIFF: I'll see Oliver tomorrow. Hap, if we could work that out . . .

LINDA: Maybe things are beginning to—

WILLY, *wildly enthused, to Linda:* Stop interrupting! *To Biff:* But don't wear sport jacket and slacks when you see Oliver.

BIFF: No, I'll—

WILLY: A business suit, and talk as little as possible, and don't crack any jokes.

BIFF: He did like me. Always liked me.

LINDA: He loved you!

WILLY, *to Linda:* Will you stop! *To Biff:* Walk in very serious. You are not applying for a boy's job. Money is to pass. Be quiet, fine, and serious. Everybody likes a kidder, but nobody lends him money.

HAPPY: I'll try to get some myself, Biff. I'm sure I can.

WILLY: I see great things for you kids, I think your troubles are over. But remember, start big and you'll end big. Ask for fifteen. How much you gonna ask for?

BIFF: Gee, I don't know—

WILLY: And don't say "Gee." "Gee" is a boy's word. A man walking in for fifteen thousand dollars does not say "Gee!"

BIFF: Ten, I think, would be top though.

WILLY: Don't be so modest. You always started too low. Walk in with a big laugh. Don't look worried. Start off with a couple of your good stories to lighten things up. It's not what you say, it's how you say it—because personality always wins the day.

LINDA: Oliver always thought the highest of him—

WILLY: Will you let me talk?

BIFF: Don't yell at her, Pop, will ya?

WILLY, *angrily:* I was talking, wasn't I?

BIFF: I don't like you yelling at her all the time, and I'm tellin' you, that's all.

WILLY: What're you, takin' over this house?

LINDA: Willy—

WILLY, *turning on her:* Don't take his side all the time, goddammit!

BIFF, *furiously:* Stop yelling at her!

WILLY, *suddenly pulling on his cheek, beaten down, guilt-ridden:* Give my best to Bill Oliver—he may remember me. *He exits through the living-room doorway.*

LINDA, *her voice subdued:* What'd you have to start that for? *Biff turns away.* You see how sweet he was as soon as you talked hopefully? *She goes over to Biff.* Come up and say good night to him. Don't let him go to bed that way.

HAPPY: Come on, Biff, let's buck him up.

LINDA: Please, dear. Just say good night. It takes so little to make him happy. Come. *She goes through the living-room doorway, calling upstairs from within the living room:* Your pajamas are hanging in the bathroom, Willy!

HAPPY, *looking toward where Linda went out:* What a woman! They broke the mold when they made her. You know that, Biff?

BIFF: He's off salary. My God, working on commission!

HAPPY: Well, let's face it: he's no hot-shot selling man. Except that sometimes, you have to admit, he's a sweet personality.

BIFF, *deciding:* Lend me ten bucks, will ya? I want to buy some new ties.

HAPPY: I'll take you to a place I know. Beautiful stuff. Wear one of my striped shirts tomorrow.

BIFF: She got gray. Mom got awful old. Gee, I'm gonna go in to Oliver tomorrow and knock him for a—

HAPPY: Come on up. Tell that to Dad. Let's give him a whirl. Come on.

BIFF, *steamed up:* You know, with ten thousand bucks, boy!

HAPPY, *as they go into the living room:* That's the talk, Biff, that's the first time I've heard the old confidence out of you! *From within the living room, fading off:* You're gonna live with me, kid, and any babe you want just say the word . . . *The last lines are hardly heard. They are mounting the stairs to their parents' bedroom.*

LINDA, *entering her bedroom and addressing Willy, who is in the bathroom. She is straightening the bed for him:* Can you do anything about the shower? It drips.

WILLY, *from the bathroom:* All of a sudden everything falls to pieces! Goddam plumbing, oughta be sued, those people. I hardly finished putting it in and the thing . . . *His words rumble off.*

LINDA: I'm just wondering if Oliver will remember him. You think he might?

WILLY, *coming out of the bathroom in his pajamas:* Remember him? What's the matter with you, you crazy? If he'd've stayed with Oliver he'd be on top by now! Wait'll Oliver gets a look at him. You don't know the average caliber any more. The average young man today—*he is getting into bed*—is got a caliber of zero. Greatest thing in the world for him was to bum around.

Biff and Happy enter the bedroom. Slight pause.

WILLY, *stops short, looking at Biff:* Glad to hear it, boy.

HAPPY: He wanted to say good night to you, sport.

WILLY, *to Biff:* Yeah. Knock him dead, boy. What'd you want to tell me?

BIFF: Just take it easy, Pop. Good night. *He turns to go.*

WILLY, *unable to resist:* And if anything falls off the desk while you're talking to him—like a package or something don't you pick it up. They have office boys for that.

LINDA: I'll make a big breakfast—

WILLY: Will you let me finish? *To Biff:* Tell him you were in the business in the West. Not farm work.

BIFF: All right, Dad.

LINDA: I think everything—

WILLY, *going right through her speech:* And don't undersell yourself. No less than fifteen thousand dollars.

BIFF, *unable to bear him:* Okay. Good night, Mom. *He starts moving.*

WILLY: Because you got a greatness in you, Biff, remember that. You got all kinds a greatness . . . *He lies back, exhausted. Biff walks out.*

LINDA, *calling after Biff:* Sleep well, darling!

HAPPY: I'm gonna get married, Mom. I wanted to tell you.

LINDA: Go to sleep, dear.

HAPPY, *going:* I just wanted to tell you.

WILLY: Keep up the good work. *Happy exits.* God . . . remember that Ebbets Field game? The championship of the city?

LINDA: Just rest. Should I sing to you?

WILLY: Yeah. Sing to me. *Linda hums a soft lullaby.* When that team came out—he was the tallest, remember?

LINDA: Oh, yes. And in gold.

Biff enters the darkened kitchen, takes a cigarette, and leaves the house. He comes downstage into a golden pool of light. He smokes, staring at the night.

WILLY: Like a young god. Hercules—something like that. And the sun, the sun all around him. Remember how he waved to me? Right up from the field, with the representatives of three colleges standing by? And the buyers I brought, and the cheers when he came out—Loman, Loman, Loman! God Almighty, he'll be great yet. A star like that, magnificent, can never really fade away!

The light on Willy is fading. The gas heater begins to glow through the kitchen wall, near the stairs, a blue flame beneath red coils.

LINDA, *timidly:* Willy dear, what has he got against you?

WILLY: I'm so tired. Don't talk any more.

Biff slowly returns to the kitchen. He stops, stares toward the heater.

LINDA: Will you ask Howard to let you work in New York?

WILLY: First thing in the morning. Everything'll be all right.

Biff reaches behind the heater and draws out a length of rubber tubing. He is horrified and turns his head toward Willy's room, still dimly lit, from which the strains of Linda's desperate but monotonous humming rise.

WILLY, *staring through the window into the moonlight:* Gee, look at the moon moving between the buildings!
Biff wraps the tubing around his hand and quickly goes up the stairs.

CURTAIN

Act Two

Music is heard, gay and bright. The curtain rises as the music fades away. Willy, in shirt sleeves, is sitting at the kitchen table, sipping coffee, his hat in his lap. Linda is filling his cup when she can.

WILLY: Wonderful coffee. Meal in itself.

LINDA: Can I make you some eggs?

WILLY: No. Take a breath.

LINDA: You look so rested, dear.

WILLY: I slept like a dead one. First time in months. Imagine, sleeping till ten on a Tuesday morning. Boys left nice and early, heh?

LINDA: They were out of here by eight o'clock.

WILLY: Good work!

LINDA: It was so thrilling to see them leaving together. I can't get over the shaving lotion in this house!

WILLY, *smiling:* Mmm—

LINDA: Biff was very changed this morning. His whole attitude seemed to be hopeful. He couldn't wait to get downtown to see Oliver.

WILLY: He's heading for a change. There's no question, there simply are certain men that take longer to get—solidified. How did he dress?

LINDA: His blue suit. He's so handsome in that suit. He could be a—anything in that suit!

Willy gets up from the table. Linda holds his jacket for him.

WILLY: There's no question, no question at all. Gee, on the way home tonight I'd like to buy some seeds.

LINDA, *laughing:* That'd be wonderful. But not enough sun gets back there. Nothing'll grow any more.

WILLY: You wait, kid, before it's all over we're gonna get a little place out in the country, and I'll raise some vegetables, a couple of chickens . . .

LINDA: You'll do it yet, dear.

Willy walks out of his jacket. Linda follows him.

WILLY: And they'll get married, and come for a weekend. I'd build a little guest house. 'Cause I got so many fine tools, all I'd need would be a little lumber and some peace of mind.

LINDA, *joyfully:* I sewed the lining . . .

WILLY: I could build two guest houses, so they'd both come. Did he decide how much he's going to ask Oliver for?

LINDA, *getting him into the jacket:* He didn't mention it, but I imagine ten or fifteen thousand. You going to talk to Howard today?

WILLY: Yeah. I'll put it to him straight and simple. He'll just have to take me off the road.

LINDA: And Willy, don't forget to ask for a little advance, because we've got the insurance premium. It's the grace period now.

WILLY: That's a hundred . . . ?

LINDA: A hundred and eight, sixty-eight. Because we're a little short again.

WILLY: Why are we short?

LINDA: Well, you had the motor job on the car . . .

WILLY: That goddam Studebaker!

LINDA: And you got one more payment on the refrigerator . . .

WILLY: But it just broke again!

LINDA: Well, it's old, dear.

WILLY: I told you we should've bought a well-advertised machine. Charley bought a General Electric and it's twenty years old and it's still good, that son-of-a-bitch.

LINDA: But, Willy—

WILLY: Whoever heard of a Hastings refrigerator? Once in my life I would like to own something outright before it's broken! I'm always in a race with the junkyard! I just finished paying for the car and it's on its last legs. The refrigerator consumes belts like a goddam maniac. They time those things. They time them so when you finally paid for them, they're used up.

LINDA, *buttoning up his jacket as he unbuttons it:* All told, about two hundred dollars would carry us, dear. But that includes the last payment on the mortgage. After this payment, Willy, the house belongs to us.

WILLY: It's twenty-five years!

LINDA: Biff was nine years old when we bought it.

WILLY: Well, that's a great thing. To weather a twenty-five-year mortgage is—

LINDA: It's an accomplishment.

WILLY: All the cement, the lumber, the reconstruction I put in this house! There ain't a crack to be found in it any more.

LINDA: Well, it served its purpose.

WILLY: What purpose? Some stranger'll come along, move in, and that's that. If only Biff would take this house, and raise a family . . . *He starts to go.* Good-by, I'm late.

LINDA, *suddenly remembering:* Oh, I forgot! You're supposed to meet them for dinner.

WILLY: Me?

LINDA: At Frank's Chop House on Forty-eighth near Sixth Avenue.

WILLY: Is that so! How about you?

LINDA: No, just the three of you. They're gonna blow you to a big meal!

WILLY: Don't say! Who thought of that?

LINDA: Biff came to me this morning, Willy, and he said, "Tell Dad, we want to blow him to a big meal." Be there six o'clock. You and your two boys are going to have dinner.

WILLY: Gee whiz! That's really somethin'. I'm gonna knock Howard for a loop, kid. I'll get an advance, and I'll come home with a New York job. Goddammit, now I'm gonna do it!

LINDA: Oh, that's the spirit, Willy!

WILLY: I will never get behind a wheel the rest of my life!

LINDA: It's changing, Willy, I can feel it changing!

WILLY: Beyond a question. G'by, I'm late. *He starts to go again.*

LINDA, *calling after him as she runs to the kitchen table for a handkerchief:* You got your glasses?

WILLY—*he feels for them, then comes back in:* Yeah, yeah, got my glasses.

LINDA, *giving him the handkerchief:* And a handkerchief.

WILLY: Yeah, handkerchief.

LINDA: And your saccharine?

Willy: Yeah, my saccharine.

LINDA: Be careful on the subway stairs.

She kisses him, and a silk stocking is seen hanging from her hand. Willy notices it.

WILLY: Will you stop mending stockings? At least while I'm in the house. It gets me nervous. I can't tell you. Please.

Linda hides the stocking in her hand as she follows Willy across the forestage in front of the house.

LINDA: Remember, Frank's Chop House.

WILLY, *passing the apron:* Maybe beets would grow out there.

LINDA, *laughing:* But you tried so many times.

WILLY: Yeah. Well, don't work hard today. *He disappears around the right corner of the house.*

LINDA: Be careful!

As Willy vanishes, Linda waves to him. Suddenly the phone rings. She runs across the stage and into the kitchen and lifts it.

LINDA: Hello? Oh, Biff! I'm so glad you called, I just . . . Yes, sure, I just told him. Yes, he'll be there for dinner at six o'clock, I didn't forget. Listen, I was just dying to tell you. You know that little rubber pipe I told you about? That he connected to the gas heater? I finally decided to go down the cellar this morning and take it away and destroy it. But it's gone! Imagine? He took it away himself, it isn't there! *She lis-*

tens. When? Oh, then you took it. Oh—nothing, it's just that I'd hoped he'd taken it away himself. Oh, I'm not worried, darling, because this morning he left in such high spirits, it was like the old days! I'm not afraid any more. Did Mr. Oliver see you? . . . Well, you wait there then. And make a nice impression on him, darling. Just don't perspire too much before you see him. And have a nice time with Dad. He may have big news too! . . . That's right, a New York job. And be sweet to him tonight, dear. Be loving to him. Because he's only a little boat looking for a harbor. *She is trembling with sorrow and joy.* Oh, that's wonderful, Biff, you'll save his life. Thanks, darling. Just put your arm around him when he comes into the restaurant. Give him a smile. That's the boy . . . Good-by, dear. . . . You got your comb? . . . That's fine. Good-by, Biff dear.

In the middle of her speech, Howard Wagner, thirty-six, wheels on a small typewriter table on which is a wire-recording machine and proceeds to plug it in. This is on the left forestage. Light slowly fades on Linda as it rises on Howard. Howard is intent on threading the machine and only glances over his shoulder as Willy appears.

WILLY: Pst! Pst!

HOWARD: Hello, Willy, come in.

WILLY: Like to have a little talk with you, Howard.

HOWARD: Sorry to keep you waiting. I'll be with you in a minute.

WILLY: What's that, Howard?

HOWARD: Didn't you ever see one of these? Wire recorder.

WILLY: Oh. Can we talk a minute?

HOWARD: Records things. Just got delivery yesterday. Been driving me crazy, the most terrific machine I ever saw in my life. I was up all night with it.

WILLY: What do you do with it?

HOWARD: I bought it for dictation, but you can do anything with it. Listen to this. I had it home last night. Listen to what I picked up. The first one is my daughter. Get this. *He flicks the switch and "Roll out the Barrel" is heard being whistled.* Listen to that kid whistle.

WILLY: That is lifelike, isn't it?

HOWARD: Seven years old. Get that tone.

WILLY: Ts, ts. Like to ask a little favor if you . . .

The whistling breaks off, and the voice of Howard's daughter is heard.

HIS DAUGHTER: "Now you, Daddy."

HOWARD: She's crazy for me! *Again the same song is whistled.* That's me! Ha! *He winks.*

WILLY: You're very good!

The whistling breaks off again. The machine runs silent for a moment.

HOWARD: Sh! Get this now, this is my son.

HIS SON: "The capital of Alabama is Montgomery; the capital of Arizona is Phoenix; the capital of Arkansas is Little Rock; the capital of California is Sacramento . . ." *and on, and on.*

HOWARD, *holding up five fingers:* Five years old, Willy!

WILLY: He'll make an announcer some day!

HIS SON, *continuing:* "The capital . . ."

HOWARD: Get that—alphabetical order! *The machine breaks off suddenly.* Wait a minute. The maid kicked the plug out.

WILLY: It certainly is a—

HOWARD: Sh, for God's sake!

HIS SON: "It's nine o'clock, Bulova watch time. So I have to go to sleep."

WILLY: That really is—

HOWARD: Wait a minute! The next is my wife.

They wait.

HOWARD'S VOICE: "Go on, say something." *Pause.* "Well, you gonna talk?"

HIS WIFE: "I can't think of anything."

HOWARD'S VOICE: "Well, talk—it's turning."

HIS WIFE, *shyly, beaten:* "Hello." *Silence.* "Oh, Howard, I can't talk into this . . ."

HOWARD, *snapping the machine off:* That was my wife.

WILLY: That is a wonderful machine. Can we—

HOWARD: I tell you, Willy, I'm gonna take my camera, and my bandsaw, and all my hobbies, and out they go. This is the most fascinating relaxation I ever found.

WILLY: I think I'll get one myself.

HOWARD: Sure, they're only a hundred and a half. You can't do without it. Supposing you wanna hear Jack Benny, see? But you can't be at home at that hour. So you tell the maid to turn the radio on when Jack Benny comes on, and this automatically goes on with the radio . . .

WILLY: And when you come home you . . .

HOWARD: You can come home twelve o'clock, one o'clock, any time you like, and you get yourself a Coke and sit yourself down, throw the switch, and there's Jack Benny's program in the middle of the night!

WILLY: I'm definitely going to get one. Because lots of time

I'm on the road, and I think to myself, what I must be missing on the radio!

HOWARD: Don't you have a radio in the car?

WILLY: Well, yeah, but who ever thinks of turning it on?

HOWARD: Say, aren't you supposed to be in Boston?

WILLY: That's what I want to talk to you about, Howard. You got a minute? *He draws a chair in from the wing.*

HOWARD: What happened? What're you doing here?

WILLY: Well . . .

HOWARD: You didn't crack up again, did you?

WILLY: Oh, no. No . . .

HOWARD: Geez, you had me worried there for a minute. What's the trouble?

WILLY: Well, tell you the truth, Howard. I've come to the decision that I'd rather not travel any more.

HOWARD: Not travel! Well, what'll you do?

WILLY: Remember, Christmas time, when you had the party here? You said you'd try to think of some spot for me here in town.

HOWARD: With us?

WILLY: Well, sure.

HOWARD: Oh, yeah, yeah. I remember. Well, I couldn't think of anything for you, Willy.

WILLY: I tell ya, Howard. The kids are all grown up, y'know. I don't need much any more. If I could take home—well, sixty-five dollars a week, I could swing it.

HOWARD: Yeah, but Willy, see I—

WILLY: I tell ya why, Howard. Speaking frankly and between the two of us, y'know—I'm just a little tired.

HOWARD: Oh, I could understand that, Willy. But you're a road man, Willy, and we do a road business. We've only got a half-dozen salesmen on the floor here.

WILLY: God knows, Howard, I never asked a favor of any man. But I was with the firm when your father used to carry you in here in his arms.

HOWARD: I know that, Willy, but—

WILLY: Your father came to me the day you were born and asked me what I thought of the name of Howard, may he rest in peace.

HOWARD: I appreciate that, Willy, but there just is no spot here for you. If I had a spot I'd slam you right in, but I just don't have a single solitary spot.

He looks for his lighter. Willy has picked it up and gives it to him. Pause.

WILLY, *with increasing anger:* Howard, all I need to set my table is fifty dollars a week.

HOWARD: But where am I going to put you, kid?

WILLY: Look, it isn't a question of whether I can sell merchandise, is it?

HOWARD: No, but it's a business, kid, and everybody's gotta pull his own weight.

WILLY, *desperately:* Just let me tell you a story, Howard—

HOWARD: 'Cause you gotta admit, business is business.

WILLY, *angrily:* Business is definitely business, but just listen for a minute. You don't understand this. When I was a boy—eighteen, nineteen—I was already on the road. And there was a question in my mind as to whether selling had a future for me. Because in those days I had a yearning to go to Alaska. See, there were three gold strikes in one month in Alaska, and I felt like going out. Just for the ride, you might say.

HOWARD, *barely interested:* Don't say.

WILLY: Oh, yeah, my father lived many years in Alaska. He was an adventurous man. We've got quite a little streak of self-reliance in our family. I thought I'd go out with my older brother and try to locate him, and maybe settle in the North with the old man. And I was almost decided to go, when I met a salesman in the Parker House. His name was Dave Single-man. And he was eighty-four years old, and he'd drummed merchandise in thirty-one states. And old Dave, he'd go up to his room, y'understand, put on his green velvet slippers—I'll never forget—and pick up his phone and call the buyers, and without ever leaving his room, at the age of eighty-four, he made his living. And when I saw that, I realized that selling was the greatest career a man could want. 'Cause what could be more satisfying than to be able to go, at the age of eighty-four, into twenty or thirty different cities, and pick up a phone, and be remembered and loved and helped by so many different people? Do you know? when he died—and by the way he died the death of a salesman, in his green velvet slippers in the smoker of the New York, New Haven and Hartford, going into Boston—when he died, hundreds of salesmen and buyers were at his funeral. Things were sad on a lotta trains for months after that. *He stands up. Howard has not looked at him.* In those days there was personality in it, Howard. There was respect, and comradeship, and gratitude in it. Today, it's all cut and dried, and there's no chance for bringing friendship to bear—or personality. You see what I mean? They don't know me any more.

HOWARD, *moving away, to the right:* That's just the thing, Willy.

WILLY: If I had forty dollars a week—that's all I'd need. Forty dollars, Howard.

HOWARD: Kid, I can't take blood from a stone, I—

WILLY, *desperation is on him now:* Howard, the year Al Smith was nominated, your father came to me and—

HOWARD, *starting to go off:* I've got to see some people, kid.

WILLY, *stopping him:* I'm talking about your father! There were promises made across this desk! You mustn't tell me you've got people to see—I put thirty-four years into this firm, Howard, and now I can't pay my insurance! You can't eat the orange and throw the peel away—a man is not a piece of fruit! *After a pause:* Now pay attention. Your father—in 1928 I had a big year, I averaged a hundred and seventy dollars a week in commissions.

HOWARD, *impatiently:* Now, Willy, you never averaged—

WILLY, *banging his hand on the desk:* I averaged a hundred and seventy dollars a week in the year of 1928! And your father came to me—or rather, I was in the office here—it was right over this desk—and he put his hand on my shoulder—

HOWARD, *getting up:* You'll have to excuse me, Willy, I gotta see some people. Pull yourself together. *Going out:* I'll be back in a little while.

On Howard's exit, the light on his chair grows very bright and strange.

WILLY: Pull myself together! What the hell did I say to him? My God, I was yelling at him! How could I! *Willy breaks off, staring at the light, which occupies the chair, animating it. He approaches this chair, standing across the desk from it.* Frank, Frank, don't you remember what you told me that time? How you put your hand on my shoulder, and Frank . . . *He leans on the desk and as he speaks the dead man's name he accidentally switches on the recorder, and instantly*

HOWARD'S SON: ". . . of New York is Albany. The capital of Ohio is Cincinnati, the capital of Rhode Island is . . ." *The recitation continues.*

WILLY, *leaping away with fright, shouting:* Ha! Howard! Howard! Howard!

HOWARD, *rushing in:* What happened?

WILLY, *pointing at the machine, which continues nasally, childishly, with the capital cities:* Shut it off! Shut it off!

HOWARD, *pulling the plug out:* Look, Willy . . .

WILLY, *pressing his hands to his eyes:* I gotta get myself some coffee. I'll get some coffee . . .

Willy starts to walk out. Howard stops him.

HOWARD, *rolling up the cord:* Willy, look . . .

WILLY: I'll go to Boston.

HOWARD: Willy, you can't go to Boston for us.

WILLY: Why can't I go?

HOWARD: I don't want you to represent us. I've been meaning to tell you for a long time now.

WILLY: Howard, are you firing me?

HOWARD: I think you need a good long rest, Willy.

Willy: Howard—

HOWARD: And when you feel better, come back, and we'll see if we can work something out.

WILLY: But I gotta earn money, Howard. I'm in no position to—

HOWARD: Where are your sons? Why don't your sons give you a hand?

WILLY: They're working on a very big deal.

HOWARD: This is no time for false pride, Willy. You go to your sons and you tell them that you're tired. You've got two great boys, haven't you?

WILLY: Oh, no question, no question, but in the meantime . . .

HOWARD: Then that's that, heh?

WILLY: All right, I'll go to Boston tomorrow.

HOWARD: No, no.

WILLY: I can't throw myself on my sons. I'm not a cripple!

HOWARD: Look, kid, I'm busy this morning.

WILLY, *grasping Howard's arm:* Howard, you've got to let me go to Boston!

HOWARD, *hard, keeping himself under control:* I've got a line of people to see this morning. Sit down, take five minutes, and pull yourself together, and then go home, will ya? I need the office, Willy. *He starts to go; turns, remembering the recorder, starts to push off the table holding the recorder.* Oh, yeah. Whenever you can this week, stop by and drop off the samples. You'll feel better, Willy, and then come back and we'll talk. Pull yourself together, kid, there's people outside.

Howard exits, pushing the table off left. Willy stares into space, exhausted. Now the music is heard—Ben's music—first distantly, then closer, closer. As Willy speaks, Ben enters from the right. He carries valise and umbrella.

WILLY: Oh, Ben, how did you do it? What is the answer? Did you wind up the Alaska deal already?

BEN: Doesn't take much time if you know what you're doing. Just a short business trip. Boarding ship in an hour. Wanted to say good-by.

WILLY: Ben, I've got to talk to you.

BEN, *glancing at his watch:* Haven't the time, William.

WILLY, *crossing the apron to Ben:* Ben, nothing's working out. I don't know what to do.

BEN: Now, look here, William. I've bought timberland in Alaska and I need a man to look after things for me.

WILLY: God, timberland! Me and my boys in those grand outdoors!

BEN: You've a new continent at your doorstep, William. Get out of these cities, they're full of talk and time payments and courts of law. Screw on your fists and you can fight for a fortune up there.

WILLY: Yes, yes! Linda, Linda!

Linda enters as of old, with the wash.

LINDA: Oh, you're back?

BEN: I haven't much time.

WILLY: No, wait! Linda, he's got a proposition for me in Alaska.

LINDA: But you've got— *To Ben:* He's got a beautiful job here.

WILLY: But in Alaska, kid, I could—

LINDA: You're doing well enough, Willy!

BEN, *to Linda:* Enough for what, my dear?

LINDA, *frightened of Ben and angry at him:* Don't say those things to him! Enough to be happy right here, right now. *To Willy, while Ben laughs:* Why must everybody conquer the world? You're well liked, and the boys love you, and some-day—*to Ben*—why, old man Wagner told him just the other day that if he keeps it up he'll be a member of the firm, didn't he, Willy?

WILLY: Sure, sure. I am building something with this firm, Ben, and if a man is building something he must be on the right track, mustn't he?

BEN: What are you building? Lay your hand on it. Where is it?

WILLY, *hesitantly:* That's true, Linda, there's nothing.

LINDA: Why? *To Ben:* There's a man eighty-four years old—

WILLY: That's right, Ben, that's right. When I look at that man I say, what is there to worry about?

BEN: Bah!

WILLY: It's true, Ben. All he has to do is go into any city, pick up the phone, and he's making his living and you know why?

BEN, *picking up his valise:* I've got to go.

WILLY, *holding Ben back:* Look at this boy!

Biff, in his high school sweater, enters carrying suitcase. Happy carries Biff's shoulder guards, gold helmet, and football pants.

WILLY: Without a penny to his name, three great universities are begging for him, and from there the sky's the limit, because it's not what you do, Ben. It's who you know and the smile on your face! It's contacts, Ben, contacts! The whole wealth of Alaska passes over the lunch table at the Commodore Hotel, and that's the wonder, the wonder of this country, that a man can end with diamonds here on the basis of being liked! *He turns to Biff.* And that's why when you get out on that field today it's important. Because thousands of people will be rooting for you and loving you. *To Ben, who has again begun to leave:* And Ben! when he walks into a business office his name will sound out like a bell and all the doors will open to him! I've seen it, Ben, I've seen it a thousand times! You can't feel it with your hand like timber, but it's there!

BEN: Good-by, William.

WILLY: Ben, am I right? Don't you think I'm right? I value your advice.

BEN: There's a new continent at your doorstep, William. You could walk out rich. Rich! *He is gone.*

WILLY: We'll do it here, Ben! You hear me? We're gonna do it here!

Young Bernard rushes in. The gay music of the Boys is heard.

BERNARD: Oh, gee, I was afraid you left already!

WILLY: Why? What time is it?

BERNARD: It's half-past one!

WILLY: Well, come on, everybody! Ebbets Field next stop! Where's the pennants? *He rushes through the wall-line of the kitchen and out into the living room.*

LINDA, *to Biff:* Did you pack fresh underwear?

BIFF, *who has been limbering up:* I want to go!

BERNARD: Biff, I'm carrying your helmet, ain't I?

HAPPY: No, I'm carrying the helmet.

BERNARD: Oh, Biff, you promised me.

HAPPY: I'm carrying the helmet.

BERNARD: How am I going to get in the locker room?

LINDA: Let him carry the shoulder guards. *She puts her coat and hat on in the kitchen.*

BERNARD: Can I, Biff? 'Cause I told everybody I'm going to be in the locker room.

HAPPY: In Ebbets Field it's the clubhouse.

BERNARD: I meant the clubhouse. Biff!

HAPPY: Biff!

BIFF, *grandly, after a slight pause:* Let him carry the shoulder guards.

HAPPY, *as he gives Bernard the shoulder guards:* Stay close to us now.

Willy rushes in with the pennants.

WILLY, *handing them out:* Everybody wave when Biff comes out on the field. *Happy and Bernard run off.* You set now, boy?

The music has died away.

BIFF: Ready to go, Pop. Every muscle is ready.

WILLY, *at the edge of the apron:* You realize what this means?

BIFF: That's right, Pop.

WILLY, *feeling Biff's muscles:* You're comin' home this afternoon captain of the All-Scholastic Championship Team of the City of New York.

BIFF: I got it, Pop. And remember, pal, when I take off my helmet, that touchdown is for you.

WILLY: Let's go! *He is starting out, with his arms around Biff, when Charley enters, as of old, in knickers.* I got no room for you, Charley.

CHARLEY: Room? For what?

WILLY: In the car.

CHARLEY: You goin' for a ride? I wanted to shoot some casino.

WILLY, *furiously:* Casino! *Incredulously:* Don't you realize what today is?

LINDA: Oh, he knows, Willy. He's just kidding you.

WILLY: That's nothing to kid about!

CHARLEY: No, Linda, what's goin' on?

LINDA: He's playing in Ebbets Field.

CHARLEY: Baseball in this weather?

WILLY: Don't talk to him. Come on, come on! *He is pushing them out.*

CHARLEY: Wait a minute, didn't you hear the news?

WILLY: What?

CHARLEY: Don't you listen to the radio? Ebbets Field just blew up.

WILLY: You go to hell! *Charley laughs. Pushing them out:* Come on, come on! We're late.

CHARLEY, *as they go:* Knock a homer, Biff, knock a homer!

WILLY, *the last to leave, turning to Charley:* I don't think that was funny, Charley. This is the greatest day of his life.

CHARLEY: Willy, when are you going to grow up?

WILLY: Yeah, heh? When this game is over, Charley, you'll be laughing out of the other side of your face. They'll be calling him another Red Grange. Twenty-five thousand a year.

CHARLEY, *kidding:* Is that so?

WILLY: Yeah, that's so.

CHARLEY: Well, then, I'm sorry, Willy. But tell me something.

WILLY: What?

CHARLEY: Who is Red Grange?

WILLY: Put up your hands. Goddam you, put up your hands!

Charley, chuckling, shakes his head and walks away, around the left corner of the stage. Willy follows him. The music rises to a mocking frenzy.

WILLY: Who the hell do you think you are, better than everybody else? You don't know everything, you big, ignorant, stupid . . . Put up your hands!

Light rises, on the right side of the forestage, on a small table in the reception room of Charley's office. Traffic sounds are heard. Bernard, now mature, sits whistling to himself. A pair of tennis rackets and an overnight bag are on the floor beside him.

WILLY, *offstage:* What are you walking away for? Don't walk away! If you're going to say something say it to my face! I know you laugh at me behind my back. You'll laugh out of the other side of your goddam face after this game. Touchdown! Touchdown! Eighty thousand people! Touchdown! Right between the goal posts.

Bernard is a quiet, earnest, but self-assured young man. Willy's voice is coming from right upstage now. Bernard lowers his feet off the table and listens. Jenny, his father's secretary, enters.

JENNY, *distressed:* Say, Bernard, will you go out in the hall?

BERNARD: What is that noise? Who is it?

JENNY: Mr. Loman. He just got off the elevator.

BERNARD, *getting up:* Who's he arguing with?

JENNY: Nobody. There's nobody with him. I can't deal with him any more, and your father gets all upset everytime he comes. I've got a lot of typing to do, and your father's waiting to sign it. Will you see him?

WILLY, *entering:* Touchdown! Touch— *He sees Jenny.* Jenny, Jenny, good to see you. How're ya? Workin'? Or still honest?

JENNY: Fine. How've you been feeling?

WILLY: Not much any more, Jenny. Ha, ha! *He is surprised to see the rackets.*

BERNARD: Hello, Uncle Willy.

WILLY, *almost shocked:* Bernard! Well, look who's here! *He comes quickly, guiltily, to Bernard and warmly shakes his hand.*

BERNARD: How are you? Good to see you.

WILLY: What are you doing here?

BERNARD: Oh, just stopped by to see Pop. Get off my feet till my train leaves. I'm going to Washington in a few minutes.

WILLY: Is he in?

BERNARD: Yes, he's in his office with the accountant. Sit down.

WILLY, *sitting down:* What're you going to do in Washington?

BERNARD: Oh, just a case I've got there, Willy.

WILLY: That so? *Indicating the rackets:* You going to play tennis there?

BERNARD: I'm staying with a friend who's got a court.

WILLY: Don't say. His own tennis court. Must be fine people, I bet.

BERNARD: They are, very nice. Dad tells me Biff's in town.

WILLY, *with a big smile:* Yeah, Biff's in. Working on a very big deal, Bernard.

BERNARD: What's Biff doing?

WILLY: Well, he's been doing very big things in the West. But he decided to establish himself here. Very big. We're having dinner. Did I hear your wife had a boy?

BERNARD: That's right. Our second.

WILLY: Two boys! What do you know!

BERNARD: What kind of a deal has Biff got?

WILLY: Well, Bill Oliver—very big sporting-goods man—he wants Biff very badly. Called him in from the West. Long distance, carte blanche, special deliveries. Your friends have their own private tennis court?

BERNARD: You still with the old firm, Willy?

WILLY, *after a pause:* I'm—I'm overjoyed to see how you made the grade, Bernard, overjoyed. It's an encouraging thing to see a young man really—really— Looks very good for Biff —very— *He breaks off, then:* Bernard— *He is so full of emotion, he breaks off again.*

BERNARD: What is it, Willy?

WILLY, *small and alone:* What—what's the secret?

BERNARD: What secret?

WILLY: How—how did you? Why didn't he ever catch on?

BERNARD: I wouldn't know that, Willy.

WILLY, *confidentially, desperately:* You were his friend, his boyhood friend. There's something I don't understand about it. His life ended after that Ebbets Field game. From the age of seventeen nothing good ever happened to him.

BERNARD: He never trained himself for anything.

WILLY: But he did, he did. After high school he took so many correspondence courses. Radio mechanics; television; God knows what, and never made the slightest mark.

BERNARD, *taking off his glasses:* Willy, do you want to talk candidly?

WILLY, *rising, faces Bernard:* I regard you as a very brilliant man, Bernard. I value your advice.

BERNARD: Oh, the hell with the advice, Willy. I couldn't advise you. There's just one thing I've always wanted to ask you. When he was supposed to graduate, and the math teacher flunked him—

WILLY: Oh, that son-of-a-bitch ruined his life.

BERNARD: Yeah, but, Willy, all he had to do was go to summer school and make up that subject.

WILLY: That's right, that's right.

BERNARD: Did you tell him not to go to summer school?

WILLY: Me? I begged him to go. I ordered him to go!

BERNARD: Then why wouldn't he go?

WILLY: Why? Why! Bernard, that question has been trailing me like a ghost for the last fifteen years. He flunked the subject, and laid down and died like a hammer hit him!

BERNARD: Take it easy, kid.

WILLY: Let me talk to you—I got nobody to talk to. Bernard, Bernard, was it my fault? Y'see? It keeps going around in my mind, maybe I did something to him. I got nothing to give him.

BERNARD: Don't take it so hard.

WILLY: Why did he lay down? What is the story there? You were his friend!

BERNARD: Willy, I remember, it was June, and our grades came out. And he'd flunked math.

WILLY: That son-of-a-bitch!

BERNARD: No, it wasn't right then. Biff just got very angry, I remember, and he was ready to enroll in summer school.

WILLY, *surprised:* He was?

BERNARD: He wasn't beaten by it at all. But then, Willy, he disappeared from the block for almost a month. And I got the idea that he'd gone up to New England to see you. Did he have a talk with you then?

Willy stares in silence.

BERNARD: Willy?

WILLY, *with a strong edge of resentment in his voice:* Yeah, he came to Boston. What about it?

BERNARD: Well, just that when he came back—I'll never forget this, it always mystifies me. Because I'd thought so well of Biff, even though he'd always taken advantage of me. I loved him, Willy, y'know? And he came back after that month and took his sneakers—remember those sneakers with "University of Virginia" printed on them? He was so proud of those, wore them every day. And he took them down in the cellar, and burned them up in the furnace. We had a fist fight. It lasted at least half an hour. Just the two of us, punching each other down the cellar, and crying right through it. I've often thought of how strange it was that I knew he'd given up his life. What happened in Boston, Willy?

Willy looks at him as at an intruder.

BERNARD: I just bring it up because you asked me.

WILLY, *angrily:* Nothing. What do you mean, "What happened?" What's that got to do with anything?

BERNARD: Well, don't get sore.

WILLY: What are you trying to do, blame it on me? If a boy lays down is that my fault?

BERNARD: Now, Willy, don't get—

WILLY: Well, don't—don't talk to me that way! What does that mean, "What happened?"

Charley enters. He is in his vest, and he carries a bottle of bourbon.

CHARLEY: Hey, you're going to miss that train. *He waves the bottle.*

BERNARD: Yeah, I'm going. *He takes the bottle.* Thanks, Pop. *He picks up his rackets and bag.* Good-by, Willy, and don't worry about it. You know, "If at first you don't succeed . . ."

WILLY: Yes, I believe in that.

BERNARD: But sometimes, Willy, it's better for a man just to walk away.

WILLY: Walk away?

BERNARD: That's right.

WILLY: But if you can't walk away?

BERNARD, *after a slight pause:* I guess that's when it's tough. *Extending his hand:* Good-by, Willy.

WILLY, *shaking Bernard's hand:* Good-by, boy.

CHARLEY, *an arm on Bernard's shoulder:* How do you like this kid? Gonna argue a case in front of the Supreme Court.

BERNARD, *protesting:* Pop!

WILLY, *genuinely shocked, pained, and happy:* No! The Supreme Court!

BERNARD: I gotta run. 'By, Dad!

CHARLEY: Knock 'em dead, Bernard!

Bernard goes off.

WILLY, *as Charley takes out his wallet:* The Supreme Court! And he didn't even mention it!

CHARLEY, *counting out money on the desk:* He don't have to— he's gonna do it.

WILLY: And you never told him what to do, did you? You never took any interest in him.

CHARLEY: My salvation is that I never took any interest in anything. There's some money—fifty dollars. I got an accountant inside.

WILLY: Charley, look . . . *With difficulty:* I got my insurance to pay. If you can manage it—I need a hundred and ten dollars.

Charley doesn't reply for a moment; merely stops moving.

WILLY: I'd draw it from my bank but Linda would know, and I . . .

CHARLEY. Sit down, Willy.

WILLY, *moving toward the chair:* I'm keeping an account of everything, remember. I'll pay every penny back. *He sits.*

CHARLEY: Now listen to me, Willy.

WILLY: I want you to know I appreciate . . .

CHARLEY, *sitting down on the table:* Willy, what're you doin'? What the hell is goin' on in your head?

WILLY: Why? I'm simply . . .

CHARLEY: I offered you a job. You can make fifty dollars a week. And I won't send you on the road.

WILLY: I've got a job.

CHARLEY: Without pay? What kind of a job is a job without pay? *He rises.* Now, look, kid, enough is enough. I'm no genius but I know when I'm being insulted.

WILLY: Insulted!

CHARLEY: Why don't you want to work for me?

WILLY: What's the matter with you? I've got a job.

CHARLEY: Then what're you walkin' in here every week for?

WILLY, *getting up:* Well, if you don't want me to walk in here—

CHARLEY: I am offering you a job.

WILLY: I don't want your goddam job!

CHARLEY: When the hell are you going to grow up?

WILLY, *furiously:* You big ignoramus, if you say that to me again I'll rap you one! I don't care how big you are! *He's ready to fight.*

Pause.

CHARLEY, *kindly, going to him:* How much do you need, Willy?

WILLY: Charley, I'm strapped, I'm strapped. I don't know what to do. I was just fired.

CHARLEY: Howard fired you?

WILLY: That snotnose. Imagine that? I named him. I named him Howard.

CHARLEY: Willy, when're you gonna realize that them things don't mean anything? You named him Howard, but you can't sell that. The only thing you got in this world is what you can sell. And the funny thing is that you're a salesman, and you don't know that.

WILLY: I've always tried to think otherwise, I guess. I always felt that if a man was impressive, and well liked, that nothing—

CHARLEY: Why must everybody like you? Who liked J. P. Morgan? Was he impressive? In a Turkish bath he'd look like a butcher. But with his pockets on he was very well liked. Now listen, Willy, I know you don't like me, and nobody can say I'm in love with you, but I'll give you a job because—just for the hell of it, put it that way. Now what do you say?

WILLY: I—I just can't work for you, Charley.

CHARLEY: What're you, jealous of me?

WILLY: I can't work for you, that's all, don't ask me why.

CHARLEY, *angered, taking out more bills:* You been jealous of me all your life, you damned fool! Here, pay your insurance. *He puts the money in Willy's hand.*

WILLY: I'm keeping strict accounts.

CHARLEY: I've got some work to do. Take care of yourself. And pay your insurance.

WILLY, *moving to the right:* Funny, y'know? After all the highways, and the trains, and the appointments, and the years, you end up worth more dead than alive.

CHARLEY: Willy, nobody's worth nothin' dead. *After a slight pause:* Did you hear what I said?

Willy stands still, dreaming.

CHARLEY: Willy!

WILLY: Apologize to Bernard for me when you see him. I didn't mean to argue with him. He's a fine boy. They're all fine boys, and they'll end up big—all of them. Someday they'll all play tennis together. Wish me luck, Charley. He saw Bill Oliver today.

CHARLEY: Good luck.

WILLY, *on the verge of tears:* Charley, you're the only friend I got. Isn't that a remarkable thing? *He goes out.*

CHARLEY: Jesus!

Charley stares after him a moment and follows. All light blacks out. Suddenly raucous music is heard, and a red glow rises behind the screen at right. Stanley, a young waiter, appears, carrying a table, followed by Happy, who is carrying two chairs.

STANLEY, *putting the table down:* That's all right, Mr. Loman, I can handle it myself. *He turns and takes the chairs from Happy and places them at the table.*

HAPPY, *glancing around:* Oh, this is better.

STANLEY: Sure, in the front there you're in the middle of all kinds a noise. Whenever you got a party, Mr. Loman, you just tell me and I'll put you back here. Y'know, there's a lotta people they don't like it private, because when they go out they like to see a lotta action around them because they're sick and tired to stay in the house by theirself. But I know you, you ain't from Hackensack. You know what I mean?

HAPPY, *sitting down:* So how's it coming, Stanley?

STANLEY: Ah, it's a dog's life. I only wish during the war they'd a took me in the Army. I coulda been dead by now.

HAPPY: My brother's back, Stanley.

STANLEY: Oh, he come back, heh? From the Far West.

HAPPY: Yeah, big cattle man, my brother, so treat him right. And my father's coming too.

STANLEY: Oh, your father too!

HAPPY: You got a couple of nice lobsters?

STANLEY: Hundred per cent, big.

HAPPY: I want them with the claws.

STANLEY: Don't worry, I don't give you no mice. *Happy laughs.* How about some wine? It'll put a head on the meal.

HAPPY: No. You remember, Stanley, that recipe I brought you from overseas? With the champagne in it?

STANLEY: Oh, yeah, sure. I still got it tacked up yet in the kitchen. But that'll have to cost a buck apiece anyways.

HAPPY: That's all right.

STANLEY: What'd you, hit a number or somethin'?

HAPPY: No, it's a little celebration. My brother is—I think he pulled off a big deal today. I think we're going into business together.

STANLEY: Great! That's the best for you. Because a family business, you know what I mean?—that's the best.

HAPPY: That's what I think.

STANLEY: 'Cause what's the difference? Somebody steals? It's in the family. Know what I mean? *Sotto voce:* Like this bartender here. The boss is goin' crazy what kinda leak he's got in the cash register. You put it in but it don't come out.

HAPPY, *raising his head:* Sh!

STANLEY: What?

HAPPY: You notice I wasn't lookin' right or left, was I?

STANLEY: No.

HAPPY: And my eyes are closed.

STANLEY: So what's the—?

HAPPY: Strudel's comin'.

STANLEY, *catching on, looks around:* Ah, no, there's no—

He breaks off as a furred, lavishly dressed girl enters and sits at the next table. Both follow her with their eyes.

STANLEY: Geez, how'd ya know?

HAPPY: I got radar or something. *Staring directly at her profile:* Oooooooo . . . Stanley.

STANLEY: I think that's for you, Mr. Loman.

HAPPY: Look at that mouth. Oh, God. And the binoculars.

STANLEY: Geez, you got a life, Mr. Loman.

HAPPY: Wait on her.

STANLEY, *going to the girl's table:* Would you like a menu, ma'am?

GIRL: I'm expecting someone, but I'd like a—

HAPPY: Why don't you bring her—excuse me, miss, do you mind? I sell champagne, and I'd like you to try my brand. Bring her a champagne, Stanley.

GIRL: That's awfully nice of you.

HAPPY: Don't mention it. It's all company money. *He laughs.*

GIRL: That's a charming product to be selling, isn't it?

HAPPY: Oh, gets to be like everything else. Selling is selling, y'know.

GIRL: I suppose.

HAPPY: You don't happen to sell, do you?

GIRL: No, I don't sell.

HAPPY: Would you object to a compliment from a stranger? You ought to be on a magazine cover.

GIRL, *looking at him a little archly:* I have been.

Stanley comes in with a glass of champagne.

HAPPY: What'd I say before, Stanley? You see? She's a cover girl.

STANLEY: Oh, I could see, I could see.

HAPPY, *to the Girl:* What magazine?

GIRL: Oh, a lot of them. *She takes the drink.* Thank you.

HAPPY: You know what they say in France, don't you? "Champagne is the drink of the complexion"—Hiya, Biff!

Biff has entered and sits with Happy.

BIFF: Hello, kid. Sorry I'm late.

HAPPY: I just got here. Uh, Miss—?

GIRL: Forsythe.

HAPPY: Miss Forsythe, this is my brother.

BIFF: Is Dad here?

HAPPY: His name is Biff. You might've heard of him. Great football player.

GIRL: Really? What team?

HAPPY: Are you familiar with football?

GIRL: No, I'm afraid I'm not.

HAPPY: Biff is quarterback with the New York Giants.

GIRL: Well, that is nice, isn't it? *She drinks.*

HAPPY: Good health.

GIRL: I'm happy to meet you.

HAPPY: That's my name. Hap. It's really Harold, but at West Point they called me Happy.

GIRL, *now really impressed:* Oh, I see. How do you do? *She turns her profile.*

BIFF: Isn't Dad coming?

HAPPY: You want her?

BIFF: Oh, I could never make that.

HAPPY: I remember the time that idea would never come into your head. Where's the old confidence, Biff?

BIFF: I just saw Oliver—

HAPPY: Wait a minute. I've got to see that old confidence again. Do you want her? She's on call.

BIFF: Oh, no. *He turns to look at the Girl.*

HAPPY: I'm telling you. Watch this. *Turning to the Girl:* Honey? *She turns to him.* Are you busy?

GIRL: Well, I am . . . but I could make a phone call.

HAPPY: Do that, will you, honey? And see if you can get a friend. We'll be here for a while. Biff is one of the greatest football players in the country.

GIRL, *standing up:* Well, I'm certainly happy to meet you.

HAPPY: Come back soon.

GIRL: I'll try.

HAPPY: Don't try, honey, try hard.

The Girl exits. Stanley follows, shaking his head in bewildered admiration.

HAPPY: Isn't that a shame now? A beautiful girl like that? That's why I can't get married. There's not a good woman in a thousand. New York is loaded with them, kid!

BIFF: Hap, look—

HAPPY: I told you she was on call!

BIFF, *strangely unnerved:* Cut it out, will ya? I want to say something to you.

HAPPY: Did you see Oliver?

BIFF: I saw him all right. Now look, I want to tell Dad a couple of things and I want you to help me.

HAPPY: What? Is he going to back you?

BIFF: Are you crazy? You're out of your goddam head, you know that?

HAPPY: Why? What happened?

BIFF, *breathlessly:* I did a terrible thing today, Hap. It's been the strangest day I ever went through. I'm all numb, I swear.

HAPPY: You mean he wouldn't see you?

BIFF: Well, I waited six hours for him, see? All day. Kept sending my name in. Even tried to date his secretary so she'd get me to him, but no soap.

HAPPY: Because you're not showin' the old confidence, Biff. He remembered you, didn't he?

BIFF, *stopping Happy with a gesture:* Finally, about five o'clock, he comes out. Didn't remember who I was or anything. I felt like such an idiot, Hap.

HAPPY: Did you tell him my Florida idea?

BIFF: He walked away. I saw him for one minute. I got so mad I could've torn the walls down! How the hell did I ever get the idea I was a salesman there? I even believed myself that I'd been a salesman for him! And then he gave me one look and —I realized what a ridiculous lie my whole life has been! We've been talking in a dream for fifteen years. I was a shipping clerk.

HAPPY: What'd you do?

BIFF, *with great tension and wonder:* Well, he left, see. And the secretary went out. I was all alone in the waiting room. I don't know what came over me, Hap. The next thing I know I'm in his office—paneled walls, everything. I can't explain it. I— Hap, I took his fountain pen.

HAPPY: Geez, did he catch you?

BIFF: I ran out. I ran down all eleven flights. I ran and ran and ran.

HAPPY: That was an awful dumb—what'd you do that for?

BIFF, *agonized:* I don't know, I just—wanted to take something, I don't know. You gotta help me, Hap, I'm gonna tell Pop.

HAPPY: You crazy? What for?

BIFF: Hap, he's got to understand that I'm not the man somebody lends that kind of money to. He thinks I've been spiting him all these years and it's eating him up.

HAPPY: That's just it. You tell him something nice.

BIFF: I can't.

HAPPY: Say you got a lunch date with Oliver tomorrow.

BIFF: So what do I do tomorrow?

HAPPY: You leave the house tomorrow and come back at night and say Oliver is thinking it over. And he thinks it over for a couple of weeks, and gradually it fades away and nobody's the worse.

BIFF: But it'll go on forever!

HAPPY: Dad is never so happy as when he's looking forward to something!

Willy enters.

HAPPY: Hello, scout!

WILLY: Gee, I haven't been here in years!

Stanley has followed Willy in and sets a chair for him. Stanley starts off but Happy stops him.

HAPPY: Stanley!

Stanley stands by, waiting for an order.

BIFF, *going to Willy with guilt, as to an invalid:* Sit down, Pop. You want a drink?

WILLY: Sure, I don't mind.

BIFF: Let's get a load on.

WILLY: You look worried.

BIFF: N-no. *To Stanley:* Scotch all around. Make it doubles.

STANLEY: Doubles, right. *He goes.*

WILLY: You had a couple already, didn't you?

BIFF: Just a couple, yeah.

WILLY: Well, what happened, boy? *Nodding affirmatively, with a smile:* Everything go all right?

BIFF, *takes a breath, then reaches out and grasps Willy's hand:* Pal . . . *He is smiling bravely, and Willy is smiling too.* I had an experience today.

HAPPY: Terrific, Pop.

WILLY: That so? What happened?

BIFF, *high, slightly alcoholic, above the earth:* I'm going to tell you everything from first to last. It's been a strange day. *Silence. He looks around, composes himself as best he can, but his breath keeps breaking the rhythm of his voice.* I had to wait quite a while for him, and—

WILLY: Oliver?

BIFF: Yeah, Oliver. All day, as a matter of cold fact. And a lot of instances—facts, Pop, facts about my life came back to me. Who was it, Pop? Who ever said I was a salesman with Oliver?

WILLY: Well, you were.

BIFF: No, Dad, I was a shipping clerk.

WILLY: But you were practically—

BIFF, *with determination:* Dad, I don't know who said it first, but I was never a salesman for Bill Oliver.

WILLY: What're you talking about?

BIFF: Let's hold on to the facts tonight, Pop. We're not going to get anywhere bullin' around. I was a shipping clerk.

WILLY, *angrily:* All right, now listen to me—

BIFF: Why don't you let me finish?

WILLY: I'm not interested in stories about the past or any crap of that kind because the woods are burning, boys, you understand? There's a big blaze going on all around. I was fired today.

BIFF, *shocked:* How could you be?

WILLY: I was fired, and I'm looking for a little good news to tell your mother, because the woman has waited and the woman has suffered. The gist of it is that I haven't got a story left in my head, Biff. So don't give me a lecture about facts and aspects. I am not interested. Now what've you got to say to me?

Stanley enters with three drinks. They wait until he leaves.

WILLY: Did you see Oliver?

BIFF: Jesus, Dad!

WILLY: You mean you didn't go up there?

HAPPY: Sure he went up there.

BIFF: I did. I—saw him. How could they fire you?

WILLY, *on the edge of his chair:* What kind of a welcome did he give you?

BIFF: He won't even let you work on commission?

WILLY: I'm out! *Driving:* So tell me, he gave you a warm welcome?

HAPPY: Sure, Pop, sure!

BIFF, *driven:* Well, it was kind of—

WILLY: I was wondering if he'd remember you. *To Happy:* Imagine, man doesn't see him for ten, twelve years and gives him that kind of a welcome!

HAPPY: Damn right!

BIFF, *trying to return to the offensive:* Pop, look—

WILLY: You know why he remembered you, don't you? Because you impressed him in those days.

BIFF: Let's talk quietly and get this down to the facts, huh?

WILLY, *as though Biff had been interrupting:* Well, what happened? It's great news, Biff. Did he take you into his office or'd you talk in the waiting room?

BIFF: Well, he came in, see, and—

WILLY, *with a big smile:* What'd he say? Betcha he threw his arm around you.

BIFF: Well, he kinda—

WILLY: He's a fine man. *To Happy:* Very hard man to see, y'know.

HAPPY, *agreeing:* Oh, I know.

WILLY, *to Biff:* Is that where you had the drinks?

BIFF: Yeah, he gave me a couple of—no, no!

HAPPY, *cutting in:* He told him my Florida idea.

WILLY: Don't interrupt. *To Biff:* How'd he react to the Florida idea?

BIFF: Dad, will you give me a minute to explain?

WILLY: I've been waiting for you to explain since I sat down here! What happened? He took you into his office and what?

BIFF: Well—I talked. And—and he listened, see.

WILLY: Famous for the way he listens, y'know. What was his answer?

BIFF: His answer was— *He breaks off, suddenly angry.* Dad, you're not letting me tell you what I want to tell you!

WILLY, *accusing, angered:* You didn't see him, did you?

BIFF: I did see him!

WILLY: What'd you insult him or something? You insulted him, didn't you?

BIFF: Listen, will you let me out of it, will you just let me out of it!

HAPPY: What the hell!

WILLY: Tell me what happened!

BIFF, *to Happy:* I can't talk to him!

A single trumpet note jars the ear. The light of green leaves stains the house, which holds the air of night and a dream. Young Bernard enters and knocks on the door of the house.

YOUNG BERNARD, *frantically:* Mrs. Loman, Mrs. Loman!

HAPPY: Tell him what happened!

BIFF, *to Happy:* Shut up and leave me alone!

WILLY: No, no! You had to go and flunk math!

BIFF: What math? What're you talking about?

YOUNG BERNARD: Mrs. Loman, Mrs. Loman!

Linda appears in the house, as of old.

WILLY, *wildly:* Math, math, math!

BIFF: Take it easy, Pop!

YOUNG BERNARD: Mrs. Loman!

WILLY, *furiously:* If you hadn't flunked you'd've been set by now!

BIFF: Now, look, I'm gonna tell you what happened, and you're going to listen to me.

YOUNG BERNARD: Mrs. Loman!

BIFF: I waited six hours—

HAPPY: What the hell are you saying?

BIFF: I kept sending in my name but he wouldn't see me. So finally he . . . *He continues unheard as light fades low on the restaurant.*

YOUNG BERNARD: Biff flunked math!

LINDA: No!

YOUNG BERNARD: Birnbaum flunked him! They won't graduate him!

LINDA: But they have to. He's gotta go to the university. Where is he? Biff! Biff!

YOUNG BERNARD: No, he left. He went to Grand Central.

LINDA: Grand— You mean he went to Boston!

YOUNG BERNARD: Is Uncle Willy in Boston?

LINDA: Oh, maybe Willy can talk to the teacher. Oh, the poor, poor boy!

Light on house area snaps out.

BIFF, *at the table, now audible, holding up a gold fountain pen:* . . . so I'm washed up with Oliver, you understand? Are you listening to me?

WILLY, *at a loss:* Yeah, sure. If you hadn't flunked—

BIFF: Flunked what? What're you talking about?

WILLY: Don't blame everything on me! I didn't flunk math—you did! What pen?

HAPPY: That was awful dumb, Biff, a pen like that is worth—

WILLY, *seeing the pen for the first time:* You took Oliver's pen?

BIFF, *weakening:* Dad, I just explained it to you.

WILLY: You stole Bill Oliver's fountain pen!

BIFF: I didn't exactly steal it! That's just what I've been explaining to you!

HAPPY: He had it in his hand and just then Oliver walked in, so he got nervous and stuck it in his pocket!

WILLY: My God, Biff!

BIFF: I never intended to do it, Dad!

OPERATOR'S VOICE: Standish Arms, good evening!

WILLY, *shouting:* I'm not in my room!

BIFF, *frightened:* Dad, what's the matter? *He and Happy stand up.*

OPERATOR: Ringing Mr. Loman for you!

WILLY: I'm not there, stop it!

BIFF, *horrified, gets down on one knee before Willy:* Dad, I'll make good, I'll make good. *Willy tries to get to his feet. Biff holds him down.* Sit down now.

WILLY: No, you're no good, you're no good for anything.

BIFF: I am, Dad, I'll find something else, you understand? Now don't worry about anything. *He holds up Willy's face:* Talk to me, Dad.

OPERATOR: Mr. Loman does not answer. Shall I page him?

WILLY, *attempting to stand, as though to rush and silence the Operator:* No, no, no!

HAPPY: He'll strike something, Pop.

WILLY: No, no . . .

BIFF, *desperately, standing over Willy:* Pop, listen! Listen to me! I'm telling you something good. Oliver talked to his partner about the Florida idea. You listening? He—he talked to his partner, and he came to me . . . I'm going to be all right, you hear? Dad, listen to me, he said it was just a question of the amount!

WILLY: Then you . . . got it?

HAPPY: He's gonna be terrific, Pop!

WILLY, *trying to stand:* Then you got it, haven't you? You got it! You got it!

BIFF, *agonized, holds Willy down:* No, no. Look, Pop. I'm supposed to have lunch with them tomorrow. I'm just telling you this so you'll know that I can still make an impression, Pop. And I'll make good somewhere, but I can't go tomorrow, see?

WILLY: Why not? You simply—

BIFF: But the pen, Pop!

WILLY: You give it to him and tell him it was an oversight!

HAPPY: Sure, have lunch tomorrow!

BIFF: I can't say that—

WILLY: You were doing a crossword puzzle and accidentally used his pen!

BIFF: Listen, kid, I took those balls years ago, now I walk in with his fountain pen? That clinches it, don't you see? I can't face him like that! I'll try elsewhere.

PAGE'S VOICE: Paging Mr. Loman!

WILLY: Don't you want to be anything?

BIFF: Pop, how can I go back?

WILLY: You don't want to be anything, is that what's behind it?

BIFF, *now angry at Willy for not crediting his sympathy:* Don't take it that way! You think it was easy walking into that office after what I'd done to him? A team of horses couldn't have dragged me back to Bill Oliver!

WILLY: Then why'd you go?

BIFF: Why did I go? Why did I go! Look at you! Look at what's become of you!

Off left, The Woman laughs.

WILLY: Biff, you're going to go to that lunch tomorrow, or—

BIFF: I can't go. I've got no appointment!

HAPPY: Biff, for . . . !

WILLY: Are you spiting me?

BIFF: Don't take it that way! Goddammit!

WILLY—*he strikes Biff and falters away from the table:* You rotten little louse! Are you spiting me?

THE WOMAN: Someone's at the door, Willy!

BIFF: I'm no good, can't you see what I am?

HAPPY, *separating them:* Hey, you're in a restaurant! Now cut it out, both of you! *The girls enter.* Hello, girls, sit down.

The Woman laughs, off left.

MISS FORSYTHE: I guess we might as well. This is Letta.

THE WOMAN: Willy, are you going to wake up?

BIFF, *ignoring Willy:* How're ya, miss, sit down. What do you drink?

MISS FORSYTHE: Letta might not be able to stay long.

LETTA: I gotta get up very early tomorrow. I got jury duty. I'm so excited! Were you fellows ever on a jury?

BIFF: No, but I been in front of them! *The girls laugh.* This is my father.

LETTA: Isn't he cute? Sit down with us, Pop.

HAPPY: Sit him down, Biff!

BIFF, *going to him:* Come on, slugger, drink us under the table. To hell with it! Come on, sit down, pal.

On Biff's last insistence, Willy is about to sit.

THE WOMAN, *now urgently:* Willy, are you going to answer the door!

The Woman's call pulls Willy back. He starts right, befuddled.

BIFF: Hey, where are you going?

WILLY: Open the door.

BIFF: The door?

WILLY: The washroom . . . the door . . . where's the door?

BIFF, *leading Willy to the left:* Just go straight down.

Willy moves left.

THE WOMAN: Willy, Willy, are you going to get up, get up, get up, get up?

Willy exits left.

LETTA: I think it's sweet you bring your daddy along.

MISS FORSYTHE: Oh, he isn't really your father!

BIFF, *at left, turning to her resentfully:* Miss Forsythe, you've just seen a prince walk by. A fine, troubled prince. A hard-working, unappreciated prince. A pal, you understand? A good companion. Always for his boys.

LETTA: That's so sweet.

HAPPY: Well, girls, what's the program? We're wasting time. Come on, Biff. Gather round. Where would you like to go?

BIFF: Why don't you do something for him?

HAPPY: Me!

BIFF: Don't you give a damn for him, Hap?

HAPPY: What're you talking about? I'm the one who—

BIFF: I sense it, you don't give a good goddam about him. *He takes the rolled-up hose from his pocket and puts it on the table in front of Happy.* Look what I found in the cellar, for Christ's sake. How can you bear to let it go on?

HAPPY: Me? Who goes away? Who runs off and—

BIFF: Yeah, but he doesn't mean anything to you. You could help him—I can't! Don't you understand what I'm talking about? He's going to kill himself, don't you know that?

HAPPY: Don't I know it! Me!

BIFF: Hap, help him! Jesus . . . help him . . . Help me, help me, I can't bear to look at his face! *Ready to weep, he hurries out, up right.*

HAPPY, *starting after him:* Where are you going?

MISS FORSYTHE: What's he so mad about?

HAPPY: Come on, girls, we'll catch up with him.

MISS FORSYTHE, *as Happy pushes her out:* Say, I don't like that temper of his!

HAPPY: He's just a little overstrung, he'll be all right!

WILLY, *off left, as The Woman laughs:* Don't answer! Don't answer!

LETTA: Don't you want to tell your father—

HAPPY: No, that's not my father. He's just a guy. Come on, we'll catch Biff, and, honey, we're going to paint this town! Stanley, where's the check! Hey, Stanley!

They exit. Stanley looks toward left.

STANLEY, *calling to Happy indignantly:* Mr. Loman! Mr. Loman!

Stanley picks up a chair and follows them off. Knocking is heard off left. The Woman enters, laughing. Willy follows her. She is in a black slip; he is buttoning his shirt. Raw, sensuous music accompanies their speech.

WILLY: Will you stop laughing? Will you stop?

THE WOMAN: Aren't you going to answer the door? He'll wake the whole hotel.

WILLY: I'm not expecting anybody.

THE WOMAN: Whyn't you have another drink, honey, and stop being so damn self-centered?

WILLY: I'm so lonely.

THE WOMAN: You know you ruined me, Willy? From now on, whenever you come to the office, I'll see that you go right through to the buyers. No waiting at my desk any more, Willy. You ruined me.

WILLY: That's nice of you to say that.

THE WOMAN: Gee, you are self-centered! Why so sad? You are the saddest, self-centeredest soul I ever did see-saw. *She laughs. He kisses her.* Come on inside, drummer boy. It's silly to be dressing in the middle of the night. *As knocking is heard:* Aren't you going to answer the door?

WILLY: They're knocking on the wrong door.

THE WOMAN: But I felt the knocking. And he heard us talking in here. Maybe the hotel's on fire!

WILLY, *his terror rising:* It's a mistake.

THE WOMAN: Then tell him to go away!

WILLY: There's nobody there.

THE WOMAN: It's getting on my nerves, Willy. There's somebody standing out there and it's getting on my nerves!

WILLY, *pushing her away from him:* All right, stay in the bathroom here, and don't come out. I think there's a law in Massachusetts about it, so don't come out. It may be that new room clerk. He looked very mean. So don't come out. It's a mistake, there's no fire.

The knocking is heard again. He takes a few steps away from her, and she vanishes into the wing. The light follows him, and now he is facing Young Biff, who carries a suitcase. Biff steps toward him. The music is gone.

BIFF: Why didn't you answer?

WILLY: Biff! What are you doing in Boston?

BIFF: Why didn't you answer? I've been knocking for five minutes, I called you on the phone—

WILLY: I just heard you. I was in the bathroom and had the door shut. Did anything happen home?

BIFF: Dad—I let you down.

WILLY: What do you mean?

BIFF: Dad . . .

WILLY: Biffo, what's this about? *Putting his arm around Biff:* Come on, let's go downstairs and get you a malted.

BIFF: Dad, I flunked math.

WILLY: Not for the term?

BIFF: The term. I haven't got enough credits to graduate.

WILLY: You mean to say Bernard wouldn't give you the answers?

BIFF: He did, he tried, but I only got a sixty-one.

WILLY: And they wouldn't give you four points?

BIFF: Birnbaum refused absolutely. I begged him, Pop, but he won't give me those points. You gotta talk to him before they close the school. Because if he saw the kind of man you are, and you just talked to him in your way, I'm sure he'd come through for me. The class came right before practice, see, and I didn't go enough. Would you talk to him? He'd like you, Pop. You know the way you could talk.

WILLY: You're on. We'll drive right back.

BIFF: Oh, Dad, good work! I'm sure he'll change it for you!

WILLY: Go downstairs and tell the clerk I'm checkin' out. Go right down.

BIFF: Yes, sir! See, the reason he hates me, Pop—one day he was late for class so I got up at the blackboard and imitated him. I crossed my eyes and talked with a lithp.

WILLY, *laughing:* You did? The kids like it?

BIFF: They nearly died laughing!

WILLY: Yeah? What'd you do?

BIFF: The thquare root of thixthy twee is . . . *Willy bursts out laughing; Biff joins him.* And in the middle of it he walked in!

Willy laughs, and The Woman joins in offstage.

WILLY, *without hesitation:* Hurry downstairs and—

BIFF: Somebody in there?

WILLY: No, that was next door.

The Woman laughs offstage.

BIFF: Somebody got in your bathroom!

WILLY: No, it's the next room, there's a party—

THE WOMAN, *enters, laughing. She lisps this:* Can I come in? There's something in the bathtub, Willy, and it's moving!

Willy looks at Biff, who is staring open-mouthed and horrified at The Woman.

WILLY: Ah—you better go back to your room. They must be finished painting by now. They're painting her room so I let her take a shower here. Go back, go back . . . *He pushes her.*

THE WOMAN, *resisting:* But I've got to get dressed, Willy, I can't—

WILLY: Get out of here! Go back, go back . . . *Suddenly striving for the ordinary:* This is Miss Francis, Biff, she's a buyer. They're painting her room. Go back, Miss Francis, go back . . .

THE WOMAN: But my clothes, I can't go out naked in the hall!

WILLY, *pushing her offstage:* Get outa here! Go back, go back!

Biff slowly sits down on his suitcase as the argument continues offstage.

THE WOMAN: Where's my stockings? You promised me stockings, Willy!

WILLY: I have no stockings here!

THE WOMAN: You had two boxes of size nine sheers for me, and I want them!

WILLY: Here, for God's sake, will you get outa here!

THE WOMAN, *entering, holding a box of stockings:* I just hope there's nobody in the hall. That's all I hope. *To Biff:* Are you football or baseball?

BIFF: Football.

THE WOMAN, *angry, humiliated:* That's me too. G'night. *She snatches her clothes from Willy, and walks out.*

WILLY, *after a pause:* Well, better get going. I want to get to the school first thing in the morning. Get my suits out of the closet. I'll get my valise. *Biff doesn't move.* What's the matter? *Biff remains motionless, tears falling.* She's a buyer. Buys for J. H. Simmons. She lives down the hall—they're painting. You don't imagine— *He breaks off. After a pause:* Now listen, pal, she's just a buyer. She sees merchandise in her room and they have to keep it looking just so . . . *Pause. Assuming command:* All right, get my suits. *Biff doesn't move.* Now stop crying and do as I say. I gave you an order. Biff, I gave you an order! Is that what you do when I give you an order? How dare you cry! *Putting his arm around Biff:* Now look, Biff, when you grow up you'll understand about these things. You mustn't— you mustn't overemphasize a thing like this. I'll see Birnbaum first thing in the morning.

BIFF: Never mind.

WILLY, *getting down beside Biff:* Never mind! He's going to give you those points. I'll see to it.

BIFF: He wouldn't listen to you.

WILLY: He certainly will listen to me. You need those points for the U. of Virginia.

BIFF: I'm not going there.

WILLY: Heh? If I can't get him to change that mark you'll make it up in summer school. You've got all summer to—

BIFF, *his weeping breaking from him:* Dad . . .

WILLY, *infected by it:* Oh, my boy . . .

BIFF: Dad . . .

WILLY: She's nothing to me, Biff. I was lonely, I was terribly lonely.

BIFF: You—you gave her Mama's stockings! *His tears break through and he rises to go.*

WILLY, *grabbing for Biff:* I gave you an order!

BIFF: Don't touch me, you—liar!

WILLY: Apologize for that!

BIFF: You fake! You phony little fake! You fake! *Overcome, he turns quickly and weeping fully goes out with his suitcase. Willy is left on the floor on his knees.*

WILLY: I gave you an order! Biff, come back here or I'll beat you! Come back here! I'll whip you!

Stanley comes quickly in from the right and stands in front of Willy.

WILLY, *shouting at Stanley:* I gave you an order . . .

STANLEY: Hey, let's pick it up, pick it up, Mr. Loman. *He helps Willy to his feet.* Your boys left with the chippies. They said they'll see you home.

A second waiter watches some distance away.

WILLY: But we were supposed to have dinner together.

Music is heard, Willy's theme.

STANLEY: Can you make it?

WILLY: I'll—sure, I can make it. *Suddenly concerned about his clothes:* Do I—I look all right?

STANLEY: Sure, you look all right. *He flicks a speck off Willy's lapel.*

WILLY: Here—here's a dollar.

STANLEY: Oh, your son paid me. It's all right.

WILLY, *putting it in Stanley's hand:* No, take it. You're a good boy.

STANLEY: Oh, no, you don't have to . . .

WILLY: Here—here's some more, I don't need it any more. *After a slight pause:* Tell me—is there a seed store in the neighborhood?

STANLEY: Seeds? You mean like to plant?

As Willy turns, Stanley slips the money back into his jacket pocket.

WILLY: Yes. Carrots, peas . . .

STANLEY: Well, there's hardware stores on Sixth Avenue, but it may be too late now.

WILLY, *anxiously:* Oh, I'd better hurry. I've got to get some seeds. *He starts off to the right.* I've got to get some seeds, right away. Nothing's planted. I don't have a thing in the ground.

Willy hurries out as the light goes down. Stanley moves over to the right after him, watches him off. The other waiter has been staring at Willy.

STANLEY, *to the waiter:* Well, whatta you looking at?

The waiter picks up the chairs and moves off right. Stanley takes the table and follows him. The light fades on this area. There is a long pause, the sound of the flute coming over. The light gradually rises on the kitchen, which is empty. Happy appears at the door of the house, followed by Biff. Happy is carrying a large bunch of long-stemmed roses. He enters the kitchen, looks around for Linda. Not seeing her, he turns to Biff, who is just outside the house door, and makes a gesture with his hands, indicating "Not here, I guess." He looks into the living room and freezes. Inside, Linda, unseen, is seated, Willy's coat on her lap. She rises ominously and quietly and moves toward Happy, who backs up into the kitchen, afraid.

HAPPY: Hey, what're you doing up? *Linda says nothing but moves toward him implacably.* Where's Pop? *He keeps backing to the right, and now Linda is in full view in the doorway to the living room.* Is he sleeping?

LINDA: Where were you?

HAPPY, *trying to laugh it off:* We met two girls, Mom, very fine types. Here, we brought you some flowers. *Offering them to her:* Put them in your room, Ma.

She knocks them to the floor at Biff's feet. He has now come inside and closed the door behind him. She stares at Biff, silent.

HAPPY: Now what'd you do that for? Mom, I want you to have some flowers—

LINDA, *cutting Happy off, violently to Biff:* Don't you care whether he lives or dies?

HAPPY, *going to the stairs:* Come upstairs, Biff.

BIFF, *with a flare of disgust, to Happy:* Go away from me! *To Linda:* What do you mean, lives or dies? Nobody's dying around here, pal.

LINDA: Get out of my sight! Get out of here!

BIFF: I wanna see the boss.

LINDA: You're not going near him!

BIFF: Where is he? *He moves into the living room and Linda follows.*

LINDA, *shouting after Biff:* You invite him for dinner. He looks forward to it all day—*Biff appears in his parents' bedroom, looks around, and exits*—and then you desert him there. There's no stranger you'd do that to!

HAPPY: Why? He had a swell time with us. Listen, when I—*Linda comes back into the kitchen*—desert him I hope I don't outlive the day!

LINDA: Get out of here!

HAPPY: Now look, Mom . . .

LINDA: Did you have to go to women tonight? You and your lousy rotten whores!

Biff re-enters the kitchen.

HAPPY: Mom, all we did was follow Biff around trying to cheer him up! *To Biff:* Boy, what a night you gave me!

LINDA: Get out of here, both of you, and don't come back! I don't want you tormenting him any more. Go on now, get your things together! *To Biff:* You can sleep in his apartment. *She starts to pick up the flowers and stops herself.* Pick up this stuff, I'm not your maid any more. Pick it up, you bum, you!

Happy turns his back to her in refusal. Biff slowly moves over and gets down on his knees, picking up the flowers.

LINDA: You're a pair of animals! Not one, not another living soul would have had the cruelty to walk out on that man in a restaurant!

BIFF, *not looking at her:* Is that what he said?

LINDA: He didn't have to say anything. He was so humiliated he nearly limped when he came in.

HAPPY: But, Mom, he had a great time with us—

BIFF, *cutting him off violently:* Shut up!

Without another word, Happy goes upstairs.

LINDA: You! You didn't even go in to see if he was all right!

BIFF, *still on the floor in front of Linda, the flowers in his hand; with self-loathing:* No. Didn't. Didn't do a damned thing. How do you like that, heh? Left him babbling in a toilet.

LINDA: You louse. You . . .

BIFF: Now you hit it on the nose! *He gets up, throws the flowers in the wastebasket.* The scum of the earth, and you're looking at him!

LINDA: Get out of here!

BIFF: I gotta talk to the boss, Mom. Where is he?

LINDA: You're not going near him. Get out of this house!

BIFF, *with absolute assurance, determination:* No. We're gonna have an abrupt conversation, him and me.

LINDA: You're not talking to him!

Hammering is heard from outside the house, off right. Biff turns toward the noise.

LINDA, *suddenly pleading:* Will you please leave him alone?

BIFF: What's he doing out there?

LINDA: He's planting the garden!

BIFF, *quietly:* Now? Oh, my God!

Biff moves outside, Linda following. The light dies down on them and comes up on the center of the apron as Willy walks into it. He is carrying a flashlight, a hoe, and a handful of seed packets. He raps the top of the hoe sharply to fix it firmly, and then moves to the left, measuring off the distance with his foot. He holds the flashlight to look at the seed packets, reading off the instructions. He is in the blue of night.

WILLY: Carrots . . . quarter-inch apart. Rows . . . one-foot rows. *He measures it off.* One foot. *He puts down a package and measures off.* Beets. *He puts down another package and measures again.* Lettuce. *He reads the package, puts it down.* One foot— *He breaks off as Ben appears at the right and moves slowly down to him.* What a proposition, ts, ts. Terrific, terrific. 'Cause she's suffered, Ben, the woman has suffered. You understand me? A man can't go out the way he came in, Ben, a man has got to add up to something. You can't, you can't— *Ben moves toward him as though to interrupt.* You gotta consider, now. Don't answer so quick. Remember, it's a guaranteed twenty-thousand-dollar proposition. Now look, Ben, I want you to go through the ins and outs of this thing with me. I've got nobody to talk to, Ben, and the woman has suffered, you hear me?

BEN, *standing still, considering:* What's the proposition?

WILLY: It's twenty thousand dollars on the barrelhead. Guaranteed, gilt-edged, you understand?

BEN: You don't want to make a fool of yourself. They might not honor the policy.

WILLY: How can they dare refuse? Didn't I work like a coolie to meet every premium on the nose? And now they don't pay off? Impossible!

BEN: It's called a cowardly thing, William.

WILLY: Why? Does it take more guts to stand here the rest of my life ringing up a zero?

BEN, *yielding:* That's a point, William. *He moves, thinking, turns.* And twenty thousand—that *is* something one can feel with the hand, it is there.

WILLY, *now assured, with rising power:* Oh, Ben, that's the whole beauty of it! I see it like a diamond, shining in the dark, hard and rough, that I can pick up and touch in my hand. Not like—like an appointment! This would not be another damned-fool appointment, Ben, and it changes all the aspects. Because he thinks I'm nothing, see, and so he spites me. But the funeral— *Straightening up:* Ben, that funeral will be massive! They'll come from Maine, Massachusetts, Vermont, New Hampshire! All the old-timers with the strange license plates —that boy will be thunder-struck, Ben, because he never realized—I am known! Rhode Island, New York, New Jersey—I am known, Ben, and he'll see it with his eyes once and for all. He'll see what I am, Ben! He's in for a shock, that boy!

BEN, *coming down to the edge of the garden:* He'll call you a coward.

WILLY, *suddenly fearful:* No, that would be terrible.

BEN: Yes. And a damned fool.

WILLY: No, no, he mustn't, I won't have that! *He is broken and desperate.*

BEN: He'll hate you, William.

The gay music of the Boys is heard.

WILLY: Oh, Ben, how do we get back to all the great times? Used to be so full of light, and comradeship, the sleigh-riding in winter, and the ruddiness on his cheeks. And always some kind of good news coming up, always something nice coming up ahead. And never even let me carry the valises in the house, and simonizing, simonizing that little red car! Why, why can't I give him something and not have him hate me?

BEN: Let me think about it. *He glances at his watch.* I still have a little time. Remarkable proposition, but you've got to be sure you're not making a fool of yourself.

Ben drifts off upstage and goes out of sight. Biff comes down from the left.

WILLY, *suddenly conscious of Biff, turns and looks up at him, then begins picking up the packages of seeds in confusion:* Where the hell is that seed? *Indignantly:* You can't see nothing out here! They boxed in the whole goddam neighborhood!

BIFF: There are people all around here. Don't you realize that?

WILLY: I'm busy. Don't bother me.

BIFF, *taking the hoe from Willy:* I'm saying good-by to you, Pop. *Willy looks at him, silent, unable to move.* I'm not coming back any more.

WILLY: You're not going to see Oliver tomorrow?

BIFF: I've got no appointment, Dad.

WILLY: He put his arm around you, and you've got no appointment?

BIFF: Pop, get this now, will you? Every time I've left it's been a fight that sent me out of here. Today I realized something about myself and I tried to explain it to you and I—I think I'm just not smart enough to make any sense out of it for you. To hell with whose fault it is or anything like that. *He takes Willy's arm.* Let's just wrap it up, heh? Come on in, we'll tell Mom. *He gently tries to pull Willy to left.*

WILLY, *frozen, immobile, with guilt in his voice:* No, I don't want to see her.

BIFF: Come on! *He pulls again, and Willy tries to pull away.*

WILLY, *highly nervous:* No, no, I don't want to see her.

BIFF, *trying to look into Willy's face, as if to find the answer there:* Why don't you want to see her?

WILLY, *more harshly now:* Don't bother me, will you?

BIFF: What do you mean, you don't want to see her? You don't want them calling you yellow, do you? This isn't your fault; it's me, I'm a bum. Now come inside! *Willy strains to get away.* Did you hear what I said to you?

Willy pulls away and quickly goes by himself into the house. Biff follows.

LINDA, *to Willy:* Did you plant, dear?

BIFF, *at the door, to Linda:* All right, we had it out. I'm going and I'm not writing any more.

LINDA, *going to Willy in the kitchen:* I think that's the best way, dear. 'Cause there's no use drawing it out, you'll just never get along.

Willy doesn't respond.

BIFF: People ask where I am and what I'm doing, you don't know, and you don't care. That way it'll be off your mind and you can start brightening up again. All right? That clears it, doesn't it? *Willy is silent, and Biff goes to him.* You gonna wish me luck, scout? *He extends his hand.* What do you say?

LINDA: Shake his hand, Willy.

WILLY, *turning to her, seething with hurt:* There's no necessity to mention the pen at all, y'know.

BIFF, *gently:* I've got no appointment, Dad.

WILLY, *erupting fiercely:* He put his arm around . . . ?

BIFF: Dad, you're never going to see what I am, so what's the use of arguing? If I strike oil I'll send you a check. Meantime forget I'm alive.

WILLY, *to Linda:* Spite, see?

BIFF: Shake hands, Dad.

WILLY: Not my hand.

BIFF: I was hoping not to go this way.

WILLY: Well, this is the way you're going. Good-by.

Biff looks at him a moment, then turns sharply and goes to the stairs.

WILLY, *stops him with:* May you rot in hell if you leave this house!

BIFF, *turning:* Exactly what is it that you want from me?

WILLY: I want you to know, on the train, in the mountains, in the valleys, wherever you go, that you cut down your life for spite!

BIFF: No, no.

WILLY: Spite, spite, is the word of your undoing! And when you're down and out, remember what did it. When you're rotting somewhere beside the railroad tracks, remember, and don't you dare blame it on me!

BIFF: I'm not blaming it on you!

WILLY: I won't take the rap for this, you hear?

Happy comes down the stairs and stands on the bottom step, watching.

BIFF: That's just what I'm telling you!

WILLY, *sinking into a chair at the table, with full accusation:* You're trying to put a knife in me—don't think I don't know what you're doing!

BIFF: All right, phony! Then let's lay it on the line. *He whips the rubber tube out of his pocket and puts it on the table.*

HAPPY: You crazy—

Linda: Biff! *She moves to grab the hose, but Biff holds it down with his hand.*

BIFF: Leave it there! Don't move it!

WILLY, *not looking at it:* What is that?

BIFF: You know goddam well what that is.

WILLY, *caged, wanting to escape:* I never saw that.

BIFF: You saw it. The mice didn't bring it into the cellar! What is this supposed to do, make a hero out of you? This supposed to make me sorry for you?

WILLY: Never heard of it.

BIFF: There'll be no pity for you, you hear it? No pity!

WILLY, *to Linda:* You hear the spite!

BIFF: No, you're going to hear the truth—what you are and what I am!

LINDA: Stop it!

WILLY: Spite!

HAPPY, *coming down toward Biff:* You cut it now!

BIFF, *to Happy:* The man don't know who we are! The man is gonna know! *To Willy:* We never told the truth for ten minutes in this house!

HAPPY: We always told the truth!

BIFF, *turning on him:* You big blow, are you the assistant buyer? You're one of the two assistants to the assistant, aren't you?

HAPPY: Well, I'm practically—

BIFF: You're practically full of it! We all are! And I'm through with it. *To Willy:* Now hear this, Willy, this is me.

WILLY: I know you!

BIFF: You know why I had no address for three months? I stole a suit in Kansas City and I was in jail. *To Linda, who is sobbing:* Stop crying. I'm through with it.

Linda turns away from them, her hands covering her face.

WILLY: I suppose that's my fault!

BIFF: I stole myself out of every good job since high school!

WILLY: And whose fault is that?

BIFF: And I never got anywhere because you blew me so full of hot air I could never stand taking orders from anybody! That's whose fault it is!

WILLY: I hear that!

LINDA: Don't, Biff!

BIFF: It's goddam time you heard that! I had to be boss big shot in two weeks, and I'm through with it!

WILLY: Then hang yourself! For spite, hang yourself!

BIFF: No! Nobody's hanging himself, Willy! I ran down eleven flights with a pen in my hand today. And suddenly I stopped, you hear me? And in the middle of that office building, do you hear this? I stopped in the middle of that building and I saw—the sky. I saw the things that I love in this world. The work and the food and time to sit and smoke. And I looked at the pen and said to myself, what the hell am I grabbing this for? Why am I trying to become what I don't want to be? What am I doing in an office, making a contemptuous, begging fool of myself, when all I want is out there, waiting for me the minute I say I know who I am! Why can't I say that, Willy? *He tries to make Willy face him, but Willy pulls away and moves to the left.*

WILLY, *with hatred, threateningly:* The door of your life is wide open!

BIFF: Pop! I'm a dime a dozen, and so are you!

WILLY, *turning on him now in an uncontrolled outburst:* I am not a dime a dozen! I am Willy Loman, and you are Biff Loman!

Biff starts for Willy, but is blocked by Happy. In his fury, Biff seems on the verge of attacking his father.

BIFF: I am not a leader of men, Willy, and neither are you. You were never anything but a hard-working drummer who landed in the ash can like all the rest of them! I'm one dollar an hour, Willy! I tried seven states and couldn't raise it. A buck an hour! Do you gather my meaning? I'm not bringing home any prizes any more, and you're going to stop waiting for me to bring them home!

WILLY, *directly to Biff:* You vengeful, spiteful mut!

Biff breaks from Happy. Willy, in fright, starts up the stairs. Biff grabs him.

BIFF, *at the peak of his fury:* Pop, I'm nothing! I'm nothing, Pop. Can't you understand that? There's no spite in it any more. I'm just what I am, that's all.

Biff's fury has spent itself, and he breaks down, sobbing, holding on to Willy, who dumbly fumbles for Biff's face.

WILLY, *astonished:* What're you doing? What're you doing? *To Linda:* Why is he crying?

BIFF, *crying, broken:* Will you let me go, for Christ's sake? Will you take that phony dream and burn it before something happens? *Struggling to contain himself, he pulls away and moves to the stairs.* I'll go in the morning. Put him—put him to bed. *Exhausted, Biff moves up the stairs to his room.*

WILLY, *after a long pause, astonished, elevated:* Isn't that—isn't that remarkable? Biff—he likes me!

LINDA: He loves you, Willy!

HAPPY, *deeply moved:* Always did, Pop.

WILLY: Oh, Biff! *Staring wildly:* He cried! Cried to me. *He is choking with his love, and now cries out his promise:* That boy—that boy is going to be magnificent!

Ben appears in the light just outside the kitchen.

BEN: Yes, outstanding, with twenty thousand behind him.

LINDA, *sensing the racing of his mind, fearfully, carefully:* Now come to bed, Willy. It's all settled now.

WILLY, *finding it difficult not to rush out of the house:* Yes, we'll sleep. Come on. Go to sleep, Hap.

BEN: And it does take a great kind of a man to crack the jungle.

In accents of dread, Ben's idyllic music starts up.

HAPPY, *his arm around Linda:* I'm getting married, Pop, don't forget it. I'm changing everything. I'm gonna run that department before the year is up. You'll see, Mom. *He kisses her.*

BEN: The jungle is dark but full of diamonds, Willy.

Willy turns, moves, listening to Ben.

LINDA: Be good. You're both good boys, just act that way, that's all.

HAPPY: 'Night, Pop. *He goes upstairs.*

LINDA, *to Willy:* Come, dear.

BEN, *with greater force:* One must go in to fetch a diamond out.

WILLY, *to Linda, as he moves slowly along the edge of the kitchen, toward the door:* I just want to get settled down, Linda. Let me sit alone for a little.

LINDA, *almost uttering her fear:* I want you upstairs.

WILLY, *taking her in his arms:* In a few minutes, Linda. I couldn't sleep right now. Go on, you look awful tired. *He kisses her.*

BEN: Not like an appointment at all. A diamond is rough and hard to the touch.

WILLY: Go on now. I'll be right up.

LINDA: I think this is the only way, Willy.

WILLY: Sure, it's the best thing.

BEN: Best thing!

WILLY: The only way. Everything is gonna be—go on, kid, get to bed. You look so tired.

LINDA: Come right up.

WILLY: Two minutes.

Linda goes into the living room, then reappears in her bedroom. Willy moves just outside the kitchen door.

WILLY: Loves me. *Wonderingly:* Always loved me. Isn't that a remarkable thing? Ben, he'll worship me for it!

BEN, *with promise:* It's dark there, but full of diamonds.

WILLY: Can you imagine that magnificence with twenty thousand dollars in his pocket?

LINDA, *calling from her room:* Willy! Come up!

WILLY, *calling into the kitchen:* Yes! Yes. Coming! It's very smart, you realize that, don't you, sweetheart? Even Ben sees it. I gotta go, baby. 'By! 'By! *Going over to Ben, almost dancing:* Imagine? When the mail comes he'll be ahead of Bernard again!

BEN: A perfect proposition all around.

WILLY: Did you see how he cried to me? Oh, if I could kiss him, Ben!

BEN: Time, William, time!

WILLY: Oh, Ben, I always knew one way or another we were gonna make it, Biff and I!

BEN, *looking at his watch:* The boat. We'll be late. *He moves slowly off into the darkness.*

WILLY, *elegiacally, turning to the house:* Now when you kick off, boy, I want a seventy-yard boot, and get right down the field under the ball, and when you hit, hit low and hit hard, because it's important, boy. *He swings around and faces the audience.* There's all kinds of important people in the stands, and the first thing you know . . . *Suddenly realizing he is alone:* Ben! Ben, where do I . . . ? *He makes a sudden movement of search.* Ben, how do I . . . ?

LINDA, *calling:* Willy, you coming up?

WILLY, *uttering a gasp of fear, whirling about as if to quiet her:* Oh! *He turns around as if to find his way; sounds, faces, voices, seem to be swarming in upon him and he flicks at them, crying, Sh! Sh! Suddenly music, faint and high, stops him. It rises in intensity, almost to an unbearable scream. He goes up and down on his toes, and rushes off around the house.* Shhh!

LINDA: Willy?

There is no answer. Linda waits. Biff gets up off his bed. He is still in his clothes. Happy sits up. Biff stands listening.

LINDA, *with real fear:* Willy, answer me! Willy!

There is the sound of a car starting and moving away at full speed.

LINDA: No!

BIFF, *rushing down the stairs:* Pop!

As the car speeds off, the music crashes down in a frenzy of sound, which becomes the soft pulsation of a single cello string. Biff slowly returns to his bedroom. He and Happy gravely don their jackets. Linda slowly walks out of her room. The music has developed into a dead march. The leaves of day are appearing over everything. Charley and Bernard, somberly dressed, appear and knock on the kitchen door. Biff and Happy slowly descend the stairs to the kitchen as Charley and Bernard enter. All stop a moment when Linda, in clothes of mourning, bearing a little bunch of roses, comes through the draped doorway into the kitchen. She goes to Charley and takes his arm. Now all move toward the audience, through the wall-line of the kitchen. At the limit of the apron, Linda lays down the flowers, kneels, and sits back on her heels. All stare down at the grave.

Requiem

CHARLEY: It's getting dark, Linda.

Linda doesn't react. She stares at the grave.

BIFF: How about it, Mom? Better get some rest, heh? They'll be closing the gate soon.

Linda makes no move. Pause.

HAPPY, *deeply angered:* He had no right to do that. There was no necessity for it. We would've helped him.

CHARLEY, *grunting:* Hmmm.

BIFF: Come along, Mom.

LINDA: Why didn't anybody come?

CHARLEY: It was a very nice funeral.

LINDA: But where are all the people he knew? Maybe they blame him.

CHARLEY: Naa. It's a rough world, Linda. They wouldn't blame him.

LINDA: I can't understand it. At this time especially. First time in thirty-five years we were just about free and clear. He only needed a little salary. He was even finished with the dentist.

CHARLEY: No man only needs a little salary.

LINDA: I can't understand it.

BIFF: There were a lot of nice days. When he'd come home from a trip; or on Sundays, making the stoop; finishing the cellar; putting on the new porch; when he built the extra bathroom; and put up the garage. You know something, Charley, there's more of him in that front stoop than in all the sales he ever made.

CHARLEY: Yeah. He was a happy man with a batch of cement.

LINDA: He was so wonderful with his hands.

BIFF: He had the wrong dreams. All, all, wrong.

HAPPY, *almost ready to fight Biff:* Don't say that!

BIFF: He never knew who he was.

CHARLEY, *stopping Happy's movement and reply. To Biff:* Nobody dast blame this man. You don't understand: Willy was a salesman. And for a salesman, there is no rock bottom to the life. He don't put a bolt to a nut, he don't tell you the law or give you medicine. He's a man way out there in the blue, riding on a smile and a shoeshine. And when they start not smiling back—that's an earthquake. And then you get yourself a couple of spots on your hat, and you're finished. Nobody dast blame this man. A salesman is got to dream, boy. It comes with the territory.

BIFF: Charley, the man didn't know who he was.

HAPPY, *infuriated:* Don't say that!

BIFF: Why don't you come with me, Happy?

HAPPY: I'm not licked that easily. I'm staying right in this city, and I'm gonna beat this racket! *He looks at Biff, his chin set.* The Loman Brothers!

BIFF: I know who I am, kid.

HAPPY: All right, boy. I'm gonna show you and everybody else that Willy Loman did not die in vain. He had a good dream. It's the only dream you can have—to come out number-one man. He fought it out here, and this is where I'm gonna win it for him.

BIFF—*with a hopeless glance at Happy, he bends toward his mother:* Let's go, Mom.

LINDA: I'll be with you in a minute. Go on, Charley. *He hesitates.* I want to, just for a minute. I never had a chance to say good-by.

Charley moves away, followed by Happy. Biff remains a slight distance up and left of Linda. She sits there, summoning herself. The flute begins, not far away, playing behind her speech.

LINDA: Forgive me, dear. I can't cry. I don't know what it is, but I can't cry. I don't understand it. Why did you ever do that? Help me, Willy, I can't cry. It seems to me that you're just on another trip. I keep expecting you. Willy, dear, I can't cry. Why did you do it? I search and search and I search, and I can't understand it, Willy. I made the last payment on the house today. Today, dear. And there'll be nobody home. *A sob rises in her throat.* We're free and clear. *Sobbing more fully, released:* We're free. *Biff comes slowly toward her.* We're free . . . We're free . . .

Biff lifts her to her feet and moves out up right with her in his arms. Linda sobs quietly. Bernard and Charley come together and follow them, followed by Happy. Only the music of the flute is left on the darkening stage as over the house the hard towers of the apartment buildings rise into sharp focus, and

THE CURTAIN FALLS

The Crucible

THE CAST

(in order of appearance)

REVEREND PARRIS	Fred Stewart
BETTY PARRIS	Janet Alexander
TITUBA	Jacqueline Andre
ABIGAIL WILLIAMS	Madeleine Sherwood
SUSANNA WALCOTT	Barbara Stanton
MRS. ANN PUTNAM	Jane Hoffman
THOMAS PUTNAM	Raymond Bramley
MERCY LEWIS	Dorothy Joliffe
MARY WARREN	Jennie Egan
JOHN PROCTOR	Arthur Kennedy
REBECCA NURSE	Jean Adair
GILES COREY	Joseph Sweeney
REVEREND JOHN HALE	E. G. Marshall
ELIZABETH PROCTOR	Beatrice Straight
FRANCIS NURSE	Graham Velsey
EZEKIEL CHEEVER	Don McHenry
MARSHAL HERRICK	George Mitchell
JUDGE HATHORNE	Philip Coolidge
DEPUTY GOVERNOR DANFORTH	Walter Hampden
SARAH GOOD	Adele Fortin
HOPKINS	Donald Marye

Directed by Jed Harris; produced by Kermit Bloomgarden. Opened January 22, 1953, Martin Beck Theatre, New York City.

A NOTE ON
THE HISTORICAL ACCURACY
OF THIS PLAY

This play is not history in the sense in which the word is used by the academic historian. Dramatic purposes have sometimes required many characters to be fused into one; the number of girls involved in the "crying-out" has been reduced; Abigail's age has been raised; while there were several judges of almost equal authority, I have symbolized them all in Hathorne and Danforth. However, I believe that the reader will discover here the essential nature of one of the strangest and most awful chapters in human history. The fate of each character is exactly that of his historical model, and there is no one in the drama who did not play a similar—and in some cases exactly the same—role in history.

As for the characters of the persons, little is known about most of them excepting what may be surmised from a few letters, the trial record, certain broadsides written at the time, and references to their conduct in sources of varying reliability. They may therefore be taken as creations of my own, drawn to the best of my ability in conformity with their known behavior, except as indicated in the commentary I have written for this text.

Act One

A small upper bedroom in the home of Reverend Samuel Parris, Salem, Massachusetts, in the spring of the year 1692.

There is a narrow window at the left. Through its leaded panes the morning sunlight streams. A candle still burns near the bed, which is at the right. A chest, a chair, and a small table are the other furnishings. At the back a door opens on the landing of the stairway to the ground floor. The room gives off an air of clean spareness. The roof rafters are exposed, and the wood colors are raw and unmellowed.

As the curtain rises, Reverend Parris is discovered kneeling beside the bed, evidently in prayer. His daughter, Betty Parris, aged ten, is lying on the bed, inert.

At the time of these events Parris was in his middle forties. In history he cut a villainous path, and there is very little good to be said for him. He believed he was being persecuted wherever he went, despite his best efforts to win people and God to his side. In meeting, he felt insulted if someone rose to shut the door without first asking his permission. He was a widower with no interest in children, or talent with them. He regarded them as young adults, and until this strange crisis he, like the rest of Salem, never conceived that the children were anything but thankful for being permitted to walk straight, eyes slightly lowered, arms at the sides, and mouths shut until bidden to speak.

His house stood in the "town"—but we today would hardly

call it a village. The meeting house was nearby, and from this point outward—toward the bay or inland—there were a few small-windowed, dark houses snuggling against the raw Massachusetts winter. Salem had been established hardly forty years before. To the European world the whole province was a barbaric frontier inhabited by a sect of fanatics who, nevertheless, were shipping out products of slowly increasing quantity and value.

No one can really know what their lives were like. They had no novelists—and would not have permitted anyone to read a novel if one were handy. Their creed forbade anything resembling a theater or "vain enjoyment." They did not celebrate Christmas, and a holiday from work meant only that they must concentrate even more upon prayer.

Which is not to say that nothing broke into this strict and somber way of life. When a new farmhouse was built, friends assembled to "raise the roof," and there would be special foods cooked and probably some potent cider passed around. There was a good supply of ne'er-do-wells in Salem, who dallied at the shovelboard in Bridget Bishop's tavern. Probably more than the creed, hard work kept the morals of the place from spoiling, for the people were forced to fight the land like heroes for every grain of corn, and no man had very much time for fooling around.

That there were some jokers, however, is indicated by the practice of appointing a two-man patrol whose duty was to "walk forth in the time of God's worship to take notice of such as either lye about the meeting house, without attending to the word and ordinances, or that lye at home or in the fields without giving good account thereof, and to take the names of such persons, and to present them to the magistrates, whereby they may be accordingly proceeded against." This predilection for minding other people's business was time-honored among the people of Salem, and it undoubtedly created many of the suspicions which were to feed the coming madness. It was also, in my opinion, one of the things that a John Proctor would rebel against, for the time of the armed camp had almost passed, and since the country was reasonably—although not wholly—safe, the old disciplines were beginning to rankle. But, as in all such matters, the issue was not clear-cut, for danger was still a possibility, and in unity still lay the best promise of safety.

The edge of the wilderness was close by. The American continent stretched endlessly west, and it was full of mystery for them. It stood, dark and threatening, over their shoulders night and day, for out of it Indian tribes marauded from time to time, and Reverend Parris had parishioners who had lost relatives to these heathen.

The parochial snobbery of these people was partly responsible for their failure to convert the Indians. Probably they also preferred to take land from heathens rather than from fellow Christians. At any rate, very few Indians were converted, and the Salem folk believed that the virgin forest was the Devil's last preserve, his home base and the citadel of his final stand. To the best of their knowledge the American forest was the last place on earth that was not paying homage to God.

For these reasons, among others, they carried about an air of innate resistance, even of persecution. Their fathers had, of course, been persecuted in England. So now they and their church found it necessary to deny any other sect its freedom, lest their New Jerusalem be defiled and corrupted by wrong ways and deceitful ideas.

They believed, in short, that they held in their steady hands the candle that would light the world. We have inherited this belief, and it has helped and hurt us. It helped them with the discipline it gave them. They were a dedicated folk, by and large, and they had to be to survive the life they had chosen or been born into in this country.

The proof of their belief's value to them may be taken from the opposite character of the first Jamestown settlement, farther south, in Virginia. The Englishmen who landed there were motivated mainly by a hunt for profit. They had thought to pick off the wealth of the new country and then return rich to England. They were a band of individualists, and a much more ingratiating group than the Massachusetts men. But Virginia destroyed them. Massachusetts tried to kill off the Puritans, but they combined; they set up a communal society which, in the beginning, was little more than an armed camp with an autocratic and very devoted leadership. It was, however, an autocracy by consent, for they were united from top to bottom by a commonly held ideology whose perpetuation was the reason and justification for all their sufferings. So their self-denial, their purposefulness, their suspicion of all vain pursuits, their hard-handed justice, were altogether perfect instruments for the conquest of this space so antagonistic to man.

But the people of Salem in 1692 were not quite the dedicated folk that arrived on the *Mayflower*. A vast differentiation had taken place, and in their own time a revolution had unseated the royal government and substituted a junta which was at this moment in power. The times, to their eyes, must have been out of joint, and to the common folk must have seemed as insoluble and complicated as do ours today. It is not hard to see how easily many could have been led to believe that the time of confusion had been brought upon them by deep and darkling forces. No hint of such speculation appears on the court record, but social disorder in any age breeds such mystical suspicions, and when, as in Salem, wonders are brought forth from below the social surface, it is too much to expect people to hold back very long from laying on the victims with all the force of their frustrations.

The Salem tragedy, which is about to begin in these pages, developed from a paradox. It is a paradox in whose grip we still live, and there is no prospect yet that we will discover its resolution. Simply, it was this: for good purposes, even high purposes, the people of Salem developed a theocracy, a combine of state and religious power whose function was to keep the community together, and to prevent any kind of disunity that might open it to destruction by material or ideological enemies. It was forged for a necessary purpose and accomplished that purpose. But all organization is and must be grounded on the idea of exclusion and prohibition, just as two objects cannot occupy the same space. Evidently the time came in New England when the repressions of order were heavier than seemed warranted by the dangers against which the order was organized. The witch-hunt was a perverse manifestation of the panic which set in among all classes when the balance began to turn toward greater individual freedom.

When one rises above the individual villainy displayed, one can only pity them all, just as we shall be pitied someday. It is still impossible for man to organize his social life without repressions, and the balance has yet to be struck between order and freedom.

The witch-hunt was not, however, a mere repression. It was also, and as importantly, a long overdue opportunity for everyone so inclined to express publicly his guilt and sins, under the cover of accusations against the victims. It suddenly became possible—and patriotic and holy—for a man to say that Martha Corey had come into his bedroom at night, and that, while his wife was sleeping at his side, Martha laid herself down on his chest and "nearly suffocated him." Of course it was her spirit only, but his satisfaction at confessing himself was no lighter than if it had been Martha herself. One could not ordinarily speak such things in public.

Long-held hatreds of neighbors could now be openly expressed, and vengeance taken, despite the Bible's charitable injunctions. Land-lust which had been expressed by constant bickering over bounderies and deeds, could now be elevated to the arena of morality; one could cry witch against one's neighbor and feel perfectly justified in the bargain. Old scores could be settled on a plane of heavenly combat between Lucifer and the Lord; suspicions and the envy of the miserable toward the happy could and did burst out in the general revenge.

Reverend Parris is praying now, and, though we cannot hear his words, a sense of his confusion hangs about him. He mumbles, then seems about to weep; then he weeps, then prays again; but his daughter does not stir on the bed.

The door opens, and his Negro slave enters. Tituba is in her forties. Parris brought her with him from Barbados, where he spent some years as a merchant before entering the ministry. She enters as one does who can no longer bear to be barred from the sight of her beloved, but she is also very frightened because her slave sense has warned her that, as always, trouble in this house eventually lands on her back.

TITUBA, *already taking a step backward:* My Betty be hearty soon?

PARRIS: Out of here!

TITUBA, *backing to the door:* My Betty not goin' die . . .

PARRIS, *scrambling to his feet in a fury:* Out of my sight! *She is gone.* Out of my— *He is overcome with sobs. He clamps his teeth against them and closes the door and leans against it, exhausted.* Oh, my God! God help me! *Quaking with fear, mumbling to himself through his sobs, he goes to the bed and gently takes Betty's hand.* Betty. Child. Dear child. Will you wake, will you open up your eyes! Betty, little one . . .

He is bending to kneel again when his niece, Abigail Williams, seventeen, enters—a strikingly beautiful girl, an orphan, with an endless capacity for dissembling. Now she is all worry and apprehension and propriety.

ABIGAIL: Uncle? *He looks to her.* Susanna Walcott's here from Doctor Griggs.

PARRIS: Oh? Let her come, let her come.

ABIGAIL, *leaning out the door to call to Susanna, who is down the hall a few steps:* Come in, Susanna.

Susanna Walcott, a little younger than Abigail, a nervous, hur-ried girl, enters.

PARRIS, *eagerly:* What does the doctor say, child?

SUSANNA, *craning around Parris to get a look at Betty:* He bid me come and tell you, reverend sir, that he cannot discover no medicine for it in his books.

PARRIS: Then he must search on.

SUSANNA: Aye, sir, he have been searchin' his books since he left you, sir. But he bid me tell you, that you might look to un-natural things for the cause of it.

PARRIS, *his eyes going wide:* No—no. There be no unnatural cause here. Tell him I have sent for Reverend Hale of Beverly, and Mr. Hale will surely confirm that. Let him look to medi-cine and put out all thought of unnatural causes here. There be none.

SUSANNA: Aye, sir. He bid me tell you. *She turns to go.*

ABIGAIL: Speak nothin' of it in the village, Susanna.

PARRIS: Go directly home and speak nothing of unnatural causes.

SUSANNA: Aye, sir. I pray for her. *She goes out.*

ABIGAIL: Uncle, the rumor of witchcraft is all about; I think you'd best go down and deny it yourself. The parlor's packed with people, sir. I'll sit with her.

PARRIS, *pressed, turns on her:* And what shall I say to them? That my daughter and my niece I discovered dancing like hea-then in the forest?

ABIGAIL: Uncle, we did dance; let you tell them I confessed it —and I'll be whipped if I must be. But they're speakin' of witchcraft. Betty's not witched.

PARRIS: Abigail, I cannot go before the congregation when I know you have not opened with me. What did you do with her in the forest?

ABIGAIL: We did dance, uncle, and when you leaped out of the bush so suddenly, Betty was frightened and then she fainted. And there's the whole of it.

PARRIS: Child. Sit you down.

ABIGAIL, *quavering, as she sits:* I would never hurt Betty. I love her dearly.

PARRIS: Now look you, child, your punishment will come in its time. But if you trafficked with spirits in the forest I must know it now, for surely my enemies will, and they will ruin me with it.

ABIGAIL: But we never conjured spirits.

PARRIS: Then why can she not move herself since midnight? This child is desperate! *Abigail lowers her eyes.* It must come out—my enemies will bring it out. Let me know what you done there. Abigail, do you understand that I have many enemies?

ABIGAIL: I have heard of it, uncle.

PARRIS: There is a faction that is sworn to drive me from my pulpit. Do you understand that?

ABIGAIL: I think so, sir.

PARRIS: Now then, in the midst of such disruption, my own household is discovered to be the very center of some obscene practice. Abominations are done in the forest—

ABIGAIL: It were sport, uncle!

PARRIS, *pointing at Betty:* You call this sport? *She lowers her eyes. He pleads:* Abigail, if you know something that may help the doctor, for God's sake tell it to me. *She is silent.* I saw Tituba waving her arms over the fire when I came on you. Why was she doing that? And I heard a screeching and gibberish coming from her mouth. She were swaying like a dumb beast over that fire!

ABIGAIL: She always sings her Barbados songs, and we dance.

PARRIS: I cannot blink what I saw, Abigail, for my enemies will not blink it. I saw a dress lying on the grass.

ABIGAIL, *innocently:* A dress?

PARRIS—*it is very hard to say:* Aye, a dress. And I thought I saw—someone naked running through the trees!

ABIGAIL, *in terror:* No one was naked! You mistake yourself, uncle!

PARRIS, *with anger:* I saw it! *He moves from her. Then, resolved:* Now tell me true, Abigail. And I pray you feel the weight of truth upon you, for now my ministry's at stake, my ministry and perhaps your cousin's life. Whatever abomination you have done, give me all of it now, for I dare not be taken unaware when I go before them down there.

ABIGAIL: There is nothin' more. I swear it, uncle.

PARRIS—*he studies her, then nods, half convinced:* Abigail, I have fought here three long years to bend these stiff-necked people to me, and now, just now when some good respect is rising for me in the parish, you compromise my very character. I have given you a home, child, I have put clothes upon your back—now give me upright answer. Your name in the town—it is entirely white, is it not?

ABIGAIL, *with an edge of resentment:* Why, I am sure it is, sir. There be no blush about my name.

PARRIS, *to the point:* Abigail, is there any other cause than you have told me, for your being discharged from Goody Proctor's service? I have heard it said, and I tell you as I heard it, that she comes so rarely to the church this year for she will not sit so close to something soiled. What signified that remark?

ABIGAIL: She hates me, uncle, she must, for I would not be her slave. It's a bitter woman, a lying, cold, sniveling woman, and I will not work for such a woman!

PARRIS: She may be. And yet it has troubled me that you are now seven month out of their house, and in all this time no other family has ever called for your service.

ABIGAIL: They want slaves, not such as I. Let them send to Barbados for that. I will not black my face for any of them! *With ill-concealed resentment at him:* Do you begrudge my bed, uncle?

PARRIS: No—no.

ABIGAIL, *in a temper:* My name is good in the village! I will not have it said my name is soiled! Goody Proctor is a gossiping liar!

Enter Mrs. Ann Putnam. She is a twisted soul of forty-five, a death-ridden woman, haunted by dreams.

PARRIS, *as soon as the door begins to open:* No—no, I cannot have anyone. *He sees her, and a certain deference springs into him, although his worry remains.* Why, Goody Putnam, come in.

MRS. PUTNAM, *full of breath, shiny-eyed:* It is a marvel. It is surely a stroke of hell upon you.

PARRIS: No, Goody Putnam, it is—

MRS. PUTNAM, *glancing at Betty:* How high did she fly, how high?

PARRIS: No, no, she never flew—

MRS. PUTNAM, *very pleased with it:* Why, it's sure she did. Mr.

Collins saw her goin' over Ingersoll's barn, and come down light as bird, he says!

PARRIS: Now, look you, Goody Putnam, she never— *Enter Thomas Putnam, a well-to-do, hard-handed landowner, near fifty.* Oh, good morning, Mr. Putnam.

PUTNAM: It is a providence the thing is out now! It is a providence. *He goes directly to the bed.*

PARRIS: What's out, sir, what's—?

Mrs. Putnam goes to the bed.

PUTNAM, *looking down at Betty:* Why, *her* eyes is closed! Look you, Ann.

MRS. PUTNAM: Why, that's strange. *To Parris:* Ours is open.

PARRIS, *shocked:* Your Ruth is sick?

MRS. PUTNAM, *with vicious certainty:* I'd not call it sick; the Devil's touch is heavier than sick. It's death, y'know, it's death drivin' into them, forked and hoofed.

PARRIS: Oh, pray not! Why, how does Ruth ail?

MRS. PUTNAM: She ails as she must—she never waked this morning, but her eyes open and she walks, and hears naught, sees naught, and cannot eat. Her soul is taken, surely.

Parris is struck.

PUTNAM, *as though for further details:* They say you've sent for Reverend Hale of Beverly?

PARRIS, *with dwindling conviction now:* A precaution only. He has much experience in all demonic arts, and I—

MRS. PUTNAM: He has indeed; and found a witch in Beverly last year, and let you remember that.

PARRIS: Now, Goody Ann, they only thought that were a witch, and I am certain there be no element of witchcraft here.

PUTNAM: No witchcraft! Now look you, Mr. Parris—

PARRIS: Thomas, Thomas, I pray you, leap not to witchcraft. I know that you—you least of all, Thomas, would ever wish so disastrous a charge laid upon me. We cannot leap to witchcraft. They will howl me out of Salem for such corruption in my house.

A word about Thomas Putnam. He was a man with many grievances, at least one of which appears justified. Some time before, his wife's brother-in-law, James Bayley, had been turned down as minister of Salem. Bayley had all the qualifications, and a two-thirds vote into the bargain, but a faction stopped his acceptance, for reasons that are not clear.

Thomas Putnam was the eldest son of the richest man in the village. He had fought the Indians at Narragansett, and was deeply interested in parish affairs. He undoubtedly felt it poor payment that the village should so blatantly disregard his candidate for one of its more important offices, especially since he regarded himself as the intellectual superior of most of the people around him.

His vindictive nature was demonstrated long before the witchcraft began. Another former Salem minister, George Burroughs, had had to borrow money to pay for his wife's funeral, and, since the parish was remiss in his salary, he was soon bankrupt. Thomas and his brother John had Burroughs jailed for debts the man did not owe. The incident is important only in that Burroughs succeeded in becoming minister where Bayley, Thomas Putnam's brother-in-law, had been rejected; the motif of resentment is clear here. Thomas Putnam felt that his own name and the honor of his family had been smirched by the village, and he meant to right matters however he could.

Another reason to believe him a deeply embittered man was his attempt to break his father's will, which left a disproportionate amount to a stepbrother. As with every other public cause in which he tried to force his way, he failed in this.

So it is not surprising to find that so many accusations against people are in the handwriting of Thomas Putnam, or that his name is so often found as a witness corroborating the supernatural testimony, or that his daughter led the crying-out at the most opportune junctures of the trials, especially when — But we'll speak of that when we come to it.

PUTNAM—*at the moment he is intent upon getting Parris, for whom he has only contempt, to move toward the abyss:* Mr. Parris, I have taken your part in all contention here, and I would continue; but I cannot if you hold back in this. There are hurtful, vengeful spirits layin' hands on these children.

PARRIS: But, Thomas, you cannot—

PUTNAM: Ann! Tell Mr. Parris what you have done.

MRS. PUTNAM: Reverend Parris, I have laid seven babies unbaptized in the earth. Believe me, sir, you never saw more hearty babies born. And yet, each would wither in my arms the very night of their birth. I have spoke nothin', but my heart has clamored intimations. And now, this year, my Ruth, my only— I see her turning strange. A secret child she has become this year, and shrivels like a sucking mouth were pullin' on her life too. And so I thought to send her to your Tituba—

PARRIS: To Tituba! What may Tituba—?

MRS. PUTNAM: Tituba knows how to speak to the dead, Mr. Parris.

PARRIS: Goody Ann, it is a formidable sin to conjure up the dead!

MRS. PUTNAM: I take it on my soul, but who else may surely tell us what person murdered my babies?

PARRIS, *horrified:* Woman!

MRS. PUTNAM: They were murdered, Mr. Parris! And mark

this proof! Mark it! Last night my Ruth were ever so close to their little spirits; I know it, sir. For how else is she struck dumb now except some power of darkness would stop her mouth? It is a marvelous sign, Mr. Parris!

PUTNAM: Don't you understand it, sir? There is a murdering witch among us, bound to keep herself in the dark. *Parris turns to Betty, a frantic terror rising in him.* Let your enemies make of it what they will, you cannot blink it more.

PARRIS, *to Abigail:* Then you were conjuring spirits last night.

ABIGAIL, *whispering:* Not I, sir—Tituba and Ruth.

PARRIS *turns now, with new fear, and goes to Betty, looks down at her, and then, gazing off:* Oh, Abigail, what proper payment for my charity! Now I am undone.

PUTNAM: You are not undone! Let you take hold here. Wait for no one to charge you—declare it yourself. You have discovered witchcraft—

PARRIS: In my house? In my house, Thomas? They will topple me with this! They will make of it a—

Enter Mercy Lewis, the Putnams' servant, a fat, sly, merciless girl of eighteen.

MERCY: Your pardons. I only thought to see how Betty is.

PUTNAM: Why aren't you home? Who's with Ruth?

MERCY: Her grandma come. She's improved a little, I think— she give a powerful sneeze before.

MRS. PUTNAM: Ah, there's a sign of life!

MERCY: I'd fear no more, Goody Putnam. It were a grand sneeze; another like it will shake her wits together, I'm sure. *She goes to the bed to look.*

PARRIS: Will you leave me now, Thomas? I would pray a while alone.

ABIGAIL: Uncle, you've prayed since midnight. Why do you not go down and—

PARRIS: No—no. *To Putnam:* I have no answer for that crowd. I'll wait till Mr. Hale arrives. *To get Mrs. Putnam to leave:* If you will, Goody Ann . . .

PUTNAM: Now look you, sir. Let you strike out against the Devil, and the village will bless you for it! Come down, speak to them—pray with them. They're thirsting for your word, Mister! Surely you'll pray with them.

PARRIS, *swayed:* I'll lead them in a psalm, but let you say nothing of witchcraft yet. I will not discuss it. The cause is yet unknown. I have had enough contention since I came; I want no more.

MRS. PUTNAM: Mercy, you go home to Ruth, d'y'hear?

MERCY: Aye, mum.

Mrs. Putnam goes out.

PARRIS, *to Abigail:* If she starts for the window, cry for me at once.

ABIGAIL: I will, uncle.

PARRIS, *to Putnam:* There is a terrible power in her arms today. *He goes out with Putnam.*

ABIGAIL, *with hushed trepidation:* How is Ruth sick?

MERCY: It's weirdish, I know not—she seems to walk like a dead one since last night.

ABIGAIL—*she turns at once and goes to Betty, and now, with fear in her voice:* Betty? *Betty doesn't move. She shakes her.* Now stop this! Betty! Sit up now! *Betty doesn't stir. Mercy comes over.*

MERCY: Have you tried beatin' her? I gave Ruth a good one and it waked her for a minute. Here, let me have her.

ABIGAIL, *holding Mercy back:* No, he'll be comin' up. Listen, now; if they be questioning us, tell them we danced—I told him as much already.

MERCY: Aye. And what more?

ABIGAIL: He knows Tituba conjured Ruth's sisters to come out of the grave.

MERCY: And what more?

ABIGAIL: He saw you naked.

MERCY, *clapping her hands together with a frightened laugh:* Oh, Jesus!

Enter Mary Warren, breathless. She is seventeen, a subservient, naïve, lonely girl.

MARY WARREN: What'll we do? The village is out! I just come from the farm; the whole country's talkin' witchcraft! They'll be callin' us witches, Abby!

MERCY, *pointing and looking at Mary Warren:* She means to tell, I know it.

MARY WARREN: Abby, we've got to tell. Witchery's a hangin' error, a hangin' like they done in Boston two year ago! We must tell the truth, Abby! You'll only be whipped for dancin', and the other things!

ABIGAIL: Oh, *we'll* be whipped!

MARY WARREN: I never done none of it, Abby. I only looked!

MERCY, *moving menacingly toward Mary:* Oh, you're a great one for lookin', aren't you, Mary Warren? What a grand peeping courage you have!

Betty, on the bed, whimpers. Abigail turns to her at once.

ABIGAIL: Betty? *She goes to Betty.* Now, Betty, dear, wake up now. It's Abigail. *She sits Betty up and furiously shakes her.* I'll beat you, Betty! *Betty whimpers.* My, you seem improving. I talked to your papa and I told him everything. So there's nothing to—

BETTY—*she darts off the bed, frightened of Abigail, and flattens herself against the wall:* I want my mama!

ABIGAIL, *with alarm, as she cautiously approaches Betty:* What ails you, Betty? Your mama's dead and buried.

BETTY: I'll fly to Mama. Let me fly! *She raises her arms as though to fly, and streaks for the window, gets one leg out.*

ABIGAIL, *pulling her away from the window:* I told him everything; he knows now, he knows everything we—

BETTY: You drank blood, Abby! You didn't tell him that!

ABIGAIL: Betty, you never say that again! You will never—

BETTY: You did, you did! You drank a charm to kill John Proctor's wife! You drank a charm to kill Goody Proctor!

ABIGAIL, *smashing her across the face:* Shut it! Now shut it!

BETTY, *collapsing on the bed:* Mama, Mama! *She dissolves into sobs.*

ABIGAIL: Now look you. All of you. We danced. And Tituba conjured Ruth Putnam's dead sisters. And that is all. And mark this. Let either of you breathe a word, or the edge of a word, about the other things, and I will come to you in the black of some terrible night and I will bring a pointy reckoning that will shudder you. And you know I can do it; I saw Indians smash my dear parents' heads on the pillow next to mine, and I have seen some reddish work done at night, and I can make you wish you had never seen the sun go down! *She goes to Betty and roughly sits her up.* Now, you—sit up and stop this! *But Betty collapses in her hands and lies inert on the bed.*

MARY WARREN, *with hysterical fright:* What's got her? *Abigail stares in fright at Betty.* Abby, she's going to die! It's a sin to conjure, and we—

ABIGAIL, *starting for Mary:* I say shut it, Mary Warren!

Enter John Proctor. On seeing him, Mary Warren leaps in fright.

Proctor was a farmer in his middle thirties. He need not have been a partisan of any faction in the town, but there is evidence to suggest that he had a sharp and biting way with hypocrites. He was the kind of man—powerful of body, even-tempered, and not easily led—who cannot refuse support to partisans without drawing their deepest resentment. In Proctor's presence a fool felt his foolishness instantly—and a Proctor is always marked for calumny therefore.

But as we shall see, the steady manner he displays does not spring from an untroubled soul. He is a sinner, a sinner not only against the moral fashion of the time, but against his own vision of decent conduct. These people had no ritual for the washing away of sins. It is another trait we inherited from them, and it has helped to discipline us as well as to breed hypocrisy among us. Proctor, respected and even feared in Salem, has come to regard himself as a kind of fraud. But no hint of this has yet appeared on the surface, and as he enters from the crowded parlor below it is a man in his prime we see, with a quiet confidence and an unexpressed, hidden force. Mary Warren, his servant, can barely speak for embarrassment and fear.

MARY WARREN: Oh! I'm just going home, Mr. Proctor.

PROCTOR: Be you foolish, Mary Warren? Be you deaf? I forbid you leave the house, did I not? Why shall I pay you? I am looking for you more often than my cows!

MARY WARREN: I only come to see the great doings in the world.

PROCTOR: I'll show you a great doin' on your arse one of these days. Now get you home; my wife is waitin' with your work! *Trying to retain a shred of dignity, she goes slowly out.*

MERCY LEWIS, *both afraid of him and strangely titillated:* I'd best be off. I have my Ruth to watch. Good morning, Mr. Proctor.

Mercy sidles out. Since Proctor's entrance, Abigail has stood as though on tiptoe, absorbing his presence, wide-eyed. He glances at her, then goes to Betty on the bed.

ABIGAIL: Gah! I'd almost forgot how strong you are, John Proctor!

PROCTOR, *looking at Abigail now, the faintest suggestion of a knowing smile on his face:* What's this mischief here?

ABIGAIL, *with a nervous laugh:* Oh, she's only gone silly somehow.

PROCTOR: The road past my house is a pilgrimage to Salem all morning. The town's mumbling witchcraft.

ABIGAIL: Oh, posh! *Winningly she comes a little closer, with a confidential, wicked air.* We were dancin' in the woods last night, and my uncle leaped in on us. She took fright, is all.

PROCTOR, *his smile widening:* Ah, you're wicked yet, aren't y'! *A trill of expectant laughter escapes her, and she dares come closer, feverishly looking into his eyes.* You'll be clapped in the stocks before you're twenty.

He takes a step to go, and she springs into his path.

ABIGAIL: Give me a word, John. A soft word. *Her concentrated desire destroys his smile.*

PROCTOR: No, no, Abby. That's done with.

ABIGAIL, *tauntingly:* You come five mile to see a silly girl fly? I know you better.

PROCTOR, *setting her firmly out of his path:* I come to see what mischief your uncle's brewin' now. *With final emphasis:* Put it out of mind, Abby.

ABIGAIL, *grasping his hand before he can release her:* John—I am waitin' for you every night.

PROCTOR: Abby, I never give you hope to wait for me.

ABIGAIL, *now beginning to anger—she can't believe it:* I have something better than hope, I think!

PROCTOR: Abby, you'll put it out of mind. I'll not be comin' for you more.

ABIGAIL: You're surely sportin' with me.

PROCTOR: You know me better.

ABIGAIL: I know how you clutched my back behind your house and sweated like a stallion whenever I come near! Or did I dream that? It's she put me out, you cannot pretend it were you. I saw your face when she put me out, and you loved me then and you do now!

PROCTOR: Abby, that's a wild thing to say—

ABIGAIL: A wild thing may say wild things. But not so wild, I think. I have seen you since she put me out; I have seen you nights.

PROCTOR: I have hardly stepped off my farm this seven month.

ABIGAIL: I have a sense for heat, John, and yours has drawn me to my window, and I have seen you looking up, burning in your loneliness. Do you tell me you've never looked up at my window?

PROCTOR: I may have looked up.

ABIGAIL, *now softening:* And you must. You are no wintry

man. I know you, John. I *know* you. *She is weeping.* I cannot sleep for dreamin'; I cannot dream but I wake and walk about the house as though I'd find you comin' through some door. *She clutches him desperately.*

PROCTOR, *gently pressing her from him, with great sympathy but firmly:* Child—

ABIGAIL, *with a flash of anger:* How do you call me child!

PROCTOR: Abby, I may think of you softly from time to time. But I will cut off my hand before I'll ever reach for you again. Wipe it out of mind. We never touched, Abby.

ABIGAIL: Aye, but we did.

PROCTOR: Aye, but we did not.

ABIGAIL, *with a bitter anger:* Oh, I marvel how such a strong man may let such a sickly wife be—

PROCTOR, *angered—at himself as well:* You'll speak nothin' of Elizabeth!

ABIGAIL: She is blackening my name in the village! She is telling lies about me! She is a cold, sniveling woman, and you bend to her! Let her turn you like a—

PROCTOR, *shaking her:* Do you look for whippin'?

A psalm is heard being sung below.

ABIGAIL, *in tears:* I look for John Proctor that took me from my sleep and put knowledge in my heart! I never knew what pretense Salem was, I never knew the lying lessons I was taught by all these Christian women and their covenanted men! And now you bid me tear the light out of my eyes? I will not, I cannot! You loved me, John Proctor, and whatever sin it is, you love me yet! *He turns abruptly to go out. She rushes to him.* John, pity me, pity me!

The words "going up to Jesus" are heard in the psalm, and Betty claps her ears suddenly and whines loudly.

ABIGAIL: Betty? *She hurries to Betty, who is now sitting up and screaming. Proctor goes to Betty as Abigail is trying to pull her hands down, calling "Betty!"*

PROCTOR, *growing unnerved:* What's she doing? Girl, what ails you? Stop that wailing!

The singing has stopped in the midst of this, and now Parris rushes in.

PARRIS: What happened? What are you doing to her? Betty! *He rushes to the bed, crying, "Betty, Betty!" Mrs. Putnam enters, feverish with curiosity, and with her Thomas Putnam and Mercy Lewis. Parris, at the bed, keeps lightly slapping Betty's face, while she moans and tries to get up.*

ABIGAIL: She heard you singin' and suddenly she's up and screamin'.

MRS. PUTNAM: The psalm! The psalm! She cannot bear to hear the Lord's name!

PARRIS: No, God forbid. Mercy, run to the doctor! Tell him what's happened here! *Mercy Lewis rushes out.*

MRS. PUTNAM: Mark it for a sign, mark it!

Rebecca Nurse, seventy-two, enters. She is white-haired, leaning upon her walking-stick.

PUTNAM, *pointing at the whimpering Betty:* That is a notorious sign of witchcraft afoot, Goody Nurse, a prodigious sign!

MRS. PUTNAM: My mother told me that! When they cannot bear to hear the name of—

PARRIS, *trembling:* Rebecca, Rebecca, go to her, we're lost. She suddenly cannot bear to hear the Lord's—

Giles Corey, eighty-three, enters. He is knotted with muscle, canny, inquisitive, and still powerful.

REBECCA: There is hard sickness here, Giles Corey, so please to keep the quiet.

GILES: I've not said a word. No one here can testify I've said a word. Is she going to fly again? I hear she flies.

PUTNAM: Man, be quiet now!

Everything is quiet. Rebecca walks across the room to the bed. Gentleness exudes from her. Betty is quietly whimpering, eyes shut. Rebecca simply stands over the child, who gradually quiets.

And while they are so absorbed, we may put a word in for Rebecca. Rebecca was the wife of Francis Nurse, who, from all accounts, was one of those men for whom both sides of the argument had to have respect. He was called upon to arbitrate disputes as though he were an unofficial judge, and Rebecca also enjoyed the high opinion most people had for him. By the time of the delusion, they had three hundred acres, and their children were settled in separate homesteads within the same estate. However, Francis had originally rented the land, and one theory has it that, as he gradually paid for it and raised his social status, there were those who resented his rise.

Another suggestion to explain the systematic campaign against Rebecca, and inferentially against Francis, is the land war he fought with his neighbors, one of whom was a Putnam. This squabble grew to the proportions of a battle in the woods between partisans of both sides, and it is said to have lasted for two days. As for Rebecca herself, the general opinion of her character was so high that to explain how anyone dared cry her out for a witch—and more, how adults could bring themselves to lay hands on her—we must look to the fields and boundaries of that time.

As we have seen, Thomas Putnam's man for the Salem ministry was Bayley. The Nurse clan had been in the faction that prevented Bayley's taking office. In addition, certain families allied to the Nurses by blood or friendship, and whose farms were contiguous with the Nurse farm or close to it, combined to break away from the Salem town authority and set up Topsfield, a new and independent entity whose existence was resented by old Salemites.

That the guiding hand behind the outcry was Putnam's is indicated by the fact that, as soon as it began, this Topsfield-Nurse faction absented themselves from church in protest and disbelief. It was Edward and Jonathan Putnam who signed the first complaint against Rebecca; and Thomas Putnam's little daughter was the one who fell into a fit at the hearing and pointed to Rebecca as her attacker. To top it all, Mrs. Putnam—who is now staring at the bewitched child on the bed—soon accused Rebecca's spirit of "tempting her to iniquity," a charge that had more truth in it than Mrs. Putnam could know.

MRS. PUTNAM, *astonished:* What have you done?

Rebecca, in thought, now leaves the bedside and sits.

PARRIS, *wondrous and relieved:* What do you make of it, Rebecca?

PUTNAM, *eagerly:* Goody Nurse, will you go to my Ruth and see if you can wake her?

REBECCA, *sitting:* I think she'll wake in time. Pray calm yourselves. I have eleven children, and I am twenty-six times a grandma, and I have seen them all through their silly seasons, and when it come on them they will run the Devil bowlegged keeping up with their mischief. I think she'll wake when she tires of it. A child's spirit is like a child, you can never catch it by running after it; you must stand still, and, for love, it will soon itself come back.

PROCTOR: Aye, that's the truth of it, Rebecca.

MRS. PUTNAM: This is no silly season, Rebecca. My Ruth is bewildered, Rebecca; she cannot eat.

REBECCA: Perhaps she is not hungered yet. *To Parris:* I hope you are not decided to go in search of loose spirits, Mr. Parris. I've heard promise of that outside.

PARRIS: A wide opinion's running in the parish that the Devil may be among us, and I would satisfy them that they are wrong.

PROCTOR: Then let you come out and call them wrong. Did you consult the wardens before you called this minister to look for devils?

PARRIS: He is not coming to look for devils!

PROCTOR: Then what's he coming for?

PUTNAM: There be children dyin' in the village, Mister!

PROCTOR: I seen none dyin'. This society will not be a bag to swing around your head, Mr. Putnam. *To Parris:* Did you call a meeting before you—?

PUTNAM: I am sick of meetings; cannot the man turn his head without he have a meeting?

PROCTOR: He may turn his head, but not to Hell!

REBECCA: Pray, John, be calm. *Pause. He defers to her.* Mr. Parris, I think you'd best send Reverend Hale back as soon as he come. This will set us all to arguin' again in the society, and we thought to have peace this year. I think we ought rely on the doctor now, and good prayer.

MRS. PUTNAM: Rebecca, the doctor's baffled!

REBECCA: If so he is, then let us go to God for the cause of it. There is prodigious danger in the seeking of loose spirits. I fear it, I fear it. Let us rather blame ourselves and—

PUTNAM: How may we blame ourselves? I am one of nine sons; the Putnam seed have peopled this province. And yet I have but one child left of eight—and now she shrivels!

REBECCA: I cannot fathom that.

MRS. PUTNAM, *with a growing edge of sarcasm:* But I must! You think it God's work you should never lose a child, nor grandchild either, and I bury all but one? There are wheels within wheels in this village, and fires within fires!

PUTNAM, *to Parris:* When Reverend Hale comes, you will proceed to look for signs of witchcraft here.

PROCTOR, *to Putnam:* You cannot command Mr. Parris. We vote by name in this society, not by acreage.

PUTNAM: I never heard you worried so on this society, Mr. Proctor. I do not think I saw you at Sabbath meeting since snow flew.

PROCTOR: I have trouble enough without I come five mile to hear him preach only hellfire and bloody damnation. Take it to heart, Mr. Parris. There are many others who stay away from church these days because you hardly ever mention God any more.

PARRIS, *now aroused:* Why, that's a drastic charge!

REBECCA: It's somewhat true; there are many that quail to bring their children—

PARRIS: I do not preach for children, Rebecca. It is not the children who are unmindful of their obligations toward this ministry.

REBECCA: Are there really those unmindful?

PARRIS: I should say the better half of Salem village—

PUTNAM: And more than that!

PARRIS: Where is my wood? My contract provides I be supplied with all my firewood. I am waiting since November for a stick, and even in November I had to show my frostbitten hands like some London beggar!

GILES: You are allowed six pound a year to buy your wood, Mr. Parris.

PARRIS: I regard that six pound as part of my salary. I am paid little enough without I spend six pound on firewood.

PROCTOR: Sixty, plus six for firewood—

PARRIS: The salary is sixty-six pound, Mr. Proctor! I am not some preaching farmer with a book under my arm; I am a graduate of Harvard College.

GILES: Aye, and well instructed in arithmetic!

PARRIS: Mr. Corey, you will look far for a man of my kind at sixty pound a year! I am not used to this poverty; I left a thrifty business in the Barbados to serve the Lord. I do not fathom it, why am I persecuted here? I cannot offer one proposition but there be a howling riot of argument. I have often wondered if the Devil be in it somewhere; I cannot understand you people otherwise.

PROCTOR: Mr. Parris, you are the first minister ever did demand the deed to this house—

PARRIS: Man! Don't a minister deserve a house to live in?

PROCTOR: To live in, yes. But to ask ownership is like you shall own the meeting house itself; the last meeting I were at you spoke so long on deeds and mortgages I thought it were an auction.

PARRIS: I want a mark of confidence, is all! I am your third preacher in seven years. I do not wish to be put out like the cat whenever some majority feels the whim. You people seem not to comprehend that a minister is the Lord's man in the parish; a minister is not to be so lightly crossed and contradicted—

PUTNAM: Aye!

PARRIS: There is either obedience or the church will burn like Hell is burning!

PROCTOR: Can you speak one minute without we land in Hell again? I am sick of Hell!

PARRIS: It is not for you to say what is good for you to hear!

PROCTOR: I may speak my heart, I think!

PARRIS, *in a fury:* What, are we Quakers? We are not Quakers here yet, Mr. Proctor. And you may tell that to your followers!

PROCTOR: My followers!

PARRIS—*now he's out with it:* There is a party in this church. I am not blind; there is a faction and a party.

PROCTOR: Against you?

PUTNAM: Against him and all authority!

PROCTOR: Why, then I must find it and join it.

There is shock among the others.

REBECCA: He does not mean that.

PUTNAM: He confessed it now!

PROCTOR: I mean it solemnly, Rebecca; I like not the smell of this "authority."

REBECCA: No, you cannot break charity with your minister. You are another kind, John. Clasp his hand, make your peace.

PROCTOR: I have a crop to sow and lumber to drag home. *He goes angrily to the door and turns to Corey with a smile.* What say you, Giles, let's find the party. He says there's a party.

GILES: I've changed my opinion of this man, John. Mr. Parris, I beg your pardon. I never thought you had so much iron in you.

PARRIS, *surprised:* Why, thank you, Giles!

GILES: It suggests to the mind what the trouble be among us all these years. *To all:* Think on it. Wherefore is everybody suing everybody else? Think on it now, it's a deep thing, and dark as a pit. I have been six time in court this year—

PROCTOR, *familiarly, with warmth, although he knows he is approaching the edge of Giles' tolerance with this:* Is it the Devil's fault that a man cannot say you good morning without you clap him for defamation? You're old, Giles, and you're not hearin' so well as you did.

GILES—*he cannot be crossed:* John Proctor, I have only last month collected four pound damages for you publicly sayin' I burned the roof off your house, and I—

PROCTOR, *laughing:* I never said no such thing, but I've paid you for it, so I hope I can call you deaf without charge. Now come along, Giles, and help me drag my lumber home.

PUTNAM: A moment, Mr. Proctor. What lumber is that you're draggin', if I may ask you?

PROCTOR: My lumber. From out my forest by the riverside.

PUTNAM: Why, we are surely gone wild this year. What anarchy is this? That tract is in my bounds, it's in my bounds, Mr. Proctor.

PROCTOR: In your bounds! *Indicating Rebecca:* I bought that tract from Goody Nurse's husband five months ago.

PUTNAM: He had no right to sell it. It stands clear in my grandfather's will that all the land between the river and—

PROCTOR: Your grandfather had a habit of willing land that never belonged to him, if I may say it plain.

GILES: That's God's truth; he nearly willed away my north pasture but he knew I'd break his fingers before he'd set his name to it. Let's get your lumber home, John. I feel a sudden will to work coming on.

PUTNAM: You load one oak of mine and you'll fight to drag it home!

GILES: Aye, and we'll win too, Putnam—this fool and I. Come on! *He turns to Proctor and starts out.*

PUTNAM: I'll have my men on you, Corey! I'll clap a writ on you!

Enter Reverend John Hale of Beverly.

Mr. Hale is nearing forty, a tight-skinned, eager-eyed intellectual. This is a beloved errand for him; on being called here to ascertain witchcraft he felt the pride of the specialist whose unique knowledge has at last been publicly called for. Like almost all men of learning, he spent a good deal of his time pondering the invisible world, especially since he had himself encountered a witch in his parish not long before. That woman, however, turned into a mere pest under his searching scrutiny, and the child she had allegedly been afflicting recovered her normal behavior after Hale had given her his kindness and a few days of rest in his own house. However, that experience never raised a doubt in his mind as to the reality of the underworld or the existence of Lucifer's many-faced lieutenants. And his belief is not to his discredit. Better minds than Hale's were—and still are—convinced that there is a society of spirits beyond our ken. One cannot help noting that one of his lines has never yet raised a laugh in any audience that has seen this play; it is his assurance that "We cannot look to superstition in this. The Devil is precise." Evidently we are not quite certain even now whether diabolism is holy and not to be scoffed at. And it is no accident that we should be so bemused.

Like Reverend Hale and the others on this stage, we conceive the Devil as a necessary part of a respectable view of cosmology. Ours is a divided empire in which certain ideas and emotions and actions are of God, and their opposites are of Lucifer. It is as impossible for most men to conceive of a morality without sin as of an earth without "sky." Since 1692 a great but superficial change has wiped out God's beard and the Devil's horns, but the world is still gripped between two diametrically opposed absolutes. The concept of unity, in which positive and negative are attributes of the same force, in which good and evil are relative, ever-changing, and always joined to the same phenomenon—such a concept is still reserved to the physical sciences and to the few who have grasped the history of ideas. When it is recalled that until the Christian era the underworld was never regarded as a hostile area, that all gods were useful and essentially friendly to man despite occasional lapses; when we see the steady and methodical inculcation into humanity of the idea of man's worthlessness—until redeemed—the necessity of the Devil may become evident as a weapon, a weapon designed and used time and time again in every age to whip men into a surrender to a particular church or church-state.

Our difficulty in believing the—for want of a better word— political inspiration of the Devil is due in great part to the fact that he is called up and damned not only by our social antagonists but by our own side, whatever it may be. The Catholic Church, through its Inquisition, is famous for cultivating Lucifer as the arch-fiend, but the Church's enemies relied no less upon the Old Boy to keep the human mind enthralled. Luther was himself accused of alliance with Hell, and he in turn accused his enemies. To complicate matters further, he believed that he had had contact with the Devil and had argued theology with him. I am not surprised at this, for at my own university a professor of history—a Lutheran, by the way—used to assemble his graduate students, draw the shades, and commune in the classroom with Erasmus. He was never, to my knowledge, officially scoffed at for this, the reason being that the university officials, like most of us, are the children of a history which still sucks at the Devil's teats. At this writing, only England has held back before the temptations of contemporary diabolism. In the countries of the Communist ideology, all resistance of any import is linked to the totally malign capitalist succubi, and in America any man who is not reactionary in his views is open to the charge of alliance with the Red hell. Political opposition, thereby, is given an inhumane overlay which then justifies the abrogation of all normally applied customs of civilized intercourse. A political policy is equated with moral right, and opposition to it with diabolical malevolence. Once such an equation is effectively made, society becomes a congeries of plots and counterplots, and the main role of government changes from that of the arbiter to that of the scourge of God.

The results of this process are no different now from what they ever were, except sometimes in the degree of cruelty inflicted, and not always even in that department. Normally the actions and deeds of a man were all that society felt comfortable in judging. The secret intent of an action was left to the ministers, priests, and rabbis to deal with. When diabolism rises, however, actions are the least important manifests of the true nature of a man. The Devil, as Reverend Hale said, is a wily one, and, until an hour before he fell, even God thought him beautiful in Heaven.

The analogy, however, seems to falter when one considers that, while there were no witches then, there are Communists and capitalists now, and in each camp there is certain proof that spies of each side are at work undermining the other. But this is a snobbish objection and not at all warranted by the facts. I have no doubt that people *were* communing with, and even worshiping, the Devil in Salem, and if the whole truth could be known in this case, as it is in others, we should discover a regular and conventionalized propitiation of the dark spirit. One certain evidence of this is the confession of Tituba, the slave of Reverend Parris, and another is the behavior of the children who were known to have indulged in sorceries with her.

There are accounts of similar *klatches* in Europe, where the daughters of the towns would assemble at night and, sometimes with fetishes, sometimes with a selected young man, give themselves to love, with some bastardly results. The Church, sharp-eyed as it must be when gods long dead are brought to life, condemned these orgies as witchcraft and interpreted them rightly, as a resurgence of the Dionysiac forces it had crushed long before. Sex, sin, and the Devil were early linked, and so they continued to be in Salem, and are today. From all accounts there are no more puritanical mores in the world than those enforced by the Communists in Russia, where women's fashions, for instance, are as prudent and all-covering as any American Baptist would desire. The divorce laws lay a tremendous responsibility on the father for the care of his children. Even the laxity of divorce regulations in the early years of the revolution was undoubtedly a revulsion from the nineteenth-century Victorian immobility of marriage and the consequent hypocrisy that developed from it. If for no other reasons, a state so powerful, so jealous of the uniformity of its citizens, cannot long tolerate the atomization of the family. And yet, in American eyes at least, there remains the conviction that the Russian attitude toward women is lascivious. It is the Devil working again, just as he is working within the Slav who is shocked at the very idea of a woman's disrobing herself in a burlesque show. Our opposites are always robed in sexual sin, and it is from this unconscious conviction that demonology gains both its attractive sensuality and its capacity to infuriate and frighten.

Coming into Salem now, Reverend Hale conceives of himself much as a young doctor on his first call. His painfully acquired armory of symptoms, catchwords, and diagnostic procedures is now to be put to use at last. The road from Beverly is unusually busy this morning, and he has passed a hundred rumors that make him smile at the ignorance of the yeomanry in this most precise science. He feels himself allied with the best minds of Europe—kings, philosophers, scientists, and ecclesiasts of all churches. His goal is light, goodness and its preservation, and he knows the exaltation of the blessed whose intelligence, sharpened by minute examinations of enormous tracts, is finally called upon to face what may be a bloody fight with the Fiend himself.

He appears loaded down with half a dozen heavy books.

HALE: Pray you, someone take these!

PARRIS, *delighted:* Mr. Hale! Oh! it's good to see you again! *Taking some books:* My, they're heavy!

HALE, *setting down his books:* They must be; they are weighted with authority.

PARRIS, *a little scared:* Well, you do come prepared!

HALE: We shall need hard study if it comes to tracking down the Old Boy. *Noticing Rebecca:* You cannot be Rebecca Nurse?

REBECCA: I am, sir. Do you know me?

HALE: It's strange how I knew you, but I suppose you look as such a good soul should. We have all heard of your great charities in Beverly.

PARRIS: Do you know this gentleman? Mr. Thomas Putnam. And his good wife Ann.

HALE: Putnam! I had not expected such distinguished company, sir.

PUTNAM, *pleased:* It does not seem to help us today, Mr. Hale. We look to you to come to our house and save our child.

HALE: Your child ails too?

MRS. PUTNAM: Her soul, her soul seems flown away. She sleeps and yet she walks . . .

PUTNAM: She cannot eat.

HALE: Cannot eat! *Thinks on it. Then, to Proctor and Giles Corey:* Do you men have afflicted children?

PARRIS: No, no, these are farmers. John Proctor—

GILES COREY: He don't believe in witches.

PROCTOR, *to Hale:* I never spoke on witches one way or the other. Will you come, Giles?

GILES: No—no, John, I think not. I have some few queer questions of my own to ask this fellow.

PROCTOR: I've heard you to be a sensible man, Mr. Hale. I hope you'll leave some of it in Salem.

Proctor goes. Hale stands embarrassed for an instant.

PARRIS, *quickly:* Will you look at my daughter, sir? *Leads Hale to the bed.* She has tried to leap out the window; we discovered her this morning on the highroad, waving her arms as though she'd fly.

HALE, *narrowing his eyes:* Tries to fly.

PUTNAM: She cannot bear to hear the Lord's name, Mr. Hale; that's a sure sign of witchcraft afloat.

HALE, *holding up his hands:* No, no. Now let me instruct you. We cannot look to superstition in this. The Devil is precise; the marks of his presence are definite as stone, and I must tell you all that I shall not proceed unless you are prepared to believe me if I should find no bruise of Hell upon her.

PARRIS: It is agreed, sir—it is agreed—we will abide by your judgment.

HALE: Good then, *He goes to the bed, looks down at Betty. To Parris:* Now, sir, what were your first warning of this strangeness?

PARRIS: Why, sir—I discovered her—*indicating Abigail*—and my niece and ten or twelve of the other girls, dancing in the forest last night.

HALE, *surprised:* You permit dancing?

PARRIS: No, no, it were secret—

MRS. PUTNAM, *unable to wait:* Mr. Parris's slave has knowledge of conjurin', sir.

PARRIS, *to Mrs. Putnam:* We cannot be sure of that, Goody Ann—

MRS. PUTNAM, *frightened, very softly:* I know it, sir. I sent my child—she should learn from Tituba who murdered her sisters.

REBECCA, *horrified:* Goody Ann! You sent a child to conjure up the dead?

MRS. PUTNAM: Let God blame me, not you, not you, Rebecca! I'll not have you judging me any more! *To Hale:* Is it a natural work to lose seven children before they live a day?

PARRIS: Sssh!

Rebecca, with great pain, turns her face away. There is a pause.

HALE: Seven dead in childbirth.

MRS. PUTNAM, *softly:* Aye. *Her voice breaks; she looks up at him. Silence. Hale is impressed. Parris looks to him. He goes to his books, opens one, turns pages, then reads. All wait, avidly.*

PARRIS, *hushed:* What book is that?

MRS. PUTNAM: What's there, sir?

HALE, *with a tasty love of intellectual pursuit:* Here is all the invisible world, caught, defined, and calculated. In these books the Devil stands stripped of all his brute disguises. Here are all your familiar spirits—your incubi and succubi; your witches that go by land, by air, and by sea; your wizards of the night and of the day. Have no fear now—we shall find him out if he has come among us, and I mean to crush him utterly if he has shown his face! *He starts for the bed.*

REBECCA: Will it hurt the child, sir?

HALE: I cannot tell. If she is truly in the Devil's grip we may have to rip and tear to get her free.

REBECCA: I think I'll go, then. I am too old for this. *She rises.*

PARRIS, *striving for conviction:* Why, Rebecca, we may open up the boil of all our troubles today!

REBECCA: Let us hope for that. I go to God for you, sir.

PARRIS, *with trepidation—and resentment:* I hope you do not mean we go to Satan here! *Slight pause.*

REBECCA: I wish I knew. *She goes out; they feel resentful of her note of moral superiority.*

PUTNAM, *abruptly:* Come, Mr. Hale, let's get on. Sit you here.

GILES: Mr. Hale, I have always wanted to ask a learned man —what signifies the readin' of strange books?

HALE: What books?

GILES: I cannot tell; she hides them.

HALE: Who does this?

GILES: Martha, my wife. I have waked at night many a time and found her in a corner, readin' of a book. Now what do you make of that?

HALE: Why, that's not necessarily—

GILES: It discomfits me! Last night—mark this—I tried and tried and could not say my prayers. And then she close her book and walks out of the house, and suddenly—mark this—I could pray again!

Old Giles must be spoken for, if only because his fate was to be so remarkable and so different from that of all the others. He was in his early eighties at this time, and was the most comical hero in the history. No man has ever been blamed for so much. If a cow was missed, the first thought was to look for her around Corey's house; a fire blazing up at night brought suspicion of arson to his door. He didn't give a hoot for public opinion, and only in his last years—after he had married Martha—did he bother much with the church. That she stopped his prayer is very probable, but he forgot to say that he'd only recently learned any prayers and it didn't take much to make him stumble over them. He was a crank and a nuisance, but withal a deeply innocent and brave man. In court, once, he was asked if it were true that he had been frightened by the strange behavior of a hog and had then said he knew it to be the Devil in an animal's shape. "What frighted you?" he was asked. He forgot everything but the word "frighted," and instantly replied, "I do not know that I ever spoke that word in my life."

HALE: Ah! The stoppage of prayer—that is strange. I'll speak further on that with you.

GILES: I'm not sayin' she's touched the Devil, now, but I'd admire to know what books she reads and why she hides them. She'll not answer me, y' see.

HALE: Aye, we'll discuss it. *To all:* Now mark me, if the Devil is in her you will witness some frightful wonders in this room, so please to keep your wits about you. Mr. Putnam, stand close in case she flies. Now, Betty, dear, will you sit up? *Putnam comes in closer, ready-handed. Hale sits Betty up, but she hangs limp in his hands.* Hmmm. *He observes her carefully. The others watch breathlessly.* Can you hear me? I am John Hale, minister of Beverly. I have come to help you, dear. Do you remember my two little girls in Beverly? *She does not stir in his hands.*

PARRIS, *in fright:* How can it be the Devil? Why would he choose my house to strike? We have all manner of licentious people in the village!

HALE: What victory would the Devil have to win a soul already bad? It is the best the Devil wants, and who is better than the minister?

GILES: That's deep, Mr. Parris, deep, deep!

PARRIS, *with resolution now:* Betty! Answer Mr. Hale! Betty!

HALE: Does someone afflict you, child? It need not be a woman, mind you, or a man. Perhaps some bird invisible to others comes to you—perhaps a pig, a mouse, or any beast at all. Is there some figure bids you fly? *The child remains limp in his hands. In silence he lays her back on the pillow. Now, holding out his hands toward her, he intones:* In nomine Domini Sabaoth sui filiique ite ad infernos. *She does not stir. He turns to Abigail, his eyes narrowing.* Abigail, what sort of dancing were you doing with her in the forest?

ABIGAIL: Why—common dancing is all.

PARRIS: I think I ought to say that I—I saw a kettle in the grass where they were dancing.

ABIGAIL: That were only soup.

HALE: What sort of soup were in this kettle, Abigail?

ABIGAIL: Why, it were beans—and lentils, I think, and—

HALE: Mr. Parris, you did not notice, did you, any living thing in the kettle? A mouse, perhaps, a spider, a frog—?

PARRIS, *fearfully:* I—do believe there were some movement—in the soup.

ABIGAIL: That jumped in, we never put it in!

HALE, *quickly:* What jumped in?

ABIGAIL: Why, a very little frog jumped—

PARRIS: A frog, Abby!

HALE, *grasping Abigail:* Abigail, it may be your cousin is dying. Did you call the Devil last night?

ABIGAIL: I never called him! Tituba, Tituba . . .

PARRIS, *blanched:* She called the Devil?

HALE: I should like to speak with Tituba.

PARRIS: Goody Ann, will you bring her up? *Mrs. Putnam exits.*

HALE: How did she call him?

ABIGAIL: I know not—she spoke Barbados.

HALE: Did you feel any strangeness when she called him? A sudden cold wind, perhaps? A trembling below the ground?

ABIGAIL: I didn't see no Devil! *Shaking Betty:* Betty, wake up. Betty! Betty!

HALE: You cannot evade me, Abigail. Did your cousin drink any of the brew in that kettle?

ABIGAIL: She never drank it!

HALE: Did you drink it?

ABIGAIL: No, sir!

HALE: Did Tituba ask you to drink it?

ABIGAIL: She tried, but I refused.

HALE: Why are you concealing? Have you sold yourself to Lucifer?

ABIGAIL: I never sold myself! I'm a good girl! I'm a proper girl!

Mrs. Putnam enters with Tituba, and instantly Abigail points at Tituba.

ABIGAIL: She made me do it! She made Betty do it!

TITUBA, *shocked and angry:* Abby!

ABIGAIL: She makes me drink blood!

PARRIS: Blood!!

MRS. PUTNAM: My baby's blood?

TITUBA: No, no, chicken blood. I give she chicken blood!

HALE: Woman, have you enlisted these children for the Devil?

TITUBA: No, no, sir, I don't truck with no Devil!

HALE: Why can she not wake? Are you silencing this child?

TITUBA: I love me Betty!

HALE: You have sent your spirit out upon this child, have you not? Are you gathering souls for the Devil?

ABIGAIL: She sends her spirit on me in church; she makes me laugh at prayer!

PARRIS: She have often laughed at prayer!

ABIGAIL: She comes to me every night to go and drink blood!

TITUBA: You beg *me* to conjure! She beg *me* make charm—

ABIGAIL: Don't lie! *To Hale:* She comes to me while I sleep; she's always making me dream corruptions!

TITUBA: Why you say that, Abby?

ABIGAIL: Sometimes I wake and find myself standing in the open doorway and not a stitch on my body! I always hear her laughing in my sleep. I hear her singing her Barbados songs and tempting me with—

TITUBA: Mister Reverend, I never—

HALE, *resolved now:* Tituba, I want you to wake this child.

TITUBA: I have no power on this child, sir.

HALE: You most certainly do, and you will free her from it now! When did you compact with the Devil?

TITUBA: I don't compact with no Devil!

PARRIS: You will confess yourself or I will take you out and whip you to your death, Tituba!

PUTNAM: This woman must be hanged! She must be taken and hanged!

TITUBA, *terrified, falls to her knees:* No, no, don't hang Tituba! I tell him I don't desire to work for him, sir.

PARRIS: The Devil?

HALE: Then you saw him! *Tituba weeps.* Now Tituba, I know that when we bind ourselves to Hell it is very hard to break with it. We are going to help you tear yourself free—

TITUBA, *frightened by the coming process:* Mister Reverend, I do believe somebody else be witchin' these children.

HALE: Who?

TITUBA: I don't know, sir, but the Devil got him numerous witches.

HALE: Does he! *It is a clue.* Tituba, look into my eyes. Come, look into me. *She raises her eyes to his fearfully.* You would be a good Christian woman, would you not, Tituba?

TITUBA: Aye, sir, a good Christian woman.

HALE: And you love these little children?

TITUBA: Oh, yes, sir, I don't desire to hurt little children.

HALE: And you love God, Tituba?

TITUBA: I love God with all my bein'.

HALE: Now, in God's holy name—

TITUBA: Bless Him. Bless Him. *She is rocking on her knees, sobbing in terror.*

HALE: And to His glory—

TITUBA: Eternal glory. Bless Him—bless God . . .

HALE: Open yourself, Tituba—open yourself and let God's holy light shine on you.

TITUBA: Oh, bless the Lord.

HALE: When the Devil comes to you does he ever come—with another person? *She stares up into his face.* Perhaps another person in the village? Someone you know.

PARRIS: Who came with him?

PUTNAM: Sarah Good? Did you ever see Sarah Good with him? Or Osburn?

PARRIS: Was it man or woman came with him?

TITUBA: Man or woman. Was—was woman.

PARRIS: What woman? A woman, you said. What woman?

TITUBA: It was black dark, and I—

PARRIS: You could see him, why could you not see her?

TITUBA: Well, they was always talking; they was always runnin' round and carryin' on—

PARRIS: You mean out of Salem? Salem witches?

TITUBA: I believe so, yes, sir.

Now Hale takes her hand. She is surprised.

HALE: Tituba. You must have no fear to tell us who they are, do you understand? We will protect you. The Devil can never overcome a minister. You know that, do you not?

TITUBA—*she kisses Hale's hand:* Aye, sir, oh, I do.

HALE: You have confessed yourself to witchcraft, and that speaks a wish to come to Heaven's side. And we will bless you, Tituba.

TITUBA, *deeply relieved:* Oh, God bless you, Mr. Hale!

HALE, *with rising exaltation:* You are God's instrument put in our hands to discover the Devil's agents among us. You are selected, Tituba, you are chosen to help us cleanse our village. So speak utterly, Tituba, turn your back on him and face God—face God, Tituba, and God will protect you.

TITUBA, *joining with him:* Oh, God, protect Tituba!

HALE, *kindly:* Who came to you with the Devil? Two? Three? Four? How many?

Tituba pants and begins rocking back and forth again, staring ahead.

TITUBA: There was four. There was four.

PARRIS, *pressing in on her:* Who? Who? Their names, their names!

TITUBA, *suddenly bursting out:* Oh, how many times he bid me kill you, Mr. Parris!

PARRIS: Kill me!

TITUBA, *in a fury:* He say Mr. Parris must be kill! Mr. Parris no goodly man, Mr. Parris mean man and no gentle man, and he bid me rise out of my bed and cut your throat! *They gasp.* But I tell him "No! I don't hate that man. I don't want kill that man." But he say, "You work for me, Tituba, and I make you free! I give you pretty dress to wear, and put you way high up in the air, and you gone fly back to Barbados!" And I say, "You lie, Devil, you lie!" And then he come one stormy night to me, and he say, "Look! I have *white* people belong to me." And I look—and there was Goody Good.

PARRIS: Sarah Good!

TITUBA, *rocking and weeping:* Aye, sir, and Goody Osburn.

MRS. PUTNAM: I knew it! Goody Osburn were midwife to me three times. I begged you, Thomas, did I not? I begged him not to call Osburn because I feared her. My babies always shriveled in her hands!

HALE: Take courage, you must give us all their names. How can you bear to see this child suffering? Look at her, Tituba. *He is indicating Betty on the bed.* Look at her God-given innocence; her soul is so tender; we must protect her, Tituba; the Devil is out and preying on her like a beast upon the flesh of the pure lamb. God will bless you for your help.

Abigail rises, staring as though inspired, and cries out.

ABIGAIL. I want to open myself! *They turn to her, startled. She is enraptured, as though in a pearly light.* I want the light of God, I want the sweet love of Jesus! I danced for the Devil; I saw him; I wrote in his book; I go back to Jesus; I kiss His hand. I saw Sarah Good with the Devil! I saw Goody Osburn with the Devil! I saw Bridget Bishop with the Devil!

As she is speaking, Betty is rising from the bed, a fever in her eyes, and picks up the chant.

BETTY, *staring too:* I saw George Jacobs with the Devil! I saw Goody Howe with the Devil!

PARRIS: She speaks! *He rushes to embrace Betty.* She speaks!

HALE: Glory to God! It is broken, they are free!

BETTY, *calling out hysterically and with great relief:* I saw Martha Bellows with the Devil!

ABIGAIL: I saw Goody Sibber with the Devil! *It is rising to a great glee.*

PUTNAM: The marshal, I'll call the marshal!

Parris is shouting a prayer of thanksgiving.

BETTY: I saw Alice Barrow with the Devil!

The curtain begins to fall.

HALE, *as Putnam goes out:* Let the marshal bring irons!

ABIGAIL: I saw Goody Hawkins with the Devil!

BETTY: I saw Goody Bibber with the Devil!

ABIGAIL: I saw Goody Booth with the Devil!

On their ecstatic cries

THE CURTAIN FALLS

Act Two

The common room of Proctor's house, eight days later.

At the right is a door opening on the fields outside. A fireplace is at the left, and behind it a stairway leading upstairs. It is the low, dark, and rather long living room of the time. As the curtain rises, the room is empty. From above, Elizabeth is heard softly singing to the children. Presently the door opens and John Proctor enters, carrying his gun. He glances about the room as he comes toward the fireplace, then halts for an instant as he hears her singing. He continues on to the fireplace, leans the gun against the wall as he swings a pot out of the fire and smells it. Then he lifts out the ladle and tastes. He is not quite pleased. He reaches to a cupboard, takes a pinch of salt, and drops it into the pot. As he is tasting again, her footsteps are heard on the stair. He swings the pot into the fireplace and goes to a basin and washes his hands and face. Elizabeth enters.

ELIZABETH: What keeps you so late? It's almost dark.

PROCTOR: I were planting far out to the forest edge.

ELIZABETH: Oh, you're done then.

PROCTOR: Aye, the farm is seeded. The boys asleep?

ELIZABETH: They will be soon. *And she goes to the fireplace, proceeds to ladle up stew in a dish.*

183

PROCTOR: Pray now for a fair summer.

ELIZABETH: Aye.

PROCTOR: Are you well today?

ELIZABETH: I am. *She brings the plate to the table, and, indicating the food:* It is a rabbit.

PROCTOR, *going to the table:* Oh, is it! In Jonathan's trap?

ELIZABETH: No, she walked into the house this afternoon; I found her sittin' in the corner like she come to visit.

PROCTOR: Oh, that's a good sign walkin' in.

ELIZABETH: Pray God. It hurt my heart to strip her, poor rabbit. *She sits and watches him taste it.*

PROCTOR: It's well seasoned.

ELIZABETH, *blushing with pleasure:* I took great care. She's tender?

PROCTOR: Aye. *He eats. She watches him.* I think we'll see green fields soon. It's warm as blood beneath the clods.

ELIZABETH: That's well.

Proctor eats, then looks up.

PROCTOR: If the crop is good I'll buy George Jacobs' heifer. How would that please you?

ELIZABETH: Aye, it would.

PROCTOR, *with a grin:* I mean to please you, Elizabeth.

ELIZABETH—*it is hard to say:* I know it, John.

He gets up, goes to her, kisses her. She receives it. With a certain disappointment, he returns to the table.

PROCTOR, *as gently as he can:* Cider?

ELIZABETH, *with a sense of reprimanding herself for having forgot:* Aye! *She gets up and goes and pours a glass for him. He now arches his back.*

PROCTOR: This farm's a continent when you go foot by foot droppin' seeds in it.

ELIZABETH, *coming with the cider:* It must be.

PROCTOR—*he drinks a long draught, then, putting the glass down:* You ought to bring some flowers in the house.

ELIZABETH: Oh! I forgot! I will tomorrow.

PROCTOR: It's winter in here yet. On Sunday let you come with me, and we'll walk the farm together; I never see such a load of flowers on the earth. *With good feeling he goes and looks up at the sky through the open doorway.* Lilacs have a purple smell. Lilac is the smell of nightfall, I think. Massachusetts is a beauty in the spring!

ELIZABETH: Aye, it is.

There is a pause. She is watching him from the table as he stands there absorbing the night. It is as though she would speak but cannot. Instead, now, she takes up his plate and glass and fork and goes with them to the basin. Her back is turned to him. He turns to her and watches her. A sense of their separation rises.

PROCTOR: I think you're sad again. Are you?

ELIZABETH—*she doesn't want friction, and yet she must:* You come so late I thought you'd gone to Salem this afternoon.

PROCTOR: Why? I have no business in Salem.

ELIZABETH: You did speak of going, earlier this week.

PROCTOR—*he knows what she means:* I thought better of it since.

ELIZABETH: Mary Warren's there today.

PROCTOR: Why'd you let her? You heard me forbid her to go to Salem any more!

ELIZABETH: I couldn't stop her.

PROCTOR, *holding back a full condemnation of her:* It is a fault, it is a fault, Elizabeth—you're the mistress here, not Mary Warren.

ELIZABETH: She frightened all my strength away.

PROCTOR: How may that mouse frighten you, Elizabeth? You—

ELIZABETH: It is a mouse no more. I forbid her go, and she raises up her chin like the daughter of a prince and says to me, "I must go to Salem, Goody Proctor; I am an official of the court!"

PROCTOR: Court! What court?

ELIZABETH: Aye, it is a proper court they have now. They've sent four judges out of Boston, she says, weighty magistrates of the General Court, and at the head sits the Deputy Governor of the Province.

PROCTOR, *astonished:* Why, she's mad.

ELIZABETH: I would to God she were. There be fourteen people in the jail now, she says. *Proctor simply looks at her, unable to grasp it.* And they'll be tried, and the court have power to hang them too, she says.

PROCTOR, *scoffing, but without conviction:* Ah, they'd never hang—

ELIZABETH: The Deputy Governor promise hangin' if they'll not confess, John. The town's gone wild, I think. She speak of Abigail, and I thought she were a saint, to hear her. Abigail brings the other girls into the court, and where she walks the crowd will part like the sea for Israel. And folks are brought

before them, and if they scream and howl and fall to the floor
—the person's clapped in the jail for bewitchin' them.

PROCTOR, *wide-eyed:* Oh, it is a black mischief.

ELIZABETH: I think you must go to Salem, John. *He turns to
her.* I think so. You must tell them it is a fraud.

PROCTOR, *thinking beyond this:* Aye, it is, it is surely.

ELIZABETH: Let you go to Ezekiel Cheever—he knows you
well. And tell him what she said to you last week in her uncle's
house. She said it had naught to do with witchcraft, did she
not?

PROCTOR, *in thought:* Aye, she did, she did. *Now a pause.*

ELIZABETH, *quietly, fearing to anger him by prodding:* God forbid
you keep that from the court, John. I think they must be
told.

PROCTOR, *quietly, struggling with his thought:* Aye, they must,
they must. It is a wonder they do believe her.

ELIZABETH: I would go to Salem now, John—let you go tonight.

PROCTOR: I'll think on it.

ELIZABETH, *with her courage now:* You cannot keep it, John.

PROCTOR, *angering:* I know I cannot keep it. I say I will think
on it!

ELIZABETH, *hurt, and very coldly:* Good, then, let you think on
it. *She stands and starts to walk out of the room.*

PROCTOR: I am only wondering how I may prove what she
told me, Elizabeth. If the girl's a saint now, I think it is not
easy to prove she's fraud, and the town gone so silly. She told
it to me in a room alone—I have no proof for it.

ELIZABETH: You were alone with her?

PROCTOR, *stubbornly:* For a moment alone, aye.

ELIZABETH: Why, then, it is not as you told me.

PROCTOR, *his anger rising:* For a moment, I say. The others come in soon after.

ELIZABETH, *quietly—she has suddenly lost all faith in him:* Do as you wish, then. *She starts to turn.*

PROCTOR: Woman. *She turns to him.* I'll not have your suspicion any more.

ELIZABETH, *a little loftily: I* have no—

PROCTOR: I'll not have it!

ELIZABETH: Then let you not earn it.

PROCTOR, *with a violent undertone:* You doubt me yet?

ELIZABETH, *with a smile, to keep her dignity:* John, if it were not Abigail that you must go to hurt, would you falter now? I think not.

PROCTOR: Now look you—

ELIZABETH: I see what I see, John.

PROCTOR, *with solemn warning:* You will not judge me more, Elizabeth. I have good reason to think before I charge fraud on Abigail, and I will think on it. Let you look to your own improvement before you go to judge your husband any more. I have forgot Abigail, and—

ELIZABETH: And I.

PROCTOR: Spare me! You forget nothin' and forgive nothin'. Learn charity, woman. I have gone tiptoe in this house all seven month since she is gone. I have not moved from there to there without I think to please you, and still an everlasting funeral marches round your heart. I cannot speak but I am doubted, every moment judged for lies, as though I come into a court when I come into this house!

ELIZABETH: John, you are not open with me. You saw her with a crowd, you said. Now you—

PROCTOR: I'll plead my honesty no more, Elizabeth.

ELIZABETH—*now she would justify herself:* John, I am only—

PROCTOR: No more! I should have roared you down when first you told me your suspicion. But I wilted, and, like a Christian, I confessed. Confessed! Some dream I had must have mistaken you for God that day. But you're not, you're not, and let you remember it! Let you look sometimes for the goodness in me, and judge me not.

ELIZABETH: I do not judge you. The magistrate sits in your heart that judges you. I never thought you but a good man, John *with a smile*—only somewhat bewildered.

PROCTOR, *laughing bitterly:* Oh, Elizabeth, your justice would freeze beer! *He turns suddenly toward a sound outside. He starts for the door as Mary Warren enters. As soon as he sees her, he goes directly to her and grabs her by her cloak, furious.* How do you go to Salem when I forbid it? Do you mock me? *Shaking her:* I'll whip you if you dare leave this house again! *Strangely, she doesn't resist him but hangs limply by his grip.*

MARY WARREN: I am sick, I am sick, Mr. Proctor. Pray, pray, hurt me not. *Her strangeness throws him off, and her evident pallor and weakness. He frees her.* My insides are all shuddery; I am in the proceedings all day, sir.

PROCTOR, *with draining anger—his curiosity is draining it:* And what of these proceedings here? When will you proceed to keep this house, as you are paid nine pound a year to do—and my wife not wholly well? *As though to compensate, Mary Warren goes to Elizabeth with a small rag doll.*

MARY WARREN: I made a gift for you today, Goody Proctor. I had to sit long hours in a chair, and passed the time with sewing.

ELIZABETH, *perplexed, looking at the doll:* Why, thank you, it's a fair poppet.

MARY WARREN, *with a trembling, decayed voice:* We must all love each other now, Goody Proctor.

ELIZABETH, *amazed at her strangeness:* Aye, indeed, we must.

MARY WARREN, *glancing at the room:* I'll get up early in the morning and clean the house. I must sleep now. *She turns and starts off.*

PROCTOR: Mary. *She halts.* Is it true? There be fourteen women arrested?

MARY WARREN: No, sir. There be thirty-nine now— *She suddenly breaks off and sobs and sits down, exhausted.*

ELIZABETH: Why, she's weepin'! What ails you, child?

MARY WARREN: Goody Osburn—will hang! *There is a shocked pause, while she sobs.*

PROCTOR: Hang! *He calls into her face.* Hang, y'say?

MARY WARREN, *through her weeping:* Aye.

PROCTOR: The Deputy Governor will permit it?

MARY WARREN: He sentenced her. He must. *To ameliorate it:* But not Sarah Good. For Sarah Good confessed, y'see.

PROCTOR: Confessed! To what?

MARY WARREN: That she—*in horror at the memory*—she sometimes made a compact with Lucifer, and wrote her name in his black book—with her blood—and bound herself to torment Christians till God's thrown down—and we all must worship Hell forevermore.

Pause.

PROCTOR: But—surely you know what a jabberer she is. Did you tell them that?

MARY WARREN: Mr. Proctor, in open court she near to choked us all to death.

PROCTOR: How, choked you?

MARY WARREN: She sent her spirit out.

ELIZABETH: Oh, Mary, Mary, surely you—

MARY WARREN, *with an indignant edge:* She tried to kill me many times, Goody Proctor!

ELIZABETH: Why, I never heard you mention that before.

MARY WARREN: I never knew it before. I never knew anything before. When she come into the court I say to myself, I must not accuse this woman, for she sleep in ditches, and so very old and poor. But then—then she sit there, denying and denying, and I feel a misty coldness climbin' up my back, and the skin on my skull begin to creep, and I feel a clamp around my neck and I cannot breathe air; and then—*entranced*—I hear a voice, a screamin' voice, and it were my voice—and all at once I remember everything she done to me!

PROCTOR: Why? What did she do to you?

MARY WARREN, *like one awakened to a marvelous secret insight:* So many time, Mr. Proctor, she come to this very door, beggin' bread and a cup of cider—and mark this: whenever I turned her away empty, she *mumbled*.

ELIZABETH: Mumbled! She may mumble if she's hungry.

MARY WARREN: But *what* does she mumble? You must remember, Goody Proctor. Last month—a Monday, I think—she walked away, and I thought my guts would burst for two days after. Do you remember it?

ELIZABETH: Why—I do, I think, but—

MARY WARREN: And so I told that to Judge Hathorne, and he asks her so. "Goody Osburn," says he, "what curse do you

mumble that this girl must fall sick after turning you away?"
And then she replies—*mimicking an old crone*—"Why, your
excellence, no curse at all. I only say my commandments; I
hope I may say my commandments," says she!

ELIZABETH: And that's an upright answer.

MARY WARREN: Aye, but then Judge Hathorne say, "Recite
for us your commandments!"—*leaning avidly toward them*—
and of all the ten she could not say a single one. She never
knew no commandments, and they had her in a flat lie!

PROCTOR: And so condemned her?

MARY WARREN, *now a little strained, seeing his stubborn doubt:*
Why, they must when she condemned herself.

PROCTOR: But the proof, the proof!

MARY WARREN, *with greater impatience with him:* I told you
the proof. It's hard proof, hard as rock, the judges said.

PROCTOR—*he pauses an instant, then:* You will not go to court
again, Mary Warren.

MARY WARREN: I must tell you, sir, I will be gone every day
now. I am amazed you do not see what weighty work we do.

PROCTOR: What work you do! It's strange work for a Christian girl to hang old women!

MARY WARREN: But, Mr. Proctor, they will not hang them if
they confess. Sarah Good will only sit in jail some time—*recalling*—and here's a wonder for you; think on this. Goody
Good is pregnant!

ELIZABETH: Pregnant! Are they mad? The woman's near to
sixty!

MARY WARREN: They had Doctor Griggs examine her, and
she's full to the brim. And smokin' a pipe all these years, and
no husband either! But she's safe, thank God, for they'll not

hurt the innocent child. But be that not a marvel? You must see it, sir, it's God's work we do. So I'll be gone every day for some time. I'm—I am an official of the court, they say, and I— *She has been edging toward offstage.*

PROCTOR: I'll official you! *He strides to the mantel, takes down the whip hanging there.*

MARY WARREN, *terrified, but coming erect, striving for her authority:* I'll not stand whipping any more!

ELIZABETH, *hurriedly, as Proctor approaches:* Mary, promise now you'll stay at home—

MARY WARREN, *backing from him, but keeping her erect posture, striving, striving for her way:* The Devil's loose in Salem, Mr. Proctor; we must discover where he's hiding!

PROCTOR: I'll whip the Devil out of you! *With whip raised he reaches out for her, and she streaks away and yells.*

MARY WARREN, *pointing at Elizabeth:* I saved her life today!

Silence. His whip comes down.

ELIZABETH, *softly:* I am accused?

MARY WARREN, *quaking:* Somewhat mentioned. But I said I never see no sign you ever sent your spirit out to hurt no one, and seeing I do live so closely with you, they dismissed it.

ELIZABETH: Who accused me?

MARY WARREN: I am bound by law, I cannot tell it. *To Proctor:* I only hope you'll not be so sarcastical no more. Four judges and the King's deputy sat to dinner with us but an hour ago. I—I would have you speak civilly to me, from this out.

PROCTOR, *in horror, muttering in disgust at her:* Go to bed.

MARY WARREN, *with a stamp of her foot:* I'll not be ordered to bed no more, Mr. Proctor! I am eighteen and a woman, however single!

PROCTOR: Do you wish to sit up? Then sit up.

MARY WARREN: I wish to go to bed!

PROCTOR, *in anger:* Good night, then!

MARY WARREN: Good night. *Dissatisfied, uncertain of herself, she goes out. Wide-eyed, both Proctor and Elizabeth stand staring.*

ELIZABETH, *quietly:* Oh, the noose, the noose is up!

PROCTOR: There'll be no noose.

ELIZABETH: She wants me dead. I knew all week it would come to this!

PROCTOR, *without conviction:* They dismissed it. You heard her say—

ELIZABETH: And what of tomorrow? She will cry me out until they take me!

PROCTOR: Sit you down.

ELIZABETH: She wants me dead, John, you know it!

PROCTOR: I say sit down! *She sits, trembling. He speaks quietly, trying to keep his wits.* Now we must be wise, Elizabeth.

ELIZABETH, *with sarcasm, and a sense of being lost:* Oh, indeed, indeed!

PROCTOR: Fear nothing. I'll find Ezekiel Cheever. I'll tell him she said it were all sport.

ELIZABETH: John, with so many in the jail, more than Cheever's help is needed now, I think. Would you favor me with this? Go to Abigail.

PROCTOR, *his soul hardening as he senses* . . . . What have I to say to Abigail?

ELIZABETH, *delicately:* John—grant me this. You have a faulty understanding of young girls. There is a promise made in any bed—

PROCTOR, *striving against his anger:* What promise!

ELIZABETH: Spoke or silent, a promise is surely made. And she may dote on it now—I am sure she does—and thinks to kill me, then to take my place.

Proctor's anger is rising; he cannot speak.

ELIZABETH: It is her dearest hope, John, I know it. There be a thousand names; why does she call mine? There be a certain danger in calling such a name—I am no Goody Good that sleeps in ditches, nor Osburn, drunk and half-witted. She'd dare not call out such a farmer's wife but there be monstrous profit in it. She thinks to take my place, John.

PROCTOR: She cannot think it! *He knows it is true.*

ELIZABETH, *"reasonably":* John, have you ever shown her somewhat of contempt? She cannot pass you in the church but you will blush—

PROCTOR: I may blush for my sin.

ELIZABETH: I think she sees another meaning in that blush.

PROCTOR: And what see you? What see you, Elizabeth?

ELIZABETH, *"conceding":* I think you be somewhat ashamed, for I am there, and she so close.

PROCTOR: When will you know me, woman? Were I stone I would have cracked for shame this seven month!

ELIZABETH: Then go and tell her she's a whore. Whatever promise she may sense—break it, John, break it.

PROCTOR, *between his teeth:* Good, then. I'll go. *He starts for his rifle.*

ELIZABETH, *trembling, fearfully:* Oh, how unwillingly!

PROCTOR, *turning on her, rifle in hand:* I will curse her hotter than the oldest cinder in hell. But pray, begrudge me not my anger!

ELIZABETH: Your anger! I only ask you—

PROCTOR: Woman, am I so base? Do you truly think me base?

ELIZABETH: I never called you base.

PROCTOR: Then how do you charge me with such a promise? The promise that a stallion gives a mare I gave that girl!

ELIZABETH: Then why do you anger with me when I bid you break it?

PROCTOR: Because it speaks deceit, and I am honest! But I'll plead no more! I see now your spirit twists around the single error of my life, and I will never tear it free!

ELIZABETH, *crying out:* You'll tear it free—when you come to know that I will be your only wife, or no wife at all! She has an arrow in you yet, John Proctor, and you know it well!

Quite suddenly, as though from the air, a figure appears in the doorway. They start slightly. It is Mr. Hale. He is different now —drawn a little, and there is a quality of deference, even of guilt, about his manner now.

HALE: Good evening.

PROCTOR, *still in his shock:* Why, Mr. Hale! Good evening to you, sir. Come in, come in.

HALE, *to Elizabeth:* I hope I do not startle you.

ELIZABETH: No, no, it's only that I heard no horse—

HALE: You are Goodwife Proctor.

PROCTOR: Aye; Elizabeth.

HALE—*he nods, then:* I hope you're not off to bed yet.

PROCTOR, *setting down his gun:* No, no. *Hale comes further into the room. And Proctor, to explain his nervousness:* We are not used to visitors after dark, but you're welcome here. Will you sit you down, sir?

HALE; I will. *He sits.* Let you sit, Goodwife Proctor. *She does, never letting him out of her sight. There is a pause as Hale looks about the room.*

PROCTOR, *to break the silence:* Will you drink cider, Mr. Hale?

HALE: No, it rebels my stomach; I have some further traveling yet tonight. Sit you down, sir. *Proctor sits.* I will not keep you long, but I have some business with you.

PROCTOR: Business of the court?

HALE: No—no, I come of my own, without the court's authority. Hear me. *He wets his lips.* I know not if you are aware, but your wife's name is—mentioned in the court.

PROCTOR: We know it, sir. Our Mary Warren told us. We are entirely amazed.

HALE: I am a stranger here, as you know. And in my ignorance I find it hard to draw a clear opinion of them that come accused before the court. And so this afternoon, and now tonight, I go from house to house—I come now from Rebecca Nurse's house and—

ELIZABETH, *shocked:* Rebecca's charged!

HALE: God forbid such a one be charged. She is, however—mentioned somewhat.

ELIZABETH, *with an attempt at a laugh:* You will never believe, I hope, that Rebecca trafficked with the Devil.

HALE: Woman, it is possible.

PROCTOR, *taken aback:* Surely you cannot think so.

HALE: This is a strange time, Mister. No man may longer doubt the powers of the dark are gathered in monstrous attack upon this village. There is too much evidence now to deny it. You will agree, sir?

PROCTOR, *evading:* I—have no knowledge in that line. But it's hard to think so pious a woman be secretly a Devil's bitch after seventy year of such good prayer.

HALE: Aye. But the Devil is a wily one, you cannot deny it. However, she is far from accused, and I know she will not be. *Pause.* I thought, sir, to put some questions as to the Christian character of this house, if you'll permit me.

PROCTOR, *coldly, resentful:* Why, we—have no fear of questions, sir.

HALE: Good, then. *He makes himself more comfortable.* In the book of record that Mr. Parris keeps, I note that you are rarely in the church on Sabbath Day.

PROCTOR: No, sir, you are mistaken.

HALE: Twenty-six time in seventeen month, sir. I must call that rare. Will you tell me why you are so absent?

PROCTOR: Mr. Hale, I never knew I must account to that man for I come to church or stay at home. My wife were sick this winter.

HALE: So I am told. But you, Mister, why could you not come alone?

PROCTOR: I surely did come when I could, and when I could not I prayed in this house.

HALE: Mr. Proctor, your house is not a church; your theology must tell you that.

PROCTOR: It does, sir, it does; and it tells me that a minister may pray to God without he have golden candlesticks upon the altar.

HALE: What golden candlesticks?

PROCTOR: Since we built the church there were pewter candlesticks upon the altar; Francis Nurse made them, y'know, and a sweeter hand never touched the metal. But Parris came, and for twenty week he preach nothin' but golden candlesticks until he had them. I labor the earth from dawn of day to blink of night, and I tell you true, when I look to heaven and see my money glaring at his elbows—it hurt my prayer, sir, it hurt my prayer. I think, sometimes, the man dreams cathedrals, not clapboard meetin' houses.

HALE—*he thinks, then:* And yet, Mister, a Christian on Sabbath Day must be in church. *Pause.* Tell me—you have three children?

PROCTOR: Aye. Boys.

HALE: How comes it that only two are baptized?

PROCTOR—*he starts to speak, then stops, then, as though unable to restrain this:* I like it not that Mr. Parris should lay his hand upon my baby. I see no light of God in that man. I'll not conceal it.

HALE: I must say it, Mr. Proctor; that is not for you to decide. The man's ordained, therefore the light of God is in him.

PROCTOR, *flushed with resentment but trying to smile:* What's your suspicion, Mr. Hale?

HALE: No, no, I have no—

PROCTOR: I nailed the roof upon the church, I hung the door—

HALE: Oh, did you! That's a good sign, then.

PROCTOR: It may be I have been too quick to bring the man to book, but you cannot think we ever desired the destruction of religion. I think that's in your mind, is it not?

HALE, *not altogether giving way:* I—have—there is a softness in your record, sir, a softness.

ELIZABETH: I think, maybe, we have been too hard with Mr. Parris, I think so. But sure we never loved the Devil here.

HALE—*he nods, deliberating this. Then, with the voice of one administering a secret test:* Do you know your Commandments, Elizabeth?

ELIZABETH, *without hesitation, even eagerly:* I surely do. There be no mark of blame upon my life, Mr. Hale. I am a convenanted Christian woman.

HALE: And you, Mister?

PROCTOR, *a trifle unsteadily:* I—am sure I do, sir.

HALE—*he glances at her open face, then at John, then:* Let you repeat them, if you will.

PROCTOR: The Commandments.

HALE: Aye.

PROCTOR, *looking off, beginning to sweat:* Thou shalt not kill.

HALE: Aye.

PROCTOR, *counting on his fingers:* Thou shalt not steal. Thou shalt not covet thy neighbor's goods, nor make unto thee any graven image. Thou shalt not take the name of the Lord in vain; thou shalt have no other gods before me. *With some hesitation:* Thou shalt remember the Sabbath Day and keep it holy. *Pause. Then:* Thou shalt honor thy father and mother. Thou shalt not bear false witness. *He is stuck. He counts back on his fingers, knowing one is missing.* Thou shalt not make unto thee any graven image.

HALE: You have said that twice, sir.

PROCTOR, *lost:* Aye. *He is flailing for it.*

ELIZABETH, *delicately:* Adultery, John.

PROCTOR, *as though a secret arrow had pained his heart:* Aye. *Trying to grin it away—to Hale:* You see, sir, between the two of us we do know them all. *Hale only looks at Proctor, deep in his attempt to define this man. Proctor grows more uneasy.* I think it be a small fault.

HALE: Theology, sir, is a fortress; no crack in a fortress may be accounted small. *He rises; he seems worried now. He paces a little, in deep thought.*

PROCTOR: There be no love for Satan in this house, Mister.

HALE: I pray it, I pray it dearly. *He looks to both of them, an attempt at a smile on his face, but his misgivings are clear.* Well, then—I'll bid you good night.

ELIZABETH, *unable to restrain herself:* Mr. Hale. *He turns.* I do think you are suspecting me somewhat? Are you not?

HALE, *obviously disturbed—and evasive:* Goody Proctor, I do not judge you. My duty is to add what I may to the godly wisdom of the court. I pray you both good health and good fortune. *To John:* Good night, sir. *He starts out.*

ELIZABETH, *with a note of desperation:* I think you must tell him, John.

HALE: What's that?

ELIZABETH, *restraining a call:* Will you tell him?

Slight pause. Hale looks questioningly at John.

PROCTOR, *with difficulty:* I—I have no witness and cannot prove it, except my word be taken. But I know the children's sickness had naught to do with witchcraft.

HALE, *stopped, struck:* Naught to do—?

PROCTOR: Mr. Parris discovered them sportin' in the woods. They were startled and took sick.

Pause.

HALE: Who told you this?

PROCTOR—*he hesitates, then:* Abigail Williams.

HALE: Abigail!

PROCTOR: Aye.

HALE, *his eyes wide:* Abigail Williams told you it had naught to do with witchcraft!

PROCTOR: She told me the day you came, sir.

HALE, *suspiciously:* Why—why did you keep this?

PROCTOR: I never knew until tonight that the world is gone daft with this nonsense.

HALE: Nonsense! Mister, I have myself examined Tituba, Sarah Good, and numerous others that have confessed to dealing with the Devil. They have *confessed* it.

PROCTOR: And why not, if they must hang for denyin' it? There are them that will swear to anything before they'll hang; have you never thought of that?

HALE: I have. I—I have indeed. *It is his own suspicion, but he resists it. He glances at Elizabeth, then at John.* And you—would you testify to this in court?

PROCTOR: I—had not reckoned with goin' into court. But if I must I will.

HALE: Do you falter here?

PROCTOR: I falter nothing, but I may wonder if my story will be credited in such a court. I do wonder on it, when such a steady-minded minister as you will suspicion such a woman that never lied, and cannot, and the world knows she cannot! I may falter somewhat, Mister; I am no fool.

HALE, *quietly—it has impressed him:* Proctor, let you open with me now, for I have a rumor that troubles me. It's said you hold no belief that there may even be witches in the world. Is that true, sir?

PROCTOR—*he knows this is critical, and is striving against his disgust with Hale and with himself for even answering:* I know not what I have said, I may have said it. I have wondered if there be witches in the world—although I cannot believe they come among us now.

HALE: Then you do not believe—

PROCTOR: I have no knowledge of it; the Bible speaks of witches, and I will not deny them.

HALE: And you, woman?

ELIZABETH: I—I cannot believe it.

HALE, *shocked:* You cannot!

PROCTOR: Elizabeth, you bewilder him!

ELIZABETH, *to Hale:* I cannot think the Devil may own a woman's soul, Mr. Hale, when she keeps an upright way, as I have. I am a good woman, I know it; and if you believe I may do only good work in the world, and yet be secretly bound to Satan, then I must tell you, sir, I do not believe it.

HALE: But, woman, you do believe there are witches in—

ELIZABETH: If you think that I am one, then I say there are none.

HALE: You surely do not fly against the Gospel, the Gospel—

PROCTOR: She believe in the Gospel, every word!

ELIZABETH: Question Abigail Williams about the Gospel, not myself!

Hale stares at her.

PROCTOR: She do not mean to doubt the Gospel, sir, you cannot think it. This be a Christian house, sir, a Christian house.

HALE: God keep you both; let the third child be quickly baptized, and go you without fail each Sunday in to Sabbath prayer; and keep a solemn, quiet way among you. I think—

Giles Corey appears in doorway.

GILES: John!

PROCTOR: Giles! What's the matter?

GILES: They take my wife.

Francis Nurse enters.

GILES: And his Rebecca!

PROCTOR, *to Francis:* Rebecca's in the *jail!*

FRANCIS: Aye, Cheever come and take her in his wagon. We've only now come from the jail, and they'll not even let us in to see them.

ELIZABETH: They've surely gone wild now, Mr. Hale!

FRANCIS, *going to Hale:* Reverend Hale! Can you not speak to the Deputy Governor? I'm sure he mistakes these people—

HALE: Pray calm yourself, Mr. Nurse.

FRANCIS: My wife is the very brick and mortar of the church, Mr. Hale—*indicating Giles*—and Martha Corey, there cannot be a woman closer yet to God than Martha.

HALE: How is Rebecca charged, Mr. Nurse?

FRANCIS, *with a mocking, half-hearted laugh:* For murder, she's charged! *Mockingly quoting the warrant:* "For the marvelous and supernatural murder of Goody Putnam's babies." What am I to do, Mr. Hale?

HALE, *he turns from Francis, deeply troubled, then:* Believe me,

Mr. Nurse, if Rebecca Nurse be tainted, then nothing's left to stop the whole green world from burning. Let you rest upon the justice of the court; the court will send her home, I know it.

FRANCIS: You cannot mean she will be tried in court!

HALE, *pleading:* Nurse, though our hearts break, we cannot flinch; these are new times, sir. There is a misty plot afoot so subtle we should be criminal to cling to old respects and ancient friendships. I have seen too many frightful proofs in court—the Devil is alive in Salem, and we dare not quail to follow wherever the accusing finger points!

PROCTOR, *angered:* How may such a woman murder children?

HALE, *in great pain:* Man, remember, until an hour before the Devil fell, God thought him beautiful in Heaven.

GILES: I never said my wife were a witch, Mr. Hale; I only said she were reading books!

HALE: Mr. Corey, exactly what complaint were made on your wife?

GILES: That bloody mongrel Walcott charge her. Y'see, he buy a pig of my wife four or five year ago, and the pig died soon after. So he come dancin' in for his money back. So my Martha, she says to him, "Walcott, if you haven't the wit to feed a pig properly, you'll not live to own many," she says. Now he goes to court and claims that from that day to this he cannot keep a pig alive for more than four weeks because my Martha bewitch them with her books!

Enter Ezekiel Cheever. A shocked silence.

CHEEVER: Good evening to you, Proctor.

PROCTOR: Why, Mr. Cheever. Good evening.

CHEEVER: Good evening, all. Good evening, Mr. Hale.

PROCTOR: I hope you come not on business of the court.

CHEEVER: I do, Proctor, aye. I am clerk of the court now, y'know.

Enter Marshal Herrick, a man in his early thirties, who is somewhat shamefaced at the moment.

GILES: It's a pity, Ezekiel, that an honest tailor might have gone to Heaven must burn in Hell. You'll burn for this, do you know it?

CHEEVER: You know yourself I must do as I'm told. You surely know that, Giles. And I'd as lief you'd not be sending me to Hell. I like not the sound of it, I tell you; I like not the sound of it. *He fears Proctor, but starts to reach inside his coat.* Now believe me, Proctor, how heavy be the law, all its tonnage I do carry on my back tonight. *He takes out a warrant.* I have a warrant for your wife.

PROCTOR, *to Hale:* You said she were not charged!

HALE: I know nothin' of it. *To Cheever:* When were she charged?

CHEEVER: I am given sixteen warrant tonight, sir, and she is one.

PROCTOR: Who charged her?

CHEEVER: Why, Abigail Williams charge her.

PROCTOR: On what proof, what proof?

CHEEVER, *looking about the room:* Mr. Proctor, I have little time. The court bid me search your house, but I like not to search a house. So will you hand me any poppets that your wife may keep here?

Proctor: Poppets?

ELIZABETH: I never kept no poppets, not since I were a girl.

CHEEVER, *embarrassed, glancing toward the mantel where sits Mary Warren's poppet:* I spy a poppet, Goody Proctor.

ELIZABETH: Oh! *Going for it:* Why, this is Mary's.

CHEEVER, *shyly:* Would you please to give it to me?

ELIZABETH, *handing it to him, asks Hale:* Has the court discovered a text in poppets now?

CHEEVER, *carefully holding the poppet:* Do you keep any others in this house?

PPROCTOR: No, nor this one either till tonight. What signifies a poppet?

CHEEVER: Why, a poppet—*he gingerly turns the poppet over*—a poppet may signify— Now, woman, will you please to come with me?

PROCTOR: She will not! *To Elizabeth:* Fetch Mary here.

CHEEVER, *ineptly reaching toward Elizabeth:* No, no, I am forbid to leave her from my sight.

PROCTOR, *pushing his arm away:* You'll leave her out of sight and out of mind, Mister. Fetch Mary, Elizabeth. *Elizabeth goes upstairs.*

HALE: What signifies a poppet, Mr. Cheever?

CHEEVER, *turning the poppet over in his hands:* Why, they say it may signify that she— *He has lifted the poppet's skirt, and his eyes widen in astonished fear.* Why, this, this—

PROCTOR, *reaching for the poppet:* What's there?

CHEEVER: Why—*he draws out a long needle from the poppet*—it is a needle! Herrick, Herrick, it is a needle!

Herrick comes toward him.

PROCTOR, *angrily, bewildered:* And what signifies a needle!

CHEEVER, *his hands shaking:* Why, this go hard with her, Proctor, this—I had my doubts, Proctor, I had my doubts, but here's calamity. *To Hale, showing the needle:* You see it, sir, it is a needle!

HALE: Why? What meanin' has it?

CHEEVER, *wide-eyed, trembling:* The girl, the Williams girl, Abigail Williams, sir. She sat to dinner in Reverend Parris's house tonight, and without word nor warnin' she falls to the floor. Like a struck beast, he says, and screamed a scream that a bull would weep to hear. And he goes to save her, and, stuck two inches in the flesh of her belly, he draw a needle out. And demandin' of her how she come to be so stabbed, she—*to Proctor now*—testify it were your wife's familiar spirit pushed it in.

PROCTOR: Why, she done it herself! *To Hale:* I hope you're not takin' this for proof, Mister!

Hale, struck by the proof, is silent.

CHEEVER: 'Tis hard proof! *To Hale:* I find here a poppet Goody Proctor keeps. I have found it, sir. And in the belly of the poppet a needle's stuck. I tell you true, Proctor, I never warranted to see such proof of Hell, and I bid you obstruct me not, for I—

Enter Elizabeth with Mary Warren. Proctor, seeing Mary Warren, draws her by the arm to Hale.

PROCTOR: Here now! Mary, how did this poppet come into my house?

MARY WARREN, *frightened for herself, her voice very small:* What poppet's that, sir?

PROCTOR, *impatiently, pointing at the doll in Cheever's hand:* This poppet, this poppet.

MARY WARREN, *evasively, looking at it:* Why, I—I think it is mine.

PROCTOR: It is your poppet, is it not?

MARY WARREN, *not understanding the direction of this:* It—is, sir.

PROCTOR: And how did it come into this house?

MARY WARREN, *glancing about at the avid faces:* Why—I made it in the court, sir, and—give it to Goody Proctor tonight.

PROCTOR, *to Hale:* Now, sir—do you have it?

HALE: Mary Warren, a needle have been found inside this poppet.

MARY WARREN, *bewildered:* Why, I meant no harm by it, sir.

PROCTOR, *quickly:* You stuck that needle in yourself?

MARY WARREN: I—I believe I did, sir, I—

PROCTOR, *to Hale:* What say you now?

HALE, *watching Mary Warren closely:* Child, you are certain this be your natural memory? May it be, perhaps, that some- one conjures you even now to say this?

MARY WARREN: Conjures me? Why, no, sir, I am entirely my- self, I think. Let you ask Susanna Walcott—she saw me sewin' it in court. *Or better still:* Ask Abby, Abby sat beside me when I made it.

PROCTOR, *to Hale, of Cheever:* Bid him begone. Your mind is surely settled now. Bid him out, Mr. Hale.

ELIZABETH: What signifies a needle?

HALE: Mary—you charge a cold and cruel murder on Abigail.

MARY WARREN: Murder! I charge no—

HALE: Abigail were stabbed tonight; a needle were found stuck into her belly—

ELIZABETH: And she charges me?

HALE: Aye.

ELIZABETH, *her breath knocked out:* Why—! The girl is murder! She must be ripped out of the world!

CHEEVER, *pointing at Elizabeth:* You've heard that, sir! Ripped out of the world! Herrick, you heard it!

PROCTOR, *suddenly snatching the warrant out of Cheever's hands:* Out with you.

CHEEVER: Proctor, you dare not touch the warrant.

PROCTOR, *ripping the warrant:* Out with you!

CHEEVER: You've ripped the Deputy Governor's warrant, man!

PROCTOR: Damn the Deputy Governor! Out of my house!

HALE: Now, Proctor, Proctor!

PROCTOR: Get y'gone with them! You are a broken minister.

HALE: Proctor, if she is innocent, the court—

PROCTOR: If *she* is innocent! Why do you never wonder if Parris be innocent, or Abigail? Is the accuser always holy now? Were they born this morning as clean as God's fingers? I'll tell you what's walking Salem—vengeance is walking Salem. We are what we always were in Salem, but now the little crazy children are jangling the keys of the kingdom, and common vengeance writes the law! This warrant's vengeance! I'll not give my wife to vengeance!

ELIZABETH: I'll go, John—

Proctor: You will not go!

HERRICK: I have nine men outside. You cannot keep her. The law binds me, John, I cannot budge.

PROCTOR, *to Hale, ready to break him:* Will you see her taken?

HALE: Proctor, the court is just—

PROCTOR: Pontius Pilate! God will not let you wash your hands of this!

ELIZABETH: John—I think I must go with them. *He cannot bear to look at her.* Mary, there is bread enough for the morning; you will bake, in the afternoon. Help Mr. Proctor as you were his daughter—you owe me that, and much more. *She is fighting her weeping. To Proctor:* When the children wake, speak nothing of witchcraft—it will frighten them. *She cannot go on.*

PROCTOR: I will bring you home. I will bring you soon.

ELIZABETH: Oh, John, bring me soon!

PROCTOR: I will fall like an ocean on that court! Fear nothing, Elizabeth.

ELIZABETH, *with great fear:* I will fear nothing. *She looks about the room, as though to fix it in her mind.* Tell the children I have gone to visit someone sick.

She walks out the door, Herrick and Cheever behind her. For a moment, Proctor watches from the doorway. The clank of chain is heard.

PROCTOR: Herrick! Herrick, don't chain her! *He rushes out the door. From outside:* Damn you, man, you will not chain her! Off with them! I'll not have it! I will not have her chained!

There are other men's voices against his. Hale, in a fever of guilt and uncertainty, turns from the door to avoid the sight; Mary Warren bursts into tears and sits weeping. Giles Corey calls to Hale.

GILES: And yet silent, minister? It is fraud, you know it is fraud! What keeps you, man?

Proctor is half braced, half pushed into the room by two deputies and Herrick.

PROCTOR: I'll pay you, Herrick, I will surely pay you!

HERRICK, *panting:* In God's name, John, I cannot help myself. I must chain them all. Now let you keep inside this house till I am gone! *He goes out with his deputies.*

Proctor stands there, gulping air. Horses and a wagon creaking are heard.

HALE, *in great uncertainty:* Mr. Proctor—

PROCTOR: Out of my sight!

HALE: Charity, Proctor, charity. What I have heard in her favor, I will not fear to testify in court. God help me, I cannot judge her guilty or innocent—I know not. Only this consider: the world goes mad, and it profit nothing you should lay the cause to the vengeance of a little girl.

PROCTOR: You are a coward! Though you be ordained in God's own tears, you are a coward now!

HALE: Proctor, I cannot think God be provoked so grandly by such a petty cause. The jails are packed—our greatest judges sit in Salem now—and hangin's promised. Man, we must look to cause proportionate. Were there murder done, perhaps, and never brought to light? Abomination? Some secret blasphemy that stinks to Heaven? Think on cause, man, and let you help me to discover it. For there's your way, believe it, there is your only way, when such confusion strikes upon the world. *He goes to Giles and Francis.* Let you counsel among yourselves; think on your village and what may have drawn from heaven such thundering wrath upon you all. I shall pray God open up our eyes.

Hale goes out.

FRANCIS, *struck by Hale's mood:* I never heard no murder done in Salem.

PROCTOR—*he has been reached by Hale's words:* Leave me, Francis, leave me.

GILES, *shaken:* John—tell me, are we lost?

PROCTOR: Go home now, Giles. We'll speak on it tomorrow.

GILES: Let you think on it. We'll come early, eh?

PROCTOR: Aye. Go now, Giles.

GILES: Good night, then.

Giles Corey goes out. After a moment:

MARY WARREN, *in a fearful squeak of a voice:* Mr. Proctor, very likely they'll let her come home once they're given proper evidence.

PROCTOR: You're coming to the court with me, Mary. You will tell it in the court.

MARY WARREN: I cannot charge murder on Abigail.

PROCTOR, *moving menacingly toward her:* You will tell the court how that poppet come here and who stuck the needle in.

MARY WARREN: She'll kill me for sayin' that! *Proctor continues toward her.* Abby'll charge lechery on you, Mr. Proctor!

PROCTOR, *halting:* She's told you!

MARY WARREN: I have known it, sir. She'll ruin you with it, I know she will.

PROCTOR, *hesitating, and with deep hatred of himself:* Good. Then her saintliness is done with. *Mary backs from him.* We will slide together into our pit; you will tell the court what you know.

MARY WARREN, *in terror:* I cannot, they'll turn on me—

Proctor strides and catches her, and she is repeating, "I cannot, I cannot!"

PROCTOR: My wife will never die for me! I will bring your guts into your mouth but that goodness will not die for me!

MARY WARREN, *struggling to escape him:* I cannot do it, I cannot!

PROCTOR, *grasping her by the throat as though he would strangle her:* Make your peace with it! Now Hell and Heaven grapple on our backs, and all our old pretense is ripped away—make your peace! *He throws her to the floor, where she sobs, "I cannot, I cannot . . ." And now, half to himself, staring, and turning to the open door:* Peace. It is a providence, and no great change; we are only what we always were, but naked now. *He walks as though toward a great horror, facing the open sky.* Aye, naked! And the wind, God's icy wind, will blow!

And she is over and over again sobbing, "I cannot, I cannot, I cannot," as

THE CURTAIN FALLS*

---

* Act II, Scene 2, which appeared in the original production, was dropped by the author from the published reading version, the *Collected Plays,* and all Compass editions prior to 1970. It has not been included in most productions subsequent to the revival at New York's Martinique Theatre in 1958 and was dropped by Sir Laurence Olivier in his London production in 1965. It is included here as an appendix on page 277.

Act Three

The vestry room of the Salem meeting house, now serving as the anteroom of the General Court.

As the curtain rises, the room is empty, but for sunlight pouring through two high windows in the back wall. The room is solemn, even forbidding. Heavy beams jut out, boards of random widths make up the walls. At the right are two doors leading into the meeting house proper, where the court is being held. At the left another door leads outside.

There is a plain bench at the left, and another at the right. In the center a rather long meeting table, with stools and a considerable armchair snugged up to it.

Through the partitioning wall at the right we hear a prosecutor's voice, Judge Hathorne's, asking a question; then a woman's voice, Martha Corey's, replying.

HATHORNE'S VOICE: Now, Martha Corey, there is abundant evidence in our hands to show that you have given yourself to the reading of fortunes. Do you deny it?

MARTHA COREY'S VOICE: I am innocent to a witch. I know not what a witch is.

HATHORNE'S VOICE: How do you know, then, that you are not a witch?

MARTHA COREY'S VOICE: If I were, I would know it.

HATHORNE'S VOICE: Why do you hurt these children?

MARTHA COREY'S VOICE: I do not hurt them. I scorn it!

GILES' VOICE, *roaring:* I have evidence for the court!

Voices of townspeople rise in excitement.

DANFORTH'S VOICE: You will keep your seat!

GILES' VOICE: Thomas Putnam is reaching out for land!

DANFORTH'S VOICE: Remove that man, Marshal!

GILES' VOICE: You're hearing lies, lies!

A roaring goes up from the people.

HATHORNE'S VOICE: Arrest him, excellency!

GILES' VOICE: I have evidence. Why will you not hear my evidence?

The door opens and Giles is half carried into the vestry room by Herrick.

GILES: Hands off, damn you, let me go!

HERRICK: Giles, Giles!

GILES: Out of my way, Herrick! I bring evidence—

HERRICK: You cannot go in there, Giles; it's a court!

Enter Hale from the court.

HALE: Pray be calm a moment.

GILES: You, Mr. Hale, go in there and demand I speak.

HALE: A moment, sir, a moment.

GILES: They'll be hangin' my wife!

Judge Hathorne enters. He is in his sixties, a bitter, remorseless Salem judge.

HATHORNE: How do you dare come roarin' into this court! Are you gone daft, Corey?

GILES: You're not a Boston judge yet, Hathorne. You'll not call me daft!

Enter Deputy Governor Danforth and, behind him, Ezekiel Cheever and Parris. On his appearance, silence falls. Danforth is a grave man in his sixties, of some humor and sophistication that do not, however, interfere with an exact loyalty to his position and his cause. He comes down to Giles, who awaits his wrath.

DANFORTH, *looking directly at Giles:* Who is this man?

PARRIS: Giles Corey, sir, and a more contentious—

GILES, *to Parris:* I am asked the question, and I am old enough to answer it! *To Danforth, who impresses him and to whom he smiles through his strain:* My name is Corey, sir, Giles Corey. I have six hundred acres, and timber in addition. It is my wife you be condemning now. *He indicates the courtroom.*

DANFORTH: And how do you imagine to help her cause with such contemptuous riot? Now be gone. Your old age alone keeps you out of jail for this.

GILES, *beginning to plead:* They be tellin' lies about my wife, sir, I

DANFORTH: Do you take it upon yourself to determine what this court shall believe and what it shall set aside?

GILES: Your Excellency, we mean no disrespect for—

DANFORTH: Disrespect indeed! It is disruption, Mister. This is the highest court of the supreme government of this province, do you know it?

GILES, *beginning to weep:* Your Excellency, I only said she were readin' books, sir, and they come and take her out of my house for—

DANFORTH, *mystified:* Books! What books?

GILES, *through helpless sobs:* It is my third wife, sir; I never had no wife that be so taken with books, and I thought to find the cause of it, d'y'see, but it were no witch I blamed her for. *He is openly weeping.* I have broke charity with the woman, I have broke charity with her. *He covers his face, ashamed. Danforth is respectfully silent.*

HALE: Excellency, he claims hard evidence for his wife's defense. I think that in all justice you must—

DANFORTH: Then let him submit his evidence in proper affidavit. You are certainly aware of our procedure here, Mr. Hale. *To Herrick:* Clear this room.

HERRICK: Come now, Giles. *He gently pushes Corey out.*

FRANCIS: We are desperate, sir; we come here three days now and cannot be heard.

DANFORTH: Who is this man?

FRANCIS: Francis Nurse, Your Excellency.

HALE: His wife's Rebecca that were condemned this morning.

DANFORTH: Indeed! I am amazed to find you in such uproar. I have only good report of your character, Mr. Nurse.

HATHORNE: I think they must both be arrested in contempt, sir.

DANFORTH, *to Francis:* Let you write your plea, and in due time I will—

FRANCIS: Excellency, we have proof for your eyes; God forbid you shut them to it. The girls, sir, the girls are frauds.

DANFORTH: What's that?

FRANCIS: We have proof of it, sir. They are all deceiving you.

Danforth is shocked, but studying Francis.

HATHORNE: This is contempt, sir, contempt!

DANFORTH: Peace, Judge Hathorne. Do you know who I am, Mr. Nurse?

FRANCIS: I surely do, sir, and I think you must be a wise judge to be what you are.

DANFORTH: And do you know that near to four hundred are in the jails from Marblehead to Lynn, and upon my signature?

FRANCIS: I—

DANFORTH: And seventy-two condemned to hang by that signature?

FRANCIS: Excellency, I never thought to say it to such a weighty judge, but you are deceived.

Enter Giles Corey from left. All turn to see as he beckons in Mary Warren with Proctor. Mary is keeping her eyes to the ground; Proctor has her elbow as though she were near collapse.

PARRIS, *on seeing her, in shock:* Mary Warren! *He goes directly to bend close to her face.* What are you about here?

PROCTOR, *pressing Parris away from her with a gentle but firm motion of protectiveness:* She would speak with the Deputy Governor.

DANFORTH—*shocked by this, he turns to Herrick:* Did you not tell me Mary Warren were sick in bed?

HERRICK: She were, Your Honor. When I go to fetch her to the court last week, she said she were sick.

GILES: She has been strivin' with her soul all week, Your Honor; she comes now to tell the truth of this to you.

DANFORTH: Who is this?

PROCTOR: John Proctor, sir. Elizabeth Proctor is my wife.

PARRIS: Beware this man, Your Excellency, this man is mischief.

HALE, *excitedly:* I think you must hear the girl, sir, she—

DANFORTH, *who has become very interested in Mary Warren and only raises a hand toward Hale:* Peace. What would you tell us, Mary Warren?

Proctor looks at her, but she cannot speak.

PROCTOR: She never saw no spirits, sir.

DANFORTH, *with great alarm and surprise, to Mary:* Never saw no spirits!

GILES, *eagerly:* Never.

PROCTOR, *reaching into his jacket:* She has signed a deposition, sir—

DANFORTH, *instantly:* No, no, I accept no depositions. *He is rapidly calculating this; he turns from her to Proctor.* Tell me, Mr. Proctor, have you given out this story in the village?

PROCTOR: We have not.

PARRIS: They've come to overthrow the court, sir! This man is—

DANFORTH: I pray you, Mr. Parris. Do you know, Mr. Proctor, that the entire contention of the state in these trials is that the voice of Heaven is speaking through the children?

PROCTOR: I know that, sir.

DANFORTH—*he thinks, staring at Proctor, then turns to Mary Warren:* And you, Mary Warren, how came you to cry out people for sending their spirits against you?

MARY WARREN: It were pretense, sir.

DANFORTH: I cannot hear you.

PROCTOR: It were pretense, she says.

DANFORTH: Ah? And the other girls? Susanna Walcott, and— the others? They are also pretending?

MARY WARREN: Aye, sir.

DANFORTH, *wide-eyed:* Indeed. *Pause. He is baffled by this. He turns to study Proctor's face.*

PARRIS, *in a sweat:* Excellency, you surely cannot think to let so vile a lie be spread in open court!

DANFORTH: Indeed not, but it strike hard upon me that she will dare come here with such a tale. Now, Mr. Proctor, before I decide whether I shall hear you or not, it is my duty to tell you this. We burn a hot fire here; it melts down all concealment.

PROCTOR: I know that, sir.

DANFORTH: Let me continue. I understand well, a husband's tenderness may drive him to extravagance in defense of a wife. Are you certain in your conscience, Mister, that your evidence is the truth?

PROCTOR: It is. And you will surely know it.

DANFORTH: And you thought to declare this revelation in the open court before the public?

PROCTOR: I thought I would, aye—with your permission.

DANFORTH, *his eyes narrowing:* Now, sir, what is your purpose in so doing?

PROCTOR: Why, I—I would free my wife, sir.

DANFORTH: There lurks nowhere in your heart, nor hidden in your spirit, any desire to undermine this court?

PROCTOR, *with the faintest faltering:* Why, no, sir.

CHEEVER—*he clears his throat, awakening:* I— Your Excellency.

DANFORTH: Mr. Cheever.

CHEEVER: I think it be my duty, sir— *Kindly, to Proctor:* You'll not deny it, John. *To Danforth:* When we come to take his wife, he damned the court and ripped your warrant.

PARRIS: Now you have it!

DANFORTH: He did that, Mr. Hale?

HALE—*he takes a breath:* Aye, he did.

PROCTOR: It were a temper, sir. I knew not what I did.

DANFORTH, *studying him:* Mr. Proctor.

PROCTOR: Aye, sir.

DANFORTH, *straight into his eyes:* Have you ever seen the Devil?

PROCTOR: No, sir.

DANFORTH: You are in all respects a Gospel Christian?

PROCTOR: I am, sir.

PARRIS: Such a Christian that will not come to church but once in a month!

DANFORTH, *restrained—he is curious:* Not come to church?

PROCTOR: I—I have no love for Mr. Parris. It is no secret. But God I surely love.

CHEEVER: He plow on Sunday, sir.

DANFORTH: Plow on Sunday!

CHEEVER, *apologetically:* I think it be evidence, John. I am an official of the court, I cannot keep it.

PROCTOR: I—I have once or twice plowed on Sunday. I have three children, sir, and until last year my land give little.

GILES: You'll find other Christians that do plow on Sunday if the truth be known.

HALE: Your Honor, I cannot think you may judge the man on such evidence.

DANFORTH: I judge nothing. *Pause. He keeps watching Proctor, who tries to meet his gaze.* I tell you straight, Mister—I have seen marvels in this court. I have seen people choked before my eyes by spirits; I have seen them stuck by pins and slashed by daggers. I have until this moment not the slightest reason to suspect that the children may be deceiving me. Do you understand my meaning?

PROCTOR: Excellency, does it not strike upon you that so many of these women have lived so long with such upright reputation, and—

PARRIS: Do you read the Gospel, Mr. Proctor?

PROCTOR: I read the Gospel.

PARRIS: I think not, or you should surely know that Cain were an upright man, and yet he did kill Abel.

PROCTOR: Aye, God tells us that. *To Danforth:* But who tells us Rebecca Nurse murdered seven babies by sending out her spirit on them? It is the children only, and this one will swear she lied to you.

Danforth considers, then beckons Hathorne to him. Hathorne leans in, and he speaks in his ear. Hathorne nods.

HATHORNE: Aye, she's the one.

DANFORTH: Mr. Proctor, this morning, your wife send me a claim in which she states that she is pregnant now.

PROCTOR: My wife pregnant!

DANFORTH: There be no sign of it—we have examined her body.

PROCTOR: But if she say she is pregnant, then she must be! That woman will never lie, Mr. Danforth.

DANFORTH: She will not?

PROCTOR: Never, sir, never.

DANFORTH: We have thought it too convenient to be credited. However, if I should tell you now that I will let her be kept another month; and if she begin to show her natural signs, you shall have her living yet another year until she is delivered—what say you to that? *John Proctor is struck silent.* Come now. You say your only purpose is to save your wife. Good, then, she is saved at least this year, and a year is long. What say you, sir? It is done now. *In conflict, Proctor glances at Francis and Giles.* Will you drop this charge?

PROCTOR: I—I think I cannot.

DANFORTH, *now an almost imperceptible hardness in his voice:* Then your purpose is somewhat larger.

PARRIS: He's come to overthrow this court, Your Honor!

PROCTOR: These are my friends. Their wives are also accused—

DANFORTH, *with a sudden briskness of manner:* I judge you not, sir. I am ready to hear your evidence.

PROCTOR: I come not to hurt the court; I only—

DANFORTH, *cutting him off:* Marshal, go into the court and bid Judge Stoughton and Judge Sewall declare recess for one hour. And let them go to the tavern, if they will. All witnesses and prisoners are to be kept in the building.

HERRICK: Aye, sir. *Very deferentially:* If I may say it, sir, I know this man all my life. It is a good man, sir.

DANFORTH—*it is the reflection on himself he resents:* I am sure of it, Marshal. *Herrick nods, then goes out.* Now, what deposition do you have for us, Mr. Proctor? And I beg you be clear, open as the sky, and honest.

PROCTOR, *as he takes out several papers:* I am no lawyer, so I'll—

DANFORTH: The pure in heart need no lawyers. Proceed as you will.

PROCTOR, *handing Danforth a paper:* Will you read this first, sir? It's a sort of testament. The people signing it declare their good opinion of Rebecca, and my wife, and Martha Corey. *Danforth looks down at the paper.*

PARRIS, *to enlist Danforth's sarcasm:* Their good opinion! *But Danforth goes on reading, and Proctor is heartened.*

PROCTOR: These are all landholding farmers, members of the church. *Delicately, trying to point out a paragraph:* If you'll notice, sir—they've known the women many years and never saw no sign they had dealings with the Devil.

Parris nervously moves over and reads over Danforth's shoulder.

DANFORTH, *glancing down a long list:* How many names are here?

FRANCIS: Ninety-one, Your Excellency.

PARRIS, *sweating:* These people should be summoned. *Danforth looks up at him questioningly.* For questioning.

FRANCIS, *trembling with anger:* Mr. Danforth, I gave them all my word no harm would come to them for signing this.

PARRIS: This is a clear attack upon the court!

HALE, *to Parris, trying to contain himself:* Is every defense an attack upon the court? Can no one—?

PARRIS: All innocent and Christian people are happy for the courts in Salem! These people are gloomy for it. *To Danforth directly:* And I think you will want to know, from each and every one of them, what discontents them with you!

HATHORNE: I think they ought to be examined, sir.

DANFORTH: It is not necessarily an attack, I think. Yet—

FRANCIS: These are all covenanted Christians, sir.

DANFORTH: Then I am sure they may have nothing to fear. *Hands Cheever the paper.* Mr. Cheever, have warrants drawn for all of these—arrest for examination. *To Proctor:* Now, Mister, what other information do you have for us? *Francis is still standing, horrified.* You may sit, Mr. Nurse.

FRANCIS: I have brought trouble on these people; I have—

DANFORTH: No, old man, you have not hurt these people if they are of good conscience. But you must understand, sir, that a person is either with this court or he must be counted against it, there be no road between. This is a sharp time, now, a precise time—we live no longer in the dusky afternoon when evil mixed itself with good and befuddled the world. Now, by God's grace, the shining sun is up, and them that fear not light will surely praise it. I hope you will be one of those. *Mary Warren suddenly sobs.* She's not hearty, I see.

PROCTOR: No, she's not, sir. *To Mary, bending to her, holding her hand, quietly:* Now remember what the angel Raphael said to the boy Tobias. Remember it.

MARY WARREN, *hardly audible:* Aye.

PROCTOR: "Do that which is good, and no harm shall come to thee."

MARY WARREN: Aye.

DANFORTH: Come, man, we wait you.

Marshal Herrick returns, and takes his post at the door.

GILES: John, my deposition, give him mine.

PROCTOR: Aye. *He hands Danforth another paper.* This is Mr. Corey's deposition.

DANFORTH: Oh? *He looks down at it. Now Hathorne comes behind him and reads with him.*

HATHORNE, *suspiciously:* What lawyer drew this, Corey?

GILES: You know I never hired a lawyer in my life, Hathorne.

DANFORTH, *finishing the reading:* It is very well phrased. My compliments. Mr. Parris, if Mr. Putnam is in the court, will you bring him in? *Hathorne takes the deposition, and walks to the window with it. Parris goes into the court.* You have no legal training, Mr. Corey?

GILES, *very pleased:* I have the best, sir—I am thirty-three time in court in my life. And always plaintiff, too.

DANFORTH: Oh, then you're much put-upon.

GILES: I am never put-upon; I know my rights, sir, and I will have them. You know, your father tried a case of mine—might be thirty-five year ago, I think.

DANFORTH: Indeed.

GILES: He never spoke to you of it?

DANFORTH: No, I cannot recall it.

GILES: That's strange, he give me nine pound damages. He were a fair judge, your father. Y'see, I had a white mare that time, and this fellow come to borrow the mare— *Enter Parris with Thomas Putnam. When he sees Putnam, Giles' ease goes; he is hard.* Aye, there he is.

DANFORTH: Mr. Putnam, I have here an accusation by Mr. Corey against you. He states that you coldly prompted your daughter to cry witchery upon George Jacobs that is now in jail.

PUTNAM: It is a lie.

DANFORTH, *turning to Giles:* Mr. Putnam states your charge is a lie. What say you to that?

GILES, *furious, his fists clenched:* A fart on Thomas Putnam, that is what I say to that!

DANFORTH: What proof do you submit for your charge, sir?

GILES: My proof is there! *Pointing to the paper.* If Jacobs hangs for a witch he forfeit up his property—that's law! And there is none but Putnam with the coin to buy so great a piece. This man is killing his neighbors for their land!

DANFORTH: But proof, sir, proof.

GILES, *pointing at his deposition:* The proof is there! I have it from an honest man who heard Putnam say it! The day his daughter cried out on Jacobs, he said she'd given him a fair gift of land.

HATHORNE: And the name of this man?

GILES, *taken aback:* What name?

HATHORNE: The man that give you this information.

GILES—*he hesitates, then:* Why, I—I cannot give you his name.

HATHORNE: And why not?

GILES—*he hesitates, then bursts out:* You know well why not! He'll lay in jail if I give his name!

HATHORNE: This is contempt of the court, Mr. Danforth!

DANFORTH, *to avoid that:* You will surely tell us the name.

GILES: I will not give you no name. I mentioned my wife's

name once and I'll burn in hell long enough for that. I stand mute.

DANFORTH: In that case, I have no choice but to arrest you for contempt of this court, do you know that?

GILES: This is a hearing; you cannot clap me for contempt of a hearing.

DANFORTH: Oh, it is a proper lawyer! Do you wish me to declare the court in full session here? Or will you give me good reply?

GILES, *faltering:* I cannot give you no name, sir, I cannot.

DANFORTH: You are a foolish old man. Mr. Cheever, begin the record. The court is now in session. I ask you, Mr. Corey—

PROCTOR, *breaking in:* Your Honor—he has the story in confidence, sir, and he—

PARRIS: The Devil lives on such confidences! *To Danforth:* Without confidences there could be no conspiracy, Your Honor!

HATHORNE: I think it must be broken, sir.

DANFORTH, *to Giles:* Old man, if your informant tells the truth let him come here openly like a decent man. But if he hide in anonymity I must know why. Now sir, the government and central church demand of you the name of him who reported Mr. Thomas Putnam a common murderer.

HALE: Excellency—

DANFORTH: Mr. Hale.

HALE: We cannot blink it more. There is a prodigious fear of this court in the country—

DANFORTH: Then there is a prodigious guilt in the country. Are *you* afraid to be questioned here?

HALE: I may only fear the Lord, sir, but there is fear in the country nevertheless.

DANFORTH, *angered now:* Reproach me not with the fear in the country; there is fear in the country because there is a moving plot to topple Christ in the country!

HALE: But it does not follow that everyone accused is part of it.

DANFORTH: No uncorrupted man may fear this court, Mr. Hale! None! *To Giles:* You are under arrest in contempt of this court. Now sit you down and take counsel with yourself, or you will be set in the jail until you decide to answer all questions.

Giles Corey makes a rush for Putnam. Proctor lunges and holds him.

PROCTOR: No, Giles!

GILES, *over Proctor's shoulder at Putnam:* I'll cut your throat, Putnam, I'll kill you yet!

PROCTOR, *forcing him into a chair:* Peace, Giles, peace. *Releasing him.* We'll prove ourselves. Now we will. *He starts to turn to Danforth.*

GILES: Say nothin' more, John. *Pointing at Danforth:* He's only playin' you! He means to hang us all!

Mary Warren bursts into sobs.

DANFORTH: This is a court of law, Mister. I'll have no effrontery here!

PROCTOR: Forgive him, sir, for his old age. Peace, Giles, we'll prove it all now. *He lifts up Mary's chin.* You cannot weep, Mary. Remember the angel, what he say to the boy. Hold to it, now; there is your rock. *Mary quiets. He takes out a paper, and turns to Danforth.* This is Mary Warren's deposition. I—I would ask you remember, sir, while you read it, that until two week ago she were no different than the other children are today. *He is speaking reasonably, restraining all his fears, his anger, his anxiety.* You saw her scream, she howled, she swore familiar spirits choked her; she even testified that Satan, in the form of women now in jail, tried to win her soul away, and then when she refused—

DANFORTH: We know all this.

PROCTOR: Aye, sir. She swears now that she never saw Satan; nor any spirit, vague or clear, that Satan may have sent to hurt her. And she declares her friends are lying now.

Proctor starts to hand Danforth the deposition, and Hale comes up to Danforth in a trembling state.

HALE: Excellency, a moment. I think this goes to the heart of the matter.

DANFORTH, *with deep misgivings:* It surely does.

HALE: I cannot say he is an honest man; I know him little. But in all justice, sir, a claim so weighty cannot be argued by a farmer. In God's name, sir, stop here; send him home and let him come again with a lawyer—

DANFORTH, *patiently:* Now look you, Mr. Hale—

HALE: Excellency, I have signed seventy-two death warrants; I am a minister of the Lord, and I dare not take a life without there be a proof so immaculate no slightest qualm of conscience may doubt it.

DANFORTH: Mr. Hale, you surely do not doubt my justice.

HALE: I have this morning signed away the soul of Rebecca Nurse, Your Honor. I'll not conceal it, my hand shakes yet as with a wound! I pray you, sir, *this* argument let lawyers present to you.

DANFORTH: Mr. Hale, believe me; for a man of such terrible learning you are most bewildered—I hope you will forgive me. I have been thirty-two year at the bar, sir, and I should be confounded were I called upon to defend these people. Let you consider, now— *To Proctor and the others:* And I bid you all do likewise. In an ordinary crime, how does one defend the accused? One calls up witnesses to prove his innocence. But witchcraft is *ipso facto,* on its face and by its nature, an invisible crime, is it not? Therefore, who may possibly be witness to it? The witch and the victim. None other. Now we cannot hope the witch will accuse herself; granted? Therefore, we must rely upon her victims—and they do testify, the children certainly do testify. As for the witches, none will deny that we are most eager for all their confessions. Therefore, what is left for a lawyer to bring out? I think I have made my point. Have I not?

HALE: But this child claims the girls are not truthful, and if they are not—

DANFORTH: That is precisely what I am about to consider, sir. What more may you ask of me? Unless you doubt my probity?

HALE, *defeated:* I surely do not, sir. Let you consider it, then.

DANFORTH: And let you put your heart to rest. Her deposition, Mr. Proctor.

Proctor hands it to him. Hathorne rises, goes beside Danforth, and starts reading. Parris comes to his other side. Danforth looks at John Proctor, then proceeds to read. Hale gets up, finds position near the judge, reads too. Proctor glances at Giles. Francis prays silently, hands pressed together. Cheever waits placidly, the sublime official, dutiful. Mary Warren sobs once. John Proctor touches her head reassuringly. Presently Danforth lifts his eyes, stands up, takes out a kerchief and blows his nose. The others stand aside as he moves in thought toward the window.

PARRIS, *hardly able to contain his anger and fear:* I should like to question—

DANFORTH—*his first real outburst, in which his contempt for Parris is clear:* Mr. Parris, I bid you be silent! *He stands in silence, looking out the window. Now, having established that he will set the gait:* Mr. Cheever, will you go into the court and bring the children here? *Cheever gets up and goes out upstage. Danforth now turns to Mary.* Mary Warren, how came you to this turnabout? Has Mr. Proctor threatened you for this deposition?

MARY WARREN: No, sir.

DANFORTH: Has he ever threatened you?

MARY WARREN, *weaker:* No, sir.

DANFORTH, *sensing a weakening:* Has he threatened you?

MARY WARREN: No, sir.

DANFORTH: Then you tell me that you sat in my court, callously lying, when you knew that people would hang by your evidence? *She does not answer.* Answer me!

MARY WARREN, *almost inaudibly:* I did, sir.

DANFORTH: How were you instructed in your life? Do you not know that God damns all liars? *She cannot speak.* Or is it now that you lie?

MARY WARREN: No, sir—I am with God now.

DANFORTH: You are with God now.

MARY WARREN: Aye, sir.

DANFORTH, *containing himself:* I will tell you this—you are either lying now, or you were lying in the court, and in either case you have committed perjury and you will go to jail for it. You cannot lightly say you lied, Mary. Do you know that?

MARY WARREN: I cannot lie no more. I am with God, I am with God.

But she breaks into sobs at the thought of it, and the right door opens, and enter Susanna Walcott, Mercy Lewis, Betty Parris, and finally Abigail. Cheever comes to Danforth.

CHEEVER: Ruth Putnam's not in the court, sir, nor the other children.

DANFORTH: These will be sufficient. Sit you down, children. *Silently they sit.* Your friend, Mary Warren, has given us a deposition. In which she swears that she never saw familiar spirits, apparitions, nor any manifest of the Devil. She claims as well that none of you have seen these things either. *Slight pause.* Now, children, this is a court of law. The law, based upon the Bible, and the Bible, writ by Almighty God, forbid the practice of witchcraft, and describe death as the penalty thereof. But likewise, children, the law and Bible damn all bearers of false witness. *Slight pause.* Now then. It does not escape me that this deposition may be devised to blind us; it may well be that Mary Warren has been conquered by Satan, who sends her here to distract our sacred purpose. If so, her neck will break for it. But if she speak true, I bid you now drop your guile and confess your pretense, for a quick confession will go easier with you. *Pause.* Abigail Williams, rise. *Abigail slowly rises.* Is there any truth in this?

ABIGAIL: No, sir.

DANFORTH—*he thinks, glances at Mary, then back to Abigail:* Children, a very augur bit will now be turned into your souls until your honesty is proved. Will either of you change your positions now, or do you force me to hard questioning?

ABIGAIL: I have naught to change, sir. She lies.

DANFORTH, *to Mary:* You would still go on with this?

MARY WARREN, *faintly:* Aye, sir.

DANFORTH, *turning to Abigail:* A poppet were discovered in Mr. Proctor's house, stabbed by a needle. Mary Warren claims that you sat beside her in the court when she made it, and that you saw her make it and witnessed how she herself stuck her needle into it for safe-keeping. What say you to that?

ABIGAIL, *with a slight note of indignation:* It is a lie, sir.

DANFORTH, *after a slight pause:* While you worked for Mr. Proctor, did you see poppets in that house?

ABIGAIL: Goody Proctor always kept poppets.

PROCTOR: Your Honor, my wife never kept no poppets. Mary Warren confesses it was her poppet.

CHEEVER: Your Excellency.

DANFORTH: Mr. Cheever.

CHEEVER: When I spoke with Goody Proctor in that house, she said she never kept no poppets. But she said she did keep poppets when she were a girl.

PROCTOR: She has not been a girl these fifteen years, Your Honor.

HATHORNE: But a poppet will keep fifteen years, will it not?

PROCTOR: It will keep if it is kept, but Mary Warren swears she never saw no poppets in my house, nor anyone else.

PARRIS: Why could there not have been poppets hid where no one ever saw them?

PROCTOR, *furious:* There might also be a dragon with five legs in my house, but no one has ever seen it.

PARRIS: We are here, Your Honor, precisely to discover what no one has ever seen.

PROCTOR: Mr. Danforth, what profit this girl to turn herself about? What may Mary Warren gain but hard questioning and worse?

DANFORTH: You are charging Abigail Williams with a marvelous cool plot to murder, do you understand that?

PROCTOR: I do, sir. I believe she means to murder.

DANFORTH, *pointing at Abigail, incredulously:* This child would murder your wife?

PROCTOR: It is not a child. Now hear me, sir. In the sight of the congregation she were twice this year put out of this meetin' house for laughter during prayer.

DANFORTH, *shocked, turning to Abigail:* What's this? Laughter during—!

PARRIS: Excellency, she were under Tituba's power at that time, but she is solemn now.

GILES: Aye, now she is solemn and goes to hang people!

DANFORTH: Quiet, man.

HATHORNE: Surely it have no bearing on the question, sir. He charges contemplation of murder.

DANFORTH: Aye. *He studies Abigail for a moment, then:* Continue, Mr. Proctor.

PROCTOR: Mary. Now tell the Governor how you danced in the woods.

PARRIS, *instantly:* Excellency, since I come to Salem this man is blackening my name. He—

DANFORTH: In a moment, sir. *To Mary Warren, sternly, and surprised:* What is this dancing?

MARY WARREN: I— *She glances at Abigail, who is staring down at her remorselessly. Then, appealing to Proctor:* Mr. Proctor—

PROCTOR, *taking it right up:* Abigail leads the girls to the woods, Your Honor, and they have danced there naked—

PARRIS: Your Honor, this—

PROCTOR, *at once:* Mr. Parris discovered them himself in the dead of night! There's the "child" she is!

DANFORTH—*it is growing into a nightmare, and he turns, astonished, to Parris:* Mr. Parris—

PARRIS: I can only say, sir, that I never found any of them naked, and this man is—

DANFORTH: But you discovered them dancing in the woods? *Eyes on Parris, he points at Abigail.* Abigail?

HALE: Excellency, when I first arrived from Beverly, Mr. Parris told me that.

DANFORTH: Do you deny it, Mr. Parris?

PARRIS: I do not, sir, but I never saw any of them naked

DANFORTH: But she have *danced?*

PARRIS, *unwillingly:* Aye, sir.

Danforth, as though with new eyes, looks at Abigail.

HATHORNE: Excellency, will you permit me? *He points at Mary Warren.*

DANFORTH, *with great worry:* Pray, proceed.

HATHORNE: You say you never saw no spirits, Mary, were never threatened or afflicted by any manifest of the Devil or the Devil's agents.

MARY WARREN, *very faintly:* No, sir.

HATHORNE, *with a gleam of victory:* And yet, when people accused of witchery confronted you in court, you would faint, saying their spirits came out of their bodies and choked you—

MARY WARREN: That were pretense, sir.

DANFORTH: I cannot hear you.

MARY WARREN: Pretense, sir.

PARRIS: But you did turn cold, did you not? I myself picked you up many times, and your skin were icy. Mr. Danforth, you—

DANFORTH: I saw that many times.

PROCTOR: She only pretended to faint, Your Excellency. They're all marvelous pretenders.

HATHORNE: Then can she pretend to faint now?

PROCTOR: Now?

PARRIS: Why not? Now there are no spirits attacking her, for none in this room is accused of witchcraft. So let her turn herself cold now, let her pretend she is attacked now, let her faint. *He turns to Mary Warren.* Faint!

MARY WARREN: Faint?

PARRIS: Aye, faint. Prove to us how you pretended in the court so many times.

MARY WARREN, *looking to Proctor:* I—cannot faint now, sir.

PROCTOR, *alarmed, quietly:* Can you not pretend it?

MARY WARREN: I— *She looks about as though searching for the passion to faint.* I—have no *sense* of it now, I—

DANFORTH: Why? What is lacking now?

MARY WARREN: I—cannot tell, sir, I—

DANFORTH: Might it be that here we have no afflicting spirit loose, but in the court there were some?

MARY WARREN: I never saw no spirits.

PARRIS: Then see no spirits now, and prove to us that you can faint by your own will, as you claim.

MARY WARREN—*she stares, searching for the emotion of it, and then shakes her head:* I—cannot do it.

PARRIS: Then you will confess, will you not? It were attacking spirits made you faint!

MARY WARREN: No, sir, I—

PARRIS: Your Excellency, this is a trick to blind the court!

MARY WARREN: It's not a trick! *She stands.* I—I used to faint because I—I thought I saw spirits.

DANFORTH: *Thought* you saw them!

MARY WARREN: But I did not, Your Honor.

HATHORNE: How could you think you saw them unless you saw them?

MARY WARREN: I—I cannot tell how, but I did. I—I heard the other girls screaming, and you, Your Honor, you seemed to believe them, and I— It were only sport in the beginning, sir, but then the whole world cried spirits, spirits, and I—I promise you, Mr. Danforth, I only thought I saw them but I did not.

Danforth peers at her.

PARRIS, *smiling, but nervous because Danforth seems to be struck by Mary Warren's story:* Surely Your Excellency is not taken by this simple lie.

DANFORTH, *turning worriedly to Abigail:* Abigail. I bid you now search your heart and tell me this—and beware of it, child, to God every soul is precious and His vengeance is terrible on them that take life without cause. Is it possible, child, that the spirits you have seen are illusion only, some deception that may cross your mind when—

ABIGAIL: Why, this—this—is a base question, sir.

DANFORTH: Child, I would have you consider it—

ABIGAIL: I have been hurt, Mr. Danforth; I have seen my

blood runnin' out! I have been near to murdered every day because I done my duty pointing out the Devil's people—and this is my reward? To be mistrusted, denied, questioned like a—

DANFORTH, *weakening:* Child, I do not mistrust you—

ABIGAIL, *in an open threat:* Let *you* beware, Mr. Danforth. Think you to be so mighty that the power of Hell may not turn *your* wits? Beware of it! There is— *Suddenly, from an accusatory attitude, her face turns, looking into the air above—it is truly frightened.*

DANFORTH, *apprehensively:* What is it, child?

ABIGAIL, *looking about in the air, clasping her arms about her as though cold:* I—I know not. A wind, a cold wind, has come. *Her eyes fall on Mary Warren.*

MARY WARREN, *terrified, pleading:* Abby!

MERCY LEWIS, *shivering:* Your Honor, I freeze!

PROCTOR: They're pretending!

HATHORNE, *touching Abigail's hand:* She is cold, Your Honor, touch her!

MERCY LEWIS, *through chattering teeth:* Mary, do you send this shadow on me?

MARY WARREN: Lord, save me!

SUSANNA WALCOTT: I freeze, I freeze!

ABIGAIL, *shivering visibly:* It is a wind, a wind!

MARY WARREN: Abby, don't do that!

DANFORTH, *himself engaged and entered by Abigail:* Mary Warren, do you witch her? I say to you, do you send your spirit out?

With a hysterical cry Mary Warren starts to run. Proctor catches her.

MARY WARREN, *almost collapsing:* Let me go, Mr. Proctor, I cannot, I cannot—

ABIGAIL, *crying to Heaven:* Oh, Heavenly Father, take away this shadow!

Without warning or hesitation, Proctor leaps at Abigail and, grabbing her by the hair, pulls her to her feet. She screams in pain. Danforth, astonished, cries, "What are you about?" and Hathorne and Parris call, "Take your hands off her!" and out of it all comes Proctor's roaring voice.

PROCTOR: How do you call Heaven! Whore! Whore!

Herrick breaks Proctor from her.

HERRICK: John!

DANFORTH: Man! Man, what do you—

PROCTOR, *breathless and in agony:* It is a whore!

DANFORTH, *dumfounded:* You charge—?

ABIGAIL: Mr. Danforth, he is lying!

PROCTOR: Mark her! Now she'll suck a scream to stab me with, but—

DANFORTH: You will prove this! This will not pass!

PROCTOR, *trembling, his life collapsing about him:* I have known her, sir. I have known her.

DANFORTH: You—you are a lecher?

FRANCIS, *horrified:* John, you cannot say such a—

PROCTOR: Oh, Francis, I wish you had some evil in you that you might know me! *To Danforth:* A man will not cast away his good name. You surely know that.

DANFORTH, *dumfounded:* In—in what time? In what place?

PROCTOR, *his voice about to break, and his shame great:* In the proper place—where my beasts are bedded. On the last night of my joy, some eight months past. She used to serve me in my house, sir. *He has to clamp his jaw to keep from weeping.* A man may think God sleeps, but God sees everything, I know it now. I beg you, sir, I beg you—see her what she is. My wife, my dear good wife, took this girl soon after, sir, and put her out on the highroad. And being what she is, a lump of vanity, sir— *He is being overcome.* Excellency, forgive me, forgive me. *Angrily against himself, he turns away from the Governor for a moment. Then, as though to cry out is his only means of speech left:* She thinks to dance with me on my wife's grave! And well she might, for I thought of her softly. God help me, I lusted, and there *is* a promise in such sweat. But it is a whore's vengeance, and you must see it; I set myself entirely in your hands. I know you must see it now.

DANFORTH, *blanched, in horror, turning to Abigail:* You deny every scrap and tittle of this?

ABIGAIL: If I must answer that, I will leave and I will not come back again!

Danforth seems unsteady.

PROCTOR: I have made a bell of my honor! I have rung the doom of my good name—you will believe me, Mr. Danforth! My wife is innocent, except she knew a whore when she saw one!

ABIGAIL, *stepping up to Danforth:* What look do you give me? *Danforth cannot speak.* I'll not have such looks! *She turns and starts for the door.*

DANFORTH: You will remain where you are! *Herrick steps into her path. She comes up short, fire in her eyes.* Mr. Parris, go into the court and bring Goodwife Proctor out.

PARRIS, *objecting:* Your Honor, this is all a—

DANFORTH, *sharply to Parris:* Bring her out! And tell her not one word of what's been spoken here. And let you knock before you enter. *Parris goes out.* Now we shall touch the bottom of this swamp. *To Proctor:* Your wife, you say, is an honest woman.

PROCTOR: In her life, sir, she have never lied. There are them that cannot sing, and them that cannot weep—my wife cannot lie. I have paid much to learn it, sir.

DANFORTH: And when she put this girl out of your house, she put her out for a harlot?

PROCTOR: Aye, sir.

DANFORTH: And knew her for a harlot?

PROCTOR: Aye, sir, she knew her for a harlot.

DANFORTH: Good then. *To Abigail:* And if she tell me, child, it were for harlotry, may God spread His mercy on you! *There is a knock. He calls to the door.* Hold! *To Abigail:* Turn your back. Turn your back. *To Proctor:* Do likewise. *Both turn their backs—Abigail with indignant slowness.* Now let neither of you turn to face Goody Proctor. No one in this room is to speak one word, or raise a gesture aye or nay. *He turns toward the door, calls:* Enter! *The door opens. Elizabeth enters with Parris. Parris leaves her. She stands alone, her eyes looking for Proctor.* Mr. Cheever, report this testimony in all exactness. Are you ready?

CHEEVER: Ready, sir.

DANFORTH: Come here, woman. *Elizabeth comes to him, glancing at Proctor's back.* Look at me only, not at your husband. In my eyes only.

ELIZABETH, *faintly:* Good, sir.

DANFORTH: We are given to understand that at one time you dismissed your servant, Abigail Williams.

ELIZABETH: That is true, sir.

DANFORTH: For what cause did you dismiss her? *Slight pause. Then Elizabeth tries to glance at Proctor.* You will look in my eyes only and not at your husband. The answer is in your memory and you need no help to give it to me. Why did you dismiss Abigail Williams?

ELIZABETH, *not knowing what to say, sensing a situation, wetting her lips to stall for time:* She—dissatisfied me. *Pause.* And my husband.

DANFORTH: In what way dissatisfied you?

ELIZABETH: She were— *She glances at Proctor for a cue.*

DANFORTH: Woman, look at me! *Elizabeth does.* Were she slovenly? Lazy? What disturbance did she cause?

ELIZABETH: Your Honor, I—in that time I were sick. And I— My husband is a good and righteous man. He is never drunk as some are, nor wastin' his time at the shovelboard, but always at his work. But in my sickness—you see, sir, I were a long time sick after my last baby, and I thought I saw my husband somewhat turning from me. And this girl— *She turns to Abigail.*

DANFORTH: Look at me.

ELIZABETH: Aye, sir. Abigail Williams— *She breaks off.*

DANFORTH: What of Abigail Williams?

ELIZABETH: I came to think he fancied her. And so one night I lost my wits, I think, and put her out on the highroad.

DANFORTH: Your husband—did he indeed turn from you?

ELIZABETH, *in agony:* My husband—is a goodly man, sir.

DANFORTH: Then he did not turn from you.

ELIZABETH, *starting to glance at Proctor:* He—

DANFORTH, *reaches out and holds her face, then:* Look at me! To your own knowledge, has John Proctor ever committed the crime of lechery? *In a crisis of indecision she cannot speak.* Answer my question! Is your husband a lecher!

ELIZABETH, *faintly:* No, sir.

DANFORTH: Remove her, Marshal.

PROCTOR: Elizabeth, tell the truth!

DANFORTH: She has spoken. Remove her!

PROCTOR, *crying out:* Elizabeth, I have confessed it!

ELIZABETH: Oh, God! *The door closes behind her.*

PROCTOR: She only thought to save my name!

HALE: Excellency, it is a natural lie to tell; I beg you, stop now before another is condemned! I may shut my conscience to it no more—private vengeance is working through this testimony! From the beginning this man has struck me true. By my oath to Heaven, I believe him now, and I pray you call back his wife before we—

DANFORTH: She spoke nothing of lechery, and this man has lied!

HALE: I believe him! *Pointing at Abigail:* This girl has always struck me false! She has—

Abigail, with a weird, wild, chilling cry, screams up to the ceiling.

ABIGAIL: You will not! Begone! Begone, I say!

DANFORTH: What is it, child? *But Abigail, pointing with fear, is now raising up her frightened eyes, her awed face, toward the ceiling—the girls are doing the same—and now Hathorne, Hale,*

Putnam, Cheever, Herrick, and Danforth do the same. What's there? *He lowers his eyes from the ceiling, and now he is frightened; there is real tension in his voice.* Child! *She is transfixed—with all the girls, she is whimpering open-mouthed, agape at the ceiling.* Girls! Why do you—?

MERCY LEWIS, *pointing:* It's on the beam! Behind the rafter!

DANFORTH, *looking up:* Where!

ABIGAIL: Why—? *She gulps.* Why do you come, yellow bird?

PROCTOR: Where's a bird? I see no bird!

ABIGAIL, *to the ceiling:* My face? My face?

PROCTOR: Mr. Hale—

DANFORTH: Be quiet!

PROCTOR, *to Hale:* Do you see a bird?

DANFORTH: Be quiet!!

ABIGAIL, *to the ceiling, in a genuine conversation with the "bird," as though trying to talk it out of attacking her:* But God made my face; you cannot want to tear my face. Envy is a deadly sin, Mary.

MARY WARREN, *on her feet with a spring, and horrified, pleading:* Abby!

ABIGAIL, *unperturbed, continuing to the "bird":* Oh, Mary, this is a black art to change your shape. No, I cannot, I cannot stop my mouth; it's God's work I do.

MARY WARREN: Abby, I'm *here!*

PROCTOR, *frantically:* They're pretending, Mr. Danforth!

ABIGAIL—*now she takes a backward step, as though in fear the bird will swoop down momentarily:* Oh, please, Mary! Don't come down.

SUSANNA WALCOTT: Her claws, she's stretching her claws!

PROCTOR: Lies, lies.

ABIGAIL, *backing further, eyes still fixed above:* Mary, please don't hurt me!

MARY WARREN, *to Danforth:* I'm not hurting her!

DANFORTH, *to Mary Warren:* Why does she see this vision?

MARY WARREN: She sees nothin'!

ABIGAIL, *now staring full front as though hypnotized, and mimicking the exact tone of Mary Warren's cry:* She sees nothin'!

MARY WARREN, *pleading:* Abby, you mustn't!

ABIGAIL AND ALL THE GIRLS, *all transfixed:* Abby, you mustn't!

MARY WARREN, *to all the girls:* I'm here, I'm here!

GIRLS: I'm here, I'm here!

DANFORTH, *horrified:* Mary Warren! Draw back your spirit out of them!

MARY WARREN: Mr. Danforth!

GIRLS, *cutting her off:* Mr. Danforth!

DANFORTH: Have you compacted with the Devil? Have you?

MARY WARREN: Never, never!

GIRLS: Never, never!

DANFORTH, *growing hysterical:* Why can they only repeat you?

PROCTOR: Give me a whip—I'll stop it!

MARY WARREN: They're sporting. They—!

GIRLS: They're sporting!

MARY WARREN, *turning on them all hysterically and stamping her feet:* Abby, stop it!

GIRLS, *stamping their feet:* Abby, stop it!

MARY WARREN: Stop it!

GIRLS: Stop it!

MARY WARREN, *screaming it out at the top of her lungs, and raising her fists:* Stop it!!

GIRLS, *raising their fists:* Stop it!!

Mary Warren, utterly confounded, and becoming overwhelmed by Abigail's—and the girls'—utter conviction, starts to whimper, hands half raised, powerless, and all the girls begin whimpering exactly as she does.

DANFORTH: A little while ago you were afflicted. Now it seems you afflict others; where did you find this power?

MARY WARREN, *staring at Abigail:* I—have no power.

GIRLS: I have no power.

PROCTOR: They're gulling you, Mister!

DANFORTH: Why did you turn about this past two weeks? You have seen the Devil, have you not?

HALE, *indicating Abigail and the girls:* You cannot believe them!

MARY WARREN: I—

PROCTOR, *sensing her weakening:* Mary, God damns all liars!

DANFORTH, *pounding it into her:* You have seen the Devil, you have made compact with Lucifer, have you not?

PROCTOR: God damns liars, Mary!

Mary utters something unintelligible, staring at Abigail, who keeps watching the "bird" above.

DANFORTH: I cannot hear you. What do you say? *Mary utters again unintelligibly.* You will confess yourself or you will hang! *He turns her roughly to face him.* Do you know who I am? I say you will hang if you do not open with me!

PROCTOR: Mary, remember the angel Raphael—do that which is good and—

ABIGAIL, *pointing upward:* The wings! Her wings are spreading! Mary, please, don't, don't—!

HALE: I see nothing, Your Honor!

DANFORTH: Do you confess this power! *He is an inch from her face.* Speak!

ABIGAIL: She's going to come down! She's walking the beam!

DANFORTH: Will you speak!

MARY WARREN, *staring in horror:* I cannot!

GIRLS: I cannot!

PARRIS: Cast the Devil out! Look him in the face! Trample him! We'll save you, Mary, only stand fast against him and—

ABIGAIL, *looking up:* Look out! She's coming down!

She and all the girls run to one wall, shielding their eyes. And now, as though cornered, they let out a gigantic scream, and Mary, as though infected, opens her mouth and screams with them. Gradually Abigail and the girls leave off, until only Mary is left there, staring up at the "bird," screaming madly. All watch her, horrified by this evident fit. Proctor strides to her.

PROCTOR: Mary, tell the Governor what they— *He has hardly got a word out, when, seeing him coming for her, she rushes out of his reach, screaming in horror.*

MARY WARREN: Don't touch me—don't touch me! *At which the girls halt at the door.*

PROCTOR, *astonished:* Mary!

MARY WARREN, *pointing at Proctor:* You're the Devil's man!

He is stopped in his tracks.

PARRIS: Praise God!

GIRLS: Praise God!

PROCTOR, *numbed:* Mary, how—?

MARY WARREN: I'll not hang with you! I love God, I love God.

DANFORTH, *to Mary:* He bid you do the Devil's work?

MARY WARREN, *hysterically, indicating Proctor:* He come at me by night and every day to sign, to sign, to—

DANFORTH: Sign what?

PARRIS: The Devil's book? He come with a book?

MARY WARREN, *hysterically, pointing at Proctor, fearful of him:* My name, he want my name. "I'll murder you," he says, "if my wife hangs! We must go and overthrow the court," he says!

Danforth's head jerks toward Proctor, shock and horror in his face.

PROCTOR, *turning, appealing to Hale:* Mr. Hale!

MARY WARREN, *her sobs beginning:* He wake me every night, his eyes were like coals and his fingers claw my neck, and I sign, I sign . . .

HALE: Excellency, this child's gone wild!

PROCTOR, *as Danforth's wide eyes pour on him:* Mary, Mary!

MARY WARREN, *screaming at him:* No, I love God; I go your way no more. I love God, I bless God. *Sobbing, she rushes to*

Abigail. Abby, Abby, I'll never hurt you more! *They all watch, as Abigail, out of her infinite charity, reaches out and draws the sobbing Mary to her, and then looks up to Danforth.*

DANFORTH, *to Proctor:* What are you? *Proctor is beyond speech in his anger.* You are combined with anti-Christ, are you not? I have seen your power; you will not deny it! What say you, Mister?

HALE: Excellency—

DANFORTH: I will have nothing from you, Mr. Hale! *To Proctor:* Will you confess yourself befouled with Hell, or do you keep that black allegiance yet? What say you?

PROCTOR, *his mind wild, breathless:* I say—I say—God is dead!

PARRIS: Hear it, hear it!

PROCTOR—*he laughs insanely, then:* A fire, a fire is burning! I hear the boot of Lucifer, I see his filthy face! And it is my face, and yours, Danforth! For them that quail to bring men out of ignorance, as I have quailed, and as you quail now when you know in all your black hearts that this be fraud—God damns our kind especially, and we will burn, we will burn together!

DANFORTH: Marshal! Take him and Corey with him to the jail!

HALE, *starting across to the door:* I denounce these proceedings!

PROCTOR: You are pulling Heaven down and raising up a whore!

HALE: I denounce these proceedings, I quit this court! *He slams the door to the outside behind him.*

DANFORTH, *calling to him in a fury:* Mr. Hale! Mr. Hale!

THE CURTAIN FALLS

Act Four

A cell in Salem jail, that fall.

At the back is a high barred window; near it, a great, heavy door. Along the walls are two benches.

The place is in darkness but for the moonlight seeping through the bars. It appears empty. Presently footsteps are heard coming down a corridor beyond the wall, keys rattle, and the door swings open. Marshal Herrick enters with a lantern.

He is nearly drunk, and heavy-footed. He goes to a bench and nudges a bundle of rags lying on it.

HERRICK: Sarah, wake up! Sarah Good! *He then crosses to the other bench.*

SARAH GOOD, *rising in her rags:* Oh, Majesty! Comin', comin'! Tituba, he's here, His Majesty's come!

HERRICK: Go to the north cell; this place is wanted now. *He hangs his lantern on the wall. Tituba sits up.*

TITUBA: That don't look to me like His Majesty; look to me like the marshal.

HERRICK, *taking out a flask:* Get along with you now, clear this place. *He drinks, and Sarah Good comes and peers up into his face.*

SARAH GOOD: Oh, is it you, Marshal! I thought sure you be the Devil comin' for us. Could I have a sip of cider for me goin'-away?

HERRICK, *handing her the flask:* And where are you off to, Sarah?

TITUBA, *as Sarah drinks:* We goin' to Barbados, soon the Devil gits here with the feathers and the wings.

HERRICK: Oh? A happy voyage to you.

SARAH GOOD: A pair of bluebirds wingin' southerly, the two of us! Oh, it be a grand transformation, Marshal! *She raises the flask to drink again.*

HERRICK, *taking the flask from her lips:* You'd best give me that or you'll never rise off the ground. Come along now.

TITUBA: I'll speak to him for you, if you desires to come along, Marshal.

HERRICK: I'd not refuse it, Tituba; it's the proper morning to fly into Hell.

TITUBA: Oh, it be no Hell in Barbados. Devil, him be pleasure-man in Barbados, him be singin' and dancin' in Barbados. It's you folks—you riles him up 'round here; it be too cold 'round here for that Old Boy. He freeze his soul in Massachusetts, but in Barbados he just as sweet and— *A bellowing cow is heard, and Tituba leaps up and calls to the window:* Aye, sir! That's him, Sarah!

SARAH GOOD: I'm here, Majesty! *They hurriedly pick up their rags as Hopkins, a guard, enters.*

HOPKINS: The Deputy Governor's arrived.

HERRICK, *grabbing Tituba:* Come along, come along.

TITUBA, *resisting him:* No, he comin' for me. I goin' home!

HERRICK, *pulling her to the door:* That's not Satan, just a poor old cow with a hatful of milk. Come along now, out with you!

TITUBA, *calling to the window:* Take me home, Devil! Take me home!

SARAH GOOD, *following the shouting Tituba out:* Tell him I'm goin', Tituba! Now you tell him Sarah Good is goin' too!

In the corridor outside Tituba calls on—"Take me home, Devil; Devil take me home!" and Hopkins' voice orders her to move on. Herrick returns and begins to push old rags and straw into a corner. Hearing footsteps, he turns, and enter Danforth and Judge Hathorne. They are in greatcoats and wear hats against the bitter cold. They are followed in by Cheever, who carries a dispatch case and a flat wooden box containing his writing materials.

HERRICK: Good morning, Excellency.

DANFORTH: Where is Mr. Parris?

HERRICK: I'll fetch him. *He starts for the door.*

DANFORTH: Marshal. *Herrick stops.* When did Reverend Hale arrive?

HERRICK: It were toward midnight, I think.

DANFORTH, *suspiciously:* What is he about here?

HERRICK: He goes among them that will hang, sir. And he prays with them. He sits with Goody Nurse now. And Mr. Parris with him.

DANFORTH: Indeed. That man have no authority to enter here, Marshal. Why have you let him in?

HERRICK: Why, Mr. Parris command me, sir. I cannot deny him.

DANFORTH: Are you drunk, Marshal?

HERRICK: No, sir; it is a bitter night, and I have no fire here.

DANFORTH, *containing his anger:* Fetch Mr. Parris.

HERRICK: Aye, sir.

DANFORTH: There is a prodigious stench in this place.

HERRICK: I have only now cleared the people out for you.

DANFORTH: Beware hard drink, Marshal.

HERRICK: Aye, sir. *He waits an instant for further orders. But Danforth, in dissatisfaction, turns his back on him, and Herrick goes out. There is a pause. Danforth stands in thought.*

HATHORNE: Let you question Hale, Excellency; I should not be surprised he have been preaching in Andover lately.

DANFORTH: We'll come to that; speak nothing of Andover. Parris prays with him. That's strange. *He blows on his hands, moves toward the window, and looks out.*

HATHORNE: Excellency, I wonder if it be wise to let Mr. Parris so continuously with the prisoners. *Danforth turns to him, interested.* I think, sometimes, the man has a mad look these days.

DANFORTH: Mad?

HATHORNE: I met him yesterday coming out of his house, and I bid him good morning—and he wept and went his way. I think it is not well the village sees him so unsteady.

DANFORTH: Perhaps he have some sorrow.

CHEEVER, *stamping his feet against the cold:* I think it be the cows, sir.

DANFORTH: Cows?

CHEEVER: There be so many cows wanderin' the highroads, now their masters are in the jails, and much disagreement who they will belong to now. I know Mr. Parris be arguin' with farmers all yesterday—there is great contention, sir, about the cows. Contention make him weep, sir; it were always a man that weep for contention. *He turns, as do Hathorne and Danforth, hearing someone coming up the corridor. Danforth raises his head as Parris enters. He is gaunt, frightened, and sweating in his greatcoat.*

PARRIS, *to Danforth, instantly:* Oh, good morning, sir, thank you for coming, I beg your pardon wakin' you so early. Good morning, Judge Hathorne.

DANFORTH: Reverend Hale have no right to enter this—

PARRIS: Excellency, a moment. *He hurries back and shuts the door.*

HATHORNE: Do you leave him alone with the prisoners?

DANFORTH: What's his business here?

PARRIS, *prayerfully holding up his hands:* Excellency, hear me. It is a providence. Reverend Hale has returned to bring Rebecca Nurse to God.

DANFORTH, *surprised:* He bids her confess?

PARRIS, *sitting:* Hear me. Rebecca have not given me a word this three month since she came. Now she sits with him, and her sister and Martha Corey and two or three others, and he pleads with them, confess their crimes and save their lives.

DANFORTH: Why—this is indeed a providence. And they soften, they soften?

PARRIS: Not yet, not yet. But I thought to summon you, sir, that we might think on whether it be not wise, to— *He dares not say it.* I had thought to put a question, sir, and I hope you will not—

DANFORTH: Mr. Parris, be plain, what troubles you?

PARRIS: There is news, sir, that the court—the court must reckon with. My niece, sir, my niece—I believe she has vanished.

DANFORTH: Vanished!

PARRIS: I had thought to advise you of it earlier in the week, but—

DANFORTH: Why? How long is she gone?

PARRIS: This be the third night. You see, sir, she told me she would stay a night with Mercy Lewis. And next day, when she does not return, I send to Mr. Lewis to inquire. Mercy told him she would sleep in *my* house for a night.

DANFORTH: They are both gone?!

PARRIS, *in fear of him:* They are, sir.

DANFORTH, *alarmed:* I will send a party for them. Where may they be?

PARRIS: Excellency, I think they be aboard a ship. *Danforth stands agape.* My daughter tells me how she heard them speaking of ships last week, and tonight I discover my—my strong-box is broke into. *He presses his fingers against his eyes to keep back tears.*

HATHORNE, *astonished:* She have robbed you?

PARRIS: Thirty-one pound is gone. I am penniless. *He covers his face and sobs.*

DANFORTH: Mr. Parris, you are a brainless man! *He walks in thought, deeply worried.*

PARRIS: Excellency, it profit nothing you should blame me. I cannot think they would run off except they fear to keep in Salem any more. *He is pleading.* Mark it, sir, Abigail had close knowledge of the town, and since the news of Andover has broken here—

DANFORTH: Andover is remedied. The court returns there on Friday, and will resume examinations.

PARRIS: I am sure of it, sir. But the rumor here speaks rebellion in Andover, and it—

DANFORTH: There is no rebellion in Andover!

PARRIS: I tell you what is said here, sir. Andover have thrown out the court, they say, and will have no part of witchcraft. There be a faction here, feeding on that news, and I tell you true, sir, I fear there will be riot here.

HATHORNE: Riot! Why at every execution I have seen naught but high satisfaction in the town.

PARRIS: Judge Hathorne—it were another sort that hanged till now. Rebecca Nurse is no Bridget that lived three year with Bishop before she married him. John Proctor is not Isaac Ward that drank his family to ruin. *To Danforth:* I would to God it were not so, Excellency, but these people have great weight yet in the town. Let Rebecca stand upon the gibbet and send up some righteous prayer, and I fear she'll wake a vengeance on you.

HATHORNE: Excellency, she is condemned a witch. The court have—

DANFORTH, *in deep concern, raising a hand to Hathorne:* Pray you. *To Parris:* How do you propose, then?

PARRIS: Excellency, I would postpone these hangin's for a time.

DANFORTH: There will be no postponement.

PARRIS: Now Mr. Hale's returned, there is hope, I think—for if he bring even one of these to God, that confession surely damns the others in the public eye, and none may doubt more that they are all linked to Hell. This way, unconfessed and claiming innocence, doubts are multiplied, many honest people will weep for them, and our good purpose is lost in their tears.

DANFORTH, *after thinking a moment, then going to Cheever:*
Give me the list.

Cheever opens the dispatch case, searches.

PARRIS: It cannot be forgot, sir, that when I summoned the
congregation for John Proctor's excommunication there were
hardly thirty people come to hear it. That speak a discontent,
I think, and—

DANFORTH, *studying the list:* There will be no postponement.

PARRIS: Excellency—

DANFORTH: Now, sir—which of these in your opinion may be
brought to God? I will myself strive with him till dawn. *He
hands the list to Parris, who merely glances at it.*

PARRIS: There is not sufficient time till dawn.

DANFORTH: I shall do my utmost. Which of them do you have
hope for?

PARRIS, *not even glancing at the list now, and in a quavering
voice, quietly:* Excellency—a dagger— *He chokes up.*

DANFORTH: What do you say?

PARRIS: Tonight, when I open my door to leave my house—a
dagger clattered to the ground. *Silence. Danforth absorbs this.
Now Parris cries out:* You cannot hang this sort. There is danger for me. I dare not step outside at night!

*Reverend Hale enters. They look at him for an instant in silence.
He is steeped in sorrow, exhausted, and more direct than he ever
was.*

DANFORTH: Accept my congratulations, Reverend Hale; we
are gladdened to see you returned to your good work.

HALE, *coming to Danforth now:* You must pardon them. They
will not budge.

Herrick enters, waits.

DANFORTH, *conciliatory:* You misunderstand, sir; I cannot pardon these when twelve are already hanged for the same crime. It is not just.

PARRIS, *with failing heart:* Rebecca will not confess?

HALE: The sun will rise in a few minutes. Excellency, I must have more time.

DANFORTH: Now hear me, and beguile yourselves no more. I will not receive a single plea for pardon or postponement. Them that will not confess will hang. Twelve are already executed; the names of these seven are given out, and the village expects to see them die this morning. Postponement now speaks a floundering on my part; reprieve or pardon must cast doubt upon the guilt of them that died till now. While I speak God's law, I will not crack its voice with whimpering. If retaliation is your fear, know this—I should hang ten thousand that dared to rise against the law, and an ocean of salt tears could not melt the resolution of the statutes. Now draw yourselves up like men and help me, as you are bound by Heaven to do. Have you spoken with them all, Mr. Hale?

HALE: All but Proctor. He is in the dungeon.

DANFORTH, *to Herrick:* What's Proctor's way now?

HERRICK: He sits like some great bird; you'd not know he lived except he will take food from time to time.

DANFORTH, *after thinking a moment:* His wife—his wife must be well on with child now.

HERRICK: She is, sir.

DANFORTH: What think you, Mr. Parris? You have closer knowledge of this man; might her presence soften him?

PARRIS: It is possible, sir. He have not laid eyes on her these three months. I should summon her.

DANFORTH, *to Herrick:* Is he yet adamant? Has he struck at you again?

HERRICK: He cannot, sir, he is chained to the wall now.

DANFORTH, *after thinking on it:* Fetch Goody Proctor to me. Then let you bring him up.

HERRICK: Aye, sir. *Herrick goes. There is silence.*

HALE: Excellency, if you postpone a week and publish to the town that you are striving for their confessions, that speak mercy on your part, not faltering.

DANFORTH: Mr. Hale, as God have not empowered me like Joshua to stop this sun from rising, so I cannot withhold from them the perfection of their punishment.

HALE, *harder now:* If you think God wills you to raise rebellion, Mr. Danforth, you are mistaken!

DANFORTH, *instantly:* You have heard rebellion spoken in the town?

HALE: Excellency, there are orphans wandering from house to house; abandoned cattle bellow on the highroads, the stink of rotting crops hangs everywhere, and no man knows when the harlots' cry will end his life—and you wonder yet if rebellion's spoke? Better you should marvel how they do not burn your province!

DANFORTH: Mr. Hale, have you preached in Andover this month?

HALE: Thank God they have no need of me in Andover.

DANFORTH: You baffle me, sir. Why have you returned here?

HALE: Why, it is all simple. I come to do the Devil's work. I come to counsel Christians they should belie themselves. *His sarcasm collapses.* There is blood on my head! Can you not see the blood on my head!!

PARRIS: Hush! *For he has heard footsteps. They all face the door. Herrick enters with Elizabeth. Her wrists are linked by heavy chain, which Herrick now removes. Her clothes are dirty; her face is pale and gaunt. Herrick goes out.*

DANFORTH, *very politely:* Goody Proctor. *She is silent.* I hope you are hearty?

ELIZABETH, *as a warning reminder:* I am yet six month before my time.

DANFORTH: Pray be at your ease, we come not for your life. We—*uncertain how to plead, for he is not accustomed to it.* Mr. Hale, will you speak with the woman?

HALE: Goody Proctor, your husband is marked to hang this morning.

Pause.

ELIZABETH, *quietly:* I have heard it.

HALE: You know, do you not, that I have no connection with the court? *She seems to doubt it.* I come of my own, Goody Proctor. I would save your husband's life, for if he is taken I count myself his murderer. Do you understand me?

ELIZABETH: What do you want of me?

HALE: Goody Proctor, I have gone this three month like our Lord into the wilderness. I have sought a Christian way, for damnation's doubled on a minister who counsels men to lie.

HATHORNE: It is no lie, you cannot speak of lies.

HALE: It is a lie! They are innocent!

DANFORTH: I'll hear no more of that!

HALE, *continuing to Elizabeth:* Let you not mistake your duty as I mistook my own. I came into this village like a bride-groom to his beloved, bearing gifts of high religion; the very crowns of holy law I brought, and what I touched with my bright confidence, it died; and where I turned the eye of my great faith, blood flowed up. Beware, Goody Proctor—cleave to no faith when faith brings blood. It is mistaken law that leads you to sacrifice. Life, woman, life is God's most precious gift; no principle, however glorious, may justify the taking of it. I beg you, woman, prevail upon your husband to confess. Let him give his lie. Quail not before God's judgment in this, for it may well be God damns a liar less than he that throws his life away for pride. Will you plead with him? I cannot think he will listen to another.

ELIZABETH, *quietly:* I think that be the Devil's argument.

HALE, *with a climactic desperation:* Woman, before the laws of God we are as swine! We cannot read His will!

ELIZABETH: I cannot dispute with you, sir; I lack learning for it.

DANFORTH, *going to her:* Goody Proctor, you are not summoned here for disputation. Be there no wifely tenderness within you? He will die with the sunrise. Your husband. Do you understand it? *She only looks at him.* What say you? Will you contend with him? *She is silent.* Are you stone? I tell you true, woman, had I no other proof of your unnatural life, your dry eyes now would be sufficient evidence that you delivered up your soul to Hell! A very ape would weep at such calamity! Have the Devil dried up any tear of pity in you? *She is silent.* Take her out. It profit nothing she should speak to him!

ELIZABETH, *quietly:* Let me speak with him, Excellency.

PARRIS, *with hope:* You'll strive with him? *She hesitates.*

DANFORTH: Will you plead for his confession or will you not?

ELIZABETH: I promise nothing. Let me speak with him.

A sound—the sibilance of dragging feet on stone. They turn. A pause. Herrick enters with John Proctor. His wrists are chained. He is another man, bearded, filthy, his eyes misty as though webs had overgrown them. He halts inside the doorway, his eye caught by the sight of Elizabeth. The emotion flowing between them prevents anyone from speaking for an instant. Now Hale, visibly affected, goes to Danforth and speaks quietly.

HALE: Pray, leave them, Excellency.

DANFORTH, *pressing Hale impatiently aside:* Mr. Proctor, you have been notified, have you not? *Proctor is silent, staring at Elizabeth.* I see light in the sky, Mister; let you counsel with your wife, and may God help you turn your back on Hell. *Proctor is silent, staring at Elizabeth.*

HALE, *quietly:* Excellency, let—

Danforth brushes past Hale and walks out. Hale follows. Cheever stands and follows, Hathorne behind. Herrick goes. Parris, from a safe distance, offers:

PARRIS: If you desire a cup of cider, Mr. Proctor, I am sure I— *Proctor turns an icy stare at him, and he breaks off. Parris raises his palms toward Proctor.* God lead you now. *Parris goes out.*

Alone. Proctor walks to her, halts. It is as though they stood in a spinning world. It is beyond sorrow, above it. He reaches out his hand as though toward an embodiment not quite real, and as he touches her, a strange soft sound, half laughter, half amazement, comes from his throat. He pats her hand. She covers his hand with hers. And then, weak, he sits. Then she sits, facing him.

PROCTOR: The child?

ELIZABETH: It grows.

PROCTOR: There is no word of the boys?

ELIZABETH: They're well. Rebecca's Samuel keeps them.

PROCTOR: You have not seen them?

ELIZABETH: I have not. *She catches a weakening in herself and downs it.*

PROCTOR: You are a—marvel, Elizabeth.

ELIZABETH: You—have been tortured?

PROCTOR: Aye. *Pause. She will not let herself be drowned in the sea that threatens her.* They come for my life now.

ELIZABETH: I know it.

Pause.

PROCTOR: None—have yet confessed?

ELIZABETH: There be many confessed.

PROCTOR: Who are they?

ELIZABETH: There be a hundred or more, they say. Goody Ballard is one; Isaiah Goodkind is one. There be many.

PROCTOR: Rebecca?

ELIZABETH: Not Rebecca. She is one foot in Heaven now; naught may hurt her more.

PROCTOR: And Giles?

ELIZABETH: You have not heard of it?

PROCTOR: I hear nothin', where I am kept.

ELIZABETH: Giles is dead.

He looks at her incredulously.

PROCTOR: When were he hanged?

ELIZABETH, *quietly, factually:* He were not hanged. He would not answer aye or nay to his indictment; for if he denied the charge they'd hang him surely, and auction out his property. So he stand mute, and died Christian under the law. And so his sons will have his farm. It is the law, for he could not be condemned a wizard without he answer the indictment, aye or nay.

PROCTOR: Then how does he die?

ELIZABETH, *gently:* They press him, John.

PROCTOR: Press?

ELIZABETH: Great stones they lay upon his chest until he plead aye or nay. *With a tender smile for the old man:* They say he give them but two words. "More weight," he says. And died.

PROCTOR, *numbed—a thread to weave into his agony:* "More weight."

ELIZABETH: Aye. It were a fearsome man, Giles Corey.

Pause.

PROCTOR, *with great force of will, but not quite looking at her:* I have been thinking I would confess to them, Elizabeth. *She shows nothing.* What say you? If I give them that?

ELIZABETH: I cannot judge you, John.

Pause.

PROCTOR, *simply—a pure question:* What would you have me do?

ELIZABETH: As you will, I would have it. *Slight pause.* I want you living, John. That's sure.

PROCTOR—*he pauses, then with a flailing of hope:* Giles' wife? Have she confessed?

ELIZABETH: She will not.

Pause.

PROCTOR: It is a pretense, Elizabeth.

ELIZABETH: What is?

PROCTOR: I cannot mount the gibbet like a saint. It is a fraud. I am not that man. *She is silent.* My honesty is broke, Elizabeth; I am no good man. Nothing's spoiled by giving them this lie that were not rotten long before.

ELIZABETH: And yet you've not confessed till now. That speak goodness in you.

PROCTOR: Spite only keeps me silent. It is hard to give a lie to dogs. *Pause, for the first time he turns directly to her.* I would have your forgiveness, Elizabeth.

ELIZABETH: It is not for me to give, John, I am—

PROCTOR: I'd have you see some honesty in it. Let them that never lied die now to keep their souls. It is pretense for me, a vanity that will not blind God nor keep my children out of the wind. *Pause.* What say you?

ELIZABETH, *upon a heaving sob that always threatens:* John, it come to naught that I should forgive you, if you'll not forgive yourself. *Now he turns away a little, in great agony.* It is not my soul, John, it is yours. *He stands, as though in physical pain, slowly rising to his feet with a great immortal longing to find his answer. It is difficult to say, and she is on the verge of tears.* Only be sure of this, for I know it now: Whatever you will do, it is a good man does it. *He turns his doubting, searching gaze upon her.* I have read my heart this three month, John. *Pause.* I have sins of my own to count. It needs a cold wife to prompt lechery.

PROCTOR, *in great pain:* Enough, enough—

ELIZABETH, *now pouring out her heart:* Better you should know me!

PROCTOR: I will not hear it! I know you!

ELIZABETH: You take my sins upon you, John—

PROCTOR, *in agony:* No, I take my own, my own!

ELIZABETH: John, I counted myself so plain, so poorly made, no honest love could come to me! Suspicion kissed you when I did; I never knew how I should say my love. It were a cold house I kept! *In fright, she swerves, as Hathorne enters.*

HATHORNE: What say you, Proctor? The sun is soon up.

Proctor, his chest heaving, stares, turns to Elizabeth. She comes to him as though to plead, her voice quaking.

ELIZABETH: Do what you will. But let none be your judge. There be no higher judge under Heaven than Proctor is! Forgive me, forgive me, John—I never knew such goodness in the world! *She covers her face, weeping.*

Proctor turns from her to Hathorne; he is off the earth, his voice hollow.

PROCTOR: I want my life.

HATHORNE, *electrified, surprised:* You'll confess yourself?

PROCTOR: I will have my life.

HATHORNE, *with a mystical tone:* God be praised! It is a providence! *He rushes out the door, and his voice is heard calling down the corridor:* He will confess! Proctor will confess!

PROCTOR, *with a cry, as he strides to the door:* Why do you cry it? *In great pain he turns back to her.* It is evil, is it not? It is evil.

ELIZABETH, *in terror, weeping:* I cannot judge you, John, I cannot!

PROCTOR: Then who will judge me? *Suddenly clasping his hands:* God in Heaven, what is John Proctor, what is John Proctor? *He moves as an animal, and a fury is riding in him, a tantalized search.* I think it is honest, I think so; I am no saint. *As though she had denied this he calls angrily at her:* Let Rebecca go like a saint; for me it is fraud!

Voices are heard in the hall, speaking together in suppressed excitement.

ELIZABETH: I am not your judge, I cannot be. *As though giving him release:* Do as you will, do as you will!

PROCTOR: Would you give them such a lie? Say it. Would you ever give them this? *She cannot answer.* You would not; if tongs of fire were singeing you you would not! It is evil. Good, then—it is evil, and I do it!

Hathorne enters with Danforth, and, with them, Cheever, Parris, and Hale. It is a businesslike, rapid entrance, as though the ice had been broken.

DANFORTH, *with great relief and gratitude:* Praise to God, man, praise to God; you shall be blessed in Heaven for this. *Cheever has hurried to the bench with pen, ink, and paper. Proctor watches him.* Now then, let us have it. Are you ready, Mr. Cheever?

PROCTOR, *with a cold, cold horror at their efficiency:* Why must it be written?

DANFORTH: Why, for the good instruction of the village, Mister; this we shall post upon the church door! *To Parris, urgently:* Where is the marshal?

PARRIS—*he runs to the door and calls down the corridor:* Marshal! Hurry!

DANFORTH: Now, then, Mister, will you speak slowly, and directly to the point, for Mr. Cheever's sake. *He is on record now, and is really dictating to Cheever, who writes.* Mr. Proctor, have you seen the Devil in your life? *Proctor's jaws lock.* Come, man, there is light in the sky; the town waits at the scaffold; I would give out this news. Did you see the Devil?

PROCTOR: I did.

PARRIS: Praise God!

DANFORTH: And when he come to you, what were his demand? *Proctor is silent. Danforth helps.* Did he bid you to do his work upon the earth?

PROCTOR: He did.

DANFORTH: And you bound yourself to his service? *Danforth turns, as Rebecca Nurse enters, with Herrick helping to support her. She is barely able to walk.* Come in, come in, woman!

REBECCA, *brightening as she sees Proctor:* Ah, John! You are well, then, eh?

Proctor turns his face to the wall.

DANFORTH: Courage, man, courage—let her witness your good example that she may come to God herself. Now hear it, Goody Nurse! Say on, Mr. Proctor. Did you bind yourself to the Devil's service?

REBECCA, *astonished:* Why, John!

PROCTOR, *through his teeth, his face turned from Rebecca:* I did.

DANFORTH: Now, woman, you surely see it profit nothin' to keep this conspiracy any further. Will you confess yourself with him?

REBECCA: Oh, John—God send his mercy on you!

DANFORTH: I say, will you confess yourself, Goody Nurse?

REBECCA: Why, it is a lie, it is a lie; how may I damn myself? I cannot, I cannot.

DANFORTH: Mr. Proctor. When the Devil came to you did you see Rebecca Nurse in his company? *Proctor is silent.* Come, man, take courage—did you ever see her with the Devil?

PROCTOR, *almost inaudibly:* No.

Danforth, now sensing trouble, glances at John and goes to the table, and picks up a sheet—the list of condemned.

DANFORTH: Did you ever see her sister, Mary Easty, with the Devil?

PROCTOR: No, I did not.

DANFORTH, *his eyes narrow on Proctor:* Did you ever see Martha Corey with the Devil?

PROCTOR: I did not.

DANFORTII, *realizing, slowly putting the sheet down:* Did you ever see anyone with the Devil?

PROCTOR: I did not.

DANFORTH: Proctor, you mistake me. I am not empowered to trade your life for a lie. You have most certainly seen some person with the Devil. *Proctor is silent.* Mr. Proctor, a score of people have already testified they saw this woman with the Devil.

PROCTOR: Then it is proved. Why must I say it?

DANFORTH: Why "must" you say it! Why, you should rejoice to say it if your soul is truly purged of any love for Hell!

PROCTOR: They think to go like saints. I like not to spoil their names.

DANFORTH, *inquiring, incredulous:* Mr. Proctor, do you think they go like saints?

PROCTOR, *evading:* This woman never thought she done the Devil's work.

DANFORTH: Look you, sir. I think you mistake your duty here. It matters nothing what she thought—she is convicted of the unnatural murder of children, and you for sending your spirit out upon Mary Warren. Your soul alone is the issue here, Mister, and you will prove its whiteness or you cannot live in a Christian country. Will you tell me now what persons conspired with you in the Devil's company? *Proctor is silent.* To your knowledge was Rebecca Nurse ever—

PROCTOR: I speak my own sins; I cannot judge another. *Crying out, with hatred:* I have no tongue for it.

HALE, *quickly to Danforth:* Excellency, it is enough he confess himself. Let him sign it, let him sign it.

PARRIS, *feverishly:* It is a great service, sir. It is a weighty name; it will strike the village that Proctor confess. I beg you, let him sign it. The sun is up, Excellency!

DANFORTH—*he considers; then with dissatisfaction:* Come, then, sign your testimony. *To Cheever:* Give it to him. *Cheever goes to Proctor, the confession and a pen in hand. Proctor does not look at it.* Come, man, sign it.

PROCTOR, *after glancing at the confession:* You have all witnessed it—it is enough.

DANFORTH: You will not sign it?

PROCTOR: You have all witnessed it; what more is needed?

DANFORTH: Do you sport with me? You will sign your name or it is no confession, Mister! *His breast heaving with agonized breathing, Proctor now lays the paper down and signs his name.*

PARRIS: Praise be to the Lord!

Proctor has just finished signing when Danforth reaches for the paper. But Proctor snatches it up, and now a wild terror is rising in him, and a boundless anger.

DANFORTH, *perplexed, but politely extending his hand:* If you please, sir.

PROCTOR: No.

DANFORTH, *as though Proctor did not understand:* Mr. Proctor, I must have—

PROCTOR: No, no. I have signed it. You have seen me. It is done! You have no need for this.

PARRIS: Proctor, the village must have proof that—

PROCTOR: Damn the village! I confess to God, and God has seen my name on this! It is enough!

DANFORTH: No, sir, it is—

PROCTOR: You came to save my soul, did you not? Here! I have confessed myself; it is enough!

DANFORTH: You have not con—

PROCTOR: I have confessed myself! Is there no good penitence but it be public? God does not need my name nailed upon the church! God sees my name; God knows how black my sins are! It is enough!

DANFORTH: Mr. Proctor—

PROCTOR: You will not use me! I am no Sarah Good or Tituba, I am John Proctor! You will not use me! It is no part of salvation that you should use me!

DANFORTH: I do not wish to—

PROCTOR: I have three children—how may I teach them to walk like men in the world, and I sold my friends?

DANFORTH: You have not sold your friends—

PROCTOR: Beguile me not! I blacken all of them when this is nailed to the church the very day they hang for silence!

DANFORTH: Mr. Proctor, I must have good and legal proof that you—

PROCTOR: You are the high court, your word is good enough! Tell them I confessed myself; say Proctor broke his knees and wept like a woman; say what you will, but my name cannot—

DANFORTH, *with suspicion:* It is the same, is it not? If I report it or you sign to it?

PROCTOR—*he knows it is insane:* No, it is not the same! What others say and what I sign to is not the same!

DANFORTH: Why? Do you mean to deny this confession when you are free?

PROCTOR: I mean to deny nothing!

DANFORTH: Then explain to me, Mr. Proctor, why you will not let—

PROCTOR, *with a cry of his whole soul:* Because it is my name! Because I cannot have another in my life! Because I lie and sign myself to lies! Because I am not worth the dust on the feet of them that hang! How may I live without my name? I have given you my soul; leave me my name!

DANFORTH, *pointing at the confession in Proctor's hand:* Is that document a lie? If it is a lie I will not accept it! What say you? I will not deal in lies, Mister! *Proctor is motionless.* You will give me your honest confession in my hand, or I cannot keep you from the rope. *Proctor does not reply.* Which way do you go, Mister?

His breast heaving, his eyes staring, Proctor tears the paper and crumples it, and he is weeping in fury, but erect.

DANFORTH: Marshal!

PARRIS, *hysterically, as though the tearing paper were his life:* Proctor, Proctor!

HALE: Man, you will hang! You cannot!

PROCTOR, *his eyes full of tears:* I can. And there's your first marvel, that I can. You have made your magic now, for now I do think I see some shred of goodness in John Proctor. Not enough to weave a banner with, but white enough to keep it from such dogs. *Elizabeth, in a burst of terror, rushes to him and weeps against his hand.* Give them no tear! Tears pleasure them! Show honor now, show a stony heart and sink them with it! *He has lifted her, and kisses her now with great passion.*

REBECCA: Let you fear nothing! Another judgment waits us all!

DANFORTH: Hang them high over the town! Who weeps for these, weeps for corruption! *He sweeps out past them. Herrick starts to lead Rebecca, who almost collapses, but Proctor catches her, and she glances up at him apologetically.*

REBECCA: I've had no breakfast.

HERRICK: Come, man. *Herrick escorts them out, Hathorne and Cheever behind them. Elizabeth stands staring at the empty doorway.*

PARRIS, *in deadly fear, to Elizabeth.* Go to him, Goody Proctor! There is yet time!

From outside a drumroll strikes the air. Parris is startled. Elizabeth jerks about toward the window.

PARRIS: Go to him! *He rushes out the door, as though to hold back his fate.* Proctor! Proctor!

Again, a short burst of drums.

HALE: Woman, plead with him! *He starts to rush out the door, and then goes back to her.* Woman! It is pride, it is vanity. *She avoids his eyes, and moves to the window. He drops to his knees.* Be his helper! What profit him to bleed? Shall the dust praise him? Shall the worms declare his truth? Go to him, take his shame away!

ELIZABETH, *supporting herself against collapse, grips the bars of the window, and with a cry:* He have his goodness now. God forbid I take it from him!

The final drumroll crashes, then heightens violently. Hale weeps in frantic prayer, and the new sun is pouring in upon her face, and the drums rattle like bones in the morning air.

THE CURTAIN FALLS

ECHOES DOWN THE CORRIDOR

Not long after the fever died, Parris was voted from office, walked out on the highroad, and was never heard of again.

The legend has it that Abigail turned up later as a prostitute in Boston.

Twenty years after the last execution, the government awarded compensation to the victims still living, and to the families of the dead. However, it is evident that some people still were unwilling to admit their total guilt, and also that the factionalism was still alive, for some beneficiaries were actually not victims at all, but informers.

Elizabeth Proctor married again, four years after Proctor's death.

In solemn meeting, the congregation rescinded the excommunications—this in March 1712. But they did so upon orders of the government. The jury, however, wrote a statement praying forgiveness of all who had suffered.

Certain farms which had belonged to the victims were left to ruin, and for more than a century no one would buy them or live on them.

To all intents and purposes, the power of theocracy in Massachusetts was broken.

APPENDIX:

Act Two,

SCENE TWO*

A wood. Night.

Proctor enters with lantern, glowing behind him, then halts, holding lantern raised. Abigail appears with a wrap over her nightgown, her hair down. A moment of questioning silence.

PROCTOR, *searching:* I must speak with you, Abigail. *She does not move, staring at him.* Will you sit?

ABIGAIL: How do you come?

PROCTOR: Friendly.

ABIGAIL, *glancing about:* I don't like the woods at night. Pray you, stand closer. *He comes closer to her.* I knew it must be you. When I heard the pebbles on the window, before I opened up my eyes I knew. *Sits on log.* I thought you would come a good time sooner.

PROCTOR: I had thought to come many times.

ABIGAIL: Why didn't you? I am so alone in the world now.

* See note on page 214.

277

PROCTOR, *as a fact, not bitterly:* Are you! I've heard that people ride a hundred mile to see your face these days.

ABIGAIL: Aye, my face. Can you see my face?

PROCTOR—*he holds the lantern to her face:* Then you're troubled?

ABIGAIL: Have you come to mock me?

PROCTOR—*he sets lantern on ground and sits next to her:* No, no, but I hear only that you go to the tavern every night, and play shovelboard with the Deputy Governor, and they give you cider.

ABIGAIL: I have once or twice played the shovelboard. But I have no joy in it.

PROCTOR: This is a surprise, Abby. I'd thought to find you gayer than this. I'm told a troop of boys go step for step with you wherever you walk these days.

ABIGAIL: Aye, they do. But I have only lewd looks from the boys.

PROCTOR: And you like that not?

ABIGAIL: I cannot bear lewd looks no more, John. My spirit's changed entirely. I ought be given Godly looks when I suffer for them as I do.

PROCTOR: Oh? How do you suffer, Abby?

ABIGAIL, *pulling up her dress:* Why, look at my leg. I'm holes all over from their damned needles and pins. *Touching her stomach:* The jab your wife gave me's not healed yet, y'know.

PROCTOR, *seeing her madness now:* Oh, it isn't?

ABIGAIL: I think sometimes she pricks it open again while I sleep.

PROCTOR: Ah?

ABIGAIL: And George Jacobs—*sliding up her sleeve*—he comes again and again and raps me with his stick—the same spot every night all this week. Look at the lump I have.

PROCTOR: Abby, George Jacobs is in the jail all this month.

ABIGAIL: Thank God he is, and bless the day he hangs and lets me sleep in peace again! Oh, John, the world's so full of hypocrites! *Astonished, outraged:* They pray in jail! I'm told they all pray in jail!

PROCTOR: They may not pray?

ABIGAIL: And torture me in my bed while sacred words are comin' from their mouths? Oh, it will need God Himself to cleanse this town properly!

PROCTOR: Abby—you mean to cry out still others?

ABIGAIL: If I live, if I am not murdered, I surely will, until the last hypocrite is dead.

PROCTOR: Then there is no good?

ABIGAIL: Aye, there is one. *You* are good.

PROCTOR: Am I! How am I good?

ABIGAIL: Why, you taught me goodness, therefore you are good. It were a fire you walked me through, and all my ignorance was burned away. It were a fire, John, we lay in fire. And from that night no woman dare call me wicked any more but I knew my answer. I used to weep for my sins when the wind lifted up my skirts; and blushed for shame because some old Rebecca called me loose. And then you burned my ignorance away. As bare as some December tree I saw them all— walking like saints to church, running to feed the sick, and hypocrites in their hearts! And God gave me strength to call them liars, and God made men to listen to me, and by God I will scrub the world clean for the love of Him! Oh, John, I will make you such a wife when the world is white again! *She kisses his hand.* You will be amazed to see me every day, a light of heaven in your house, a—*He rises, backs away, amazed.* Why are you cold?

PROCTOR: My wife goes to trial in the morning, Abigail.

ABIGAIL, *distantly:* Your wife?

PROCTOR: Surely you knew of it?

ABIGAIL: I do remember it now. How—how— Is she well?

PROCTOR: As well as she may be, thirty-six days in that place.

ABIGAIL: You said you came friendly.

PROCTOR: She will not be condemned, Abby.

ABIGAIL: You brought me from my bed to speak of her?

PROCTOR: I come to tell you, Abby, what I will do tomorrow in the court. I would not take you by surprise, but give you all good time to think on what to do to save yourself.

ABIGAIL: Save myself!

PROCTOR: If you do not free my wife tomorrow, I am set and bound to ruin you, Abby.

ABIGAIL, *her voice small—astonished:* How—ruin me?

PROCTOR: I have rocky proof in documents that you knew that poppet were none of my wife's; and that you yourself bade Mary Warren stab that needle into it.

ABIGAIL—*wildness stirs in her, a child is standing here who is unutterably frustrated, denied her wish, but she is still grasping for her wits: I* bade Mary Warren—?

PROCTOR: You know what you do, you are not so mad!

ABIGAIL: Oh, hypocrites! Have you won him, too? John, why do you let them send you?

PROCTOR: I warn you, Abby!

ABIGAIL: They send you! They steal your honesty and—

PROCTOR: I have found my honesty!

ABIGAIL: No, this is your wife pleading, your sniveling, envious wife! This is Rebecca's voice, Martha Corey's voice. You were no hypocrite!

PROCTOR: I will prove you for the fraud you are!

ABIGAIL: And if they ask you why Abigail would ever do so murderous a deed, what will you tell them?

PROCTOR: I will tell them why.

ABIGAIL: What will you tell? You will confess to fornication? In the court?

PROCTOR: If you will have it so, so I will tell it! *She utters a disbelieving laugh.* I say I will! *She laughs louder, now with more assurance he will never do it. He shakes her roughly.* If you can still hear, hear this! Can you hear! *She is trembling, staring up at him as though he were out of his mind.* You will tell the court you are blind to spirits; you cannot see them any more, and you will never cry witchery again, or I will make you famous for the whore you are!

ABIGAIL, *grabbing him:* Never in this world! I know you, John. You are this moment singing secret hallelujahs that your wife will hang!

PROCTOR, *throwing her down:* You mad, you murderous bitch!

ABIGAIL: Oh, how hard it is when pretense falls! But it falls, it falls! *she wraps herself up as though to go.* You have done your duty by her. I hope it is your last hypocrisy. I pray you will come again with sweeter news for me. I know you will—now that your duty's done. Good night, John. *She is backing away, raising her hand in farewell.* Fear naught. I will save you tomorrow. *As she turns and goes:* From yourself I will save you. *She is gone.*

Proctor is left alone, amazed, in terror. He takes up his lantern and slowly exits.

THE CURTAIN FALLS

Incident at Vichy

THE CAST

(in order of speaking)

LEBEAU	Michael Strong
BAYARD	Stanley Beck
MARCHAND	Paul Mann
POLICE GUARD	C. Thomas Blackwell
MONCEAU	David J. Stewart
GYPSY	Harold Scott
WAITER	Jack Waltzer
BOY	Ira Lewis
MAJOR	Hal Holbrook
FIRST DETECTIVE	Alek Primrose
OLD JEW	Will Lee
SECOND DETECTIVE	James Dukas
LEDUC	Joseph Wiseman
POLICE CAPTAIN	James Greene
VON BERG	David Wayne
PROFESSOR HOFFMAN	Clinton Kimbrough
FERRAND	Graham Jarvis
PRISONERS	Pierre Epstein, Stephen Peters, Tony Lo Bianco, John Vari

Directed by Harold Clurman for the Repertory Theatre of Lincoln Center for the Performing Arts. Opened December 3, 1964, ANTA–Washington Square Theatre, New York City.

Vichy, France, 1942. A place of detention.

At the right a corridor leads to a turning and an unseen door to the street. Across the back is a structure with two grimy window panes in it—perhaps an office, in any case a private room with a door opening from it at the left.

A long bench stands in front of this room, facing a large empty area whose former use is unclear but which suggests a warehouse, perhaps, an armory, or part of a railroad station not used by the public. Two small boxes stand apart on either side of the bench.

When light begins to rise, six men and a boy of fifteen are discovered on the bench in attitudes expressive of their personalities and functions, frozen there like members of a small orchestra at the moment before they begin to play.

As normal light comes on, their positions flow out of the frieze. It appears that they do not know one another and are sitting like people thrown together in a public place, mutually curious but self-occupied. However, they are anxious and frightened and tend to make themselves small and unobtrusive. Only one, Marchand, a fairly well-dressed businessman, keeps glancing at his watch and bits of paper and calling cards he keeps in his pockets, and seems normally impatient.

Now, out of hunger and great anxiety, Lebeau, a bearded, un-kempt man of twenty-five, lets out a dramatized blow of air and leans forward to rest his head on his hands. Others glance at him, then away. He is charged with the energy of fear, and it makes him seem aggressive.

LEBEAU: Cup of coffee would be nice. Even a sip. *No one responds. He turns to Bayard beside him; Bayard is his age, poorly but cleanly dressed, with a certain muscular austerity in his manner. Lebeau speaks in a private undertone.* You wouldn't have any idea what's going on, would you?

BAYARD, *shaking his head:* I was walking down the street.

LEBEAU: Me too. Something told me—Don't go outside today. So I went out. Weeks go by and I don't open my door. Today I go out. And I had no reason, I wasn't even going anywhere. *Looks left and right to the others. To Bayard:* They get picked up the same way?

BAYARD—*he shrugs:* I've only been here a couple of minutes myself—just before they brought you in.

LEBEAU, *looking to the others:* Does anybody know anything? *They shrug and shake their heads. Lebeau looks at the walls, the room; then he speaks to Bayard.* This isn't a police station, is it?

BAYARD: Doesn't seem so. There's always a desk. It's just some building they're using, I guess.

LEBEAU, *glancing about uneasily, curiously:* It's painted like a police station, though. There must be an international police paint, they're always the same color everywhere. Like dead clams, and a little yellow mixed in. *Pause. He glances at the other silent men, and tries to silence himself, like them. But it's impossible, and he speaks to Bayard with a nervous smile.* You begin wishing you'd committed a crime, you know? Something definite.

BAYARD—*he is not amused, but not unsympathetic:* Try to take it easy. It's no good getting excited. We'll find out soon.

LEBEAU: It's just that I haven't eaten since three o'clock yesterday afternoon. Everything gets more vivid when you're hungry—you ever notice that?

BAYARD: I'd give you something, but I forgot my lunch this morning. Matter of fact, I was just turning back to get it when they came up alongside me. Whyn't you try to sit back and relax?

LEBEAU: I'm nervous. . . . I mean I'm nervous anyway. *With a faint, frightened laugh:* I was even nervous before the war. *His little smile vanishes. He shifts in his seat. The others wait with subdued anxiety. He notices the good clothes and secure manner of Marchand, who is at the head of the line, nearest the door. He leans forward to attract him.* Excuse me. *Marchand does not turn to him. He gives a short, sharp, low whistle. Marchand, already offended, turns slowly to him.* Is that the way they picked you up? On the street? *Marchand turns forward again without answering.* Sir? *Marchand still does not turn back to him.* Well, Jesus, pardon me for living.

MARCHAND: It's perfectly obvious they're making a routine identity check.

LEBEAU: Oh.

MARCHAND: With so many strangers pouring into Vichy this past year there're probably a lot of spies and God knows what. It's just a document check, that's all.

LEBEAU, *turning to Bayard, hopefully:* You think so?

BAYARD—*he shrugs; obviously he feels there is something more to it:* I don't know.

MARCHAND, *to Bayard:* Why? There are thousands of people running around with false papers, we all know that. You can't permit such things in wartime. *The others glance uneasily at Marchand, whose sense of security is thereby confined to him alone.* Especially now with the Germans starting to take over down here you have to expect things to be more strict, it's inevitable.

A pause. Lebeau once again turns to him.

LEBEAU: You don't get any . . . special flavor, huh?

MARCHAND: What flavor?

LEBEAU, *glancing at the others:* Well like . . . some racial . . . implication?

MARCHAND: I don't see anything to fear if your papers are all right. *He turns front, concluding the conversation.*

Again silence. But Lebeau can't contain his anxiety. He studies Bayard's profile, then turns to the man on his other side and studies his. Then, turning back to Bayard, he speaks quietly.

LEBEAU: Listen, you are . . . Peruvian, aren't you?

BAYARD: What's the matter with you, asking questions like that in here? *He turns forward.*

LEBEAU: What am I supposed to do, sit here like a dumb beast?

BAYARD, *laying a calming hand on his knee:* Friend, it's no good getting hysterical.

LEBEAU: I think we've had it. I think all the Peruvians have had it in Vichy. *Suppressing a shout:* In 1939 I had an American visa. Before the invasion. I actually had it in my hand. . . .

BAYARD: Calm down—this may all be routine.

Slight pause. Then . . .

LEBEAU: Listen . . . *He leans in and whispers into Bayard's ear. Bayard glances toward Marchand, then shrugs to Lebeau.*

BAYARD: I don't know, maybe; maybe he's not.

LEBEAU, *desperately attempting familiarity:* What about you?

BAYARD: Will you stop asking idiotic questions? You're making yourself ridiculous.

LEBEAU: But I am ridiculous, aren't you? In 1939 we were packed for America. Suddenly my mother wouldn't leave the furniture. I'm here because of a brass bed and some fourth-rate crockery. And a stubborn, ignorant woman.

BAYARD: Yes, but it's not all that simple. You should try to think of why things happen. It helps to know the meaning of one's suffering.

LEBEAU: What meaning? If my mother—

BAYARD: It's not your mother. The monopolies got control of Germany. Big business is out to make slaves of everyone, that's why you're here.

LEBEAU: Well I'm not a philosopher, but I know my mother, and that's why I'm here. You're like people who look at my paintings—"What does this mean, what does that mean?" *Look* at it, don't ask what it means; you're not God, you can't tell what anything means. I'm walking down the street before, a car pulls up beside me, a man gets out and measures my nose, my ears, my mouth, the next thing I'm sitting in a police station—or whatever the hell this is here—and in the middle of Europe, the highest peak of civilization! And you know what it means? After the Romans and the Greeks and the Renaissance, and you know what this means?

BAYARD: You're talking utter confusion.

LEBEAU, *in terror:* Because I'm utterly confused! *He suddenly springs up and shouts:* Goddammit, I want some coffee!

The Police Guard appears at the end of the corridor, a revolver on his hip; he strolls down the corridor and meets Lebeau, who has come halfway up. Lebeau halts, returns to his place on the bench, and sits. The Guard starts to turn to go up the corridor when Marchand raises his hand.

MARCHAND: Excuse me, officer, is there a telephone one can use? I have an appointment at eleven o'clock and it's quite . . .

The Guard simply walks up the corridor, turns the corner, and disappears. Lebeau looks toward Marchand and shakes his head, laughing silently.

LEBEAU, *to Bayard, sotto:* Isn't it wonderful? The man is probably on his way to work in a German coal mine and he's worried about breaking an appointment. And people want realistic painting, you see what I mean? *Slight pause.* Did they measure your nose? Could you at least tell me that?

BAYARD: No, they just stopped me and asked for my papers. I showed them and they took me in.

MONCEAU, *leaning forward to address Marchand:* I agree with you, sir. *Marchand turns to him. Monceau is a bright-eyed, cheerful man of twenty-eight. His clothes were elegant, are now frayed. He holds a gray felt hat on his knee, his posture rather elegant.* Vichy must be full of counterfeit papers. I think as soon as they start, it shouldn't take long. *To Lebeau:* Try to settle down.

LEBEAU, *to Monceau:* Did they measure your nose?

MONCEAU, *disapprovingly:* I think it'd be best if we all kept quiet.

LEBEAU: What is it, my clothes? How do you know, I might be the greatest painter in France.

MONCEAU: For your sake, I hope you are.

LEBEAU: What a crew! I mean the animosity!

Pause.

MARCHAND, *leaning forward to see Monceau:* You would think, though, that with the manpower shortage they'd economize on personnel. In the car that stopped me there was a driver, two French detectives, and a German official of some kind. They could easily have put a notice in the paper—everyone would have come here to present his documents. This way it's a whole morning wasted. Aside from the embarrassment.

LEBEAU: I'm not embarrassed, I'm scared to death. *To Bayard:* You embarrassed?

BAYARD: Look, if you can't be serious just leave me alone.

Pause. Lebeau leans forward to see the man sitting on the far side of Marchand. He points.

LEBEAU: Gypsy?

GYPSY, *drawing closer a copper pot at his feet:* Gypsy.

LEBEAU, *to Monceau:* Gypsies never have papers. Why'd they bother him?

MONCEAU: In his case it might be some other reason. He probably stole that pot.

GYPSY: No. On the sidewalk. *He raises the pot from between his feet.* I fix, make nice. I sit down to fix. Come police. Pfft!

MARCHAND: But of course they'll tell you anything. . . . *To Gypsy, laughing familiarly:* Right?

Gypsy laughs and turns away to his own gloom.

LEBEAU: That's a hell of a thing to say to him. I mean, would you say that to a man with pressed pants?

MARCHAND: They don't mind. In fact, they're proud of stealing. *To Gypsy:* Aren't you? *Gypsy glances at him, shrugs.* I've got a place in the country where they come every summer. I like them, personally—especially the music. *With a broad grin he sings toward the Gypsy and laughs.* We often listen to them around their campfires. But they'll steal the eyes out of your head. *To Gypsy:* Right?

Gypsy shrugs and kisses the air contemptuously. Marchand laughs with brutal familiarity.

LEBEAU: Why shouldn't he steal? How'd you get *your* money?

MARCHAND: I happen to be in business.

LEBEAU: So what have you got against stealing?

BAYARD: Are you trying to provoke somebody? Is that it?

LEBEAU: Another businessman.

BAYARD: I happen to be an electrician. But a certain amount of solidarity wouldn't hurt right now.

LEBEAU: How about some solidarity with Gypsies? Just because they don't work nine to five?

WAITER—*a small man, middle-aged, still wearing his apron:* I know this one. I've made him go away a hundred times. He and his wife stand outside the café with a baby, and they beg. It's not even their baby.

LEBEAU: So what? They've still got a little imagination.

WAITER: Yes, but they keep whining to the customers through the shrubbery. People don't like it.

LEBEAU: You know—you all remind me of my father. Always worshiped the hard-working Germans. And now you hear it all over France—we have to learn how to work like the Germans. Good God, don't you ever read history? Whenever a people starts to work hard, watch out, they're going to kill somebody.

BAYARD: That depends on how production is organized. If it's for private profit, yes, but—

LEBEAU: What are you talking about, when did the Russians start getting dangerous? When they learned how to work. Look at the Germans—for a thousand years peaceful, disorganized people—they start working and they're on everybody's back. Nobody's afraid of the Africans, are they? Because they don't work. Read the Bible—work is a curse, you're not supposed to worship work.

MARCHAND: And how do you propose to produce anything?

LEBEAU: Well, that's the problem. *Marchand and Bayard laugh.* What are you laughing at? That is the problem! Yes! To work without making work a god! What kind of crew is this?

The office door opens and the Major comes out. He is twenty-eight, a wan but well-built man; there is something ill about him. He walks with a slight limp, passing the line of men as he goes toward the corridor.

WAITER: Good morning, Major.

MAJOR, *startled, nodding to the Waiter:* Oh. Good morning. *He continues up the corridor, where he summons the Guard around the corner—the Guard appears and they talk unheard.*

MARCHAND, *sotto:* You know him?

WAITER, *proudly:* I serve him breakfast every morning. Tell you the truth, he's really not a bad fellow. Regular army, see, not one of these SS bums. Got wounded somewhere, so they stuck him back here. Only came about a month ago, but he and I—

The Major comes back down the corridor. The Guard returns to his post out of sight at the corridor's end. As the Major passes Marchand . . .

MARCHAND, *leaping up and going to the Major:* Excuse me, sir. *The Major slowly turns his face to Marchand. Marchand affects to laugh deferentially.* I hate to trouble you, but I would be much obliged if I could use a telephone for one minute. In fact, it's business connected to the food supply. I am the manager of . . . *He starts to take out a business card, but the Major has turned away and walks to the door. But there he stops and turns back.*

MAJOR: I'm not in charge of this procedure. You will have to wait for the Captain of Police. *He goes into the office.*

MARCHAND: I beg your pardon.

The door has been closed on his line. He goes back to his place and sits, glaring at the Waiter.

WAITER: He's not a really bad fellow. *They all look at him, eager for some clue.* He even comes at night sometimes, plays a beautiful piano. Gives himself French lessons out of a book. Always has a few nice words to say, too.

LEBEAU: Does he know that you're a . . . Peruvian?

BAYARD, *instantly:* Don't discuss that here, for God's sake! What's the matter with you?

LEBEAU: Can't I find out what's going on? If it's a general identity check it's one thing, but if—

From the end of the corridor enter First Detective with the Old Jew, a man in his seventies, bearded, carrying a large sackcloth bundle; then the Second Detective, holding the arm of Leduc; then the Police Captain, uniformed, with Von Berg; and finally the Professor in civilian clothes.

The First Detective directs the Old Jew to sit, and he does, beside the Gypsy. The Second Detective directs Von Berg to sit beside the Old Jew. Only now does the Second Detective release his hold on Leduc and indicate that he is to sit beside Von Berg.

SECOND DETECTIVE, *to Leduc:* Don't you give me any more trouble now.

The door opens and the Major enters. Instantly Leduc is on his feet, approaching the Major.

LEDUC: Sir, I must ask the reason for this. I am a combat officer, captain in the French Army. There is no authority to arrest me in French territory. The Occupation has not revoked French law in southern France.

The Second Detective, infuriated, throws Leduc back into his seat. He returns to the Professor.

SECOND DETECTIVE, *to Major, of Leduc:* Speechmaker.

PROFESSOR, *doubtfully:* You think you two can carry on now?

SECOND DETECTIVE: We got the idea, Professor. *To the Major:* There's certain neighborhoods they head for when they run away from Paris or wherever they come from. I can get you as many as you can handle.

FIRST DETECTIVE: It's a question of knowing the neighborhoods, you see. In my opinion you've got at least a couple thousand in Vichy on false papers.

PROFESSOR: You go ahead, then.

As the Second Detective turns to go with the First Detective, the Police Captain calls him.

CAPTAIN: Saint-Père.

SECOND DETECTIVE: Yes sir.

The Captain walks downstage with the Detective.

CAPTAIN: Try to avoid taking anybody out of a crowd. Just cruise around the way we did before, and take them one at a time. There are all kinds of rumors. We don't want to alarm people.

SECOND DETECTIVE: Right, sir.

The Captain gestures, and both Detectives leave up the corridor.

CAPTAIN: I am just about to order coffee. Will you gentlemen have some?

PROFESSOR: Please.

WAITER, *timidly:* And a croissant for the Major.

The Major glances quickly at the Waiter and barely smiles. The Captain, who has thrown a mystified look at the Waiter, goes into the office.

MARCHAND, *to the Professor:* I believe I am first, sir.

PROFESSOR: Yes, this way.

He goes into the office, followed by the eager Marchand.

MARCHAND, *going in:* Thank you. I'm in a dreadful hurry. . . .
I was on my way to the Ministry of Supply, in fact. . . .

*His voice is lost within. As the Major reaches the door, Leduc,
who has been in a fever of calculation, calls to him.*

LEDUC: Amiens.

MAJOR—*he halts at the door, turns to Leduc, who is at the far
end of the line:* What about Amiens?

LEDUC, *suppressing his nervousness:* June ninth, 'forty. I was in
the Sixteenth Artillery, facing you. I recognize your insignia,
which of course I could hardly forget.

MAJOR: That was a bad day for you fellows.

LEDUC: Yes. And evidently for you.

MAJOR, *glancing down at his leg:* Can't complain. *He goes into
the office, shuts the door. A pause.*

LEDUC, *to all:* What's this all about?

WAITER, *to all:* I told you he wasn't a bad guy. You'll see.

MONCEAU, *to Leduc:* It seems they're checking on identification papers.

*Leduc receives the news, and obviously grows cautious and quietly
alarmed. He examines their faces.*

LEDUC: What's the procedure?

MONCEAU: They've just started—that businessman was the
first.

LEBEAU, *to Leduc and Von Berg:* They measure your noses?

LEDUC, *sharply alarmed:* Measure noses?

LEBEAU, *putting thumb and forefinger against the bridge and tip of his nose:* Ya, they measured my nose, right on the street. I tell you what I think . . . *To Bayard:* With your permission.

BAYARD: I don't mind you talking as long as you're serious.

LEBEAU: I think it's to carry stones. It just occurred to me—last Monday a girl I know came up from Marseille—the road is full of detours. They probably need labor. She said there was a crowd of people just carrying stones. Lot of them Jews, she thought; hundreds.

LEDUC: I never heard of forced labor in the Vichy Zone. Is that going on here?

BAYARD: Where do you come from?

LEDUC, *after a slight pause as he decides whether to reveal:* I live in the country. I don't get into town very often. There's been no forced-labor decree, has there?

BAYARD, *to all:* Now, listen. *Everyone turns to his straightforward, certain tone.* I'm going to tell you something, but I don't want anybody quoting me. Is that understood? *They nod. He glances at the door. He turns to Lebeau.* You hear what I said?

LEBEAU: Don't make me out some kind of an idiot. Christ's sake, I know it's serious!

BAYARD, *to the others:* I work in the railroad yards. A thirty-car freight train pulled in yesterday. The engineer is Polish, so I couldn't talk to him, but one of the switchmen says he heard people inside.

LEDUC: Inside the cars?

BAYARD: Yes. It came from Toulouse. I heard there's been a quiet roundup of Jews in Toulouse the last couple of weeks. And what's a Polish engineer doing on a train in southern France? You understand?

LEDUC: Concentration camp?

MONCEAU: Why? A lot of people have been volunteering for work in Germany. That's no secret. They're doubling the ration for anybody who goes.

BAYARD, *quietly:* The cars are locked on the outside. *Slight pause.* And they stink. You can smell the stench a hundred yards away. Babies are crying inside. You can hear them. And women. They don't lock volunteers in that way. I never heard of it.

A long pause.

LEDUC: But I've never heard of them applying the Racial Laws down here. It's still French territory, regardless of the Occupation—they've made a big point of that.

Pause.

BAYARD: The Gypsy bothers me.

LEBEAU: Why?

BAYARD: They're in the same category of the Racial Laws. Inferior.

Leduc and Lebeau slowly turn to look at the Gypsy.

LEBEAU, *turning back quickly to Bayard:* Unless he really stole that pot.

BAYARD: Well, yes, if he stole the pot then of course he—

LEBEAU, *quickly, to the Gypsy:* Hey, listen. *He gives a soft, sharp whistle. The Gypsy turns to him.* You steal that pot? *The Gypsy's face is inscrutable. Lebeau is embarrassed to press this, and more desperate.* You did, didn't you?

GYPSY: No steal, no.

LEBEAU: Look, I've got nothing against stealing. *Indicating the others:* I'm not one of these types. I've slept in parked cars, under bridges—I mean, to me all property is theft anyway so I've got no prejudice against you.

GYPSY: No steal.

LEBEAU: Look . . . I mean you're a Gypsy, so how else can you live, right?

WAITER: He steals everything.

LEBEAU, *to Bayard:* You hear? He's probably in for stealing, that's all.

VON BERG: Excuse me . . . *They turn to him.* Have you all been arrested for being Jewish? *They are silent, suspicious and surprised.* I'm terribly sorry. I had no idea.

BAYARD: I said nothing about being Jewish. As far as I know, nobody here is Jewish.

VON BERG: I'm terribly sorry. *Silence. The moment lengthens. In his embarrassment he laughs nervously.* It's only that I . . . I was buying a newspaper and this gentleman came out of a car and told me I must have my documents checked. I . . . I had no idea.

Silence. Hope is rising in them.

LEBEAU, *to Bayard:* So what'd they grab *him* for?

BAYARD—*he looks at Von Berg for a moment, then addresses all:* I don't understand it, but take my advice. If anything like that happens and you find yourself on that train . . . there are four bolts halfway up the doors on the inside. Try to pick up a nail or a screwdriver, even a sharp stone—you can chisel the wood out around those bolts and the doors will open. I warn you, don't believe anything they tell you—I heard they're working Jews to death in the Polish camps.

MONCEAU: I happen to have a cousin; they sent him to Auschwitz; that's in Poland, you know. I have several letters from him saying he's fine. They've even taught him bricklaying.

BAYARD: Look, friend, I'm telling you what I heard from people who know. *He hesitates.* People who make it their business to know, you understand? Don't listen to any stories about resettlement, or that they're going to teach you a trade or something. If you're on that train get out before it gets where it's going.

Pause.

LEDUC: I've heard the same thing. *They turn to him, and he turns to Bayard.* How would one find tools, you have any idea?

MONCEAU: This is so typical! We're in the French Zone, nobody has said one word to us, and we're already on a train for a concentration camp where we'll be dead in a year.

LEDUC: But if the engineer is a Pole . . .

MONCEAU: So he's a Pole, what does that prove?

BAYARD: All I'm saying is that if you have some kind of tool . . .

LEDUC: I think what this man says should be taken seriously.

MONCEAU: In my opinion you're hysterical. After all, they were picking up Jews in Germany for years before the war, they've been doing it in Paris since they came in—are you telling me all those people are dead? Is that really conceivable to you? War is war, but you still have to keep a certain sense of proportion. I mean Germans are still *people*.

LEDUC: I don't speak this way because they're Germans.

BAYARD: It's that they're Fascists.

LEDUC: Excuse me, no. It's exactly because they are people that I speak this way.

BAYARD: I don't agree with *that*.

MONCEAU—*he looks at Leduc for an instant:* You must have

had a pecular life, is all I can say. I happen to have played in Germany; I know the German people.

LEDUC: I studied in Germany for five years, and in Austria, and I—

VON BERG, *happily:* In Austria! Where?

LEDUC—*again he hesitates, then reveals:* The Psychoanalytic Institute in Vienna.

VON BERG: Imagine!

MONCEAU: You're a psychiatrist. *To the others:* No wonder he's so pessimistic!

VON BERG: Where did you live? I am Viennese.

LEDUC: Excuse me, but perhaps it would be wiser not to speak in . . . detail.

VON BERG, *glancing about as though he had committed a gaffe:* I'm terribly sorry . . . yes, of course. *Slight pause.* I was only curious if you knew Baron Kessler. He was very interested in the medical school.

LEDUC, *with an odd coolness:* No, I was never in that circle.

VON BERG: Oh, but he is extremely democratic. He . . . Shyly: He is my cousin, you see. . . .

LEBEAU: You're a nobleman?

VON BERG: Yes.

LEDUC: What is your name?

VON BERG: Wilhelm Johann Von Berg.

MONCEAU, *astonished, impressed:* The prince?

VON BERG: Yes . . . forgive me, have we met?

MONCEAU, *excited by the honor:* Oh, no. But naturally I've

heard your name. I believe it's one of the oldest houses in Austria.

VON BERG: Oh, that's of no importance any more.

LEBEAU, *turning to Bayard, bursting with hope:* Now, what the hell would they want with an Austrian prince? *Bayard looks at Von Berg, mystified.* I mean . . . *Turning back to Von Berg:* You're Catholic, right?

VON BERG: Yes.

LEDUC: But is your title on your papers?

VON BERG: Oh, yes, my passport.

Pause. They sit silent, on the edge of hope, but bewildered.

BAYARD: Were you . . . political or something?

VON BERG: No, no, I never had any interest in that direction. *Slight pause.* Of course, there is this resentment toward the nobility. That might explain it.

LEDUC: In the Nazis? Resentment?

VON BERG, *surprised:* Yes, certainly.

LEDUC, *with no evident viewpoint but with a neutral but pressing interest in drawing the nobleman out:* Really. I've never been aware of that.

VON BERG: Oh, I assure you.

LEDUC: But on what ground?

VON BERG—*he laughs, embarrassed even to have to suggest he is offended:* You're not asking that seriously.

LEDUC: Don't be offended, I'm simply ignorant of that situation. I suppose I have taken for granted that the aristocracy is . . . always behind a reactionary regime.

VON BERG: Oh, there are some, certainly. But for the most part they never took responsibility, in any case.

LEDUC: That interests me. So you still take seriously the . . . the title and . . .

VON BERG: It is not a "title"; it is my name, my family. Just as you have a name, and a family. And you are not inclined to dishonor them, I presume.

LEDUC: I see. And by responsibility, you mean, I suppose, that—

VON BERG: Oh, I don't know; whatever that means. *He glances at his watch. Pause.*

LEDUC: Please forgive me, I didn't mean to pry into your affairs. *Pause.* I'd never thought about it, but it's obvious now —they *would* want to destroy whatever power you have.

VON BERG: Oh, no, I have no power. And if I did it would be a day's work for them to destroy it. That's not the issue. *Pause.*

LEDUC, *fascinated—he is drawn to some truth in Von Berg:* What is it, then? Believe me, I'm not being critical. Quite the contrary . . .

VON BERG: But these are obvious answers! *He laughs.* I have a certain . . . standing. My name is a thousand years old, and they know the danger if someone like me is perhaps . . . not vulgar enough.

LEDUC: And by vulgar you mean . . .

VON BERG: Well, don't you think Nazism . . . whatever else it may be . . . is an outburst of vulgarity? An ocean of vulgarity?

BAYARD: I'm afraid it's a lot more than that, my friend.

VON BERG, *politely, to Bayard:* I am sure it is, yes.

BAYARD: You make it sound like they have bad table manners, that's all.

VON BERG: They certainly do, yes. Nothing angers them more than a sign of any . . . refinement. It is decadent, you see.

BAYARD: What kind of statement is that? You mean you left Austria because of their table manners?

VON BERG: Table manners, yes; and their adoration of dreadful art; and grocery clerks in uniform telling the orchestra what music it may not play. Vulgarity can be enough to send a man out of his country, yes, I think so.

BAYARD: In other words, if they had good taste in art, and elegant table manners, and let the orchestra play whatever it liked, they'd be all right with you.

VON BERG: But how would that be possible? Can people with respect for art go about hounding Jews? Making a prison of Europe, pushing themselves forward as a race of policemen and brutes? Is that possible for artistic people?

MONCEAU: I'd like to agree with you, Prince von Berg, but I have to say that the German audiences—I've played there— no audience is as sensitive to the smallest nuance of a performance; they sit in the theater with respect, like in a church. And nobody listens to music like a German. Don't you think so? It's a passion with them. *Pause.*

VON BERG, *appalled at the truth:* I'm afraid that is true, yes. *Pause.* I don't know what to say. *He is depressed, deeply at a loss.*

LEDUC: Perhaps it isn't those people who are doing this.

VON BERG: I'm afraid I know many cultivated people who . . . did become Nazis. Yes, they did. Art is perhaps no defense against this. It's curious how one takes certain ideas for granted. Until this moment I had thought of art as a . . . *To Bayard:* You may be right—I don't understand very much about it. Actually, I'm essentially a musician—in an amateur way, of course, and politics has never . . .

The office door opens and Marchand appears, backing out, talking to someone within. He is putting a leather document-wallet into his breast pocket, while with the other hand he holds a white pass.

MARCHAND: That's perfectly all right, I understand perfectly. Good day, gentlemen. *Holding up the pass to them:* I show the pass at the door? Thank you. *Shutting the door, he turns and hurries past the line of prisoners, and, as he passes the Boy . . .*

BOY: What'd they ask you, sir?

Marchand turns up the corridor without glancing at the Boy, and as he approaches the end the Guard, hearing him, appears there. He hands the pass to the Guard and goes out. The Guard moves around the turning of the corridor and disappears.

LEBEAU, *half mystified, half hopeful:* I could have sworn he was a Jew! *To Bayard:* Didn't you think so? *Slight pause.*

BAYARD—*clearly he did think so:* You have papers, don't you?

LEBEAU: Oh sure, I have good papers. *He takes rumpled documents out of his pants pocket.*

BAYARD: Well, just insist they're valid. Maybe that's what he did.

LEBEAU: I wish you'd take a look at them, will you?

BAYARD: I'm no expert.

LEBEAU: I'd like your opinion, though. You seem to know what's going on. How they look to you?

Bayard quickly hides the papers as the office door opens. The Professor appears and indicates the Gypsy.

PROFESSOR: Next. You. Come with me. *The Gypsy gets up and starts toward him. The Professor indicates the pot in the Gypsy's hand.* You can leave that. *The Gypsy hesitates, glances at the pot.* I said leave it there. *The Gypsy puts the pot down on the bench unwillingly.*

GYPSY: Fix. No steal.

PROFESSOR: Go in.

GYPSY, *indicating the pot, warning the others:* That's mine.

The Gypsy goes into the office. The Professor follows him in and shuts the door. Bayard takes the pot, bends the handle off, puts it in his pocket, and sets the pot back where it was.

LEBEAU, *turning back to Bayard, indicating his papers:* What do you think?

BAYARD—*he holds a paper up to the light, turns it over, gives it back to Lebeau:* Look good far as I can tell.

MONCEAU: That man did seem Jewish to me. Didn't he to you, Doctor?

LEDUC: I have no idea. Jews are not a race, you know. They can look like anybody.

LEBEAU, *with the joy of near-certainty:* He just probably had good papers. Because I know people have papers, I mean all you have to do is look at them and you know they're phony. But I mean if you have good papers, right? *Monceau has meanwhile taken out his papers and is examining them. The Boy does the same with his. Lebeau turns to Leduc.* That's true, though. My father looks like an Englishman. The trouble is, I took after my mother.

BOY, *to Bayard, offering his paper:* Could you look at mine?

BAYARD: I'm no expert, kid. Anyway, don't sit there looking at them like that.

Monceau puts his away, as the Boy does. A pause. They wait.

MONCEAU: I think it's a question of one's credibility—that man just now did carry himself with a certain confidence. . . .

The Old Jew begins to pitch forward onto the floor. Von Berg catches him and with the Boy helps him back onto the seat.

LEBEAU, *with heightened nervousness:* Christ, you'd think they'd shave off their beards. I mean, to walk around with a beard like that in a country like this! *Monceau looks at his beard, and Lebeau touches it.* Well, I just don't waste time shaving, but . . .

VON BERG, *to the Old Jew:* Are you all right, sir?

Leduc bends over Von Berg's lap and feels the Old Jew's pulse. Pause. He lets his hand go, and looks toward Lebeau.

LEDUC: Were you serious? They actually measured your nose?

LEBEAU: With his fingers. That civilian. They called him "professor." *Pause. Then, to Bayard:* I think you're right; it's all a question of your papers. That businessman certainly looked Jewish. . . .

MONCEAU: I'm not so sure now.

LEBEAU, *angrily:* A minute ago you were sure, now suddenly . . . !

MONCEAU: Well, even if he wasn't—it only means it really is a general checkup. On the whole population.

LEBEAU: Hey, that's right too! *Slight pause.* Actually, I'm often taken for a gentile myself. Not that I give a damn but most of the time, I . . . *To Von Berg:* How about you, they measure your nose?

VON BERG: No, they told me to get into the car, that was all.

LEBEAU: Because actually yours looks bigger than mine.

BAYARD: Will you cut that out! Just cut it out, will you?

LEBEAU: Can't I try to find out what I'm in for?

BAYARD: Did you ever think of anything beside yourself? Just because you're an artist? You people demoralize everybody!

LEBEAU, *with unconcealed terror:* What the hell am I supposed to think of? Who're you thinking of?

The office door opens. The Police Captain appears, and gestures toward Bayard.

CAPTAIN: Come inside here. *Bayard, trying hard to keep his knees from shaking, stands. Ferrand, a café proprietor, comes hurrying down the corridor with a tray of coffee things covered with a large napkin. He has an apron on.* Ah, at last!

FERRAND: Sorry, Captain, but for you I had to make some fresh.

CAPTAIN, *as he goes into the office behind Ferrand:* Put it on my desk.

The door is closed. Bayard sits, wipes his face. Pause.

MONCEAU, *to Bayard, quietly:* Would you mind if I made a suggestion? *Bayard turns to him, already defensive.* You looked terribly uncertain of yourself when you stood up just now.

BAYARD, *taking offense:* Me uncertain? You've got the wrong man.

MONCEAU: Please, I'm not criticizing you.

BAYARD: Naturally I'm a little nervous, facing a room full of Fascists like this.

MONCEAU: But that's why one must seem especially self-confident. I'm quite sure that's what got that businessman through so quickly. I've had similar experiences on trains, and even in Paris when they stopped me several times. The important thing is not to look like a victim. Or even to feel like one. They can be very stupid, but they do have a sense for victims; they know when someone has nothing to hide.

LEDUC: But how does one avoid feeling like a victim?

MONCEAU: One must create one's own reality in this world. I'm an actor, we do this all the time. The audience, you know, is very sadistic; it looks for your first sign of weakness. So you must try to think of something that makes you feel self-assured; anything at all. Like the day, perhaps, when your father gave you a compliment, or a teacher was amazed at your cleverness . . . Any thought—*to Bayard*—that makes you feel . . . valuable. After all, you are trying to create an illusion; to make them believe you are who your papers say you are.

LEDUC: That's true, we must not play the part they have written for us. That's very wise. You must have great courage.

MONCEAU: I'm afraid not. But I have talent instead. *To Bayard:* One must show them the face of a man who is right, not a man who is suspect and wrong. They sense the difference.

BAYARD: My friend, you're in a bad way if you have to put on an act to feel your rightness. The bourgeoisie sold France; they let in the Nazis to destroy the French working class. Remember the causes of this war and you've got *real* confidence.

LEDUC: Excepting that the causes of this war keep changing so often.

BAYARD: Not if you understand the economic and political forces.

LEDUC: Still, when Germany attacked us the Communists refused to support France. They pronounced it an imperialist war. Until the Nazis turned against Russia; then in one afternoon it all changed into a sacred battle against tyranny. What confidence can one feel from an understanding that turns upside down in an afternoon?

BAYARD: My friend, without the Red Army standing up to them right now you could forget France for a thousand years!

LEDUC: I agree. But that does not require an understanding of political and economic forces—it is simply faith in the Red Army.

BAYARD: It is faith in the future; and the future is Socialist. And that is what I take in there with me. *To the others:* I warn you—I've had experience with these types. You'd better ram a viewpoint up your spine or you'll break in half.

LEDUC: I understand. You mean it's important not to feel alone, is that it?

BAYARD: None of us is alone. We're members of history. Some of us don't know it, but you'd better learn it for your own preservation.

LEDUC: That we are . . . symbols.

BAYARD, *uncertain whether to agree:* Yes. Why not? Symbols, yes.

LEDUC: And you feel that helps you. Believe me, I am genuinely interested.

BAYARD: It helps me because it's the truth. What am I to them personally? Do they know me? You react personally to this, they'll turn you into an idiot. You can't make sense of this on a personal basis.

LEDUC: I agree. *Personally:* But the difficulty is—what can one be if not oneself? For example, the thought of torture or something of that sort . . .

BAYARD, *struggling to live his conviction:* Well, it frightens me —of course. But they can't torture the future; it's out of their hands. Man was not made to be the slave of Big Business. Whatever they do, something inside me is laughing. Because they can't win. Impossible. *He has stiffened himself against his rising fear.*

LEDUC: So that in a sense . . . you aren't here. You personally.

BAYARD: In a sense. Why, what's wrong with that?

LEDUC: Nothing; it may be the best way to hold on to oneself. It's only that ordinarily one tries to experience life, to be in spirit where one's body is. For some of us it's difficult to shift gears and go into reverse. But that's not a problem for you.

BAYARD, *solicitously:* You think a man can ever be himself in this society? When millions go hungry and a few live like kings, and whole races are slaves to the stock market—how can you be yourself in such a world? I put in ten hours a day for a few francs, I see people who never bend their backs and they own the planet. . . . How can my spirit be where my body is? I'd have to be an ape.

VON BERG: Then where is your spirit?

BAYARD: In the future. In the day when the working class is master of the world. *That's* my confidence . . . *To Monceau:* Not some borrowed personality.

VON BERG, *wide-eyed, genuinely asking:* But don't you think . . . excuse me. Are not most of the Nazis . . . of the working class?

BAYARD: Well, naturally, with enough propaganda you can confuse anybody.

VON BERG: I see. *Slight pause.* But in that case, how can one have such confidence in them?

BAYARD: Who do you have confidence in, the aristocracy?

VON BERG: Very little. But in certain aristocrats, yes. And in certain common people.

BAYARD: Are you telling me that history is a question of "certain people"? Are we sitting here because we are "certain people"? Is any of us an individual to them? Class interest makes history, not individuals.

VON BERG: Yes. That seems to be the trouble.

BAYARD: Facts are not trouble. A human being has to glory in the facts.

VON BERG, *with a deep, anxious out-reaching to Bayard:* But the facts . . . Dear sir, what if the facts are dreadful? And will always be dreadful?

BAYARD: So is childbirth, so is . . .

VON BERG: But a child comes of it. What if nothing comes of the facts but endless, endless disaster? Believe me, I am happy to meet a man who is not cynical; any faith is precious these days. But to give your faith to a . . . a class of people is impossible, simply impossible—ninety-nine per cent of the Nazis are ordinary working-class people!

BAYARD: I concede it *is* possible to propagandize . . .

VON BERG, *with an untoward anxiety, as though the settlement of this issue is intimate with him:* But what can *not* be propagandized? Isn't that the . . . the only point? A few individuals. Don't you think so?

BAYARD: You're an intelligent man, Prince. Are you seriously telling me that five, ten, a thousand, ten thousand decent people of integrity are all that stand between us and the end of everything? You mean this whole world is going to hang on that thread?

VON BERG, *struck:* I'm afraid it does sound impossible.

BAYARD: If I thought that, I wouldn't have the strength to walk through that door, I wouldn't know how to put one foot in front of the other.

VON BERG, *after a slight pause:* Yes. I hadn't really considered it that way. But . . . you really think the working class will . . .

BAYARD: They will destroy Fascism because it is against their interest.

VON BERG—*he nods:* But in that case, isn't it even more of a mystery?

BAYARD: I see no mystery.

VON BERG: But they adore Hitler.

BAYARD: How can you say that? Hitler is the creation of the capitalist class.

VON BERG, *in terrible mourning and anxiety:* But they adore him! My own cook, my gardeners, the people who work in my forests, the chauffeur, the gamekeeper—they are *Nazis!* I saw it coming over them, the love for this creature—my house-keeper dreams of him in her bed, she'd serve my breakfast like a god had slept with her; in a dream slicing my toast! I saw this adoration in my own house! That, that is the dreadful fact. *Controlling himself:* I beg your pardon, but it disturbs me. I admire your faith; all faith to some degree is beautiful. And when I know that yours is based on something so untrue—it's terribly disturbing. *Quietly:* In any case, I cannot glory in the facts; there is no reassurance there. They adore him, the salt of the earth. . . . *Staring:* Adore him. *There is a burst of laughter from within the office. He glances there, as they all do.* Strange; if I did not know that some of them in there were French, I'd have said they laugh like Germans. I suppose vulgarity has no nation, after all.

The door opens. Mr. Ferrand comes out, laughing; within, the laughter is subsiding. He waves within, closing the door. His smile drops. And as he goes past the Waiter, he glances back at the door, then quickly leans over and whispers hurriedly into his ear. They all watch. Now Ferrand starts away. The Waiter reaches out and grasps his apron.

WAITER: Ferrand!

FERRAND, *brushing the Waiter's hand off his apron:* What can I do? I told you fifty times to get out of this city! Didn't I? *Starting to weep:* Didn't I?

He hurries up the corridor, wiping his tears with his apron. They all watch the Waiter, who sits there staring.

BAYARD: What? Tell me. Come on, I'm next, what'd he say?

WAITER, *whispering, staring ahead in shock:* It's not to work.

LEDUC, *leaning over toward him to hear:* What?

WAITER: They have furnaces.

BAYARD: What furnaces? . . . Talk! What is it?

WAITER: He heard the detectives; they came in for coffee just before. People get burned up in furnaces. It's not to work. They burn you up in Poland.

Silence. A long moment passes.

MONCEAU: That is the most fantastic idiocy I ever heard in my life!

LEBEAU, *to the Waiter:* As long as you have regular French papers, though . . . There's nothing about Jew on *my* papers.

WAITER, *in a loud whisper:* They're going to look at your penis.

The Boy stands up as though with an electric shock. The door of the office opens; the Police Captain appears and beckons to Bayard. The Boy quickly sits.

CAPTAIN: You can come now.

Bayard stands, assuming an artificial and almost absurd posture of confidence. But approaching the Captain he achieves an authority.

BAYARD: I'm a master electrician with the railroad, Captain. You may have seen me there. I'm classified First Priority War Worker.

CAPTAIN: Inside.

BAYARD: You can check with Transport Minister Duquesne.

CAPTAIN: You telling me my business?

BAYARD: No, but we can all use advice from time to time.

CAPTAIN: Inside.

BAYARD: Right.

Without hesitation Bayard walks into the office, the Captain following and closing the door.

A long silence. Monceau, after a moment, smooths out a rough place on the felt of his hat. Lebeau looks at his papers, slowly rubbing his beard with the back of his hand, staring in terror. The Old Jew draws his bundle deeper under his feet. Leduc takes out a nearly empty pack of cigarettes, starts to take one for himself, then silently stands, crosses the line of men, and offers it to them. Lebeau takes one.

They light up. Faintly, from the next-door building, an accordion is heard playing a popular tune.

LEBEAU: Leave it to a cop to play now.

WAITER: No, that's the boss's son, Maurice. They're starting to serve lunch.

Leduc, who has returned to his position as the last man on the bench, cranes around the corner of the corridor, observes, and sits back.

LEDUC, *quietly:* There's only one guard at the door. Three men could take him.

Pause. No one responds. Then . . .

VON BERG, *apologetically:* I'm afraid I'd only get in your way. I have no strength in my hands.

MONCEAU, *to Leduc:* You actually believe that, Doctor? About the furnaces?

LEDUC—*he thinks; then:* I believe it is possible, yes. Come, we can do something.

MONCEAU: But what good are dead Jews to them? They want free labor. It's senseless. You can say whatever you like, but the Germans are not illogical; there's no conceivable advantage for them in such a thing.

LEDUC: You can be sitting here and still speak of advantages? Is there a rational explanation for your sitting here? But you are sitting here, aren't you?

MONCEAU: But an atrocity like that is . . . beyond any belief.

VON BERG: That is exactly the point.

MONCEAU: *You* don't believe it. Prince, you can't tell me you believe such a thing.

VON BERG: I find it the most believable atrocity I have heard.

LEBEAU: But why?

Slight pause.

VON BERG: Because it *is* so inconceivably vile. That is their power. To do the inconceivable; it paralyzes the rest of us. But if that is its purpose it is not the cause. Many times I used to ask my friends—if you love your country why is it necessary to hate other countries? To be a good German why must you despise everything that is not German? Until I realized the answer. They do these things not because they are German but because they are nothing. It is the hallmark of the age—the less you exist the more important it is to make a clear impression. I can see them discussing it as a kind of . . . truthfulness. After all, what *is* self-restraint but hypocrisy? If you despise Jews the most honest thing is to burn them up. And the fact that it costs money, and uses up trains and personnel—this only guarantees the integrity, the purity, the existence of their feelings. They would even tell you that only a Jew would think of the cost. They are poets, they are striving for a new nobility, the nobility of the totally vulgar. I believe in this fire; it would prove for all time that they exist, yes, and that they were sincere. You must not calculate these people with some nine-teenth-century arithmetic of loss and gain. Their motives are musical, and people are merely sounds they play. And in my opinion, win or lose this war, they have pointed the way to the future. What one used to conceive a human being to be will have no room on this earth. I would try anything to get out.

A pause.

MONCEAU: But they arrested you. That German professor is an expert. There is nothing Jewish about you. . . .

VON BERG: I have an accent. I noticed he reacted when I started to speak. It is an Austrian inflection. He may think I am another refugee.

The door opens. The Professor comes out, and indicates the Waiter.

PROFESSOR: Next. You. *The Waiter makes himself small, pressing up against Lebeau.* Don't be alarmed, it's only to check your papers.

The Waiter suddenly bends over and runs away—around the corner and up the corridor. The Guard appears at the end, collars him, and walks him back down the corridor.

WAITER, *to the Guard:* Felix, you know me. Felix, my wife will go crazy. Felix . . .

PROFESSOR: Take him in the office.

The Police Captain appears in the office doorway.

GUARD: There's nobody at the door.

CAPTAIN—*he grabs the Waiter from the Guard:* Get in here, you Jew son-of-a-bitch. . . . *He throws the Waiter into the office; the Waiter collides with the Major, who is just coming out to see what the disturbance is. The Major grips his thigh in pain, pushing the Waiter clear. The Waiter slides to the Major's feet, weeping pleadingly. The Captain strides over and violently jerks him to his feet and pushes him into the office, going in after him. From within, unseen:* You want trouble? You want trouble?

The Waiter is heard crying out; there is the sound of blows struck. Quiet. The Professor starts toward the door. The Major takes his arm and leads him down to the extreme forward edge of the stage, out of hearing of the prisoners.

MAJOR: Wouldn't it be much simpler if they were just asked whether they . . .

Impatiently, without replying, the Professor goes over to the line of prisoners.

PROFFESSOR: Will any of you admit right now that you are carrying forged identification papers? *Silence.* So. In short, you are all bona fide Frenchmen. *Silence. He goes over to the Old Jew, bends into his face.* Are there any Jews among you? *Silence. Then he returns to the Major.* There's the problem, Major; either we go house by house investigating everyone's biography, or we make this inspection.

MAJOR: That electrician fellow just now, though—I thought he made a point there. In fact, only this morning in the hospital, while I was waiting my turn for X-ray, another officer, a German officer, a captain, in fact—his bathrobe happened to fall open . . .

PROFFESOR: It is entirely possible.

MAJOR: It was unmistakable, Professor.

PROFESSOR: Let us be clear, Major; the Race Institute does not claim that circumcision is conclusive proof of Jewish blood. The Race Institute recognizes that a small proportion of gentiles . . .

MAJOR: I don't see any reason not to say it, Professor—I happen to be, myself.

PROFESSOR: Very well, but I certainly would never mistake you for a Jew. Any more than you could mistake a pig for a horse. Science is not capricious, Major; my degree is in racial anthropology. In any case, we can certainly separate the gentiles by this kind of examination. *He has taken the Major's arm to lead him back to the office.*

MAJOR: Excuse me. I'll be back in a few minutes. *Moving to leave:* You can carry on without me.

PROFESSOR: Major; you have your orders; you are in command of this operation. I must insist you take your place beside me.

MAJOR: I think some mistake has been made. I am a line officer, I have no experience with things of this kind. My training is engineering and artillery. *Slight pause.*

PROFESSOR—*he speaks more quietly, his eyes ablaze:* We'd better be candid, Major. Are you refusing this assignment?

MAJOR, *registering the threat he feels:* I'm in pain today, Professor. They are still removing fragments. In fact, I understood I was only to . . . hold this desk down until an SS officer took over. I'm more or less on loan, you see, from the regular Army.

PROFESSOR—*he takes his arm, draws him down to the edge of the stage again:* But the Army is not exempt from carrying out the Racial Program. My orders come from the top. And my report will go to the top. You understand me.

MAJOR—*his resistance seems to fall:* I do, yes.

PROFESSOR: Look now, if you wish to be relieved, I can easily telephone General von—

MAJOR: No—no, that's all right. I . . . I'll be back in a few minutes.

PROFESSOR: This is bizarre, Major—how long am I supposed to wait for you?

MAJOR, *holding back an outburst of resentment:* I need a walk. I am not used to sitting in an office. I see nothing bizarre in it, I am a line officer, and this kind of business takes a little getting used to. *Through his teeth:* What do you find bizarre in it?

PROFESSOR: Very well.

Slight pause.

MAJOR: I'll be back in ten minutes. You can carry on.

PROFESSOR: I will not continue without you, Major. The Army's responsibility is quite as great as mine here.

MAJOR: I won't be long.

The Professor turns abruptly and strides into the office, slamming the door shut. Very much wanting to get out, the Major goes up the corridor. Leduc stands as he passes.

LEDUC: Major . . .

The Major limps past him without turning, up the corridor and out. Silence.

BOY: Mister? *Leduc turns to him.* I'd try it with you.

LEDUC, *to Monceau and Lebeau:* What about you two?

LEBEAU: Whatever you say, but I'm so hungry I wouldn't do you much good.

LEDUC: You can walk up to him and start an argument. Distract his attention. Then we—

MONCEAU: You're both crazy, they'll shoot you down.

LEDUC: Some of us might make it. There's only one man at the door. This neighborhood is full of alleyways—you could disappear in twenty yards.

MONCEAU: How long would you be free—an hour? And when they catch you they'll really tear you apart.

BOY: Please! I have to get out. I was on my way to the pawnshop. *Takes out a ring.* It's my mother's wedding ring, it's all that's left. She's waiting for the money. They have nothing in the house to eat.

MONCEAU: You take my advice, boy; don't do anything, they'll let you go.

LEDUC: Like the electrician?

MONCEAU: He was obviously a Communist. And the waiter irritated the Captain.

LEBEAU: Look, I'll try it with you but don't expect too much; I'm weak as a chicken, I haven't eaten since yesterday.

LEDUC, *to Monceau:* It would be better with another man. The boy is very light. If you and the boy rush him I'll get his gun away.

VON BERG, *to Leduc, looking at his hands:* Forgive me.

Monceau springs up, goes to a box, and sits.

MONCEAU: I am not going to risk my life for nothing. That businessman had a Jewish face. *To Lebeau:* You said so yourself.

LEBEAU, *to Leduc, appeasingly:* I did. I thought so. Look, if your papers are good, maybe that's it.

LEDUC, *to Lebeau and Monceau:* You know yourself the Germans have been moving into the Southern Zone; you see they are picking up Jews; a man has just told you that you are marked for destruction. . . .

MONCEAU, *indicating Von Berg:* They took him in. Nobody's explained it.

VON BERG: My accent . . .

MONCEAU: My dear Prince, only an idiot could mistake you

for anything but an Austrian of the upper class. I took you for nobility the minute you walked in.

LEDUC: But if it's a general checkup why would they be looking at penises?

MONCEAU: There's no evidence of that!

LEDUC: The waiter's boss . . .

MONCEAU, *suppressing a nervous shout:* He overheard two French detectives who can't possibly know anything about what happens in Poland. And if they do that kind of thing, it's not the end either—I had Jew stamped on my passport in Paris and I was playing Cyrano at the same time.

VON BERG: Really! Cyrano!

LEBEAU: Then why'd you leave Paris?

MONCEAU: It was an absolutely idiotic accident. I was rooming with another actor, a gentile. And he kept warning me to get out. But naturally one doesn't just give up a role like that. But one night I let myself be influenced by him. He pointed out that I had a number of books which were on the forbidden list—of Communist literature—I mean things like Sinclair Lewis, and Thomas Mann, and even a few things by Friedrich Engels, which everybody was reading at one time. And I decided I might as well get rid of them. So we made bundles and I lived on the fifth floor of a walkup and we'd take turns going down to the street and just leaving them on benches or in doorways or anywhere at all. It was after midnight, and I was just dropping a bundle into the gutter near the Opéra, when I noticed a man standing in a doorway watching me. At that moment I realized that I had stamped my name and address in every one of those books.

VON BERG: Hah! What did you do?

MONCEAU: Started walking, and kept right on down here to

the Unoccupied Zone. *An outcry of remorse:* But in my opinion, if I'd done nothing at all I might still be working!

LEDUC, *with higher urgency, but deeply sympathetic, to Monceau:* Listen to me for one moment. I beg you. There is only one man guarding that door; we may never get another chance like this again.

LEBEAU: That's another thing; if it was all that serious, wouldn't they be guarding us more heavily? I mean, that's a point.

LEDUC: That is exactly the point. They are relying on us.

MONCEAU: Relying on us!

LEDUC: Yes. To project our own reasonable ideas into their heads. It is reasonable that a light guard means the thing is not important. They rely on our own logic to immobilize ourselves. But you have just told us how you went all over Paris advertising the fact that you owned forbidden books.

MONCEAU: But I didn't do it purposely.

LEDUC: May I guess that you could no longer bear the tension of remaining in Paris? But that you wanted to keep your role in Cyrano and had to find some absolute compulsion to save your own life? It was your unconscious mind that saved you. Do you understand? You cannot wager your life on a purely rational analysis of this situation. Listen to your feelings; you must certainly *feel* the danger here. . . .

MONCEAU, *in high anxiety:* I played in Germany. That audience could not burn up actors in a furnace. *Turning to Von Berg:* Prince, you cannot tell me you believe that!

VON BERG, *after a pause:* I supported a small orchestra. When the Germans came into Austria three of the players prepared to escape. I convinced them no harm would come to them; I brought them to my castle; we all lived together. The oboist was twenty, twenty-one—the heart stopped when he played certain tones. They came for him in the garden. They took him out of his chair. The instrument lay on the lawn like a dead bone. I made certain inquiries; he is dead now. And it was even more terrible—they came and sat down and listened until the rehearsal was over. And *then* they took him. It is as though they wished to take him at exactly the moment when he was most beautiful. I know how you feel—but I tell you nothing any longer is forbidden. Nothing. *Tears are in his eyes; he turns to Leduc.* I ask you to forgive me, Doctor. *Pause.*

BOY: Will they let you go?

VON BERG, *with a guilty glance at the Boy:* I suppose. If this is all to catch Jews, they will let me go.

BOY: Would you take this ring? And bring it back to my mother? *He stretches his hand out with the ring. Von Berg does not touch it.* Number Nine Rue Charlot. Top floor. Hirsch. Sarah Hirsch. She has long brown hair . . . be sure it's her. She has a little beauty mark on this cheek. There are two other families in the apartment, so be sure it's her.

Von Berg looks into the Boy's face. Silence. Then he turns to Leduc.

VON BERG: Come. Tell me what to do. I'll try to help you. *To Leduc:* Doctor?

LEDUC: I'm afraid it's hopeless.

VON BERG: Why?

LEDUC—*he stares ahead, then looks at Lebeau:* He's weak with hunger, and the boy's like a feather. I wanted to get away, not just slaughtered. *Pause. With bitter irony:* I live in the country, you see; I haven't talked to anybody in so long, I'm afraid I came in here with the wrong assumptions.

MONCEAU: If you're trying to bait me, Doctor, forget it.

LEDUC: Would you mind telling me, are you religious?

MONCEAU: Not at all.

LEDUC: Then why do you feel this desire to be sacrificed?

MONCEAU: I ask you to stop talking to me.

LEDUC: But you are making a gift of yourself. You are the only able-bodied man here, aside from me, and yet you feel no impulse to do something? I don't understand your air of confidence.

Pause.

MONCEAU: I refuse to play a part I do not fit. Everyone is playing the victim these days; hopeless, hysterical, they always assume the worst. I have papers; I will present them with the single idea that they must be honored. I think that is exactly what saved that businessman. You accuse us of acting the part the Germans created for us; I think you're the one who's doing that by acting so desperate.

LEDUC: And if, despite your act, they throw you into a freight car?

MONCEAU: I don't think they will.

LEDUC: But if they do. You certainly have enough imagination to visualize that.

MONCEAU: In that case, I will have done my best. I know what failure is; it took me a long time to make good; I haven't the personality for leading roles; everyone said I was crazy to stay in the profession. But I did, and I imposed my idea on others.

LEDUC: In other words, you will create yourself.

MONCEAU: Every actor creates himself.

LEDUC: But when they tell you to open your fly? *Monceau is silent, furious.* Please don't stop now; I'm very interested. How do you regard that moment? *Monceau is silent.* Believe me, I am only trying to understand this. I am incapable of penetrating such passivity; I ask you what is in your mind when you face the command to open your fly. I am being as impersonal, as scientific as I know how to be—I believe I am going to be murdered. What do you believe will happen when they point to that spot between your legs?

Pause.

MONCEAU: I have nothing to say to you.

LEBEAU: I'll tell you what I'll feel. *Indicating Von Berg:* I'll wish I was him.

LEDUC: To be someone else.

LEBEAU, *exhausted:* Yes. To have been arrested by mistake. God—to see them relaxing when they realize I am innocent.

LEDUC: You feel guilty, then.

LEBEAU—*he has gradually become closer to exhaustion:* A little, I guess. Not for anything I've done but . . . I don't know why.

LEDUC: For being a Jew, perhaps?

LEBEAU: I'm not ashamed of being a Jew.

LEDUC: Then why feel guilty?

LEBEAU: I don't know. Maybe it's that they keep saying such terrible things about us, and you can't answer. And after years and years of it, you . . . I wouldn't say you believe it, but . . . you do, a little. It's a funny thing—I used to say to my mother and father just what you're saying. We could have gone to America a month before the invasion. But they wouldn't leave Paris. She had this brass bed, and carpets, and draperies and all kinds of junk. Like him with his Cyrano. And I told them, "You're doing just what they want you to do!" But, see, people won't believe they can be killed. Not them with their brass bed and their carpets and their faces. . . .

LEDUC: But do you believe it? It seems to me you don't believe it yourself.

LEBEAU: I believe it. They only caught me this morning because I . . . I always used to walk in the morning before I sat down to work. And I wanted to do it again. I knew I shouldn't go outside. But you get tired of believing in the truth. You get tired of seeing things clearly. *Pause.* I always collected my illusions in the morning. I could never paint what I saw, only what I imagined. And this morning, danger or no danger, I just had to get out, to walk around, to see something real, something else but the inside of my head . . . and I hardly turned the corner and that motherless son-of-a-bitch of a scientist got out of the car with his fingers going for my nose. . . . *Pause.* I believe I can die. But you can get so tired . . .

LEDUC: That it's not too bad.

LEBEAU: Almost, yes.

LEDUC, *glancing at them all:* So that one way or the other, with illusions or without them, exhausted or fresh—we have been trained to die. The Jew and the gentile both.

MONCEAU: You're still trying to bait me, Doctor, but if you want to commit suicide do it alone, don't involve others. The fact is there are laws and every government enforces its laws; and I want it understood that I have nothing to do with any of this talk.

LEDUC, *angering now:* Every government does not have laws condemning people because of their race.

MONCEAU: I beg your pardon. The Russians condemn the middle class, the English have condemned the Indians, Africans, and anybody else they could lay their hands on, the French, the Italians . . . every nation has condemned somebody because of his race, including the Americans and what they do to Negroes. The vast majority of mankind is condemned because of its race. What do you advise all these people—suicide?

LEDUC: What do you advise?

MONCEAU, *seeking and finding conviction:* I go on the assumption that if I obey the law with dignity I will live in peace. I may not like the law, but evidently the majority does, or they would overthrow it. And I'm speaking now of the French majority, who outnumber the Germans in this town fifty to one. These are French police, don't forget, not German. And if by some miracle you did knock out that guard you would find yourself in a city where not one person in a thousand would help you. And it's got nothing to do with being Jewish or not Jewish. It is what the world is, so why don't you stop insulting others with romantic challenges!

LEDUC: In short, because the world is indifferent you will wait calmly and with great dignity—to open your fly.

MONCEAU—*frightened and furious, he stands:* I'll tell you what I think; I think it's people like you who brought this on us. People who give Jews a reputation for subversion, and this Talmudic analysis, and this everlasting, niggling discontent.

LEDUC: Then I will tell you that I was wrong before; you didn't advertise your name on those forbidden books in order to find a reason to leave Paris and save yourself. It was in order to get yourself caught and be put out of your misery. Your heart is conquered territory, mister.

MONCEAU: If we meet again you will pay for that remark.

LEDUC: Conquered territory! *He leans forward, his head in his hands.*

BOY, *reaching over to hand the ring to Von Berg:* Will you do it? Number nine Rue Charlot?

VON BERG, *deeply affected:* I will try. *He takes the ring. The Boy immediately stands.*

LEDUC: Where are you going? *The Boy, terrified but desperate, moves on the balls of his feet to the corridor and peeks around the corner. Leduc stands, tries to draw him back.* You can't; it'll take three men to . . . *The boy shakes loose and walks rapidly up the hallway. Leduc hesitates, then goes after him.* Wait! Wait a minute! I'm coming.

The Major enters the corridor at its far end. The Boy halts, Leduc now beside him. For a moment they stand facing him. Then they turn and come down the corridor and sit, the Major following them. He touches Leduc's sleeve, and Leduc stands and follows him downstage.

MAJOR—*he is "high," with drink and a flow of emotion:* That's impossible. Don't try it. There are sentries on both corners. *Glancing toward the office door:* Captain, I would only like to say that . . . this is all as inconceivable to me as it is to you. Can you believe that?

LEDUC: I'd believe it if you shot yourself. And better yet, if you took a few of them with you.

MAJOR, *wiping his mouth with the back of his hand:* We would all be replaced by tomorrow morning, wouldn't we?

LEDUC: We might get out alive, though; you could see to that.

MAJOR: They'd find you soon.

LEDUC: Not me.

MAJOR, *with a manic amusement, yet deeply questioning:* Why do you deserve to live more than I do?

LEDUC: Because I am incapable of doing what you are doing. I am better for the world than you.

MAJOR: It means nothing to you that I have feelings about this?

LEDUC: Nothing whatever, unless you get us out of here.

MAJOR: And then what? Then what?

LEDUC: I will remember a decent German, an honorable German.

MAJOR: Will that make a difference?

LEDUC: I will love you as long as I live. Will anyone do that now?

MAJOR: That means so much to you—that someone love you?

LEDUC: That I be worthy of someone's love, yes. And respect.

MAJOR: It's amazing; you don't understand anything. Nothing of that kind is left, don't you understand that yet?

LEDUC: It is left in me.

MAJOR, *more loudly, a fury rising in him:* There are no persons any more, don't you see that? There will never be persons again. What do I care if you love me? Are you out of your mind? What am I, a dog that I must be loved? You—*turning to all of them*—goddamned Jews! *The door opens; the Professor and the Police Captain appear.* Like dogs, Jew-dogs. Look at him—*indicating the Old Jew*—with his paws folded. Look what happens when I yell at him. Dog! He doesn't move. Does he move? Do you see him moving? *He strides to the Professor and takes him by the arm.* But we move, don't we? We measure your noses, don't we, Herr Professor, and we look at your cocks, we keep moving continually!

PROFESSOR, *with a gesture to draw him inside:* Major . . .

MAJOR: Hands off, you civilian bastard.

PROFESSOR: I think . . .

MAJOR, *drawing his revolver:* Not a word!

PROFESSOR: You're drunk.

The Major fires into the ceiling. The prisoners tense in shock.

MAJOR: Everything stops now. *He goes in thought, revolver cocked in his hand, and sits beside Lebeau.* Now it is all stopped. *His hands are shaking. He sniffs in his running nose. He crosses his legs to control them, and looks at Leduc, who is still standing.* Now you tell me. You tell me. Now nothing is moving. You tell me. Go ahead now.

LEDUC: What shall I tell you?

MAJOR: Tell me how . . . how there can be persons any more. I have you at the end of this revolver—*indicates the Professor*—he has me—and somebody has him—and somebody has somebody else. Now tell me.

LEDUC: I told you.

MAJOR: I won't repeat it. I am a man of honor. What do you make of that? I will not tell them what you advised me to do. What do you say—damned decent of me, isn't it . . . not to repeat your advice? *Leduc is silent. The Major gets up, comes to Leduc. Pause.* You are a combat veteran.

LEDUC: Yes.

MAJOR: No record of subversive activities against the German authority.

LEDUC: No.

MAJOR: If you were released, and the others were kept . . . would you refuse? *Leduc starts to turn away. The Major nudges him with the pistol, forcing him face to face.* Would you refuse?

LEDUC: No.

MAJOR: And walk out of that door with a light heart?

LEDUC—*he is looking at the floor now:* I don't know. *He starts to put his trembling hands into his pockets.*

MAJOR: Don't hide your hands. I am trying to understand why you are better for the world than me. Why do you hide your hands? Would you go out that door with a light heart, run to your woman, drink a toast to your skin? . . . Why are you better than anybody else?

LEDUC: I have no duty to make a gift of myself to your sadism.

MAJOR: But I do? To others' sadism? Of myself? I have that duty and you do not? To make a gift of myself?

LEDUC—*he looks at the Professor and the Police Captain, glances back at the Major:* I have nothing to say.

MAJOR: That's better. *He suddenly gives Leduc an almost comradely push and nearly laughs. He puts his gun away, turns swaying to the Professor and with a victorious shout:* Next! *The Major brushes past the Professor into the office. Lebeau has not moved.*

PROFESSOR: This way.

Lebeau stands up, starts sleepily toward the corridor, turns about, and moves into the office, the Professor following him.

CAPTAIN, *to Leduc:* Get back there.

Leduc returns to his seat. The Captain goes into the office; the door shuts. Pause.

MONCEAU: You happy now? You got him furious. You happy?

The door opens; the Captain appears, beckoning to Monceau.

CAPTAIN: Next.

Monceau gets up at once; taking papers out of his jacket, he fixes a smile on his face and walks with erect elegance to the Captain and with a slight bow, his voice cheerful:

MONCEAU: Good morning, Captain. *He goes right into the office; the Captain follows and shuts the door. Pause.*

BOY: Number nine Rue Charlot. Please.

VON BERG: I'll give it to her.

BOY: I'm a minor. I'm not even fifteen. Does it apply to minors? *Captain opens the door, beckons to the Boy. Standing:* I'm a minor. I'm not fifteen until February . . .

CAPTAIN: Inside.

BOY, *halting before the Captain:* I could get my birth certificate for you.

CAPTAIN, *prodding him along:* Inside, inside.

They go in. The door shuts. The accordion is heard again from next door. The Old Jew begins to rock back and forth slightly, praying softly. Von Berg, his hand trembling as it passes down his cheek, stares at the Old Jew, then turns to Leduc on his other side. The three are alone now.

VON BERG: Does he realize what is happening?

LEDUC, *with an edgy note of impatience:* As much as anyone can, I suppose.

VON BERG: He seems to be watching it all from the stars. *Slight pause.* I wish we could have met under other circumstances. There are a great many things I'd like to have asked you.

LEDUC, *rapidly, sensing the imminent summons:* I'd appreciate it if you'd do me a favor.

VON BERG: Certainly.

LEDUC: Will you go and tell my wife?

VON BERG: Where is she?

LEDUC: Take the main highway north two kilometers. You'll see a small forest on the left and a dirt road leading into it. Go about a kilometer until you see the river. Follow the river to a small mill. They are in the tool shed behind the wheel.

VON BERG, *distressed:* And . . . what shall I say?

LEDUC: That I've been arrested. And that there may be a possibility I can . . . *Breaks off.* No, tell her the truth.

VON BERG, *alarmed:* What do you mean?

LEDUC: The furnaces. Tell her that.

VON BERG: But actually . . . that's only a rumor, isn't it?

LEDUC, *turning to him, sharply:* I don't regard it as a rumor. It should be known. I never heard of it before. It must be known. Just take her aside—there's no need for the children to hear it, but tell her.

VON BERG: It's only that it would be difficult for me. To tell such a thing to a woman.

LEDUC: If it's happening, you can find a way to say it, can't you?

VON BERG—*he hesitates, sensing Leduc's resentment:* Very well. I'll tell her. It's only that I have no great . . . facility with women. But I'll do as you say. *Pause. He glances to the door.* They're taking longer with that boy. Maybe he *is* too young, you suppose? *Leduc does not answer. Von Berg seems suddenly hopeful.* They would stick to the rules, you know. . . . In fact, with the shortage of physicians, you suppose they—*He breaks off.* I'm sorry if I said anything to offend you.

LEDUC, *struggling with his anger:* That's all right. *Slight pause. His voice is trembling with anger.* It's just that you keep finding these little shreds of hope, and it's a little difficult.

VON BERG: Yes, I see. I beg your pardon. I understand. *Pause. Leduc glances at the door; he is shifting about in high tension.* Would you like to talk of something else, perhaps? Are you interested in . . . in music?

LEDUC, *desperately trying to control himself:* It's really quite simple. It's that you'll survive, you see.

VON BERG: But I can't help that, can I?

LEDUC: That only makes it worse! I'm sorry, one isn't always in control of one's emotions.

VON BERG: Doctor, I can promise you—it will not be easy for me to walk out of here. You don't know me.

LEDUC—*he tries not to reply; then:* I'm afraid it will only be difficult because it is so easy.

VON BERG: I think that's unfair.

LEDUC: Well, it doesn't matter.

VON BERG: It does to me. I . . . I can tell you that I was very close to suicide in Austria. Actually, that is why I left. When they murdered my musicians—not that alone, but when I told the story to many of my friends there was hardly any reaction. That was almost worse. Do you understand such indifference?

LEDUC—*he seems on the verge of an outbreak:* You have a curious idea of human nature. It's astounding you can go on with it in these times.

VON BERG, *with hand on heart:* But what is left if one gives up one's ideals? What *is* there?

LEDUC: Who are you talking about? You? Or me?

VON BERG: I'm terribly sorry. . . . I understand.

LEDUC: Why don't you just stop talking. I can't listen to anything. *Slight pause.* Forgive me. I do appreciate your feeling. *Slight pause.* I see it too clearly, perhaps—I know the violence inside these people's heads. It's difficult to listen to amelioration, even if it's well-meant.

VON BERG: I had no intention of ameliorating—

LEDUC: I think you do. And you must; you will survive, you will have to ameliorate it; just a little, just enough. It's no reflection on you. *Slight pause.* But, you see, this is why one gets so furious. Because all this suffering is so pointless—it can never be a lesson, it can never have a meaning. And that is why it will be repeated again and again forever.

VON BERG: Because it cannot be shared?

LEDUC: Yes. Because it cannot be shared. It is total, absolute waste. *He leans forward suddenly, trying to collect himself against his terror. He glances at the door.* How strange—one can even become impatient. *A groan as he shakes his head with wonder and anger at himself.* Hm!—what devils they are.

VON BERG, *with an overtone of closeness to Leduc:* You understand now why I left Vienna. They can make death seductive. It is their worst sin. I had dreams at night—Hitler in a great flowing cloak, almost like a gown, almost like a woman. He was beautiful.

LEDUC: Listen—don't mention the furnaces to my wife.

VON BERG: I'm glad you say that, I feel very relieved, there's really no point . . .

LEDUC, *in a higher agony as he realizes:* No, it's . . . it's . . . You see there was no reason for me to be caught here. We have a good hideout. They'd never have found us. But she has an exposed nerve in one tooth and I thought I might find some codein. Just say I was arrested.

VON BERG: Does she have sufficient money?

LEDUC: You could help her that way if you like. Thank you.

VON BERG: The children are small?

LEDUC: Two and three.

VON BERG: How dreadful. How dreadful. *He looks with a glance of fury at the door.* Do you suppose if I offered him something? I can get hold of a good deal of money. I know so little about people—I'm afraid he's rather an idealist. It could infuriate him more.

LEDUC: You might try to feel him out. I don't know what to tell you.

VON BERG: How upside down everything is—to find oneself wishing for a money-loving cynic!

LEDUC: It's perfectly natural. We have learned the price of idealism.

VON BERG: And yet can one wish for a world without ideals? That's what's so depressing—one doesn't know what to wish for.

LEDUC, *in anger:* You see, I knew it when I walked down the road, I knew it was senseless! For a goddamned toothache! So what, so she doesn't sleep for a couple of weeks! It was perfectly clear I shouldn't be taking the chance.

VON BERG: Yes, but if one loves someone . . .

LEDUC: We are not in love any more. It's just too difficult to separate in these times.

VON BERG: Oh, how terrible.

LEDUC, *more softly, realizing a new idea:* Listen . . . about the furnaces . . . don't mention that to her. Not a word, please. *With great self-contempt:* God, at a time like this—to think of taking vengeance on her! What scum we are! *He almost sways in despair.*

Pause. Von Berg turns to Leduc; tears are in his eyes.

VON BERG: There is nothing, is that it? For you there is nothing?

LEDUC, *flying out at him suddenly:* Well, what do you propose? Excuse me, but what in hell are you talking about?

The door opens. The Professor comes out and beckons to the Old Jew. He seems upset, by an argument he had in the office, possibly.

PROFESSOR: Next. *The Old Jew does not turn to him.* You hear me, why do you sit there? *He strides to the Old Jew and lifts him to his feet brusquely. The man reaches down to pick up his bundle, but the Professor tries to push it back to the floor.* Leave that. *With a wordless little cry, the Old Jew clings to his bundle.* Leave it! *The Professor strikes at the Old Jew's hand, but he only holds on tighter, uttering his wordless little cries. The Police Captain comes out as the Professor pulls at the bundle.* Let go of that! *The bundle rips open. A white cloud of feathers blows up out of it. For an instant everything stops as the Professor looks in surprise at the feathers floating down. The Major appears in the doorway as the feathers settle.*

CAPTAIN: Come on.

The Captain and the Professor lift the Old Jew and carry him past the Major into the office. The Major with deadened eyes glances at the feathers and limps in, closing the door behind him.
  Leduc and Von Berg stare at the feathers, some of which have fallen on them. They silently brush them off. Leduc picks the last one off his jacket, opens his fingers, and lets it fall to the floor.
  Silence. Suddenly a short burst of laughter is heard from the office.

VON BERG, *with great difficulty, not looking at Leduc:* I would like to be able to part with your friendship. Is that possible?

Pause.

LEDUC: Prince, in my profession one gets the habit of looking at oneself quite impersonally. It is not you I am angry with. In one part of my mind it is not even this Nazi. I am only angry that I should have been born before the day when man has accepted his own nature; that he is *not* reasonable, that he is full of murder, that his ideas are only the little tax he pays for the right to hate and kill with a clear conscience. I am only angry that, knowing this, I still deluded myself. That there was not time to truly make part of myself what I know, and to teach others the truth.

VON BERG, *angered, above his anxiety:* There are ideals, Doctor, of another kind. There are people who would find it easier to die than stain one finger with this murder. They exist. I swear it to you. People for whom everything is *not* permitted, foolish people and ineffectual, but they do exist and will not dishonor their tradition. *Desperately:* I ask your friendship.

Again laughter is heard from within the office. This time it is louder. Leduc slowly turns to Von Berg.

LEDUC: I owe you the truth, Prince; you won't believe it now, but I wish you would think about it and what it means. I have never analyzed a gentile who did not have, somewhere hidden in his mind, a dislike if not a hatred for the Jews.

VON BERG, *clapping his ears shut, springing up:* That is impossible, it is not true of me!

LEDUC, *standing, coming to him, a wild pity in his voice:* Until you know it is true of you, you will destroy whatever truth can come of this atrocity. Part of knowing who we are is knowing we are not someone else. And Jew is only the name we give to that stranger, that agony we cannot feel, that death we look at like a cold abstraction. Each man has his Jew; it is the other. And the Jews have their Jews. And now, now above all, you must see that you have yours—the man whose death leaves you relieved that you are not him, despite your decency. And that is why there is nothing and will be nothing—until you face your own complicity with this . . . your own humanity.

VON BERG: I deny that. I deny that absolutely. I have never in my life said a word against your people. Is that your implication? That I have something to do with this monstrousness! I have put a pistol to my head! To my head!

Laughter is heard again.

LEDUC, *hopelessly:* I'm sorry; it doesn't really matter.

VON BERG: It matters very much to me. Very much to me!

LEDUC, *in a level tone full of mourning; and yet behind it a howling horror:* Prince, you asked me before if I knew your cousin, Baron Kessler. *Von Berg looks at him, already with anxiety.* Baron Kessler is a Nazi. He helped to remove all the Jewish doctors from the medical school. *Von Berg is struck; his eyes glance about.* You were aware of that, weren't you? *Half-hysterical laughter comes from the office.* You must have heard that at some time or another, didn't you?

VON BERG, *stunned, inward-seeing:* Yes. I heard it. I . . . had forgotten it. You see, he was . . .

LEDUC: . . . Your cousin. I understand. *They are quite joined; and Leduc is mourning for the Prince as much as for himself, despite his anger.* And in any case, it is only a small part of Baron Kessler to you. I do understand it. But it is all of Baron Kessler to me. When you said his name it was with love; and I'm sure he must be a man of some kindness, with whom you can see eye to eye in many things. But when I hear that name I see a knife. You see now why I say there is nothing, and will be nothing, when even you cannot really put yourself in my place? Even you! And that is why your thoughts of suicide do not move me. It's not your guilt I want, it's your responsibility—that might have helped. Yes, if you had understood that Baron Kessler was in part, in some part, in some small and frightful part—doing your will. You might have done something then, with your standing, and your name and your decency, aside from shooting yourself!

VON BERG, *in full horror, his face upthrust, calling:* What can ever save us? *He covers his face with his hands.*

The door opens. The Professor comes out.

PROFESSOR, *beckoning to the Prince:* Next. *Von Berg does not turn, but holds Leduc in his horrified, beseeching gaze. The Professor approaches the Prince.* Come! *The Professor reaches down to take Von Berg's arm. Von Berg angrily brushes away his abhorrent hand.*

VON BERG: *Hände weg!*

The Professor retracts his hand, immobilized, surprised, and for a moment has no strength against his own recognition of authority. Von Berg turns back to Leduc, who glances up at him and smiles with warmth, then turns away.

Von Berg turns toward the door and, reaching into his breast pocket for a wallet of papers, goes into the office. The Professor follows and closes the door.

Alone, Leduc sits motionless. Now he begins the movements of the trapped; he swallows with difficulty, crosses and recrosses his legs. Now he is still again and bends over and cranes around the corner of the corridor to look for the guard. A movement of his foot stirs up feathers. The accordion is heard outside. He angrily kicks a feather off his foot. Now he makes a decision; he quickly reaches into his pocket, takes out a clasp knife, opens the blade, and begins to get to his feet, starting for the corridor.

The door opens and Von Berg comes out. In his hand is a white pass. The door shuts behind him. He is looking at the pass as he goes by Leduc, and suddenly turns, walks back, and thrusts the pass into Leduc's hand.

VON BERG, *in a strangely angered whisper, motioning him out:* Take it! Go! *Von Berg sits quickly on the bench, taking out the wedding ring. Leduc stares at him, a horrified look on his face. Von Berg hands him the ring.* Number nine Rue Charlot. Go.

LEDUC, *in a desperate whisper:* What will happen to you?

VON BERG, *angrily waving him away:* Go, go!

Leduc backs away, his hands springing to cover his eyes in the awareness of his own guilt.

LEDUC, *a plea in his voice:* I wasn't asking you to do this! You don't owe me this!

VON BERG: Go!

Leduc, his eyes wide in awe and terror, suddenly turns and strides up the corridor. At the end of it the Guard appears, hearing his footsteps. He gives the Guard the pass and disappears.

A long pause. The door opens. The Professor appears.

PROFESSOR: Ne— *He breaks off, looks about, then, to Von Berg:* Where's your pass? *Von Berg stares ahead. The Professor calls into the office.* Man escaped! *He runs up the corridor, calling.* Man escaped! Man escaped!

The Police Captain rushes out of the office. Voices are heard outside calling orders. The accordion stops. The Major hurries out of the office. The Police Captain rushes past him.

CAPTAIN: What? *Glancing back at Von Berg, he realizes and rushes up the corridor, calling:* Who let him out! Find that man! What happened?

The voices outside are swept away by a siren going off. The Major has gone to the opening of the corridor, following the Police Captain. For a moment he remains looking up the corridor. All that can be heard now is the siren moving off in pursuit. It dies away, leaving the Major's rapid and excited breaths, angry breaths, incredulous breaths.

Now he turns slowly to Von Berg, who is staring straight ahead. Von Berg turns and faces him. Then he gets to his feet. The moment lengthens, and lengthens yet. A look of anguish and fury is stiffening the Major's face; he is closing his fists. They stand there, forever incomprehensible to one another, looking into each other's eyes.

At the head of the corridor four new men, prisoners, appear. Herded by the Detectives, they enter the detention room and sit on the bench, glancing about at the ceiling, the walls, the feathers on the floor, and the two men who are staring at each other so strangely. CURTAIN

The Price

THE CAST

(in order of appearance)

VICTOR FRANZ	Pat Hingle
ESTHER FRANZ	Kate Reid
GREGORY SOLOMON	Harold Gary
WALTER FRANZ	Arthur Kennedy

Directed by Ulu Grosbard; produced by Robert Whitehead.
Opened February 7, 1968, Morosco Theatre, New York City.

Act One

Today. New York.

Two windows are seen at the back of the stage. Daylight filters through their sooty panes, which have been X'd out with fresh whitewash to prepare for the demolition of the building.

Now daylight seeps through a skylight in the ceiling, grayed by the grimy panes. The light from above first strikes an overstuffed armchair in center stage. It has a faded rose slipcover. Beside it on its right, a small table with a filigreed radio of the Twenties on it and old newspapers; behind it a bridge lamp. At its left an old wind-up Victrola and a pile of records on a low table. A white cleaning cloth and a mop and pail are nearby.

The room is progressively seen. The area around the armchair alone appears to be lived-in, with other chairs and a couch related to it. Outside this area, to the sides and back limits of the room and up the walls, is the chaos of ten rooms of furniture squeezed into this one.

There are four couches and three settees strewn at random over the floor; armchairs, wingbacks, a divan, occasional chairs. On the floor and stacked against the three walls up to the ceiling are bureaus, armoires, a tall secretary, a breakfront, a long, elaborately carved serving table, end tables, a library table, desks, glass-front bookcases, bow-front glass cabinets, and so forth. Several long rolled-up rugs and some shorter ones. A long sculling oar, bedsteads, trunks. And overhead one large and one smaller

345

*crystal chandelier hang from ropes, not connected to electric
wires. Twelve dining-room chairs stand in a row along a dining-
room table at left.*

*There is a rich heaviness, something almost Germanic, about
the furniture, a weight of time upon the bulging fronts and curving
chests marshalled against the walls. The room is monstrously
crowded and dense, and it is difficult to decide if the stuff is impressive or merely over-heavy and ugly.*

*An uncovered harp, its gilt chipped, stands alone downstage,
right. At the back, behind a rather makeshift drape, long since
faded, can be seen a small sink, a hotplate, and an old icebox. Up
right, a door to the bedroom. Down left, a door to the corridor
and stairway, which are unseen.*

*We are in the attic of a Manhattan brownstone soon to be torn
down.*

*From the down-left door, Police Sergeant Victor Franz enters
in uniform. He halts inside the room, glances about, walks at random a few feet, then comes to a halt. Without expression, yet
somehow stilled by some emanation from the room, he lets his
gaze move from point to point, piece to piece, absorbing its
sphinxlike presence.*

*He moves to the harp with a certain solemnity, as toward a
coffin, and, halting before it, reaches out and plucks a string. He
turns and crosses to the dining-room table and removes his gun
belt and jacket, hanging them on a chair which he has taken off
the table, where it had been set upside down along with two others.*

*He looks at his watch, waiting for time to pass. Then his eye
falls on the pile of records in front of the phonograph. He raises
the lid of the machine, sees a record already on the turntable,
cranks, and sets the tone arm on the record. Gallagher and Shean
sing. He smiles at the corniness.*

*With the record going he moves to the long sculling oar which
stands propped against furniture and touches it. Now he recalls
something, reaches in behind a chest, and takes out a fencing foil*

*and mask. He snaps the foil in the air, his gaze held by memory.
He puts the foil and mask on the table, goes through two or three
records on the pile, and sees a title that makes him smile widely.
He replaces the Gallagher and Shean record with this. It is a
Laughing Record—two men trying unsuccessfully to get out a
whole sentence through their wild hysteria.*

*He smiles. Broader. Chuckles. Then really laughs. It gets into
him; he laughs more fully. Now he bends over with laughter, taking an unsteady step as helplessness rises in him.*

*Esther, his wife, enters from the down-left door. His back is to
her. A half-smile is already on her face as she looks about to see
who is laughing with him. She starts toward him, and he hears
her heels and turns.*

ESTHER: What in the world is that?

VICTOR, *surprised:* Hi! *He lifts the tone arm, smiling, a little embarrassed.*

ESTHER: Sounded like a party in here! *He gives her a peck. Of
the record:* What *is* that?

VICTOR, *trying not to disapprove openly:* Where'd you get a
drink?

ESTHER: I told you. I went for my checkup. *She laughs with a
knowing abandonment of good sense.*

VICTOR: Boy, you and that doctor. I thought he told you not
to drink.

ESTHER—*she laughs:* I had one! One doesn't hurt me. Everything's normal anyway. He sent you his best. *She looks about.*

VICTOR: Well, that's nice. The dealer's due in a few minutes, if
you want to take anything.

ESTHER, *looking around with a sigh:* Oh, dear God—here it is
again.

VICTOR: The old lady did a nice job.

ESTHER: Ya—I never saw it so clean. *Indicating the room:* Make you feel funny?

VICTOR, *shrugging:* No, not really. She didn't recognize me, imagine?

ESTHER: Dear boy, it's a hundred and fifty years. *Shaking her head as she stares about:* Huh.

VICTOR: What?

ESTHER: Time.

VICTOR: I know.

ESTHER: There's something different about it.

VICTOR: No, it's all the way it was. *Indicating one side of the room:* I had my desk on that side and my cot. The rest is the same.

ESTHER: Maybe it's that it always used to seem so pretentious to me, and kind of bourgeois. But it does have a certain character. I think some of it's in style again. It's surprising.

VICTOR: Well, you want to take anything?

ESTHER, *looking about, hesitating:* I don't know if I want it around. It's all so massive . . . where would we put any of it? That chest is lovely. *She goes to it.*

VICTOR: That was mine. *Indicating one across the room:* The one over there was Walter's. They're a pair.

ESTHER, *comparing:* Oh ya! Did you get hold of him?

VICTOR—*he rather glances away, as though this has been an issue:* I called again this morning—he was in consultation.

ESTHER: Was he in the office?

VICTOR: Ya. The nurse went and talked to him for a minute—it doesn't matter. As long as he's notified so I can go ahead.

She suppresses comment, picks up a lamp. That's probably real porcelain. Maybe it'd go in the bedroom.

ESTHER, *putting the lamp down:* Why don't I meet you somewhere? The whole thing depresses me.

VICTOR: Why? It won't take long. Relax. Come on, sit down; the dealer'll be here any minute.

ESTHER, *sitting on a couch:* There's just something so damned rotten about it. I can't help it; it always was. The whole thing is infuriating.

VICTOR: Well, don't get worked up. We'll sell it and that'll be the end of it. I picked up the tickets, by the way.

ESTHER: Oh, good. *Laying her head back:* Boy, I hope it's a good picture.

VICTOR: Better be. Great, not good. Two-fifty apiece.

ESTHER, *with sudden protest:* I don't care! I want to go somewhere. *She aborts further response, looking around.* God, what's it all about? When I was coming up the stairs just now, and all the doors hanging open . . . It doesn't seem possible . . .

VICTOR: They tear down old buildings every day in the week, kid.

ESTHER: I know, but it makes you feel a hundred years old. I hate empty rooms. *She muses.* What was that screwball's name?—rented the front parlor, remember?—repaired saxophones?

VICTOR, *smiling:* Oh—Saltzman. *Extending his hand sideways:* With the one eye went out that way.

ESTHER: Ya! Every time I came down the stairs, there he was waiting for me with his four red hands! How'd he ever get all those beautiful girls?

VICTOR—*he laughs:* God knows. He must've smelled good.

She laughs, and he does. He'd actually come running up here sometimes; middle of the afternoon—"Victor, come down quick, I got extras!"

ESTHER: And you did, too!

VICTOR: Why not? If it was free, you took it.

ESTHER, *blushing:* You never told me that.

VICTOR: No, that was before you. Mostly.

ESTHER: You dog.

VICTOR: So what? It was the Depression. *She laughs at the non sequitur.* No, really—I think people were friendlier; lot more daytime screwing in those days. Like the McLoughlin sisters —remember, with the typing service in the front bedroom? *He laughs.* My father used to say, "In that typing service it's two dollars a copy."

She laughs. It subsides.

ESTHER: And they're probably all dead.

VICTOR: I guess Saltzman would be—he was well along. Although—*He shakes his head, laughs softly in surprise.* Jeeze, he wasn't either. I think he was about . . . my age now. Huh!

Caught by the impact of time, they stare for a moment in silence.

ESTHER—*she gets up, goes to the harp:* Well, where's your dealer?

VICTOR, *glancing at his watch:* It's twenty to six. He should be here soon. *She plucks the harp.* That should be worth something.

ESTHER: I think a lot of it is. But you're going to have to bargain, you know. You can't just take what they say . . .

VICTOR, *with an edge of protest: I* can bargain; don't worry, I'm not giving it away.

ESTHER: Because they *expect* to bargain.

VICTOR: Don't get depressed already, will you? We didn't even start. *I* intend to bargain, I know the score with these guys.

ESTHER—*she withholds further argument, goes to the phonograph; firing up some slight gaiety:* What's this record?

VICTOR: It's a Laughing Record. It was a big thing in the Twenties.

ESTHER, *curiously:* You remember it?

VICTOR: Very vaguely. I was only five or six. Used to play them at parties. You know—see who could keep a straight face. Or maybe they just sat around laughing; I don't know.

ESTHER: That's a wonderful idea!

Their relation is quite balanced, so to speak; he turns to her.

VICTOR: You look good. *She looks at him, an embarrassed smile.* I mean it. I *said* I'm going to bargain, why do you . . . ?

ESTHER: I believe you. This is the suit.

VICTOR: Oh, is that it! And how much? Turn around.

ESTHER, *turning:* Forty-five, imagine? He said nobody'd buy it, it was too simple.

VICTOR, *seizing the agreement:* Boy, women are dumb; that is really handsome. See, I don't mind if you get something for your money, but half the stuff they sell is such crap . . . *Going to her:* By the way, look at this collar. Isn't this one of the ones you just bought?

ESTHER, *examining it:* No, that's an older one.

VICTOR: Well, even so. *Turning up a heel:* Ought to write to Consumers Union about these heels. Three weeks—look at them!

ESTHER: Well, you don't walk straight. You're not going in uniform, I hope.

VICTOR: I could've murdered that guy! I'd just changed, and McGowan was trying to fingerprint some bum and he didn't want to be printed; so he swings out his arm just as I'm going by, right into my container.

ESTHER, *as though this symbolized:* Oh, God . . .

VICTOR: I gave it to that quick cleaner, he'll try to have it by six.

ESTHER: Was there cream and sugar in the coffee?

VICTOR: Ya.

ESTHER: He'll never have it by six.

VICTOR, *assuagingly:* He's going to try.

ESTHER: Oh, forget it.

Slight pause. Seriously disconsolate, she looks around at random.

VICTOR: Well, it's only a movie . . .

ESTHER: But we go out so rarely—why must everybody know your salary? I want an evening! I want to sit down in a restaurant without some drunken ex-cop coming over to the table to talk about old times.

VICTOR: It happened twice. After all these years, Esther, it would seem to me . . .

ESTHER: I know it's unimportant—but like that man in the museum; he really did—he thought you were the sculptor.

VICTOR: So I'm a sculptor.

ESTHER, *bridling:* Well, it was nice, that's all! You really do, Vic—you look distinguished in a suit. Why not? *Laying her head back on the couch:* I should've taken down the name of that scotch.

VICTOR: All scotch is chemically the same.

ESTHER: I know; but some is better.

VICTOR, *looking at his watch:* Look at that, will you? Five-thirty sharp, he tells me. People say anything. *He moves with a heightened restlessness, trying to down his irritation with her mood. His eye falls on a partly opened drawer of a chest, and he opens it and takes out an ice skate.* Look at that, they're still good! *He tests the edge with his fingernail; she merely glances at him.* They're even sharp. We ought to skate again sometime. *He sees her unremitting moodiness.* Esther, I said I would bargain! You see?—you don't know how to drink; it only depresses you.

ESTHER: Well, it's the kind of depression I enjoy!

VICTOR: Hot diggity dog.

ESTHER: I have an idea.

VICTOR: What?

ESTHER: Why don't you leave me? Just send me enough for coffee and cigarettes.

VICTOR: Then you'd *never* have to get out of bed.

ESTHER: I'd get out. Once in a while.

VICTOR: I got a better idea. Why don't you go off for a couple of weeks with your doctor? Seriously. It might change your viewpoint.

ESTHER: I wish I could.

VICTOR: Well, do it. He's got a suit. You could even take the dog—especially the dog. *She laughs.* It's not funny. Every time you go out for one of those walks in the rain I hold my breath what's going to come back with you.

ESTHER, *laughing:* Oh, go on, you love her.

VICTOR: I love her! You get plastered, you bring home strange animals, and I "love" them! I do not love that goddamned dog!

She laughs with affection, as well as with a certain feminine defiance.

ESTHER: Well, I want her!

VICTOR, *after a pause:* It won't be solved by a dog, Esther. You're an intelligent, capable woman, and you can't lay around all day. Even something part-time, it would give you a place to go.

ESTHER: I don't need a place to go. *Slight pause.* I'm not quite used to Richard not being there, that's all.

VICTOR: He's gone, kid. He's a grown man; you've got to do something with yourself.

ESTHER: I can't go to the same place day after day. I never could and I never will. Did you *ask* to speak to your brother?

VICTOR: I asked the nurse. Yes. He couldn't break away.

ESTHER: That son of a bitch. It's sickening.

VICTOR: Well, what are you going to do? He never had that kind of feeling.

ESTHER: What feeling? To come to the phone after sixteen years? It's common decency. *With sudden intimate sympathy:* You're furious, aren't you?

VICTOR: Only at myself. Calling him again and again all week like an idiot . . . To hell with him, I'll handle it alone. It's just as well.

ESTHER: What about his share? *He shifts; pressed and annoyed.* I don't want to be a pest—but I think there could be some money here, Vic. *He is silent.* You're going to raise that with him, aren't you?

VICTOR, *with a formed decision:* I've been thinking about it. He's got a right to his half, why should he give up anything?

ESTHER: I thought you'd decided to put it to him?

VICTOR: I've changed my mind. I don't really feel he owes me anything, I can't put on an act.

ESTHER: But how many Cadillacs can he drive?

VICTOR: That's why he's got Cadillacs. People who love money don't give it away.

ESTHER: I don't know why you keep putting it like charity. There's such a thing as a moral debt. Vic, you made his whole career possible. What law said that only he could study medicine—?

VICTOR: Esther, please—let's not get back on that, will you?

ESTHER: I'm not back on anything—you were even the better student. That's a real debt, and he ought to be made to face it. He could never have finished medical school if you hadn't taken care of Pop. I mean we ought to start talking the way people talk! There could be some real money here.

VICTOR: I doubt that. There are no antiques or—

ESTHER: Just because it's ours why must it be worthless?

VICTOR: Now what's that for?

ESTHER: Because that's the way we think! We do!

VICTOR, *sharply:* The man won't even come to the phone, how am I going to—?

ESTHER: Then you write him a letter, bang on his door. This *belongs* to you!

VICTOR, *surprised, seeing how deadly earnest she is:* What are you so excited about?

ESTHER: Well, for one thing it might help you make up your mind to take your retirement.

A slight pause.

VICTOR, *rather secretively, unwillingly:* It's not the money been stopping me.

ESTHER: Then what is it? *He is silent.* I just thought that with a little cushion you could take a month or two until something occurs to you that you want to do.

VICTOR: It's all I think about right now, I don't have to quit to think.

ESTHER: But nothing seems to come of it.

VICTOR: Is it that easy? I'm going to be fifty. You don't just start a whole new career. I don't understand why it's so urgent all of a sudden.

ESTHER—*she laughs:* All of a sudden! It's all I've been talking about since you became eligible. I've been saying the same thing for three years!

VICTOR: Well, it's not three years—

ESTHER: It'll be three years in March! It's *three years.* If you'd gone back to school then you'd almost have your Master's by now; you might have had a chance to get into something you'd love to do. Isn't that true? Why can't you make a move?

VICTOR, *after a pause—he is almost ashamed:* I'll tell you the truth. I'm not sure the whole thing wasn't a little unreal. I'd be fifty-three, fifty-four by the time I could start doing anything.

ESTHER: But you always knew that.

VICTOR: It's different when you're right on top of it. I'm not sure it makes any sense now.

ESTHER, *moving away, the despair in her voice:* Well . . . this is exactly what I tried to tell you a thousand times. It makes the same sense it ever made. But you might have twenty more years, and that's still a long time. Could do a lot of interesting things in that time. *Slight pause.* You're so young, Vic.

VICTOR: I am?

ESTHER: Sure! I'm not, but you are. God, all the girls goggle at you, what do you want?

VICTOR—*he laughs emptily:* It's hard to discuss it, Es, because I don't understand it.

ESTHER: Well, why not talk about what you don't understand? Why do you expect yourself to be an authority?

VICTOR: Well, one of us is got to stay afloat, kid.

ESTHER: You want me to pretend everything is great? I'm bewildered and I'm going to act bewildered! *It flies out as though long suppressed:* I've asked you fifty times to write a letter to Walter—

VICTOR, *like a repeated story:* What's this with Walter again? What's Walter going to—?

ESTHER: He is an important scientist, and that hospital's building a whole new research division. I saw it in the paper, it's his hospital.

VICTOR: Esther, the man hasn't called me in sixteen years.

ESTHER: But neither have you called him! *He looks at her in surprise.* Well, you haven't. That's also a fact.

VICTOR, *as though the idea were new and incredible:* What would I call him for?

ESTHER: Because, he's your brother, he's influential, and he could help—Yes, that's how people do, Vic! Those articles he wrote had a real idealism, there was a genuine human quality. I mean people do change, you know.

VICTOR, *turning away:* I'm sorry, I don't need Walter.

ESTHER: I'm not saying you have to approve of him; he's a selfish bastard, but he just might be able to put you on the track of something. I don't see the humiliation.

VICTOR, *pressed, irritated:* I don't understand why it's all such an emergency.

ESTHER: Because I don't know where in hell I am, Victor! *To her own surprise, she has ended nearly screaming. He is silent. She retracts.* I'll do anything if I know why, but all these years we've been saying, once we get the pension we're going to start to live. . . . It's like pushing against a door for twenty-five years and suddenly it opens . . . and we stand there. Sometimes I wonder, maybe I misunderstood you, maybe you like the department.

VICTOR: I've hated every minute of it.

ESTHER: I did everything wrong! I swear, I think if I demanded more it would have helped you more.

VICTOR: That's not true. You've been a terrific wife—

ESTHER: I don't think so. But the security meant so much to you I tried to fit into that; but I was wrong. God—just before coming here, I looked around at the apartment to see if we could use any of this—and it's all so ugly. It's worn and shabby and tasteless. And I have good taste! I know I do! It's that everything was always temporary with us. It's like we never were anything, we were always about-to-be. I think back to the war when any idiot was making so much money— that's when you should have quit, and I knew it, I knew it!

VICTOR: That's when I wanted to quit.

ESTHER: I only had one drink, Victor, so don't—

VICTOR: Don't change the whole story, kid. I wanted to quit, and you got scared.

ESTHER: Because you said there was going to be a depression after the war.

VICTOR: Well, go to the library, look up the papers around 1945, see what they were saying!

ESTHER: I don't care! *She turns away—from her own irrationality.*

VICTOR: I swear, Es, sometimes you make it sound like we've had no life at all.

ESTHER: God—my mother was so right! I can never believe what I see. I knew you'd never get out if you didn't during the war—I saw it happening, and I said nothing. You know what the goddamned trouble is?

VICTOR, *glancing at his watch, as he senses the end of her revolt:* What's the goddamned trouble?

ESTHER: We can never keep our minds on money! We worry about it, we talk about it, but we can't seem to *want* it. I do, but you don't. I really do, Vic. I want it. Vic? *I want money!*

VICTOR: Congratulations.

ESTHER: You go to hell!

VICTOR: I wish you'd stop comparing yourself to other people, Esther! That's all you're doing lately.

ESTHER: Well, I can't help it!

VICTOR: Then you've got to be a failure, kid, because there's always going to be somebody up ahead of you. What happened? I have a certain nature; just as you do—I didn't change—

ESTHER: But you have changed. You've been walking around like a zombie ever since the retirement came up. You've gotten so vague—

VICTOR: Well, it's a decision. And I'd like to feel a little more certain about it. . . . Actually, I've even started to fill out the forms a couple of times.

ESTHER, *alerted:* And?

VICTOR, *with difficulty—he cannot understand it himself:* I suppose there's some kind of finality about it that . . . *He breaks off.*

ESTHER: But what else did you expect?

VICTOR: It's stupid; I admit it. But you look at that goddamned form and you can't help it. You sign your name to twenty-eight years and you ask yourself, Is that all? Is that it? And it is, of course. The trouble is, when I think of starting something new, that number comes up—five oh—and the steam goes out. But I'll do something. I will! *With a greater closeness to her now:* I don't know what it is; every time I think about it all—it's almost frightening.

ESTHER: What?

VICTOR: Well, like when I walked in here before . . . *He looks around.* This whole thing—it hit me like some kind of craziness. Piling up all this stuff here like it was made of gold. *He half-laughs, almost embarrassed.* I brought up every stick; damn near saved the carpet tacks. *He turns to the center chair.* That whole way I was with him—it's inconceivable to me now.

ESTHER, *with regret over her sympathy:* Well . . . you loved him.

VICTOR: I know, but it's all words. What was he? A busted businessman like thousands of others, and I acted like some kind of a mountain crashed. I tell you the truth, every now and then the whole thing is like a story somebody told me. You ever feel that way?

ESTHER: All day, every day.

VICTOR: Oh, come on—

ESTHER: It's the truth. The first time I walked up those stairs I was nineteen years old. And when you opened that box with your first uniform in it—remember that? When you put it on the first time?—how we laughed? If anything happened you said you'd call a cop! *They both laugh.* It was like a masquerade. And we were right. That's when we were right.

VICTOR, *pained by her pain:* You know, Esther, every once in a while you try to sound childish and it—

ESTHER: I mean to be! I'm sick of the— Oh, forget it, I want a drink. *She goes for her purse.*

VICTOR, *surprised:* What's that, the great adventure? Where are you going all of a sudden?

ESTHER: I can't stand it in here, I'm going for a walk.

VICTOR: Now you cut out this nonsense!

ESTHER: I am not an alcoholic!

VICTOR: You've had a good life compared to an awful lot of people! You trying to turn into a goddamned teenager or something?

ESTHER, *indicating the furniture:* Don't talk childishness to me, Victor—not in this room! You let it lay here all these years because you can't have a simple conversation with your own brother, and I'm childish? You're still eighteen years old with that man! I mean I'm stuck, but I admit it!

VICTOR, *hurt:* Okay. Go ahead.

ESTHER—*she can't quite leave:* You got a receipt? I'll get your suit. *He doesn't move. She makes it rational:* I just want to get out of here.

VICTOR—*he takes out a receipt and gives it to her; his voice is cold:* It's right off Seventh. The address is on it. *He moves from her.*

ESTHER: I'm coming back right away.

VICTOR, *freeing her to her irresponsibility:* Do as you please, kid. I mean it.

ESTHER: You were grinding your teeth again last night. Did you know that?

VICTOR: Oh! No wonder my ear hurts.

ESTHER: I wish I had a tape recorder. I mean it, it's gruesome; sounds like a lot of rocks coming down a mountain. I wish you could hear it, you wouldn't take this self-sufficient attitude.

He is silent, alarmed, hurt. He moves upstage as though looking at the furniture.

VICTOR: It's okay. I think I get the message.

ESTHER, *afraid—she tries to smile and goes back toward him:* Like what?

VICTOR—*he moves a chair and does a knee bend and draws out the chassis of an immense old radio:* What other message is there? *Slight pause.*

ESTHER, *to retrieve the contact:* What's that?

VICTOR: Oh, one of my old radios that I made. Mamma mia, look at those tubes.

ESTHER, *more wondering than she feels about radios:* Would that work?

VICTOR: No, you need a storage battery. . . . *Recalling, he suddenly looks up at the ceiling.*

ESTHER, *looking up:* What?

VICTOR: One of my batteries exploded, went right through there someplace. *He points.* There! See where the plaster is different?

ESTHER, *striving for some spark between them:* Is this the one you got Tokyo on?

VICTOR, *not relenting, his voice dead:* Ya, this is the monster.

ESTHER, *with a warmth:* Why don't you take it?

VICTOR: Ah, it's useless.

ESTHER: Didn't you once say you had a lab up here? Or did I dream that?

VICTOR: Sure, I took it apart when Pop and I moved up here. Walter had that wall, and I had this. We did some great tricks up here. *She is fastened on him. He avoids her eyes and moves waywardly.* I'll be frank with you, kid—I look at my life and the whole thing is incomprehensible to me. I know all the reasons and all the reasons and all the reasons, and it ends up nothing. *He goes to the harp, touches it.* It's strange, you know? I forgot all about it—we'd work up here all night sometimes, and it was often full of music. My mother'd play for hours down in the library. Which is peculiar, because a harp is so soft. But it penetrates, I guess.

ESTHER: You're dear. You are, Vic. *She starts toward him, but he thwarts her by looking at his watch.*

VICTOR: I'll have to call another man. Come on, let's get out of here. *With a hollow, exhausted attempt at joy:* We'll get my suit and act rich!

ESTHER: Vic, I didn't mean that I—

VICTOR: Forget it. Wait, let me put these away before somebody walks off with them. *He takes up the foil and mask.*

ESTHER: Can you still do it?

VICTOR, *his sadness, his distance clinging to him:* Oh, no, you gotta be in shape for this. It's all in the thighs—

ESTHER: Well, let me see, I never saw you do it!

VICTOR, *giving the inch:* All right, but I can't get down far enough any more. *He takes position, feet at right angles, bouncing himself down to a difficult crouch.*

ESTHER: Maybe you could take it up again.

VICTOR: Oh no, it's a lot of work, it's the toughest sport there is. *Resuming position:* Okay, just stand there.

ESTHER: Me?

VICTOR: Don't be afraid. *Snapping the tip:* It's a beautiful foil, see how alive it is? I beat Princeton with this. *He laughs tiredly and makes a tramping lunge from yards away; the button touches her stomach.*

ESTHER, *springing back:* God! Victor!

VICTOR: What?

ESTHER: You looked beautiful.

He laughs, surprised and half-embarrassed—when both of them are turned to the door by a loud, sustained coughing out in the corridor. The coughing increases.

Enter Gregory Solomon. In brief, a phenomenon; a man nearly ninety but still straight-backed and the air of his massiveness still with him. He has perfected a way of leaning on his cane without appearing weak.

He wears a worn fur-felt black fedora, its brim turned down on the right side like Jimmy Walker's—although much dustier—and a shapeless topcoat. His frayed tie has a thick knot, askew under a curled-up collar tab. His vest is wrinkled, his trousers are baggy. A large diamond ring is on his left index finger. Tucked under his arm, a wrung-out leather portfolio. He hasn't shaved today.

Still coughing, catching his breath, trying to brush his cigar ashes off his lapel in a hopeless attempt at businesslike decorum, he is nodding at Esther and Victor and has one hand raised in a promise to speak quite soon. Nor has he failed to glance with some suspicion at the foil in Victor's hand.

VICTOR: Can I get you a glass of water?

Solomon gestures an imperious negative, trying to stop coughing.

ESTHER: Why don't you sit down? *Solomon gestures thanks, sits in the center armchair, the cough subsiding.* You sure you don't want some water?

SOLOMON, *in a Russian-Yiddish accent:* Water I don't need; a little blood I could use. Thank you. *He takes deep breaths, his attention on Victor, who now puts down the foil.* Oh boy. That's some stairs.

ESTHER: You all right now?

SOLOMON: Another couple steps you'll be in heaven. Ah—excuse me, Officer, I am looking for a party. The name is . . . *He fingers in his vest.*

VICTOR: Franz.

SOLOMON: That's it, Franz.

VICTOR: That's me. *Solomon looks incredulous.* Victor Franz.

SOLOMON: So it's a policeman!

VICTOR, *grinning:* Uh-huh.

SOLOMON: What do you know! *Including Esther:* You see? There's only one beauty to this lousy business, you meet all kinda people. But I never dealed with a policeman. *Reaching over to shake hands:* I'm very happy to meet you. My name is Solomon, Gregory Solomon.

VICTOR, *shaking hands:* This is my wife.

ESTHER: How do you do.

SOLOMON, *nodding appreciatively to Esther:* Very nice. *To Victor:* That's a nice-looking woman. *He extends his hands to her.* How do you do, darling. Beautiful suit.

ESTHER—*she laughs:* The fact is, I just bought it!

SOLOMON: You got good taste. Congratulations, wear it in good health. *He lets go her hand.*

ESTHER: I'll go to the cleaner, dear. I'll be back soon. *With a step toward the door—to Solomon:* Will you be very long?

SOLOMON, *glancing around at the furniture as at an antagonist:* With furniture you never know, can be short, can be long, can be medium.

ESTHER: Well, you give him a good price now, you hear?

SOLOMON: Ah ha! *Waving her out:* Look, you go to the cleaner, and we'll take care everything one hundred per cent.

ESTHER: Because there's some very beautiful stuff here. I know it, but he doesn't.

SOLOMON: I'm not sixty-two years in the business by taking advantage. Go, enjoy the cleaner.

She and Victor laugh.

ESTHER, *shaking her finger at him:* I hope I'm going to like you!

SOLOMON: Sweetheart, all the girls like me, what can I do?

ESTHER, *still smiling—to Victor as she goes to the door:* You be careful.

VICTOR, *nodding:* See you later.

She goes.

SOLOMON: I like her, she's suspicious.

VICTOR, *laughing in surprise:* What do you mean by that?

SOLOMON: Well, a girl who believes everything, how you gonna trust her? *Victor laughs appreciatively.* I had a wife . . . *He breaks off with a wave of the hand.* Well, what's the difference? Tell me, if you don't mind, how did you get my name?

VICTOR: In the phone book.

SOLOMON: You don't say! The phone book.

VICTOR: Why?

SOLOMON, *cryptically:* No-no, that's fine, that's fine.

VICTOR: The ad said you're a registered appraiser.

SOLOMON: Oh yes. I am registered, I am licensed, I am even vaccinated. *Victor laughs.* Don't laugh, the only thing you can do today without a license is you'll go up the elevator and jump out the window. But I don't have to tell you, you're a policeman, you know this world. *Hoping for contact:* I'm right?

VICTOR, *reserved:* I suppose.

SOLOMON, *surveying the furniture, one hand on his thigh, the other on the chair arm in a naturally elegant position:* So. *He glances about again, and with an uncertain smile:* That's a lot of furniture. This is all for sale?

VICTOR: Well, ya.

SOLOMON: Fine, fine. I just like to be sure where we are. *With a weak attempt at a charming laugh:* Frankly, in this neighborhood I never expected such a load. It's very surprising.

VICTOR: But I said it was a whole houseful.

SOLOMON, *with a leaven of unsureness:* Look, don't worry about it, we'll handle everything very nice. *He gets up from the chair and goes to one of the pair of chiffoniers, which he is obviously impressed with. He looks up at the chandeliers, then straight at Victor:* I'm not mixing in, Officer, but if you wouldn't mind— what is your connection? How do you come to this?

VICTOR: It was my family.

SOLOMON: You don't say. Looks like it's standing here a long time, no?

VICTOR: Well, the old man moved everything up here after the '29 crash. My uncles took over the house and they let him keep this floor.

SOLOMON, *as though to emphasize that he believes it: I* see. *He walks to the harp.*

VICTOR: Can you give me an estimate now, or do you have to—?

SOLOMON, *running a hand over the harp frame:* No-no, I'll give you right away, I don't waste a minute, I'm very busy. *He plucks a string, listens. Then bends down and runs a hand over the sounding board:* He passed away, your father?

VICTOR: Oh, long time ago—about sixteen years.

SOLOMON, *standing erect:* It's standing here sixteen years?

VICTOR: Well, we never got around to doing anything about it, but they're tearing the building down, so . . . It was very good stuff, you know—they had quite a little money.

SOLOMON: Very good, yes . . . I can see. *He leaves the harp with an estimating glance.* I was also very good; now I'm not so good. Time, you know, is a terrible thing. *He is a distance from the harp and indicates it.* That sounding board is cracked, you know. But don't worry about it, it's still a nice object. *He goes to an armoire and strokes the veneer.* It's a funny thing—an armoire like this, thirty years you couldn't give it away; it was a regular measles. Today all of a sudden, they want it again. Go figure it out. *He goes to one of the chests.*

VICTOR, *pleased:* Well, give me a good price and we'll make a deal.

SOLOMON: Definitely. You see, I don't lie to you. *He is pointing to the chest.* For instance, a chiffonier like this I wouldn't have to keep it a week. *Indicating the other chest:* That's a pair, you know.

VICTOR: I know.

SOLOMON: That's a nice chairs, too. *He sits on a dining-room chair, rocking to test its tightness.* I like the chairs.

VICTOR: There's more stuff in the bedroom, if you want to look.

SOLOMON: Oh? *He goes toward the bedroom.* What've you got here? *He looks into the bedroom, up and down.* I like the bed. That's a very nice carved bed. That I can sell. That's your parents' bed?

VICTOR: Yes. They may have bought that in Europe, if I'm not mistaken. They used to travel a good deal.

SOLOMON: Very handsome, very nice. I like it. *He starts to return to the center chair, eyes roving the furniture.* Looks a very nice family.

VICTOR: By the way, that dining-room table opens up. Probably seat about twelve people.

SOLOMON, *looking at the table:* I know that. Yes. In a pinch even fourteen. *He picks up the foil.* What's this? I thought you were stabbing your wife when I came in.

VICTOR, *laughing:* No, I just found it. I used to fence years ago.

SOLOMON: You went to college?

VICTOR: Couple of years, ya.

SOLOMON: That's very interesting.

VICTOR: It's the old story.

SOLOMON: No, listen—What happens to people is always the main element to me. Because when do they call me? It's either a divorce or somebody died. So it's always a new story. I mean it's the same, but it's different. *He sits in the center chair.*

VICTOR: You pick up the pieces.

SOLOMON: That's very good, yes. I pick up the pieces. It's a little bit like you, I suppose. You must have some stories, I betcha.

VICTOR: Not very often.

SOLOMON: What are you, a traffic cop, or something . . . ?

VICTOR: I'm out in Rockaway most of the time, the airports.

SOLOMON: That's Siberia, no?

VICTOR, *laughing:* I like it better that way.

SOLOMON: You keep your nose clean.

VICTOR, *smiling:* That's it. *Indicating the furniture:* So what do you say?

SOLOMON: What I say? *Taking out two cigars as he glances about:* You like a cigar?

VICTOR: Thanks, I gave it up long time ago. So what's the story here?

SOLOMON: I can see you are a very factual person.

VICTOR: You hit it.

SOLOMON: Couldn't be better. So tell me, you got some kind of paper here? To show ownership?

VICTOR: Well, no, I don't. But . . . *He half-laughs.* I'm the owner, that's all.

SOLOMON: In other words, there's no brothers, no sisters.

VICTOR: I have a brother, yes.

SOLOMON: Aha. You're friendly with him? Not that I'm mixing in, but I don't have to tell you the average family, they love each other like crazy, but the minute the parents die is all of a sudden a question who is going to get what and you're covered with cats and dogs—

VICTOR: There's no such problem here.

SOLOMON: Unless we're gonna talk about a few pieces, then it wouldn't bother me, but to take the whole load without a paper is a—

VICTOR: All right, I'll get you some kind of statement from him; don't worry about it.

SOLOMON: That's definite; because even from high-class people you wouldn't believe the shenanigans—lawyers, college professors, television personalities—five hundred dollars they'll pay a lawyer to fight over a bookcase it's worth fifty cents because you see, everybody wants to be number one, so . . .

VICTOR: I said I'd get you a statement. *He indicates the room.* Now what's the story?

Solomon: All right, so I'll tell you the story. *He looks at the dining-room table and points to it.* For instance, you mention the dining-room table. That's what they call Spanish Jacobean. Cost maybe twelve, thirteen hundred dollars. I would say—1921, '22. I'm right?

VICTOR: Probably, ya.

SOLOMON—*he clears his throat:* I see you're an intelligent man, so before I'll say another word, I ask you to remember—with used furniture you cannot be emotional.

VICTOR—*he laughs:* I haven't opened my mouth!

SOLOMON: I mean you're a policeman, I'm a furniture dealer, we both know this world. Anything Spanish Jacobean you'll sell quicker a case of tuberculosis.

VICTOR: Why? That table's in beautiful condition.

SOLOMON: Officer, you're talking reality; you cannot talk reality with used furniture. They don't like that style; not only they don't like it, they hate it. The same thing with that buffet there and that . . . *He starts to point elsewhere.*

VICTOR: You only want to take a few pieces, is that the ticket?

SOLOMON: Please, Officer, we're already talking too fast—

VICTOR: No-no, you're not going to walk off with the gravy and leave me with the bones. All or nothing or let's forget it. I told you on the phone it was a whole houseful.

SOLOMON: What're you in such a hurry? Talk a little bit, we'll see what happens. In a day they didn't build Rome. *He calculates worriedly for a moment, glancing again at the pieces he wants. He gets up, goes and touches the harp.* You see, what I had in mind—I would give you such a knockout price for these few pieces that you—

VICTOR: That's *out.*

SOLOMON, *quickly:* Out.

VICTOR: I'm not running a department store. They're tearing the building down.

SOLOMON: Couldn't be better! We understand each other, so —*with his charm*—so there's no reason to be emotional. *He goes to the records.* These records go? *He picks up one.*

VICTOR: I might keep three or four.

SOLOMON, *reading a label:* Look at that! Gallagher and Shean!

VICTOR, *with only half a laugh:* You're not going to start playing them now!

SOLOMON: Who needs to play? I was on the same bill with Gallagher and Shean maybe fifty theatres.

VICTOR, *surprised:* You were an actor?

SOLOMON: An actor! An acrobat; my whole family was acrobats. *Expanding with this first opening:* You never heard "The Five Solomons"—may they rest in peace? I was the one on the bottom.

VICTOR: Funny—I never heard of a Jewish acrobat.

SOLOMON: What's the matter with Jacob, he wasn't a wrestler? —wrestled with the Angel? *Victor laughs.* Jews been acrobats since the beginning of the world. I was a horse them days: drink, women, anything—on-the-go, on-the-go, nothing ever stopped me. Only life. Yes, my boy. *Almost lovingly putting down the record:* What do you know, Gallagher and Shean.

VICTOR, *more intimately now, despite himself; but with no less persistence in keeping to the business:* So where are we?

SOLOMON—*he glances off, then turns back to Victor with a deeply concerned look:* Tell me, what's with crime now? It's up, hey?

VICTOR: Yeah, it's up, it's up. Look, Mr. Solomon, let me make one thing clear, heh? I'm not sociable.

SOLOMON: You're not.

VICTOR: No, I'm not; I'm not a businessman, I'm not good at conversations. So let's get to a price, and finish. Okay?

SOLOMON: You don't want we should be buddies.

VICTOR: That's exactly it.

SOLOMON: So we wouldn't be buddies! *He sighs.* But just so you'll know me a little better—I'm going to show you something. *He takes out a leather folder which he flips open and hands to Victor.* There's my discharge from the British Navy. You see? "His Majesty's Service."

VICTOR, *looking at the document:* Huh! What were you doing in the British Navy?

SOLOMON: Forget the British Navy. What does it say the date of birth?

VICTOR: "Eighteen . . ." *Amazed, he looks up at Solomon.* You're almost ninety?

SOLOMON: Yes, my boy. I left Russia sixty-five years ago, I was twenty-four years old. And I smoked all my life. I drinked, and I loved every woman who would let me. So what do I need to steal from you?

VICTOR: Since when do people need a reason to steal?

SOLOMON: I never saw such a man in my life!

VICTOR: Oh yes you did. Now you going to give me a figure or—?

SOLOMON—*he is actually frightened because he can't get a hook into Victor and fears losing the good pieces:* How can I give you a figure? You don't trust one word I say!

VICTOR, *with a strained laugh:* I never saw you before, what're you asking me to trust you?!

SOLOMON, *with a gesture of disgust:* But how am I going to start to talk to you? I'm sorry; here you can't be a policeman. If you want to do business a little bit you gotta believe or you can't do it. I'm . . . I'm . . . Look, forget it. *He gets up and goes to his portfolio.*

VICTOR, *astonished:* What are you doing?

SOLOMON: I can't work this way. I'm too old every time I open my mouth you should practically call me a thief.

VICTOR: Who called you a thief?

SOLOMON, *moving toward the door:* No—I don't need it. I don't want it in my shop. *Wagging a finger into Victor's face:* And don't forget it—I never gave you a price, and look what you did to me. You see? I never gave you a price!

VICTOR, *angering:* Well, what did you come here for, to do me a favor? What are you talking about?

SOLOMON: Mister, I pity you! What is the matter with you people! You're worse than my daughter! Nothing in the world you believe, nothing you respect—how can you live? You think that's such a smart thing? That's so hard, what you're doing? Let me give you a piece advice—it's not that you can't believe nothing, that's not so hard—it's that you still got to believe it. *That's* hard. And if you can't do that, my friend—you're a dead man! *He starts toward the door.*

VICTOR, *chastened despite himself:* Oh, Solomon, come on, will you?

SOLOMON: No no. You got a certain problem with this furniture but you don't want to listen so how can I talk?

VICTOR: I'm listening! For Christ's sake, what do you want me to do, get down on my knees?

SOLOMON, *putting down his portfolio and taking out a wrinkled tape measure from his jacket pocket:* Okay, come here. I realize you are a factual person, but some facts are funny. *He stretches the tape measure across the depth of a piece.* What does that read? *Then he turns to Victor, showing him.*

VICTOR—*he comes to him, reads:* Forty inches. So?

SOLOMON: My boy, the bedroom doors in a modern apartment house are thirty, thirty-two inches maximum. So you can't get this in—

VICTOR: What about the old houses?

SOLOMON, *with a desperation growing:* All I'm trying to tell you is that my possibilities are smaller!

VICTOR: Well, can't I ask a question?

SOLOMON: I'm giving you architectural facts! Listen—*Wiping his face, he seizes on the library table, going to it.* You got there, for instance, a library table. That's a solid beauty. But go find me a modern apartment with a library. If they would build old hotels, I could sell this, but they only build new hotels. People don't live like this no more. This stuff is from another world. So I'm trying to give you a modern viewpoint. Because the price of used furniture is nothing but a viewpoint, and if you wouldn't understand the viewpoint is impossible to understand the price.

VICTOR: So what's the viewpoint—that it's all worth nothing?

SOLOMON: That's what you said, I didn't say that. The chairs is worth something, the chiffoniers, the bed, the harp—

VICTOR—*he turns away from him:* Okay, let's forget it, I'm not giving you the cream—

SOLOMON: What're you jumping!

VICTOR, *turning to him:* Good God, are you going to make me an offer or not?

SOLOMON, *walking away with a hand at his temple:* Boy, oh boy, oh boy. You must've arrested a million people by now.

VICTOR: Nineteen in twenty-eight years.

SOLOMON: So what are you so hard on me?

VICTOR: Because you talk about everything but money and I don't know what the hell you're up to.

SOLOMON, *raising a finger:* We will now talk money. *He returns to the center chair.*

VICTOR: Great. I mean you can't blame me—every time you open your mouth the price seems to go down.

SOLOMON, *sitting:* My boy, the price didn't change since I walked in.

VICTOR, *laughing:* That's even better! So what's the price? *Solomon glances about, his wit failed, a sunk look coming over his face.* What's going on? What's bothering you?

SOLOMON: I'm sorry, I shouldn't have come. I thought it would be a few pieces but . . . *Sunk, he presses his fingers into his eyes.* It's too much for me.

VICTOR: Well, what'd you come for? I told you it was the whole house.

SOLOMON, *protesting:* You called me, so I came! What should I do, lay down and die? *Striving again to save it:* Look, I want very much to make you an offer, the only question is . . . *He breaks off as though fearful of saying something.*

VICTOR: This is a hell of a note.

SOLOMON: Listen, it's a terrible temptation to me! But . . . *As though throwing himself on Victor's understanding:* You see, I'll tell you the truth; you must have looked in a very old phone book; a couple of years ago already I cleaned out my store. Except a few English andirons I got left, I sell when I need a few dollars. I figured I was eighty, eighty-five, it was time already. But I waited—and nothing happened—I even moved out of my apartment. I'm living in the back of the store with a hotplate. But nothing happened. I'm still practically a hundred per cent—not a hundred, but I feel very well. And I figured maybe you got a couple nice pieces—not that the rest can't be sold, but it could take a year, year and half. For me that's a big bet. *In conflict, he looks around.* The trouble is I love to work; I love it, but—*Giving up:* I don't know what to tell you.

VICTOR: All right, let's forget it then.

SOLOMON, *standing:* What're you jumping?

VICTOR: Well, are you in or out!

SOLOMON: How do I know where I am! You see, it's also this particular furniture—the average person he'll take one look, it'll make him very nervous.

VICTOR: Solomon, you're starting again.

SOLOMON: I'm not bargaining with you!

VICTOR: Why'll it make him nervous?

SOLOMON: Because he knows it's never gonna break.

VICTOR, *not in bad humor, but clinging to his senses:* Oh come on, will you? Have a little mercy.

SOLOMON: My boy, you don't know the psychology! If it wouldn't break there is no more possibilities. For instance, you take—*crosses to table*—this table . . . Listen! *He bangs the table.* You can't move it. A man sits down to such a table he knows not only he's married, he's got to stay married—there is no more possibilities. *Victor laughs.* You're laughing, I'm telling you the factual situation. What is the key word today? Disposable. The more you can throw it away the more it's beautiful. The car, the furniture, the wife, the children—everything has to be disposable. Because you see the main thing today is—shopping. Years ago a person, he was unhappy, didn't know what to do with himself—he'd go to church, start a revolution—*something.* Today you're unhappy? Can't figure it out? What is the salvation? Go shopping.

VICTOR, *laughing:* You're terrific, I have to give you credit.

SOLOMON: I'm telling you the truth! If they would close the stores for six months in this country there would be from coast to coast a regular massacre. With this kind of furniture the shopping is over, it's finished, there's no more possibilities, you *got* it, you see? So you got a problem here.

VICTOR, *laughing:* Solomon, you are one of the greatest. But I'm way ahead of you, it's not going to work.

SOLOMON, *offended:* What "work"? I don't know how much time I got. What is so terrible if I say that? The trouble is, you're such a young fella you don't understand these things—

VICTOR: I understand very well, I know what you're up against. I'm not so young.

SOLOMON, *scoffing:* What are you, forty? Forty-five?

VICTOR: I'm going to be fifty.

SOLOMON: Fifty! You're a baby boy!

VICTOR: Some baby.

SOLOMON: My God, if I was fifty . . . ! I got married I was seventy-five.

VICTOR: Go on.

SOLOMON: What are you talking? She's still living by Eighth Avenue over there. See, that's why I like to stay liquid, because I don't want her to get her hands on this. . . . Birds she loves. She's living there with maybe a hundred birds. She gives you a plate of soup it's got feathers. I didn't work all my life for them birds.

VICTOR: I appreciate your problems, Mr. Solomon, but I don't have to pay for them. *He stands.* I've got no more time.

SOLOMON, *holding up a restraining hand—desperately:* I'm going to buy it! *He has shocked himself, and glances around at the towering masses of furniture.* I mean I'll . . . *He moves, looking at the stuff.* I'll have to live, that's all, I'll make up my mind! I'll buy it.

VICTOR—*he is affected as Solomon's fear comes through to him:* We're talking about everything now.

SOLOMON, *angrily:* Everything, everything! *Going to his portfolio:* I'll figure it up, I'll give you a very nice price, and you'll be a happy man.

VICTOR, *sitting again:* That I doubt. *Solomon takes a hard-boiled egg out of the portfolio.* What's this now, lunch?

SOLOMON: You give me such an argument, I'm hungry! I'm not supposed to get too hungry.

VICTOR: Brother!

SOLOMON—*he cracks the shell on his diamond ring:* You want me to starve to death? I'm going to be very quick here.

VICTOR: Boy—I picked a number!

SOLOMON: There wouldn't be a little salt, I suppose.

VICTOR: I'm not going running for salt now!

SOLOMON: Please, don't be blue. I'm going to knock you off your feet with the price, you'll see. *He swallows the egg. He now faces the furniture, and, half to himself, pad and pencil poised:* I'm going to go here like an IBM. *He starts estimating on his pad.*

VICTOR: That's all right, take it easy. As long as you're serious.

SOLOMON: Thank you. *He touches the hated buffet:* Ay, yi, yi. All right, well . . . *He jots down a figure. He goes to the next piece, jots down another figure. He goes to another piece, jots down a figure.*

VICTOR, *after a moment:* You really got married at seventy-five?

SOLOMON: What's so terrible?

VICTOR: No, I think it's terrific. But what was the point?

SOLOMON: What's the point at twenty-five? You can't die twenty-six?

VICTOR, *laughing softly:* I guess so, ya.

SOLOMON: It's the same like secondhand furniture, you see;

the whole thing is a viewpoint. It's a mental world. *He jots down another figure for another piece.* Seventy-five I got married, fifty-one, and twenty-two.

VICTOR: You're kidding.

SOLOMON: I wish! *He works, jotting his estimate of each piece on the pad, opening drawers, touching everything. Peering into a dark recess, he takes out a pencil flashlight, switches it on, and begins to probe with the beam.*

VICTOR—*he has gradually turned to watch Solomon, who goes on working:* Cut the kidding now—how old are you?

SOLOMON, *sliding out a drawer:* I'm eighty-nine. It's such an accomplishment?

VICTOR: You're a hell of a guy.

SOLOMON, *smiling with the encouragement and turning to Victor:* You know, it's a funny thing. It's so long since I took on such a load like this—you forget what kind of life it puts into you. To take out a pencil again . . . it's a regular injection. Frankly, my telephone you could use for a ladle, it wouldn't interfere with nothing. I want to thank you. *He points at Victor.* I'm going to take good care of you, I mean it. I can open that?

VICTOR: Sure, anything.

SOLOMON, *going to an armoire:* Some of them had a mirror . . . *He opens the armoire, and a rolled-up fur rug falls out. It is about three by five.* What's this?

VICTOR: God knows. I guess it's a rug.

SOLOMON, *holding it up:* No-no—that's a lap robe. Like for a car.

VICTOR: Say, that's right, ya. When they went driving. God, I haven't seen that in—

SOLOMON: You had a chauffeur?

VICTOR: Ya, we had a chauffeur.

Their eyes meet. Solomon looks at him as though Victor were coming into focus. Victor turns away. Now Solomon turns back to the armoire.

SOLOMON: Look at that! *He takes down an opera hat from the shelf within.* My God! *He puts it on, looks into the interior mirror.* What a world! *He turns to Victor:* He must've been some sporty guy!

VICTOR, *smiling:* You look pretty good!

SOLOMON: And from all this he could go so broke?

VICTOR: Why not? Sure. Took five weeks. Less.

SOLOMON: You don't say. And he couldn't make a comeback?

VICTOR: Well, some men don't bounce, you know.

SOLOMON—*he grunts:* Hmm! So what did he do?

VICTOR: Nothing. Just sat here. Listened to the radio.

SOLOMON: But what did he do? What—?

VICTOR: Well, now and then he was making change at the Automat. Toward the end he was delivering telegrams.

SOLOMON, *with grief and wonder:* You don't say. And how much he had?

VICTOR: Oh . . . couple of million, I guess.

SOLOMON: My God. What was the matter with him?

VICTOR: Well, my mother died around the same time. I guess that didn't help. Some men just don't bounce, that's all.

SOLOMON: Listen, I can tell you bounces. I went busted 1932; then 1923 they also knocked me out; the panic of 1904, 1898 . . . But to lay down like *that* . . .

VICTOR: Well, you're different. He believed in it.

SOLOMON: What he believed?

VICTOR: The system, the whole thing. He thought it was his fault, I guess. You—you come in with your song and dance, it's all a gag. You're a hundred and fifty years old, you tell your jokes, people fall in love with you, and you walk away with their furniture.

SOLOMON: That's not nice.

VICTOR: Don't shame me, will ya? What do you say? You don't need to look any more, you know what I've got here. *Solomon is clearly at the end of his delaying resources. He looks about slowly; the furniture seems to loom over him like a threat or a promise. His eyes climb up to the edges of the ceiling, his hands grasping one another.* What are you afraid of? It'll keep you busy.

Solomon looks at him, wanting even more reassurance.

SOLOMON: You don't think it's foolish?

VICTOR: Who knows what's foolish? You enjoy it—

SOLOMON: Listen, I love it—

VICTOR:—so take it. You plan too much, you end up with nothing.

SOLOMON, *intimately:* I would like to tell you something. The last few months, I don't know what it is—she comes to me. You see, I had a daughter, she should rest in peace, she took her own life, a suicide. . . .

VICTOR: When was this?

SOLOMON: It was . . . 1916—the latter part. But very beautiful, a lovely face, with large eyes—she was pure like the morning. And lately, I don't know what it is—I see her clear like I see you. And every night practically, I lay down to go to sleep,

so she sits there. And you can't help it, you ask yourself—
what happened? What *happened?* Maybe I could have said
something to her . . . maybe I *did* say something . . . it's all
. . . *He looks at the furniture.* It's not that I'll die, you can't be
afraid of that. But . . . I'll tell you the truth—a minute ago I
mentioned I had three wives . . . *Slight pause. His fear rises.*
Just this minute I realize I had four. Isn't that terrible? The
first time was nineteen, in Lithuania. See, that's what I mean
—it's impossible to know what is important. Here I'm sitting
with you . . . and . . . and . . . *He looks around at the furniture.* What for? Not that I don't want it, I want it, but . . .
You see, all my life I was a terrible fighter—you could never
take nothing from me; I pushed, I pulled, I struggled in six
different countries, I nearly got killed a couple times, and it's
. . . It's like now I'm sitting here talking to you and I tell you
it's a dream, it's a dream! You see, you can't imagine it because—

VICTOR: I know what you're talking about. But it's not a
dream—it's that you've got to make decisions before you
know what's involved, but you're stuck with the results anyway. Like I was very good in science—I loved it. But I had to
drop out to feed the old man. And I figured I'd go on the
Force temporarily, just to get us through the Depression, then
go back to school. But the war came, we had the kid, and you
turn around and you've racked up fifteen years on the pension. And what you started out to do is a million miles away.
Not that I regret it all—we brought up a terrific boy, for one
thing; nobody's ever going to take that guy. But it's like you
were saying—it's impossible to know what's important. We always agreed, we stay out of the rat race and live our own life.
That was important. But you shovel the crap out the window,
it comes back in under the door—it all ends up she wants, she
wants. And I can't really blame her—there's just no respect
for anything but money.

SOLOMON: What're you got against money?

VICTOR: Nothing, I just didn't want to lay down my life for it. But I think I laid it down another way, and I'm not even sure any more what I was trying to accomplish. I look back now, and all I can see is a long, brainless walk in the street. I guess it's the old story; do anything, but just be sure you win. Like my brother; years ago I was living up here with the old man, and he used to contribute five dollars a month. A *month!* And a successful surgeon. But the few times he'd come around, the expression on the old man's face—you'd think God walked in. The respect, you know what I mean? The respect! And why not? Why not?

SOLOMON: Well, sure, he had the power.

VICTOR: Now you said it—if you got that you got it all. You're even lovable! *He laughs.* Well, what do you say? Give me the price.

Slight pause.

SOLOMON: I'll give you eleven hundred dollars.

Slight pause.

VICTOR: For everything?

SOLOMON, *in a breathless way:* Everything. *Slight pause. Victor looks around at the furniture.* I want it, so I'm giving you a good price. Believe me, you will never do better. I want it; I made up my mind. *Victor continues staring at the stuff. Solomon takes out a common envelope and removes a wad of bills.* Here . . . I'll pay you now. *He readies a bill to start counting it out.*

VICTOR: It's that I have to split it, see—

SOLOMON: All right . . . so I'll make out a receipt for you and I'll put down six hundred dollars.

VICTOR: No-no . . . *He gets up and moves at random, looking at the furniture.*

SOLOMON: Why not? He took from you so take from him. If you want, I'll put down four hundred.

VICTOR: No, I don't want to do that. *Slight pause.* I'll call you tomorrow.

SOLOMON, *smiling:* All right; with God's help if I'm there tomorrow I'll answer the phone. If I wouldn't be . . . *Slight pause.* Then I wouldn't be.

VICTOR, *annoyed, but wanting to believe:* Don't start that again, will you?

SOLOMON: Look, you convinced me, so I want it. So what should I do?

VICTOR: *I* convinced *you?*

SOLOMON, *very distressed:* Absolutely you convinced me. You saw it—the minute I looked at it I was going to walk out!

VICTOR, *cutting him off, angered at his own indecision:* Ah, the hell with it. *He holds out his hand.* Give it to me.

SOLOMON, *wanting Victor's good will:* Please, don't be blue.

VICTOR: Oh, it all stinks. *Jabbing forth his hand:* Come on.

SOLOMON, *with a bill raised over Victor's hand—protesting:* What stinks? You should be happy. Now you can buy her a nice coat, take her to Florida, maybe—

VICTOR, *nodding ironically:* Right, right! We'll all be happy now. Give it to me.

Solomon shakes his head and counts bills into his hand. Victor turns his head and looks at the piled walls of furniture.

SOLOMON: There's one hundred; two hundred; three hundred; four hundred . . . Take my advice, buy her a nice fur coat your troubles'll be over—

VICTOR: I know all about it. Come on.

SOLOMON: So you got there four, so I'm giving you . . . five, six, seven . . . I mean it's already in the Bible, the rat race. The minute she laid her hand on the apple, that's it.

VICTOR: I never read the Bible. Come on.

SOLOMON: If you'll read it you'll see—there's always a rat race, you can't stay out of it. So you got there seven, so now I'm giving you . . .

A man appears in the doorway—in his mid-fifties, well-barbered, hatless, in a camel's-hair coat, with a very healthy complexion. There is a look of sharp intelligence on his face.

Victor, seeing past Solomon, starts slightly with shock, withdrawing his hand from the next bill which Solomon is about to lay in it.

VICTOR, *suddenly flushed, his voice oddly high and boyish:* Walter!

WALTER—*he enters the room, coming to Victor with extended hand and with a reserve of warmth but a stiff smile:* How are you, kid?

Solomon has moved out of their line of sight.

VICTOR—*he shifts the money to his left hand as he shakes:* God, I never expected you.

WALTER, *of the money—half-humorously:* Sorry I'm late. What are you doing?

VICTOR, *fighting a treason to himself, thus taking on a strained humorous air:* I . . . I just sold it.

WALTER: Good! How much?

VICTOR, *as though absolutely certain now he has been had:* Ah . . . eleven hundred.

WALTER, *in a dead voice shorn of comment:* Oh. Well, good. *He turns rather deliberately—but not overly so—to Solomon:* For everything?

SOLOMON—*he comes to Walter, his hand extended; with an energized voice that braves everything:* I'm very happy to meet you, Doctor! My name is Gregory Solomon.

WALTER—*the look on his face is rather amused, but his reserve has possibilities of accusation:* How do you do? *He shakes Solomon's hand, as Victor raises his hand to smooth down his hair, a look of near-alarm for himself on his face.*

CURTAIN

Act Two

The action is continuous. As the curtain rises, Walter is just releasing Solomon's hand and turning about to face Victor. His posture is reserved, stiffened by traditional control over a nearly fierce curiosity. His grin is disciplined and rather hard, but his eyes are warm and combative.

WALTER: How's Esther?

VICTOR: Fine. Should be here any minute.

WALTER: Here? Good! And what's Richard doing?

VICTOR: He's at M.I.T.

WALTER: No kidding! M.I.T.!

VICTOR, *nodding:* They gave him a full scholarship.

WALTER, *dispelling his surprise:* What do you know. *With a wider smile, and embarrassed warmth:* You're proud.

VICTOR: I guess so. They put him in the Honors Program.

WALTER: Really. That's wonderful. You don't mind my coming, do you?

VICTOR: No! I called you a couple of times.

WALTER: Yes, my nurse told me. What's Richard interested in?

VICTOR: Science. So far, anyway. *With security:* How're yours?

WALTER—*moving, he breaks the confrontation:* I suppose Jean turned out best—but I don't think you ever saw her.

VICTOR: I never did, no.

WALTER: The *Times* gave her quite a spread last fall. Pretty fair designer.

VICTOR: Oh? That's great. And the boys? They in school?

WALTER: They often are. *Abruptly laughs, refusing his own embarrassment:* I hardly see them, Vic. With all the unsolved mysteries in the world they're investigating the guitar. But what the hell . . . I've given up worrying about them. *He walks past Solomon, glancing at the furniture:* I'd forgotten how much he had up here. There's your radio!

VICTOR, *smiling with him:* I know, I saw it.

Walter looks down at the radio, then upward to the ceiling through which the battery once exploded. Both laugh. Then he glances with open feeling at Victor.

WALTER: Long time.

VICTOR, *fending off the common emotion:* Yes. How's Dorothy?

WALTER, *cryptically:* She's all right, I guess. *He moves, glancing at the things, but again with suddenness turns back.* Looking forward to seeing Esther again. She still writing poetry?

VICTOR: No, not for years now.

SOLOMON: He's got a very nice wife. We met.

WALTER, *surprised; as though at something intrusive:* Oh? *He turns back to the furniture.* Well. Same old junk, isn't it?

VICTOR, *downing a greater protest:* I wouldn't say that. Some of it isn't bad.

SOLOMON: One or two very nice things, Doctor. We came to a very nice agreement.

VICTOR, *with an implied rebuke:* I never thought you'd show up; I guess we'd better start all over again—

WALTER: Oh, no-no, I don't want to foul up your deal.

SOLOMON: Excuse me, Doctor—better you should take what you want now than we'll argue later. What did you want?

WALTER, *surprised, turning to Victor:* Oh, I didn't want anything. I came by to say hello, that's all.

VICTOR: I see. *Fending off Walter's apparent gesture with an over-quick movement toward the oar:* I found your oar, if you want it.

WALTER: Oar? *Victor draws it out from behind furniture, a curved-blade sweep.* Hah! *He receives the oar, looks up its length, and laughs, hefting it.* I must have been out of my mind!

SOLOMON: Excuse me, Doctor; if you want the oar—

WALTER, *standing the oar before Solomon, whom he leaves holding on to it:* Don't get excited, I don't want it.

SOLOMON: No. I was going to say—a personal thing like this, I have no objection.

WALTER, *half-laughing:* That's very generous of you.

VICTOR, *apologizing for Solomon:* I threw in everything—I never thought you'd get here.

WALTER, *with a strained over-agreeableness:* Sure, that's all right. What are you taking?

VICTOR: Nothing, really. Esther might want a lamp or something like that.

SOLOMON: He's not interested, you see; he's a modern person, what are you going to do?

WALTER: You're not taking the harp?

VICTOR, *with a certain guilt:* Well, nobody plays . . . You take it, if you like.

SOLOMON: You'll excuse me, Doctor—the harp, please, that's another story . . .

WALTER—*he laughs, archly amused and put out:* You don't mind if I make a suggestion, do you?

SOLOMON: Doctor, please, don't be offended, I only—

WALTER: Well, why do you interrupt? Relax, we're only talking. We haven't seen each other for a long time.

SOLOMON: Couldn't be better; I'm very sorry. *He sits, nervously pulling his cheek.*

WALTER, *touching the harp:* Kind of a pity—this was Grandpa's wedding present, you know.

VICTOR, *looking with surprise at the harp:* Say—that's right!

WALTER, *to Solomon:* What are you giving him for this?

SOLOMON: I didn't itemize—one price for everything. Maybe three hundred dollars. That sounding board is cracked, you know.

VICTOR, *to Walter:* You want it?

SOLOMON: Please, Victor, I hope you're not going to take that away from me. *To Walter:* Look, Doctor, I'm not trying to fool you. The harp is the heart and soul of the deal. I realize it was your mother's harp, but like I tried to tell—*to Victor:* you before—*to Walter:* with used furniture you cannot be emotional.

WALTER: I guess it doesn't matter. *To Victor:* Actually, I was wondering if he kept any of Mother's evening gowns, did he?

VICTOR: I haven't really gone through it all—

SOLOMON, *raising a finger, eagerly:* Wait, wait, I think I can help you. *He goes to an armoire he had earlier looked into, and opens it.*

WALTER, *moving toward the armoire:* She had some spectacular—

SOLOMON, *drawing out the bottom of a gown elaborately embroidered in gold:* Is this what you mean?

WALTER: Yes, that's the stuff! *Solomon blows dust off and hands him the bottom of the gown.* Isn't that beautiful! Say, I think she wore this at my wedding! *He takes it out of the closet, holds it up.* Sure! You remember this?

VICTOR: What do you want with it?

WALTER, *drawing out another gown off the rack.* Look at this one! Isn't that something? I thought Jeannie might make something new out of the material. I'd like her to wear something of Mother's.

VICTOR—*it is a new, surprising idea:* Oh! Fine, that's a nice idea.

SOLOMON: Take, take—they're beautiful.

WALTER, *suddenly glancing about as he lays the gowns across a chair:* What happened to the piano?

VICTOR: Oh, we sold that while I was still in school. We lived on it for a long time.

WALTER, *very interestedly:* I never knew that.

VICTOR: Sure. And the silver.

WALTER: Of course! Stupid of me not to remember that. *He half-sits against the back of a couch. His interest is avid, and his energy immense.* I suppose you know—you've gotten to look a great deal like Dad.

VICTOR: *I* do?

WALTER: It's very striking. And your voice is very much like his.

VICTOR: I know. It has that sound to me, sometimes.

SOLOMON: So, gentlemen . . . *He moves the money in his hand.*

VICTOR, *indicating Solomon:* Maybe we'd better settle this now.

WALTER: Yes, go ahead! *He walks off, looking at the furniture.*

SOLOMON, *indicating the money Victor holds:* You got there seven—

WALTER, *oblivious of Solomon; unable, so to speak, to settle for the status quo:* Wonderful to see you looking so well.

VICTOR—*the new interruption seems odd; observing more than speaking:* You do too, you look great.

WALTER: I ski a lot; and I ride nearly every morning. . . . You know, I started to call you a dozen times this year—*He breaks off. Indicating Solomon:* Finish up, I'll talk to you later.

SOLOMON: So now I'm going to give you—*A bill is poised over Victor's hand.*

VICTOR, *to Walter:* That price all right with you?

WALTER: Oh, I don't want to interfere. It's just that I dealt with these fellows when I split up Dorothy's and my stuff last year, and I found—

VICTOR, *from an earlier impression:* You're not divorced, are you?

WALTER, *with a nervous shot of laughter:* Yes!

Esther enters on his line; she is carrying a suit in a plastic wrapper.

ESTHER, *surprised:* Walter! For heaven's sake!

WALTER, *eagerly jumping up, coming to her, shaking her hand:* How are you, Esther!

ESTHER, *between her disapproval and fascinated surprise:* What are *you* doing here?

WALTER: You've hardly changed!

ESTHER, *with a charged laugh, conflicted with herself:* Oh, go on now! *She hangs the suit on a chest handle.*

WALTER, *to Victor:* You son of a gun, she looks twenty-five!

VICTOR, *watching for Esther's reaction:* I know!

ESTHER, *flattered, and offended, too:* Oh stop it, Walter! *She sits.*

WALTER: But you do, honestly, you look marvelous.

SOLOMON: It's that suit, you see? What did I tell you, it's a very beautiful suit.

Victor laughs a little as Esther looks conflicted by Solomon's compliment.

ESTHER, *with a mock-affront, to Victor:* What are you laughing at? It is. *She is about to laugh.*

VICTOR: You looked so surprised, that's all.

ESTHER: Well, I'm not used to walking into all these compliments! *She bursts out laughing.*

WALTER, *suddenly recalling, eagerly:* Say! I'm sorry I didn't know I'd be seeing you when I left the house this morning— I'd have brought you some lovely Indian bracelets. I got a whole boxful from Bombay.

ESTHER, *still not focused on Walter, sizing him up:* How do you come to—?

WALTER: I operated on this big textile guy and he keeps sending me things. He sent me this coat, in fact.

ESTHER: I was noticing it. That's gorgeous material.

WALTER: Isn't it? Two gallstones.

ESTHER, *her impression lingering for the instant:* How's Dorothy? Did I hear you saying you were—?

WALTER, *very seriously:* We're divorced, ya. Last winter.

ESTHER: I'm sorry to hear that.

WALTER: It was coming a long time. We're both much better off—we're almost friendly now. *He laughs.*

ESTHER: Oh, stop that, you dog.

WALTER, *with naïve excitement:* It's true!

ESTHER: Look, I'm for the woman, so don't hand me that. *To Victor, seeing the money in his hand:* Have you settled everything?

VICTOR: Just about, I guess.

WALTER: I was just telling Victor—*to Victor:* when we split things up I—*to Solomon:* you ever hear of Spitzer and Fox?

SOLOMON: Thirty years I know Spitzer and Fox. Bert Fox worked for me maybe ten, twelve years.

WALTER: They did my appraisal.

SOLOMON: They're good boys. Spitzer is not as good as Fox, but between the two you're in good hands.

WALTER: Yes. That's why I—

SOLOMON: Spitzer is vice president of the Appraisers' Association.

WALTER: I see. The point I'm making—

SOLOMON: I used to be president.

WALTER: Really.

SOLOMON: Oh yes. I made it all ethical.

WALTER, *trying to keep a straight face—as is Victor as well:* Did you?

Victor suddenly bursts out laughing, which sets off Walter and Esther, and a warmth springs up among them.

SOLOMON, *smiling, but insistent:* What's so funny? Listen, before me was a jungle—you wouldn't laugh so much. I put in all the rates, what we charge, you know—I made it a profession, like doctors, lawyers. Used to be it was a regular snake-pit. But today, you got nothing to worry—all the members are hundred per cent ethical.

WALTER: Well, that was a good deed, Mr. Solomon—but I think you can do a little better on this furniture.

ESTHER, *to Victor, who has money in his hand:* How much has he offered?

VICTOR, *embarrassed, but braving it quite well:* Eleven hundred.

ESTHER, *distressed; with a transcendent protest:* Oh, I think that's . . . isn't that very low? *She looks to Walter's confirmation.*

WALTER, *familiarly:* Come on, Solomon. He's been risking his life for you every day; be generous—

SOLOMON, *to Esther:* That's a real brother! Wonderful. *To Walter:* But you can call anybody you like—Spitzer and Fox, Joe Brody, Paul Cavallo, Morris White—I know them all and I know what they'll tell you.

VICTOR, *striving to retain some assurance, to Esther:* See, the point he was making about it—

SOLOMON, *to Esther, raising his finger:* Listen to him because he—

VICTOR, *to Solomon:* Hold it one second, will you? *To Esther and Walter:* Not that I'm saying it's true, but he claims a lot of it is too big to get into the new apartments.

ESTHER, *half-laughing:* You believe that?

WALTER: I don't know, Esther, Spitzer and Fox said the same thing.

ESTHER: Walter, the city is full of big, old apartments!

SOLOMON: Darling, why don't you leave it to the boys?

ESTHER, *suppressing an outburst:* I wish you wouldn't order me around, Mr. Solomon! *To Walter, protesting:* Those two bureaus alone are worth a couple of hundred dollars!

WALTER, *delicately:* Maybe I oughtn't interfere—

ESTHER: Why? *Of Solomon:* Don't let him bulldoze you—

SOLOMON: My dear girl, you're talking without a basis—

ESTHER, *slashing:* I don't like this kind of dealing, Mr. Solomon! I just don't like it! *She is near tears. A pause. She turns back to Walter.* This money is very important to us, Walter.

WALTER, *chastised:* Yes. I . . . I'm sorry, Esther. *He looks about.* Well . . . if it was mine—

ESTHER: Why? It's yours as much as Victor's.

WALTER: Oh no, dear—I wouldn't take anything from this.

Pause.

VICTOR: No, Walter, you get half.

WALTER: I wouldn't think of it, kid. I came by to say hello, that's all.

Pause.

ESTHER—*she is very moved:* That's terrific, Walter. It's . . . Really, I . . .

VICTOR: Well, we'll talk about it.

WALTER: No-no, Vic, you've earned it. It's yours.

VICTOR, *rejecting the implication:* Why have I earned it? You take your share.

WALTER: Why don't we discuss it later? *To Solomon:* In my opinion—

SOLOMON, *to Victor:* So now you don't even have to split. *To Victor and Walter:* You're lucky they're tearing the building down—you got together, finally.

WALTER: I would have said a minimum of three thousand dollars.

ESTHER: That's exactly what I had in mind! *To Solomon:* I was going to say thirty-five hundred dollars.

WALTER, *to Victor, tactfully:* In that neighborhood.

Silence. Solomon sits there, holding back comment, not looking at Victor, blinking with protest. Victor thinks for a moment, then turns to Solomon, and there is a wide discouragement in his voice.

VICTOR: Well? What do you say?

SOLOMON, *spreading out his hands helplessly, outraged:* What can I say? It's ridiculous. Why does he give you three thousand? What's the matter with five thousand, ten thousand?

WALTER, *to Victor, without criticism:* You should've gotten a couple of other estimates, you see, that's always the—

VICTOR: I've been calling you all week for just that reason, Walter, and you never came to the phone.

WALTER, *blushing:* Why would that stop you from—?

VICTOR: I didn't think I had the right to do it alone—the nurse gave you my messages, didn't she?

WALTER: I've been terribly tied up—and I had no intention of taking anything for myself, so I assumed—

VICTOR: But how was I supposed to know that?

WALTER, *with open self-reproach:* Yes. Well, I . . . I beg your pardon. *He decides to stop there.*

SOLOMON: Excuse me, Doctor, but I can't understand you; first it's a lot of junk—

ESTHER: Nobody called it a lot of junk!

SOLOMON: He called it a lot of junk, Esther, when he walked in here.

Esther turns to Walter, puzzled and angry.

WALTER, *reacting to her look, to Solomon:* Now just a minute—

SOLOMON: No, please. *Indicating Victor:* This is a factual man, so let's be factual.

ESTHER: Well, that's an awfully strange thing to say, Walter.

WALTER, *intimately:* I didn't mean it in that sense, Esther—

SOLOMON: Doctor, please. You said junk.

WALTER, *sharply—and there is an over-meaning of much greater anger in his tone:* I didn't mean it in that sense, Mr. Solomon! *He controls himself—and, half to Esther:* When you've been brought up with things, you tend to be sick of them. . . . *To Esther:* That's all I meant.

SOLOMON: My dear man, if it was Louis Seize, Biedermeier, something like that, you wouldn't get sick.

WALTER, *pointing to a piece, and weakened by knowing he is exaggerating:* Well, there happens to be a piece right over there in Biedermeier style!

SOLOMON: Biedermeier "style"! *He picks up his hat.* I got a hat it's in Borsolino style but it's not a Borsolino. *To Victor:* I mean he don't have to charge me to make an impression.

WALTER, *striving for an air of amusement:* Now what's that supposed to mean?

VICTOR, *with a refusal to dump Solomon:* Well, what basis *do* you go on, Walter?

WALTER, *reddening but smiling:* I don't know . . . it's a feeling, that's all.

ESTHER—*there is ridicule:* Well, on what basis do you take eleven hundred, dear?

VICTOR, *angered; his manly leadership is suddenly in front:* I simply felt it was probably more or less right!

ESTHER, *as a refrain:* Oh God, here we go again. All right, throw it away—

SOLOMON, *indicating Victor:* Please, Esther, he's not throwing nothing away. This man is no fool! *To Walter as well:* Excuse me, but this is not right to do to him!

WALTER, *bridling, but retaining his smile:* You going to teach me what's right now?

ESTHER, *to Victor, expanding Walter's protest:* Really! I *mean.*

VICTOR—*obeying her protest for want of a certainty of his own, he touches Solomon's shoulder:* Mr. Solomon . . . why don't you sit down in the bedroom for a few minutes and let us talk?

SOLOMON: Certainly, whatever you say. *He gets up.* Only please, you made a very nice deal, you got no right to be ashamed. . . . *To Esther:* Excuse me, I don't want to be personal.

ESTHER—*she laughs angrily:* He's fantastic!

VICTOR, *trying to get him moving again:* Whyn't you go inside?

SOLOMON: I'm going; I only want you to understand, Victor, that if it was a different kind of man—*turning to Esther*—I would say to you that he's got the money in his hand, so the deal is concluded.

WALTER: He can't conclude any deal without me, Solomon, I'm half-owner here.

SOLOMON, *to Victor:* You see? What did I ask you the first thing I walked in here? "Who is the owner?"

WALTER: Why do you confuse everything? I'm not making any claim, I merely—

SOLOMON: Then how do you come to interfere? He's got the money; I know the law!

WALTER, *angering:* Now you stop being foolish! Just stop it! I've got the best lawyers in New York, so go inside and sit down.

VICTOR, *as he turns back to escort Solomon:* Take it easy, Walter, come on, cut it out.

ESTHER, *striving to keep a light, amused tone:* Why? He's perfectly right.

VICTOR, *with a hard glance at her, moving upstage with Solomon:* Here, you better hold on to this money.

SOLOMON: No, that's yours; you hold . . .

He sways. Victor grasps his arm. Walter gets up.

WALTER: You all right?

SOLOMON—*dizzy, he grasps his head:* Yes, yes, I'm . . .

WALTER, *coming to him:* Let me look at you. *He takes Solomon's wrists, looks into his face.*

SOLOMON: I'm only a little tired, I didn't take my nap today.

WALTER: Come in here, lie down for a moment. *He starts Solomon toward the bedroom.*

SOLOMON: Don't worry about me, I'm . . . *He halts and points back at his portfolio, leaning on a chest.* Please, Doctor, if you wouldn't mind—I got a Hershey's in there. *Walter hesitates to do his errand.* Helps me. *Walter unwillingly goes to the portfolio and reaches into it.* I'm a very healthy person, but a nap, you see, I have to have a . . . *Walter takes out an orange.* Not the orange—on the bottom is a Hershey's. *Walter takes out a Hershey bar.* That's a boy.

WALTER, *returning to him and helping him to the bedroom:* All right, come on . . . easy does it . . .

SOLOMON, *as he goes into the bedroom:* I'm all right, don't worry. You're very nice people.

Solomon and Walter exit into the bedroom. Victor glances at the money in his hand, then puts it on a table, setting the foil on it.

ESTHER: Why are you being so apologetic?

VICTOR: About what?

ESTHER: That old man. Was that his first offer?

VICTOR: Why do you believe Walter? He was obviously pulling a number out of a hat.

ESTHER: Well, I agree with him. Did you try to get him to go higher?

VICTOR: I don't know how to bargain and I'm not going to start now.

ESTHER: I wish you wouldn't be above everything, Victor, we're not twenty years old. We need this money. *He is silent.* You hear me?

VICTOR: I've made a deal, and that's it. You know, you take a tone sometimes—like I'm some kind of an incompetent.

ESTHER—*she gets up, moves restlessly:* Well anyway, you'll get the whole amount. God, he's certainly changed. It's amazing.

VICTOR, *without assent:* Seems so, ya.

ESTHER, *wanting him to join her:* He's so human! And he laughs!

VICTOR: I've seen him laugh.

ESTHER, *with a grin of trepidation:* Am I hearing something, or is that my imagination?

VICTOR: I want to think about it.

ESTHER, *quietly:* You're not taking his share?

VICTOR: I said I would like to think . . .

Assuming he will refuse Walter's share, she really doesn't know what to do or where to move, so she goes for her purse with a quick stride.

VICTOR, *getting up:* Where you going?

ESTHER, *turning back on him:* I want to know. Are you or aren't you taking his share?

VICTOR: Esther, I've been calling him all week; doesn't even bother to come to the phone, walks in here and smiles and I'm supposed to fall into his arms? I can't behave as though nothing ever happened, and you're not going to either! Now just take it easy, we're not dying of hunger.

ESTHER: I don't understand what you think you're upholding!

VICTOR, *outraged:* Where have you been?!

ESTHER: But he's doing exactly what you thought he should do! What do you *want?*

VICTOR: Certain things have happened, haven't they? I can't turn around this fast, kid. He's only been here ten minutes,

I've got twenty-eight years to shake off my back. . . . Now sit down, I want you here. *He sits. She remains standing, uncertain of what to do.* Please. You can wait a few minutes for your drink.

ESTHER, *in despair:* Vic, it's all blowing away.

VICTOR, *to diminish the entire prize:* Half of eleven hundred dollars is five-fifty, dear.

ESTHER: I'm not talking about money. *Voices are heard from the bedroom.* He's obviously making a gesture, why can't you open yourself a little? *She lays her head back.* My mother was right—I can never believe anything I see. But I'm going to. That's all I'm going to do. What I see.

A chair scrapes in the bedroom.

VICTOR: Wipe your cheek, will you? *Walter enters from the bedroom.* How is he?

WALTER: I think he'll be all right. *Warmly:* God, what a pirate! *He sits.* He's eighty-nine!

ESTHER: I don't believe it!

VICTOR: He is. He showed me his—

WALTER, *laughing:* Oh, he show you that too?

VICTOR, *smiling:* Ya, the British Navy.

ESTHER: *He* was in the British Navy?

VICTOR, *building on Walter's support:* He's got a discharge. He's not altogether phony.

WALTER: I wouldn't go that far. A guy that age, though, still driving like that . . . *As though admitting Victor was not foolish:* There *is* something wonderful about it.

VICTOR, *understating:* I think so.

ESTHER: What do you think we ought to do, Walter?

WALTER, *after a slight pause, trying to modify what he believes is his overpowering force so as not to appear to be taking over, faintly smiling toward Victor:* There is a way to get a good deal more out of it. I suppose you know that, though.

VICTOR: Look, I'm not married to this guy. If you want to call another dealer we can compare.

WALTER: You don't have to do that; he's a registered appraiser. You see, instead of selling it, you could make it a charitable contribution.

VICTOR: I don't understand.

WALTER: It's perfectly simple. He puts a value on it—let's say twenty-five thousand dollars, and—

ESTHER, *fascinated, with a laugh:* Are you kidding?

WALTER: It's done all the time. It's a dream world but it's legal. He estimates its highest retail value, which could be put at some such figure. Then I donate it to the Salvation Army. I'd have to take ownership, you see, because my tax rate is much higher than yours so it would make more sense if I took the deduction. I pay around fifty per cent tax, so if I make a twenty-five-thousand-dollar contribution I'd be saving around twelve thousand in taxes. Which we could split however you wanted to. Let's say we split it in half, I'd give you six thousand dollars. *A pause.* It's really the only sensible way to do it, Vic.

ESTHER—*she glances at Victor, but he remains silent:* Would it be costing you anything?

WALTER: On the contrary—it's found money to me. *To Victor:* I mentioned it to him just now.

VICTOR, *as though this had been the question:* What'd he say?

WALTER: It's up to you. We'd pay him an appraisal fee—fifty, sixty bucks.

VICTOR: Is he willing to do that?

WALTER: Well, of course he'd rather buy it outright, but what the hell—

ESTHER: Well, that's not his decision, is it?

VICTOR: No . . . it's just that I feel I did come to an agreement with him and I—

WALTER: Personally, I wouldn't let that bother me. He'd be making fifty bucks for filling out a piece of paper.

ESTHER: That's not bad for an afternoon.

Pause.

VICTOR: I'd like to think about it.

ESTHER: There's not much time, though, if you want to deal with *him*.

VICTOR, *cornered:* I'd like a few minutes, that's all.

WALTER, *to Esther:* Sure . . . let him think it over. *To Victor:* It's perfectly legal, if that's what's bothering you. I almost did it with my stuff but I finally decided to keep it. *He laughs.* In fact, my own apartment is so loaded up it doesn't look too different from this.

ESTHER: Well, maybe you'll get married again.

WALTER: I doubt that very much, Esther. I often feel I never should have.

ESTHER, *scoffing:* Why!

WALTER: Seriously. I'm in a strange business, you know. There's too much to learn and far too little time to learn it. And there's a price you have to pay for that. I tried awfully hard to kid myself but there's simply no time for people. Not the way a woman expects, if she's any kind of woman. *He laughs.* But I'm doing pretty well alone!

VICTOR: How would I list an amount like that on my income tax?

WALTER: Well . . . call it a gift. *Victor is silent, obviously in conflict. Walter sees the emotion.* Not that it is, but you could list it as such. It's allowed.

VICTOR: I see. I was just curious how it—

WALTER: Just enter it as a gift. There's no problem. *With the first sting of a vague resentment, Walter turns his eyes away. Esther raises her eyebrows, staring at the floor. Walter lifts the foil off the table—clearly changing the subject.* You still fence?

VICTOR, *almost gratefully pursuing this diversion:* No, you got to join a club and all that. And I work weekends often. I just found it here.

WALTER, *as though to warm the mood:* Mother used to love to watch him do this.

ESTHER, *surprised, pleased:* Really?

WALTER: Sure, she used to come to all his matches.

ESTHER, *to Victor, somehow charmed:* You never told me that.

WALTER: Of course; she's the one made him take it up. *He laughs to Victor.* She thought it was elegant!

VICTOR: Hey, that's right!

WALTER, *laughing at the memory:* He did look pretty good too! *He spreads his jacket away from his chest.* I've still got the wounds! *To Victor, who laughs:* Especially with those French gauntlets she—

VICTOR, *recalling:* Say . . . ! *Looking around with an enlivened need:* I wonder where the hell . . . *He suddenly moves toward a bureau.* Wait, I think they used to be in . . .

ESTHER, *to Walter:* French gauntlets?

WALTER: She brought them from Paris. Gorgeously embroidered. He looked like one of the musketeers.

Out of the drawer where he earlier found the ice skate, Victor takes a pair of emblazoned gauntlets.

VICTOR: Here they are! What do you know!

ESTHER, *reaching her hand out:* Aren't they beautiful! *He hands her one.*

VICTOR: God, I'd forgotten all about them. *He slips one on his hand.*

WALTER: Christmas, 1929.

VICTOR, *moving his hand in the gauntlet:* Look at that, they're still soft . . . *To Walter—a little shy in asking:* How do you remember all this stuff?

WALTER: Why not? Don't you?

ESTHER: He doesn't remember your mother very well.

VICTOR: I remember her. *Looking at the gauntlet:* It's just her face; somehow I can never *see* her.

WALTER, *warmly:* That's amazing, Vic. *To Esther:* She adored him.

ESTHER, *pleased:* Did she?

WALTER: Victor? If it started to rain she'd run all the way to school with his galoshes. Her Victor—my God! By the time he could light a match he was already Louis Pasteur.

VICTOR: It's odd . . . like the harp! I can almost hear the music . . . But I can never see her face. Somehow. *For a moment, silence, as he looks across at the harp.*

WALTER: What's the problem?

Pause. Victor's eyes are swollen with feeling. He turns and looks

up at Walter, who suddenly is embarrassed and oddly anxious.
Solomon enters from the bedroom. He looks quite distressed.
He is in his vest, his tie is open.

SOLOMON, *without coming downstage:* Please, Doctor, if you
wouldn't mind I would like to . . . *He breaks off, indicating the
bedroom.*

WALTER: What is it?

SOLOMON: Just for one minute, please.

*Walter stands. Solomon glances at Victor and Esther and returns
to the bedroom.*

WALTER: I'll be right back. *He goes rather quickly up and into
the bedroom.*

A pause. Victor is sitting in silence, unable to face her.

ESTHER, *with delicacy and pity, sensing his conflicting feelings:*
Why can't you take him as he is? *He glances at her.* Well you
can't expect him to go into an apology, Vic—he probably sees
it all differently, anyway. *He is silent. She comes to him.* I know
it's difficult, but he is trying to make a gesture, I think.

VICTOR: I guess he is, yes.

ESTHER: You know what would be lovely? If we could take a
few weeks and go to like . . . out-of-the-way places . . . just
to really break it up and see all the things that people do.
You've been around such mean, petty people for so long, and
little ugly tricks. I'm serious—it's not romantic. We're much
too suspicious of everything.

VICTOR, *staring ahead:* Strange guy.

ESTHER: Why?

VICTOR: Well, to walk in that way—as though nothing ever
happened.

ESTHER: Why not? What can be done about it?

VICTOR, *after a slight pause:* I feel I have to say something.

ESTHER, *with a slight trepidation, less than she feels:* What can you say?

VICTOR: You feel I ought to just take the money and shut up, heh?

ESTHER: But what's the point of going backwards?

VICTOR, *with a self-bracing tension:* I'm not going to take this money unless I talk to him.

ESTHER, *frightened:* You can't bear the thought that he's decent. *He looks at her sharply.* That's all it is, dear. I'm sorry, I have to say it.

VICTOR, *without raising his voice:* I can't bear that he's *decent!*

ESTHER: You throw this away, you've got to explain it to me. You can't go on blaming everything on him or the system or God knows what else! You're free and you can't make a move, Victor, and that's what's driving me crazy! *Silence. Quietly:* Now take this money. *He is silent, staring at her.* You take this money! Or I'm washed up. You hear me? If you're stuck it doesn't mean I have to be. Now that's it.

Movements are heard within the bedroom. She straightens. Victor smooths down his hair with a slow, preparatory motion of his hand, like one adjusting himself for combat. Walter enters from the bedroom, smiling, shaking his head.

WALTER, *indicating the bedroom:* Boy—we got a tiger here. What is this between you, did you know him before?

VICTOR: No. Why? What'd he say?

WALTER: He's still trying to buy it outright. *He laughs.* He talks like you added five years by calling him up.

VICTOR: Well, what's the difference, I don't mind.

WALTER, *registering the distant rebuke:* No, that's fine, that's all right. *He sits. Slight pause.* We don't understand each other, do we?

VICTOR, *with a certain thrust, matching Walter's smile:* I am a little confused, Walter . . . yes.

WALTER: Why is that? *Victor doesn't answer at once.* Come on, we'll all be dead soon!

VICTOR: All right, I'll give you one example. When I called you Monday and Tuesday and again this morning—

WALTER: I've explained that.

VICTOR: But I don't make phone calls to pass the time. Your nurse sounded like I was a pest of some kind . . . it was humiliating.

WALTER—*oddly, he is over-upset:* I'm terribly sorry, she shouldn't have done that.

VICTOR: I know, Walter, but I can't imagine she takes that tone all by herself.

WALTER, *aware now of the depth of resentment in Victor:* Oh no —she's often that way. I've never referred to you like that. *Victor is silent, not convinced.* Believe me, will you? I'm terribly sorry. I'm overwhelmed with work, that's all it is.

VICTOR: Well, you asked me, so I'm telling you.

WALTER: Yes! You should! But don't misinterpret that. *Slight pause. His tension has increased. He braves a smile.* Now about this tax thing. He'd be willing to make the appraisal twenty-five thousand. *With difficulty:* If you'd like, I'd be perfectly willing for you to have the whole amount I'd be saving.

Slight pause.

ESTHER: Twelve thousand?

WALTER: Whatever it comes to. *Pause. Esther slowly looks to Victor.* You must be near retirement now, aren't you?

ESTHER, *excitedly:* He's past it. But he's trying to decide what to do.

WALTER: Oh. *To Victor—near open embarrassment now:* It would come in handy, then, wouldn't it? *Victor glances at him as a substitute for a reply.* I don't need it, that's all, Vic. Actually, I've been about to call you for quite some time now.

VICTOR: What for?

WALTER—*suddenly, with a strange quick laugh, he reaches and touches Victor's knee:* Don't be suspicious!

VICTOR, *grinning:* I'm just trying to figure it out, Walter.

WALTER: Yes, good. All right. *Slight pause.* I thought it was time we got to know one another. That's all.

Slight pause.

VICTOR: You know, Walter, I tried to call you a couple of times before this about the furniture—must be three years ago.

WALTER: I was sick.

VICTOR, *surprised:* Oh . . . Because I left a lot of messages

WALTER: I was quite sick. I was hospitalized.

ESTHER: What happened?

WALTER, *after a slight pause, as though he were not quite sure whether to say it:* I broke down.

Slight pause.

VICTOR: I had no idea.

WALTER: Actually, I'm only beginning to catch up with things. I was out of commission for nearly three years. *With a thrust of success:* But I'm almost thankful for it now—I've never been happier!

ESTHER: You seem altogether different!

WALTER: I think I am, Esther. I live differently, I think differently. All I have now is a small apartment. And I got rid of the nursing homes—

VICTOR: What nursing homes?

WALTER, *with a removed self-amusement:* Oh, I owned three nursing homes. There's big money in the aged, you know. Helpless, desperate children trying to dump their parents—nothing like it. I even pulled out of the market. Fifty per cent of my time now is in City hospitals. And I tell you, I'm alive. For the first time. I do medicine, and that's it. *Attempting an intimate grin:* Not that I don't soak the rich occasionally, but only enough to live, really. *It is as though this was his mission here, and he waits for Victor's comment.*

VICTOR: Well, that must be great.

WALTER, *seizing on this minute encouragement:* Vic, I wish we could talk for weeks, there's so much I want to tell you. . . . *It is not rolling quite the way he would wish and he must pick examples of his new feelings out of the air.* I never had friends—you probably know that. But I do now, I have good friends. *He moves, sitting nearer Victor, his enthusiasm flowing.* It all happens so gradually. You start out wanting to be the best, and there's no question that you do need a certain fanaticism; there's so much to know and so little time. Until you've eliminated everything extraneous—*he smiles*—including people. And of course the time comes when you realize that you haven't merely been specializing in something—something has been specializing in you. You become a kind of instrument, an instrument that cuts money out of people, or fame out of the world. And it finally makes you stupid. Power can do that. You get to think that because you can frighten people they love you. Even that you love them. And the whole thing comes down to fear. One night I found myself in the middle of my living room, dead drunk, with a knife in my hand, getting ready to kill my wife.

ESTHER: Good Lord!

WALTER: Oh ya—and I nearly made it too! *He laughs.* But there's one virtue in going nuts—provided you survive, of course. You get to see the terror—not the screaming kind, but the slow, daily fear you call ambition, and cautiousness, and piling up the money. And really, what I wanted to tell you for some time now, is that you helped me to understand that in myself.

VICTOR: Me?

WALTER: Yes. *He grins warmly, embarrassed.* Because of what you did. I could never understand it, Vic—after all, you *were* the better student. And to stay with a job like that through all those years seemed . . . *He breaks off momentarily, the uncertainty of Victor's reception widening his smile.* You see, it never dawned on me until I got sick—that you'd made a choice.

VICTOR: A choice, how?

WALTER: You wanted a real life. And that's an expensive thing; it costs. *He has found his theme now, sees he has at last touched something in Victor. A breath of confidence comes through now.* I know I may sound terribly naïve, but I'm still unused to talking about anything that matters. Frankly, I didn't answer your calls this week because I was afraid. I've struggled so long for a concept of myself and I'm not sure I can make it believable to you. But I'd like to. *He sees permission to go on in Victor's perplexed eyes:* You see, I got to a certain point where . . . I dreaded my own work; I finally couldn't cut. There are times, as you know, when if you leave someone alone he might live a year or two; while if you go in you might kill him. And the decision is often—not quite, but almost—arbitrary. But the odds are acceptable, provided you think the right thoughts. Or don't think at all, which I managed to do till then. *Slight pause. He is no longer smiling; instead, a near-embarrassment is on him.* I ran into a cluster of misjudgments. It can happen, but it never had to me, not one on top of the other. And they had one thing in common; they'd all been diagnosed by other men as inoperable. And quite suddenly the . . . the whole prospect of my own motives opened up. Why had I taken risks that very competent men had declined? And the quick answer, of course, is—to pull off the impossible. Shame the competition. But suddenly I saw something else. And it was terror. In dead center, directing my brains, my hands, my ambition—for thirty years.

Slight pause.

VICTOR: Terror of what?

Pause.

WALTER, *his gaze direct on Victor now:* Of it ever happening to me—*he glances at the center chair*—as it happened to him. Overnight, for no reason, to find yourself degraded and thrown down. *With the faintest hint of impatience and challenge:* You know what I'm talking about, don't you? *Victor turns away slightly, refusing commitment.* Isn't that why you turned your back on it all?

VICTOR, *sensing the relevancy to himself now:* Partly. Not altogether, though.

WALTER: Vic, we were both running from the same thing. I thought I wanted to be tops, but what it was was untouchable. I ended in a swamp of success and bankbooks, you on civil service. The difference is that you haven't hurt other people to defend yourself. And I've learned to respect that, Vic; you simply tried to make yourself useful.

ESTHER: That's wonderful—to come to such an understanding with yourself.

WALTER: Esther, it's a strange thing; in the hospital, for the first time since we were boys, I began to feel . . . like a brother. In the sense that we shared something. *To Victor:* And I feel I would know how to be friends now.

VICTOR, *after a slight pause—he is unsure:* Well, fine. I'm glad of that.

WALTER—*he sees the reserve but feels he has made headway and presses on a bit more urgently:* You see, that's why you're still so married. That's a very rare thing. And why your boy's in such good shape. You've lived a real life. *To Esther:* But you know that better than I.

ESTHER: I don't know what I know, Walter.

WALTER: Don't doubt it, dear—believe me, you're fortunate people. *To Victor:* You know that, don't you?

VICTOR, *without looking at Esther:* I think so.

ESTHER: It's not quite as easy as you make it, Walter.

WALTER—*he hesitates, then throws himself into it:* Look, I've had a wild idea—it'll probably seem absurd to you, but I wish you'd think about it before you dismiss it. I gather you haven't decided what to do with yourself now? You're retiring . . . ?

VICTOR: I'll decide one of these days, I'm still thinking.

WALTER, *nervously:* Could I suggest something?

VICTOR: Sure, go ahead.

WALTER: We've been interviewing people for the new wing. For the administrative side. Kind of liaison people between the scientists and the board. And it occurred to me several times that you might fit in there. *Slight pause.*

ESTHER, *with a release of expectation:* That would be wonderful!

VICTOR, *after a slight pause—he glances at her with suppression, but his voice betrays excitement:* What could I do there, though?

WALTER, *sensing Victor's interest:* It's kind of fluid at the moment, but there's a place for people with a certain amount of science who—

VICTOR: I have no degree, you know.

WALTER: But you've had analytic chemistry, and a lot of math and physics, if I recall. If you thought you needed it you could take some courses in the evenings. I think you have enough background. How would you feel about that?

VICTOR, *digging in against the temptation:* Well . . . I'd like to know more about it, sure.

ESTHER, *as though to press him to accept:* It'd be great if he could work in science, it's really the only thing he ever wanted.

WALTER: I know; it's a pity he never went on with it. *Turning to Victor:* It'd be perfectly simple, Vic, I'm chairman of the committee. I could set it all up—

Solomon enters. They turn to him, surprised. He seems about to say something, but in fear changes his mind.

SOLOMON: Excuse me, go right ahead. *He goes nervously to his portfolio, reaching into it, which was not his original intention.* I'm sorry to disturb you. *He takes out an orange and starts back to the bedroom, then halts, addressing Walter:* About the harp. If you'll make me a straight out-and-out sale, I would be willing to go another fifty dollars. So it's eleven fifty, and between the two of you nobody has to do any favors.

WALTER: Well, you're getting warmer.

SOLOMON: I'm a fair person! So you don't have to bother with the appraisal and deductions, all right? *Before Walter can answer:* But don't rush, I'll wait. I'm at your service. *He goes quickly and worriedly into the bedroom.*

ESTHER, *starting to laugh, to Victor:* Where did you *find* him?

WALTER: —that wonderful? He "made it all ethical"! *Esther bursts out laughing, and Walter with her, and Victor manages to join. As it begins to subside, Walter turns to him.* What do you say, Vic? Will you come by?

The laughter is gone. The smile is just fading on Victor's face. He looks at nothing, as though deciding. The pause lengthens, and lengthens still. Now it begins to seem he may not speak at all. No one knows how to break into his puzzling silence. At last he turns to Walter with a rather quick movement of his head, as though he had made up his mind to take the step.

VICTOR: I'm not sure I know what you want, Walter.

Walter looks shocked, astonished, almost unbelieving. But Victor's gaze is steady on him.

ESTHER, *with a tone of the conciliator shrouding her shock and protest:* I don't think that's being very fair, is it?

VICTOR: Why is it unfair? We're talking about some pretty big steps here. *To Walter:* Not that I don't appreciate it, Walter, but certain things have happened, haven't they? *With a half laugh:* It just seems odd to suddenly be talking about—

WALTER, *downing his resentment:* I'd hoped we could take one step at a time, that's all. It's very complicated between us, I think, and it seemed to me we might just try to—

VICTOR: I know, but you can understand it would be a little confusing.

WALTER—*against his will, anger peaks his voice:* What do you find confusing?

VICTOR—*he considers for a moment, but he cannot go back:* You must have some idea, don't you?

WALTER: This is a little astonishing, Victor. After all these years you can't expect to settle everything in one conversation, can you? I simply felt that with a little good will we . . . we . . . *He sees Victor's adamant poise.* Oh, the hell with it. *He goes abruptly and snatches up his coat and one of the evening gowns.* Get what you can from the old man, I don't want any of it. *He goes and extends his hand to Esther, forcing a smile.* I'm sorry, Esther. It was nice seeing you anyway. *Sickened, she accepts his hand.* Maybe I'll see you again, Vic. Good luck. *He starts for the door. There are tears in his eyes.*

ESTHER, *before she can think:* Walter?

Walter halts and turns to her questioningly. She looks to Victor helplessly. But he cannot think either.

WALTER: I don't accept this resentment, Victor. It simply baffles me. I don't understand it. I just want you to know how I feel.

ESTHER, *assuaging:* It's not resentment, Walter.

VICTOR: The whole thing is a little fantastic to me, that's all. I haven't cracked a book in twenty-five years. How do I walk into a research laboratory?

ESTHER: But Walter feels that you have enough background—

VICTOR, *almost laughing over his quite concealed anger at her:* I know less chemistry than most high-school kids, Esther. *To Walter:* And physics, yet! Good God, Walter. *He laughs.* Where you been?

WALTER: I'm sure you could make a place for yourself—

VICTOR: What place? Running papers from one office to another?

WALTER: You're not serious.

VICTOR: Why? Sooner or later my being your brother is not

going to mean very much, is it? I've been walking a beat for twenty-eight years, I'm not qualified for anything technical. What's this all about?

WALTER: Why do you keep asking what it's about? I've been perfectly open with you, Victor!

VICTOR: I don't think you have.

WALTER: Why! What do you think I'm—?

VICTOR: Well, when you say what you said a few minutes ago, I—

WALTER: What did I say?

VICTOR, *with a resolutely cool smile:* What a pity it was that I didn't go on with science.

WALTER, *puzzled:* What's wrong with that?

VICTOR, *laughing:* Oh, Walter, come on, now!

WALTER: But I feel that. I've always felt that.

VICTOR, *smiling still, and pointing at the center chair; a new reverberation sounds in his voice:* There used to be a man in that chair, staring into space. Don't you remember that?

WALTER: Very well, yes. I sent him money every month.

VICTOR: You sent him five dollars every month.

WALTER: I could afford five dollars. But what's that got to do with you?

VICTOR: What it's got to do with me!

WALTER: Yes, I don't see that.

VICTOR: Where did you imagine the rest of his living was coming from?

WALTER: Victor, that was your decision, not mine.

VICTOR: My decision!

WALTER: We had a long talk in this room once, Victor.

VICTOR, *not recalling:* What talk?

WALTER, *astonished:* Victor! We came to a complete under-standing—just after you moved up here with Dad. I told you then that I was going to finish my schooling come hell or high water, and I advised you to do the same. In fact, I warned you not to allow him to strangle your life. *To Esther:* And if I'm not mistaken I told you the same at your wedding, Esther.

Victor, *with an incredulous laugh:* Who the hell was supposed to keep him alive, Walter?

WALTER, *with a strange fear, more than anger:* Why did any-body have to? He wasn't sick. He was perfectly fit to go to work.

VICTOR: Work? In 1936? With no skill, no money?

WALTER, *in an outburst:* Then he could have gone on welfare! Who *was* he, some exiled royalty? What did a hundred and fifty million other people do in 1936? He'd have survived, Vic-tor. Good God, you must know that by now, don't you?

Slight pause.

VICTOR—*suddenly at the edge of fury, and caught by Walter's voicing his own opinion, he turns to Esther:* I've had enough of this, Esther; it's the same old thing all over again, let's get out of here. *He starts rapidly upstage toward the bedroom.*

WALTER, *quickly:* Vic! Please! *He catches Victor, who frees his arm.* I'm not running him down. I loved him in many ways—

ESTHER, *as though conceding her earlier position:* Vic, listen—maybe you *ought* to talk about it.

VICTOR: It's all pointless! The whole thing doesn't matter to me! *He turns to go to the bedroom.*

WALTER: He exploited you! *Victor halts, turns to him, his anger full in his face.* Doesn't that matter to you?

VICTOR: Let's get one thing straight, Walter—I am nobody's victim.

WALTER: But that's exactly what I've tried to tell you. I'm not trying to condescend.

VICTOR: Of course you are. Would you be saying any of this if I'd made a pile of money somewhere? *Dead stop.* I'm sorry, Walter, I can't take that. I made no choice; the icebox was empty and the man was sitting there with his mouth open. *Slight pause.* I didn't start this, Walter, and the whole thing doesn't interest me, but when you talk about making choices, and I should have gone on with science, I have to say something. Just because you want things a certain way doesn't make them that way. *He has ended at a point distant from Walter.*

A slight pause.

WALTER, *with affront mixed into his trepidation:* All right, then . . . How do *you* see it?

VICTOR: Look, you've been sick, Walter, why upset yourself with all this?

WALTER: It's important to me!

VICTOR, *trying to smile, and in a friendly way:* But why? It's all over the dam. *He starts toward the bedroom again.*

ESTHER: I think he's come to you in good faith, Victor. *He turns to her angrily, but she braves his look.* I don't see why you can't consider his offer.

VICTOR: I said I'd consider it.

ESTHER, *restraining a cry:* You know you're turning it down! *In a certain fear of him, but persisting:* I mean what's so dreadful about telling the truth, can it be any worse than this?

VICTOR: What "truth"? What are you—?

Solomon suddenly appears from the bedroom.

ESTHER: For God's sake, *now* what?

SOLOMON: I just didn't want you to think I wouldn't make the appraisal; I will, I'll do it—

ESTHER, *pointing to the bedroom:* Will you please leave us alone!

SOLOMON, *suddenly, his underlying emotion coming through, indicating Victor:* What do you want from him! He's a policeman! I'm a dealer, he's a doctor, and he's a policeman, so what's the good you'll tear him to pieces?

ESTHER: Well, one of us has got to leave this room, Victor.

SOLOMON: Please, Esther, let me . . . *Going quickly to Walter:* Doctor, listen to me, take my advice—stop it. What can come of this? In the first place, if you take the deduction how do you know in two, three years they wouldn't come back to you, whereby they disallow it? I don't have to tell you, the federal government is not reliable. I understand very well you want to be sweet to him—*to Esther*—but can be two, three years before you'll know how sweet they're going to allow him. *To Victor and Walter:* In other words, what I'm trying to bring out, my boys, is that—

ESTHER: —you want the furniture.

SOLOMON, *shouting at her:* Esther, if I didn't want it I wouldn't buy it! But what can they settle here? It's still up to the federal government, don't you see? If they can't settle nothing they should stop it right now! *With a look of warning and alarm in his eyes:* Now please—do what I tell you! I'm not a fool! *He walks out into the bedroom, shaking.*

WALTER, *after a moment:* I guess he's got a point, Vic. Why don't you just sell it to him; maybe then we can sit down and talk sometime. *Glancing at the furniture:* It isn't really a very conducive atmosphere. Can I call you?

VICTOR: Sure.

ESTHER: You're both fantastic. *She tries to laugh.* We're giving this furniture away because nobody's able to say the simplest things. You're incredible, the both of you.

WALTER, *a little shamed:* It isn't that easy, Esther.

ESTHER: Oh, what the hell—I'll say it. When he went to you, Walter, for the five hundred he needed to get his degree—

VICTOR: Esther! There's no—

ESTHER: It's one of the things standing between you, isn't it? Maybe Walter can clear it up. I mean . . . Good God, is there never to be an end? *To Walter, without pause:* Because it stunned him, Walter. He'll never say it, but—*she takes the plunge*—he hadn't the slightest doubt you'd lend it to him. So when you turned him down—

VICTOR, *as though it wearies him:* Esther, he was just starting out—

ESTHER, *in effect, taking her separate road:* Not the way you told me! Please let me finish! *To Walter:* You already had the house in Rye, you were perfectly well established, weren't you?

VICTOR: So what? He didn't feel he could—

WALTER, *with a certain dread, quietly:* No, no, I . . . I could have spared the money. . . . *He sits slowly.* Please, Vic—sit down, it'll only take a moment.

VICTOR: I just don't see any point in—

WALTER: No—no; maybe it's just as well to talk now. We've never talked about this. I think perhaps we have to. *Slight pause. Toward Esther:* It *was* despicable; but I don't think I

can leave it quite that way. *Slight pause.* Two or three days afterward—*to Victor*—after you came to see me, I phoned to
offer you the money. Did you know that? *Slight pause.*

VICTOR: Where'd you phone?

WALTER: Here. I spoke to Dad. *Slight pause. Victor sits.* I saw
that I'd acted badly, and I—

VICTOR: You didn't act badly—

WALTER, *with a sudden flight of his voice:* It was frightful! *He
gathers himself against his past.* We'll have another talk, won't
we? I wasn't prepared to go into all this. . . . *Victor is expressionless.* In any case . . . when I called here he told me you'd
joined the Force. And I said—he mustn't permit you to do a
thing like that. I said—you had a fine mind and with a little
luck you could amount to something in science. That it was a
terrible waste. Etcetera. And his answer was—"Victor wants
to help me. I can't stop him."

Pause.

VICTOR: You told him you were ready to give me the money?

WALTER: Victor, you remember the . . . the helplessness in
his voice. At that time? With Mother recently gone and everything shot out from under him?

VICTOR, *persisting:* Let me understand that, Walter; did you
tell—?

WALTER, *in anguish, but hewing to himself:* There are conversations, aren't there, and looking back it's impossible to explain
why you said or didn't say certain things? I'm not defending
it, but I would like to be understood, if that's possible. You all
seemed to need each other more, Vic—more than I needed
them. I was never able to feel your kind of . . . faith in him;
that . . . confidence. His selfishness—which was perfectly
normal—was always obvious to me, but you never seemed to
notice it. To the point where I used to blame myself for a lack

of feeling. You understand? So when he said that you wanted to help him, I felt somehow that it'd be wrong for me to try to break it up between you. It seemed like interfering.

VICTOR: I see. Because he never mentioned you'd offered the money.

WALTER: All I'm trying to convey is that . . . I was never indifferent; that's the whole point. I did call here to offer the loan, but he made it impossible, don't you see?

VICTOR: I understand.

WALTER, *eagerly:* Do you?

VICTOR: Yes.

WALTER, *sensing the unsaid:* Please say what you think. It's absurd to go on this way. What do you want to say?

VICTOR, *after a slight pause:* I think it was all . . . very convenient for you.

WALTER, *appalled:* That's all?

VICTOR: I think so. If you thought Dad meant so much to me —and I guess he did in a certain way—why would five hundred bucks break us apart? I'd have gone on supporting him; it would have let me finish school, that's all. It doesn't make any sense, Walter.

WALTER, *with a hint of hysteria in his tone:* What makes sense?

VICTOR: You didn't give me the money because you didn't want to.

WALTER, *after a slight pause, hurt and quietly enraged:* It's that simple.

VICTOR: That's what it comes to, doesn't it? Not that you had any obligation, but if you want to help somebody you do it, if you don't, you don't. *He sees Walter's growing frustration and Esther's impatience.* Well, why is that so astonishing? We do what we want to do, don't we? *Walter doesn't reply. Victor's anxiety rises.* I don't understand what you're bringing this all up for.

WALTER: You don't feel the need to heal anything.

VICTOR: I wouldn't mind that, but how does this heal anything?

ESTHER: I think he's been perfectly clear, Victor. He's asking your friendship.

VICTOR: By offering me a job and twelve thousand dollars?

WALTER: Why not? What else can I offer you?

VICTOR: But why do you have to offer me anything? *Walter is silent, morally checked.* It sounds like I have to be saved, or something.

WALTER: I simply felt that there was work you could do that you'd enjoy and I—

VICTOR: Walter, I haven't got the education, what are you talking about? You can't walk in with one splash and wash out twenty-eight years. There's a price people pay. I've paid it, it's all gone, I haven't got it any more. Just like you paid, didn't you? You've got no wife, you've lost your family, you're rattling around all over the place? Can you go home and start all over again from scratch? This is where we are; now, right here, now. And as long as we're talking, I have to tell you that this is not what you say in front of a man's wife.

WALTER, *glancing at Esther, certainty shattered:* What have I said . . . ?

VICTOR, *trying to laugh:* We don't need to be saved, Walter! I've done a job that has to be done and I think I've done it straight. You talk about being out of the rat race; in my opinion, you're in it as deep as you ever were. Maybe more.

ESTHER, *standing:* I want to go, Victor.

VICTOR: Please, Esther, he's said certain things and I don't think I can leave it this way.

ESTHER, *angrily:* Well, what's the difference?

VICTOR, *suppressing an outburst:* Because for some reason you don't understand *anything* any more! *He is trembling as he turns to Walter.* What are you trying to tell me—that it was all unnecessary? Is that it? *Walter is silent.* Well, correct me, is that the message? Because that's all I get out of this.

WALTER, *toward Esther:* I guess it's impossible—

VICTOR, *the more strongly because Walter seems about to be allied with Esther:* What's impossible? . . . What do you *want*, Walter!

WALTER—*in the pause is the admission that he indeed has not leveled yet, and there is fear in his voice:* I wanted to be of some use. I've learned some painful things, but it isn't enough to know; I wanted to act on what I know.

VICTOR: Act—in what way?

WALTER, *knowing it may be a red flag, but his honor is up:* I feel . . . I could be of help. Why live, only to repeat the same mistakes again and again? I didn't want to let the chance go by, as I let it go before. *Victor is unconvinced.* And I must say, if this is as far as you can go with me, then you're only defeating yourself.

VICTOR: Like I did before. *Walter is silent.* Is that what you mean?

WALTER—*he hesitates, then with frightened but desperate acceptance of combat:* All right, yes; that's what I meant.

VICTOR: Well, that's what I thought. See, there's one thing about the cops—you get to learn how to listen to people, because if you don't hear right sometimes you end up with a knife in your back. In other words, I dreamed up the whole problem.

WALTER, *casting aside his caution, his character at issue:* Victor, my five hundred dollars was not what kept you from your degree! You could have left Pop and gone right on—he was perfectly fit.

VICTOR: And twelve million unemployed, what was that, my neurosis? I hypnotized myself every night to scrounge the outer leaves of lettuce from the Greek restaurant on the corner? The good parts we cut out of rotten grapefruit . . . ?

WALTER: I'm not trying to deny—

VICTOR, *leaning into Walter's face:* We were eating garbage here, buster!

ESTHER: But what is the point of—

VICTOR, *to Esther:* What are you trying to do, turn it all into a dream? *To Walter:* And perfectly fit! What about the inside of his head? The man was ashamed to go into the street!

ESTHER: But Victor, he's gone now.

VICTOR, *with a cry—he senses the weakness of his position:* Don't tell me he's gone now! *He is wracked, terribly alone before her.* He was here then, wasn't he? And a system broke down, did I invent that?

ESTHER: No, dear, but it's all different now.

VICTOR: What's different now? We're a goddamned army holding this city down and when it blows again you'll be thankful for a roof over your head! *To Walter:* How can you say that to me? I could have left him with your five dollars a month? I'm sorry, you can't brainwash me—if you got a hook in your mouth don't try to stick it into mine. You want to make up for things, you don't come around to make fools out of people. I didn't invent my life. Not altogether. You had a responsibility here and you walked on it. . . . You can go. I'll send you your half.

He is across the room from Walter, his face turned away. A long pause.

WALTER: If you can reach beyond anger, I'd like to tell you something. Vic? *Victor does not move.* I know I should have said this many years ago. But I did try. When you came to me I told you—remember I said, "Ask Dad for money"? I did say that.

Pause.

VICTOR: What are you talking about?

WALTER: He had nearly four thousand dollars.

ESTHER: When?

WALTER: When they were eating garbage here.

Pause.

VICTOR: How do you know that?

WALTER: He'd asked me to invest it for him.

VICTOR: Invest it.

WALTER: Yes. Not long before he sent you to me for the loan. *Victor is silent.* That's why I never sent him more than I did. And if I'd had the strength of my convictions I wouldn't have sent him that!

Victor sits down in silence. A shame is flooding into him which he struggles with. He looks at nobody.

VICTOR, *as though still absorbing the fact:* He actually had it? In the bank?

WALTER: Vic, that's what he was living on, basically, till he died. What we gave him wasn't enough; you know that.

VICTOR: But he had those jobs—

WALTER: Meant very little. He lived on his money, believe me. I told him at the time, if he would send you through I'd contribute properly. But here he's got you running from job to job to feed him—I'm damned if I'd sacrifice when he was holding out on you. You can understand that, can't you? *Victor turns to the center chair and, shaking his head, exhales a blow of anger and astonishment.* Kid, there's no point getting angry now. You know how terrified he was that he'd never earn anything any more. And there was just no reassuring him.

VICTOR, *with protest—it is still nearly incredible:* But he saw I was supporting him, didn't he?

WALTER: For how long, though?

VICTOR, *angering:* What do you mean, how long? He could see I wasn't walking out—

WALTER: I know, but he was sure you would sooner or later.

ESTHER: He was waiting for him to walk out.

WALTER—*fearing to inflame Victor, he undercuts the obvious answer:* Well . . . you could say that, yes.

ESTHER: I knew it! God, when do I believe what I see!

WALTER: He was terrified, dear, and . . . *To Victor:* I don't mean that he wasn't grateful to you, but he really couldn't understand it. I may as well say it, Vic—I myself never imagined you'd go that far. *Victor looks at him. Walter speaks with delicacy in the face of a possible explosion.* Well, you must certainly see now how extreme a thing it was, to stick with him like that? And at such cost to you?

Victor is silent.

ESTHER, *with sorrow:* He sees it.

WALTER, *to erase it all, to achieve the reconciliation:* We could work together, Vic. I know we could. And I'd love to try it. What do you say?

There is a long pause. Victor now glances at Esther to see her expression. He sees she wants him to. He is on the verge of throwing it all up. Finally he turns to Walter, a new note of awareness in his voice.

VICTOR: Why didn't you tell me he had that kind of money?

WALTER: But I did, when you came to me for the loan.

VICTOR: To "ask Dad"?

WALTER: Yes!

VICTOR: But would I have come to you if I had the faintest idea he had four thousand dollars under his ass? It was meaningless to say that to me.

WALTER: Now just a second . . . *He starts to indicate the harp.*

VICTOR: Cut it out, Walter! I'm sorry, but it's kind of insulting. I'm not five years old! What am I supposed to make of this? You knew he had that kind of money, and came here many times, you sat here, the two of you, watching me walking around in this suit? And now you expect me to—?

WALTER, *sharply:* You certainly knew he had *something*, Victor!

VICTOR: What do you want here? What do you want here!

WALTER: Well, all I can tell you is that *I* wouldn't sit around eating garbage with *that* staring me in the face! *He points at the harp.* Even then it was worth a couple of hundred, maybe more! Your degree was right there. Right there, if nothing else. *Victor is silent, trembling.* But if you want to go on with this fantasy, it's all right with me. God knows, I've had a few of my own. *He starts for his coat.*

VICTOR: Fantasy.

WALTER: It's a fantasy, Victor. Your father was penniless and your brother a son of a bitch, and you play no part at all. I said to ask him because you could see in front of your face that he had some money. You knew it then and you certainly know it now.

VICTOR: You mean if he had a few dollars left, that—?

ESTHER: What do you mean, a few dollars?

VICTOR, *trying to retract:* I didn't know he—

ESTHER: But you knew he had something?

VICTOR, *caught, as though in a dream where nothing is explicable:* I didn't say that.

ESTHER: Then what are you saying?

VICTOR, *pointing at Walter:* Don't you have anything to say to *him?*

ESTHER: I want to understand what you're saying! You knew he had money left?

VICTOR: Not four thousand dol—

ESTHER: But enough to make out?

VICTOR, *crying out in anger and for release:* I couldn't nail him to the wall, could I? He said he had nothing!

ESTHER, *stating and asking:* But you knew better.

VICTOR: I don't know what I knew! *He has called this out, and his voice and words surprise him. He sits staring, cornered by what he senses in himself.*

ESTHER: It's a farce. It's all a goddamned farce!

VICTOR: Don't. Don't say that.

ESTHER: Farce! To stick us into a furnished room so you could send him part of your pay? Even after we were married, to go on sending him money? Put off having children, live like mice—and all the time you knew he . . . ? Victor, I'm trying to understand you. Victor?—Victor!

VICTOR, *roaring out, agonized:* Stop it! Silence. *Then:* Jesus, you can't leave everything out like this. The man was a beaten dog, ashamed to walk in the street, how do you demand his last buck—?

ESTHER: You're still saying that? The man had four thousand dollars! *Victor is silent.* It was all an act! Beaten dog! He was a calculating liar! And in your heart you knew it! *He is struck silent by the fact, which is still ungraspable.* No wonder you're paralyzed—you haven't believed a word you've said all these years. We've been lying away our existence all these years; down the sewer, day after day after day . . . to protect a miserable cheap manipulator. No wonder it all seemed like a dream to me—it *was;* a goddamned nightmare. I knew it was all unreal, I knew it and I let it go by. Well, I can't any more, kid. I can't watch it another day. *I'm* not ready to die. *She moves toward her purse.*

She sits. Pause.

VICTOR, *not going to her—he can't; he is standing yards from her.* This isn't true either.

ESTHER: We are dying, that's what's true!

VICTOR: I'll tell you what happened. You want to hear it? *She catches the lack of advocacy in his tone, the simplicity. He moves from her, gathering himself, and glances at the center chair, then at Walter.* I did tell him what you'd said to me. I faced him with it. *He doesn't go on; his eyes go to the chair.* Not that I "faced" him, I just told him—"Walter said to ask you." *He stops; his stare is on the center chair, caught by memory; in effect, the last line was addressed to the chair.*

WALTER: And what happened?

Pause.

VICTOR, *quietly:* He laughed. I didn't know what to make of it. Tell you the truth—*to Esther*—I don't think a week has gone by that I haven't seen that laugh. Like it was some kind of a wild joke—because we *were* eating garbage here. *He breaks off.* I didn't know what I was supposed to do. And I went out. I went—*he sits, staring*—over to Bryant Park behind the public library. *Slight pause.* The grass was covered with men. Like a battlefield; a big open-air flophouse. And not bums—some of them still had shined shoes and good hats, busted businessmen, lawyers, skilled mechanics. Which I'd seen a hundred times. But suddenly—you know?—I *saw* it. *Slight pause.* There was no mercy. Anywhere. *Glancing at the chair at the end of the table:* One day you're the head of the house, at the head of the table, and suddenly you're shit. Overnight. And I tried to figure out that laugh. How could he be holding out on me when he loved me?

ESTHER: Loved . . .

VICTOR, *his voice swelling with protest:* He loved me, Esther! He just didn't want to end up on the grass! It's not that you don't love somebody, it's that you've got to survive. We know what that feels like, don't we! *She can't answer, feeling the barb.* We do what we have to do. *With a wide gesture including her and Walter and himself:* What else are we talking about here? If he did have something left it was—

ESTHER: "*If*" he had—

VICTOR: What does that change! I know I'm talking like a fool, but what does that change? He couldn't believe in anybody any more, and it was unbearable to me! *The unlooked-for return of his old feelings seems to anger him. Of Walter:* He'd kicked him in the face; my mother—*he glances toward Walter as he speaks; there is hardly a pause*—the night he told us he was bankrupt, my mother . . . It was right on this couch. She was all dressed up—for some affair, I think. Her hair was piled up, and long earrings? And he had his tuxedo on . . . and made us all sit down; and he told us it was all gone. And she vomited. *Slight pause. His horror and pity twist in his voice.* All over his arms. His hands. Just kept on vomiting, like thirty-five years coming up. And he sat there. Stinking like a sewer. And a look came onto his face. I'd never seen a man look like that. He was sitting there, letting it dry on his hands. *Pause. He turns to Esther.* What's the difference what you know? Do *you* do everything you know? *She avoids his eyes, his mourning shared.* Not that I excuse it; it was idiotic, nobody has to tell me that. But you're brought up to believe in one another, you're filled full of that crap—you can't help trying to keep it going, that's all. I thought if I stuck with him, if he could see that somebody was still . . . *He breaks off; the reason strangely has fallen loose. He sits.* I can't explain it; I wanted to . . . stop it from falling apart. I . . . *He breaks off again, staring.*

Pause.

WALTER, *quietly:* It won't work, Vic. *Victor looks at him, then Esther does.* You see it yourself, don't you? It's not that at all. You see that, don't you?

VICTOR, *quietly, avidly:* What?

WALTER, *with his driving need:* Is it really that something fell apart? Were we really brought up to believe in one another? We were brought up to succeed, weren't we? Why else would he respect me so and not you? What fell apart? What was here to fall apart? *Victor looks away at the burgeoning vision.* Was there ever any love here? When he needed her, she vomited. And when you needed him, he laughed. What was unbearable is not that it all fell apart, it was that there was never anything here. *Victor turns back to him, fear on his face.*

ESTHER, *as though she herself were somehow moving under the rays of judgment:* But who . . . who can ever face that, Walter?

WALTER, *to her:* You have to! *To Victor:* What you saw behind the library was not that there was no mercy in the world, kid. It's that there was no love in this house. There was no loyalty. There was nothing here but a straight financial arrangement. That's what was unbearable. And you proceeded to wipe out what you saw.

VICTOR, *with terrible anxiety:* Wipe out—

WALTER: Vic, I've been in this box. I wasted thirty years protecting myself from that catastrophe. *He indicates the chair:* And I only got out alive when I saw that there was no catastrophe, there had never been. They were never lovers—she said a hundred times that her marriage destroyed her musical career. I saw that nothing fell here, Vic—and he doesn't follow me any more with that vomit on his hands. I don't look high and low for some betrayal any more; my days belong to *me* now, I'm not afraid to risk believing someone. All I ever wanted was simply to do science, but I invented an efficient, disaster-proof, money-maker. You—*to Esther, with a warm smile:* He could never stand the sight of blood. He was shy, he was sensitive . . . *To Victor:* And what do you do? March straight into the most violent profession there is. We invent ourselves, Vic, to wipe out what we know. You invent a life of self-sacrifice, a life of duty; but what never existed here cannot be upheld. You were not upholding something, you were denying what you knew they were. And denying yourself. And that's all that is standing between us now—an illusion, Vic. That I kicked them in the face and you must uphold them against me. But I only saw then what you see now—there was nothing here to betray. I am not your enemy. It is all an illusion and if you could walk through it, we could meet . . . *His reconciliation is on him.* You see why I said before, that in the hospital—when it struck me so that we . . . we're brothers. It was only two seemingly different roads out of the same trap. It's almost as though—*he smiles warmly, uncertain still*—we're like two halves of the same guy. As though we can't quite move ahead—alone. You ever feel that? *Victor is silent.* Vic?

Pause.

VICTOR: Walter, I'll tell you—there are days when I can't remember what I've got against you. *He laughs emptily, in suffering.* It hangs in me like a rock. And I see myself in a store window, and my hair going, I'm walking the streets—and I can't remember why. And you can go crazy trying to figure it out when all the reasons disappear—when you can't even hate any more.

WALTER: Because it's unreal, Vic, and underneath you know it is.

VICTOR: Then give me something real.

WALTER: What can I give you?

VICTOR: I'm not blaming you now, I'm asking you. I can understand you walking out. I've wished a thousand times I'd done the same thing. But, to come here through all those years knowing what you knew and saying nothing . . . ?

WALTER: And if I said—Victor, if I said that I did have some wish to hold you back? What would that give you now?

VICTOR: Is that what you wanted? Walter, tell me the truth.

WALTER: I wanted the freedom to do my work. Does that mean I stole your life? *Crying out and standing:* You made those choices, Victor! And that's what you have to face!

VICTOR: But, what do you face? You're not turning me into a walking fifty-year-old mistake—we have to go home when you leave, we have to look at each other. What do *you* face?

WALTER: I have offered you everything I know how to!

VICTOR: I would know if you'd come to give me something! I would know that!

WALTER, *crossing for his coat:* You don't want the truth, you want a monster!

VICTOR: You came for the old handshake, didn't you! The okay! *Walter halts in the doorway.* And you end up with the respect, the career, the money, and the best of all, the thing that nobody else can tell you so you can believe it—that you're one hell of a guy and never harmed anybody in your life! Well, you won't get it, not till I get mine!

WALTER: And you? You never had any hatred for me? Never a wish to see me destroyed? To destroy me, to destroy me with this saintly self-sacrifice, this mockery of sacrifice? What will you give me, Victor?

VICTOR: I don't have it to give you. Not any more. And you don't have it to give me. And there's nothing to give—I see that now. I just didn't want him to end up on the grass. And he didn't. That's all it was, and I don't need anything more. I couldn't work with you, Walter. I can't. I don't trust you.

WALTER: Vengeance. Down to the end. *To Esther:* He is sacrificing his life to vengeance.

ESTHER: Nothing was sacrificed.

WALTER, *to Victor:* To prove with your failure what a treacherous son of a bitch I am!—to hang yourself in my doorway!

ESTHER: Leave him, Walter—please, don't say any more!

WALTER, *humiliated by her—he is furious, takes an unplanned step toward the door:* You quit; both of you. *To Victor as well:* You lay down and quit, and that's the long and short of all your ideology. It is all envy! *Solomon enters, apprehensive, looks from one to the other.* And to this moment you haven't the guts to face it! But your failure does not give you moral authority! Not with me! I *worked* for what I made and there are people walking around today who'd have been dead if I hadn't. Yes. *Moving toward the door, he points at the center chair.* He was smarter than all of us—he saw what you wanted and he gave it to you! *He suddenly reaches out and grabs Solo-*

mon's face and laughs. Go ahead, you old mutt—rob them blind, they love it! *Letting go, he turns to Victor.* You will never, never again make me ashamed! *He strides toward the doorway. A gown lies on the dining table, spread out, and he is halted in surprise at the sight of it. Suddenly he sweeps it up in his hands and rushes at Victor, flinging the gown at him with an outcry. Victor backs up at his wild approach.*

VICTOR: Walter!

The flicker of a humiliated smile passes across Walter's face. He wants to disappear into air. He turns, hardly glancing at Victor, makes for the door, and, straightening, goes out.

VICTOR—*he starts hesitantly to the door:* Maybe he oughtn't go into the street like that—

SOLOMON, *stopping him with his hand:* Let him go. *Victor turns to Solomon uncertainly.* What can you do?

ESTHER: Whatever you see, huh. *Solomon turns to her, questioningly.* You believe what you see.

SOLOMON, *thinking she was rebuking him:* What then?

ESTHER: No—it's wonderful. Maybe that's why you're still going. *Victor turns to her. She stares at the doorway.* I was nineteen years old when I first walked up those stairs—if that's believable. And he had a brother, who was the cleverest, most wonderful young doctor . . . in the world. As he'd be soon. Somehow, some way. *She turns to the center chair.* And a rather sweet, inoffensive gentleman, always waiting for the news to come on. . . . And next week, men we never saw or heard of will come and smash it all apart and take it all away. So many times I thought—the one thing he wanted most was to talk to his brother, and that if they could— But he's come and he's gone. And I still feel it—isn't that terrible? It always seems to me that one little step more and some crazy kind of forgiveness will come and lift up everyone. When do you stop being so . . . foolish?

SOLOMON: I had a daughter, should rest in peace, she took her own life. That's nearly fifty years. And every night I lay down to sleep, she's sitting there. I see her clear like I see you. But if it was a miracle and she came to life, what would I say to her? *He turns back to Victor, paying out.* So you got there seven; so I'm giving you eight, nine, ten, eleven—*he searches, finds a fifty*—and there's a fifty for the harp. Now you'll excuse me—I got a lot of work here tonight. *He gets his pad and pencil and begins carefully listing each piece.*

VICTOR—*he folds the money:* We could still make the picture, if you like.

ESTHER: Okay. *He goes to his suit and begins to rip the plastic wrapper off.* Don't bother. *He looks at her. She turns to Solomon.* Good-by, Mr. Solomon.

SOLOMON, *looking up from his pad:* Good-by, dear. I like that suit, that's very nice. *He returns to his work.*

ESTHER: Thank you. *She walks out with her life.*

VICTOR, *buckling on his gun belt, pulling up his tie:* When will you be taking it away?

SOLOMON: With God's help if I'll live, first thing in the morning.

VICTOR, *of the suit:* I'll be back for this later, then. And there's my foil, and the mask, and the gauntlets. *Puts on his uniform jacket.*

SOLOMON, *continuing his work:* Don't worry, I wouldn't touch it.

VICTOR, *extending his hand:* I'm glad to have met you, Solomon.

SOLOMON: Likewise. And I want to thank you.

VICTOR: What for?

SOLOMON, *with a glance at the furniture:* Well . . . who would ever believe I would start such a thing again . . . ? *He cuts himself off.* But go, go, I got a lot of work here.

VICTOR, *starting to the door, putting his cap on:* Good luck with it.

SOLOMON: Good luck you can never know till the last minute, my boy.

VICTOR, *smiling:* Right. Yes. *With a last look around at the room:* Well . . . by-by.

SOLOMON, *as Victor goes out:* By-by, by-by.

He is alone. He has the pad and pencil in his hand, and he takes the pencil to start work again. But he looks about, and the challenge of it all oppresses him and he is afraid and worried. His hand goes to his cheek, he pulls his flesh in fear, his eyes circling the room.

His eye falls on the phonograph. He goes, inspects it, winds it up, sets the tone arm on the record, and flicks the starting lever. The Laughing Record plays. As the two comedians begin their routine, his depressed expression gives way to surprise. Now he smiles. He chuckles, and remembers. Now a laugh escapes, and he nods his head in recollection. He is laughing now, and shakes his head back and forth as though to say, "It still works!" And the laughter, of the record and his own, increases and combines. He holds his head, unable to stop laughing, and sits in the center chair. He leans back sprawling in the chair, laughing with tears in his eyes, howling helplessly to the air.

SLOW CURTAIN

AUTHOR'S PRODUCTION NOTE

A fine balance of sympathy should be maintained in the playing of the roles of Victor and Walter. The actor playing Walter must not regard his attempts to win back Victor's friendship as mere manipulation. From entrance to exit, Walter is attempting to put into action what he has learned about himself, and sympathy will be evoked for him in proportion to the openness, the depth of need, the intimations of suffering with which the role is played.

This admonition goes beyond the question of theatrics to the theme of the play. As the world now operates, the qualities of both brothers are necessary to it; surely their respective psychologies and moral values conflict at the heart of the social dilemma. The production must therefore withhold judgment in favor of presenting both men in all their humanity and from their own viewpoints. Actually, each has merely proved to the other what the other has known but dared not face. At the end, demanding of one another what was forfeited to time, each is left touching the structure of his life.

The play can be performed with an intermission, as indicated at the end of Act One, if circumstances require it. But an unbroken performance is preferable.

▣ II ▣

OTHER WORKS

The Misfits [I] (*the original story*)

From *The Misfits* [II] (*a cinema novel*)

Fame (*a story*)

Fitter's Night (*a story*)

From *In Russia*

Lines from California (*a poem*)

The Misfits [I]

(THE ORIGINAL STORY)

Wind blew down from the mountains all night. A wild river of air swept and swirled across the dark sky and struck down against the blue desert and hissed back into the hills. The three cowboys slept under their blankets, their backs against the first upward curve of the circling mountains, their faces toward the desert of sage. The wind and its tidal washing seethed through their dreams, and when it stopped there was a lunar silence that caused Gay Langland to open his eyes. For the first time in three nights he could hear his own breathing, and in the new hush he looked up at the stars and saw how clear and bright they were. He felt happy and slid himself out of his blankets and stood up fully dressed.

On the silent plateau between the two mountain ranges Gay Langland was the only moving thing. He turned his head and then his body in a full circle, looking into the deep blue sky for sign of storm. He saw that it would be a good day and a quiet one. He walked a few yards from the two other sleepers and wet the sandy ground. The excitement of the stillness was awakening his body. He returned and lit the bundle of dry sage he had gathered last night, dropped some heavier wood on the quick flames, perched the blackened coffeepot on the stones surrounding the fire bed, and sat on one heel, staring at the fresh orange embers.

Gay Langland was forty-five years old but as limber as he

had ever been in his life. The light of his face brightened when
there were things to do, a nail to straighten, an animal to size
up, and it dimmed when there was nothing in his hands, and
his eyes then went sleepy. When there was something to be
done in a place he stayed there, and when there was nothing
to be done he went from it. He had a wife and two children
less than a hundred miles from here whom he had not seen in
more than three years. She had betrayed him and did not want
him, but the children were naturally better off with their
mother. When he felt lonely for them all he thought of them
longingly, and when the feeling passed he was left without any
question as to what he might do to bring them all back together again. He had been born and raised on rangeland, and
he did not know that anything could be undone that was
done, any more than falling rain could be stopped in mid-air.
And he had a smile and a look on his face that was in accord-
ance. His forehead was evenly tracked with deep ridges, as
though his brows were always raised a little expectantly,
slightly surprised, a little amused, and his mouth friendly. His
ears stuck out, as they often do with little boys or young
calves, and he had a boy's turned-up snub nose. But his skin
was browned by the wind, and his small eyes looked and saw
and, above all, were trained against showing fear.

Gay Langland looked up from the fire at the sky and saw
the first delicate stain of pink. He went over to the sleepers
and shook Guido Racanelli's arm. A grunt of salutation
sounded in Guido's head, but he remained on his side with his
eyes shut. "The sumbitch died off," Gay said to him. Guido
listened, motionless, his eyes shut against the firelight, his
bones warm in his fat. Gay wanted to shake him again and
wake him, but in the last two days he had come to wonder
whether Guido was not secretly considering not flying at all.
The plane's engine was rattling its valves and one shock absorber was weak. Gay had known the pilot for years and he
knew and respected his moods. Flying up and down these
mountain gorges within feet of the rock walls was nothing you

could pressure a man to do. But now that the wind had died Gay hoped very much that Guido would take off this morning and let them begin their work.

He got to his feet and again glanced skyward. Then he stood there thinking of Roslyn. And he had a strong desire to have money in his pocket that he had earned himself when he came to her tonight. The feeling had been returning again and again that he had somehow passed the kidding point and that he had to work again and earn his way as he always had before he met her. Not that he didn't work for her, but it wasn't the same. Driving her car, repairing her house, running errands—all that stuff wasn't what you would call work. Still, he thought, it was too. Yet, it wasn't either.

He stepped over to the other sleeper and shook him. Perce Howland opened his eyes.

"The sumbitch died, Perce," Gay said.

Perce's eyes looked toward the heavens and he nodded. Then he slid out of his blankets and walked past Gay and stood wetting the sand, breathing deeply as in sleep. Gay always found him humorous to watch when he woke up. Perce walked into things and sometimes stood wetting his own boots. He was a little like a child waking up, and his eyes now were still dreamy and soft.

Gay called over to him, "Better'n wages, huh, Perce?"

"Damn right," Perce muttered and returned to the fire, rubbing his skin against his clothes.

Gay kneeled by the fire again, scraping hot coals into a pile and setting the frying pan over them on stones. He could pick up hot things without feeling pain. Now he moved an ember with his finger.

"You make me nervous doing that," Perce said, looking down over his shoulder.

"Nothin' but fire," Gay said, pleased.

They were in silence for a moment, both of them enjoying the brightening air. "Guido goin' up?" Perce asked.

"Didn't say. I guess he's thinkin' about it."

"Be light pretty soon," Perce warned.

He glanced off to the closest range and saw the purple rocks rising in their mystery toward the faintly glowing stars. Perce Howland was twenty-two, hipless and tall, and he stood there as effortlessly as the mountains he was looking at, as though he had been created there in his dungarees, with the tight plaid shirt and the three-button cuffs, the broad-brimmed beige hat set back on his blond head, and his thumbs tucked into his belt so his fingers could touch the engraved belt buckle with his name spelled out under the raised figure of the bucking horse. It was his first bucking-horse prize, and he loved to touch it when he stood waiting, and he liked to wait.

Perce had known Gay Langland for only five weeks, and Guido for three days. He had met Gay in a Bowie bar, and Gay had asked him where he was from and what he was doing, and he had told Gay his story, which was the usual for most of the rodeo riders. He had come on down from Nevada, as he had done since he was sixteen, to follow the local rodeos and win some money riding bucking horses, but this trip had been different, because he had lost the desire to go back home again.

They had become good friends that night when Gay took him to Roslyn's house to sleep, and when he woke in the morning he had been surprised that an educated eastern woman should have been so regular and humorous and interested in his opinions. So he had been floating around with Roslyn and Gay Langland, and they were comfortable to be with; Gay mostly, because Gay never thought to say he ought to be making something of his life. Gay made him feel it was all right to go from day to day and week to week. Perce Howland did not trust anybody too far, and it was not necessary to trust Gay because Gay did not want anything of him or try to manipulate him. He just wanted a partner to go mustanging, and Perce had never done anything like that and he wanted to see how it was. And now he was here, sixty miles from the nearest town, seven thousand feet up in the air, and for two days waiting for the wind to die so the pilot could take off into the mountains where the wild horses lived.

Perce looked out toward the desert, which was beginning to show its silent horizon. "Bet the moon looks like this if anybody could get there."

Gay Langland did not answer. In his mind he could feel the wild horses grazing and moving about in the nearby mountains and he wanted to get to them. Indicating Guido Racanelli, he said, "Give him a shake, Perce. The sun's about up."

Perce started over to Guido, who moved before Perce reached him. "Gettin' light, Guido," Perce said.

Guido Racanelli rolled upright on his great behind, his belly slung over his belt, and he inspected the brightening sky in the distance as though some personal message were out there for him. The pink reflected light brightened his face. The flesh around his eyes was white where the goggles protected his face, and the rest of his skin was burned brown by wind. His silences were more profound than the silences of others because his cheeks were so deep, like the melon-half cheeks of a baboon that curve forward from the mouth. Yet they were hard cheeks, as hard as his great belly. He looked like a jungle bird now, slowly turning his head to inspect the faraway sky, a serious bird with a brown face and white eyes. His head was entirely bald. He took off his khaki army cap and rubbed his fingers into his scalp.

Gay Langland stood up and walked to him and gave him his eggs and thick bacon on a tin plate. "Wind died, Guido," Gay said, standing there and looking down at the pilot.

"It doesn't mean much what it did down here." Guido pointed skyward with his thumb. "Up there's where it counts."

"Ain't no sign of wind up there," Gay said. Gay's eyes seemed amused. He did not want to seem committed to a real argument. "We got no more eggs, Guido," he warned.

Guido ate.

Now the sky flared with true dawn, like damp paper suddenly catching fire. Perce and Gay sat down on the ground facing Guido, and they all ate their eggs.

The shroud of darkness quickly slipped off the red truck which stood a few yards away. Then, behind it, the little plane showed itself. Guido Racanelli ate and sipped his coffee, and Gay Langland watched him with a weak smile and without speaking. Perce blinked contentedly at the brightening sky, slightly detached from the other two. He finished his coffee and slipped a chew of tobacco into his mouth and sucked on it.

It was a pink day now all around the sky.

Gay Langland made a line in the sand between his thighs and said, "You goin' up, Guido?" He looked at Guido directly and he was still smiling.

Guido thought for a moment. He was older, about fifty. His pronunciation was unaccountably eastern, with sharp r's. He sounded educated sometimes. He stared off toward the squat little plane. "Every once in a while I wonder what the hell it's all about," he said.

"What is?" Gay asked.

Perce watched Guido's face, thoroughly listening.

Guido felt their attention and spoke with pleasurable ease. He still stared past them at the plane. "I got a lousy valve. I know it, Gay."

"Been that way a long time, Guido," Gay said with sympathy.

"I know," Guido said. They were not arguing but searching now. "And we won't hardly get twenty dollars apiece out of it—there's only four or five horses back in there."

"We knew that, Guido," Gay said. They were in sympathy with each other.

"I might just get myself killed, for twenty dollars."

"Hell, you know them mountains," Gay said.

"You can't see wind, Gay," the pilot said.

Gay knew now that Guido was going up right away. He saw that Guido had just wanted to get all the dangers straight in his mind so he could see them and count them; then he would go out against them.

"You're flying along in and out of those passes and then you dive for the sons of bitches, and just when you're pulling up, some goddam gust presses you down and there you are."

"I know," Gay said.

There was silence. Guido sipped his coffee, staring off at the plane. "I just wonder about it every once in a while," the pilot said.

"Well, hell," Perce Howland said, "it's better than wages."

"You damn right it is, Perce," the pilot said thoughtfully.

"I seen guys get killed who never left the ground," Perce said.

The two older men knew that his father had been killed by a bull long ago and that he had seen his father die. He had had his own arms broken in rodeos and a Brahma bull had stepped on his chest.

"One rodeo near Salinas I see a fella get his head snapped right clear off his chest by a cable busted. They had this cable drawin' horses up onto a truck. I seen his head rollin' away like a bowlin' ball. Must've roll twenty-five yards before it hit a fence post and stopped." He spat tobacco juice and turned back to look at Guido. "It had a mustache. Funny thing, I never knowed that guy had a mustache. Never noticed it. Till I see it stop rolling and there it was, dust all over the mustache."

"That was a dusty mustache," Gay said, grinning against their deepening morbidity.

They all smiled. Then time hung for a moment as they waited. And at last Guido shifted onto one buttock and said, "Well, let's get gassed up."

Guido leaned himself to one side with his palm on the ground, then got to his feet by moving in a circle around this palm, and stood up. Gay and Perce Howland were already moving off toward the truck, Perce heisting up his dungarees over his breakfast-full stomach, and the older Gay more sprightly and intent. Guido stood holding one hand open over the fire, watching them loading the six enormous truck tires onto the bed of the truck. Each tire had a twenty-foot length of rope wired to it, and at the end of each rope was a loop. Before they swung the tires onto the truck Gay inspected the ropes to be sure they were securely knotted to the tires, and the loops open and ready for throwing.

Guido blinked against the warming sun, watching the other two, then he looked off to his right where the passes were, and the fingers of his mind felt around beyond those passes into the bowls and hollows of the mountains where last week he had spotted the small herd of wild horses grazing. Now he felt the lightness he had been hoping to feel for three days, the bodiless urge to fly. For three days he had kept away from the plane because a certain carelessness had been itching at him, a feeling that he always thought would lead him to his death. About five weeks ago he had come up to this desert with Gay Langland and he had chased seven mustangs out of the mountains. But this time he had dived to within a foot of the mountainside, and afterward, as they sat around the fire eating dinner, Guido had had the feeling that he had made that deep dive so he could die. And the thought of his dead wife had come to him again, and the other thought that always came into his mind with her dead face. It was the wonderment, the quiet pressing-in of the awareness that he had never wanted a woman after she had been buried with the still-born baby beside her in the graveyard outside Bowie. Seven years now he had waited for some real yearning for a woman, and nothing at all had come to him. It pleasured him to know that he was free of that, and it sometimes made him careless in the plane, as though some great bang and a wreckage would make him again what he had been. By now he could go around in Bowie for a week and only in an odd moment recall that he hadn't even looked at a girl walking by, and the feeling of carelessness would come on him, a kind of loose gaiety, as though everything was comical. Until he had made that dive and pulled

out with his nose almost scraping the grass, and he had
climbed upward with his mouth hanging open and his body in
a sweat. So that through these past three days up here he had
refused to let himself take off until the wind had utterly died,
and he had clung to moroseness. He wanted to take off in the
absolute grip of his own wits, leaving nothing to chance. Now
there was no wind at all, and he felt he had pressed the sinister
gaiety out of his mind. He left the dying fire and walked past
Gay and Perce and down the gentle slope to the plane, looking like a stout, serious football coach before the kick-off.

He glanced over the fuselage and at the bald doughnut tires
and he loved the plane. Again, as always, he looked at the
weakened starboard shock absorber, which no longer held its
spread so that the plane stood tilted a little to one side, and
told himself that it was not serious. He heard the truck motor
starting and he unfastened the knots of the ropes holding the
plane to the spikes driven into the desert floor. Then the truck
pulled up, and young Perce Howland dropped off and went
over to the tail handle, gripped it, lifted the tail off the ground,
and swung the plane around so she faced out across the endless desert and away from the mountains. Then they unwound
the rubber hose from the gas drum on the truck and stuck the
nozzle into the gas tank behind the engine, and Perce turned
the pump crank.

Guido then walked around the wing and over to the
cockpit, whose right door was folded down, leaving the inside
open to the air. He reached in and took out his ripped leather
flight jacket and got into it.

Perce stood leaning against the truck fender now, grinning.
"That sure is a ventilated type jacket, Guido," he said.

Then Guido said, "I can't get my size any more." The jacket
had one sleeve off at the elbow, and the dried leather was split
open down the back, showing the lamb's-wool lining. He had
bombed Germany in this jacket long ago. He reached in behind the seat and took out a goggle case, slipped his goggles
out, replaced the case, set his goggles securely on his face, and

reached in again and took out a shotgun pistol and four shells from a little wooden box beside his seat. He loaded the pistol and laid it carefully under his seat. Then he got into the cockpit, sat in his seat, drew the strap over his belly and buckled it. Meantime Gay had taken his position before the propeller.

Guido called through the open doorway of the cockpit, "Turn her over, Gay-boy!"

Gay stepped up to the propeller, glanced down behind his heels to be sure no stone waited to trip him when he stepped back, pulled down on the blade, and hopped back watchfully.

"Give her another!" Guido called in the silence.

Gay stepped up again, again glancing around his heels, and pulled the blade down. The engine inhaled and exhaled, and they could all hear the oily clank of her inner shafts turning loosely.

"Ignition on, Gay-boy!" Guido called and threw the switch.

This time Gay inspected the ground around him even more carefully and pulled his hatbrim down tighter on his head. Perce stood leaning on the truck's front fender, spitting and chewing, his eyes softly squinted against the brazen sun. Gay reached up and pulled the propeller down and jumped back. A puff of smoke floated up from the engine ports.

"Goddam car gas," Guido said. "Ignition on. Go again, Gay-boy!" They were buying low octane to save money.

Gay again stepped up to the propeller, swung the blade down, and the engine said its "Chaaahh!" and the ports breathed white smoke into the morning air. Gay walked over to Perce and stood beside him, watching. The fuselage shuddered and the propeller turned into a wheel, and the dust blew pleasantly from behind the plane and toward the mountains. Guido gunned her, and she tumbled toward the open desert, bumping along over the sage clumps and crunching whitened skeletons of cattle killed by the winter. The stiff-backed plane grew smaller, shouldering its way over the broken ground, and then its nose turned upward and there was space between the

doughnut tires and the desert, and lazily it climbed, turning
back the way it had come. It flew over the heads of Perce and
Gay, and Guido waved down, a stranger now, fiercely goggled
and wrapped in leather, and they could see him exposed to the
waist, turning from them to look through the windshield at the
mountains ahead of him. The plane flew away, climbing
smoothly, losing itself against the orange and purple walls that
vaulted up from the desert to hide from the cowboys' eyes the
wild animals they wanted for themselves.

They would have at least two hours before the plane flew
out of the mountains driving the horses before it, so they
washed the three tin plates and the cups and stored them in
the aluminum grub box. If Guido did find horses they would
break camp and return to Bowie tonight, so they packed up
their bedrolls with sailors' tidiness and laid them neatly side
by side on the ground. The six great truck tires, each with its
looped rope coiled within, lay in two piles on the bed of the
truck. Gay Langland looked them over and touched them
with his hand and stood for a moment trying to think if there
was anything they were leaving behind. He jumped up on the
truck to see that the cap was screwed tight on the gas drum,
which was lashed to the back of the cab up front, and it was.
Then he hopped down to the ground and got into the cab and
started the engine. Perce was already sitting there with his hat
tipped forward against the yellow sunlight pouring through
the windshield. A thin and concerned border collie came trotting up as Gay started to close his door, and he invited her
into the cab. She leaped up, and he snugged her into the space
between the clutch and the left wall of the cab. "Damn near
forgot Belle," he said, and they started off.

Gay owned the truck and he wanted to preserve the front
end, which he knew could be twisted out of line on broken
ground. So he started off slowly. They could hear the gas
sloshing in the drum behind them outside. It was getting warm
now. They rode in silence, staring ahead at the two-track trail

they were following across the bone-cluttered sagebrush. Thirty miles ahead stood the lava mountains that were the northern border of this desert, the bed of a bowl seven thousand feet up, a place no one ever saw except the few cowboys searching for stray cattle every few months. People in Bowie, sixty miles away, did not know of this place. There were the two of them and the truck and the dog, and now that they were on the move they felt between them the comfort of purpose and their isolation, and Perce slumped in his seat, blinking as though he would go to sleep again, and Gay smoked a cigarette and let his body flow from side to side with the pitching of the truck.

There was a moving cloud of dust in the distance toward the left, and Gay said, "Antelope," and Perce tipped his hat back and looked. "Must be doin' sixty," he said, and Gay said, "More. I chased one once and I was doin' more than sixty and he lost me." Perce shook his head in wonder, and they turned to look ahead again.

After he had thought awhile Perce said, "We better get over to Largo by tomorrow if we're gonna get into that rodeo. They's gonna be a crowd trying to sign up for that one."

"We'll drive down in the morning," Gay said.

"I'll have to see about gettin' me some stock."

"We'll get there early tomorrow; you'll get stock if you come in early."

"Like to win some money," Perce said. "I just wish I get me a good horse down there."

"They be glad to fix you up, Perce. You're known pretty good around there now. They'll fix you up with some good stock," Gay said. Perce was one of the best bronc riders, and the rodeos liked to have it known he would appear.

Then there was silence. Gay had to hold the gear-shift lever in high or it would slip out into neutral when they hit bumps. The transmission fork was worn out, he knew, and the front tires were going too. He dropped one hand to his pants pocket and felt the four silver dollars he had from the ten Roslyn had given him when they had left her days ago.

As though he had read Gay's mind, Perce said, "Roslyn would've liked it up here. She'd liked to have seen that antelope, I bet." Perce grinned as both of them usually did at Roslyn's eastern surprise at everything they did and saw and said.

"Yeah," Gay said, "she likes to see things." Through the corners of his eyes he watched the younger man, who was looking ahead with a little grin on his face. "She's a damned good sport, old Roslyn," Gay said.

"Sure is," Perce Howland said. And Gay watched him for any sign of guile, but there was only a look of glad appreciation. "First woman like that I ever met," the younger man said.

"They's more," Gay said. "Some of them eastern women fool you sometimes. They got education but they're good sports. And damn good women too, some of them."

There was a silence. Then the younger man asked, "You get to know a lot of them? Eastern women?"

"Ah, I get one once in a while," Gay said.

"Only educated women I ever know, they was back home near Teachers College. Students. Y'know," he said, warming to the memory, "I used to think, hell, education's everything. But when I saw the husbands some of them got married to—schoolteachers and everything, why I don't give them much credit. And they just as soon climb on a man as tell him good morning. I was teachin' them to ride for a while near home."

"Just because a woman's educated don't mean much. Woman's a woman," Gay said. The image of his wife came into his mind. For a moment he wondered if she was still living with the same man he had beaten up when he discovered them together in a parked car six years ago.

"You divorced?" Perce asked.

"No. I never bothered with it," Gay said. It always surprised him how Perce said just what was on his mind sometimes. "How'd you know I was thinkin' of that?" he asked, grinning with embarrassment. But he was too curious to keep silent.

"Hell, I didn't know," Perce said.

"You're always doin' that. I think of somethin' and you go ahead and say it."

"That's funny," Perce said.

They rode on in silence. They were nearing the middle of the desert, where they would turn east. Gay was driving faster now because he wanted to get to the rendezvous and sit quietly waiting for the plane to appear. He held on to the gearshift lever and felt it trying to spring out of high and into neutral. It would have to be fixed. The time was coming fast when he would need about fifty dollars or have to sell the truck, because it would be useless without repairs. Without a truck and without a horse he would be down to what was in his pocket.

Perce spoke out of the silence. "If I don't win Saturday I'm gonna have to do somethin' for money."

"Goddam, you always say what's in my mind."

Perce laughed. His face looked very young and pink. "Why?"

"I was just now thinkin'," Gay said, "what I'm gonna do for money."

"Well, Roslyn give you some," Perce said.

He said it innocently, and Gay knew it was innocent, and yet he felt angry blood moving into his neck. Something had happened in these five weeks, and Gay did not know for sure what it was. Roslyn had taken to calling Perce cute, and now and again she would bend over and kiss him on the back of the neck when he was sitting in the living-room chair, drinking with them.

Not that that meant anything in itself, because he'd known eastern women before who'd do something like that and it was just their way. Especially college graduate divorced women. What he wondered at was Perce's way of hardly even noticing what she did to him. Sometimes it was like he'd already had her and could ignore her, the way a man will who knows he's boss. But then Gay thought it might just be that he really wasn't interested, or maybe that he was keeping cool in deference to Gay.

Again Gay felt a terrible longing to earn money working. He sensed the bottom of his life falling if it turned out Roslyn had really been loving this boy beside him. It had happened to him once before with his wife, but this frightened him more and he did not know exactly why. Not that he couldn't do without Roslyn. There wasn't anybody or anything he couldn't do without. She was about his age and full of laughter that was not laughter and gaiety that was not gaiety and adventurousness that was labored, and he knew all this perfectly well even as he laughed with her and was high with her in the bars and rodeos. He had only lived once, and that was when he had had his house and his wife and his children. He knew the difference, but you never kept anything, and he had never particularly thought about keeping anything or losing anything. He had been all his life like Perce Howland, sitting beside him now, a man moving on or ready to. It was only when he discovered his wife with a stranger that he knew he had had a stake to which he had been pleasurably tethered. He had not seen her or his children for years and only rarely thought about any of them. Any more than his father had thought of him very much after the day he had gotten on his pony, when he was fourteen, to go to town from the ranch, and had kept going into Montana and stayed there for three years. He lived in this country as his father did, and it was the same endless range wherever he went, and it connected him sufficiently with his father and his wife and his children. All might turn up sometime in some town or at some rodeo, where he might happen to look over his shoulder and see his daughter or one of his sons, or they might never turn up. He had neither left anyone nor not-left as long as they were all alive on these ranges, for everything here was always beyond the farthest shot of vision and far away, and mostly he had worked alone or with one or two men, between distant mountains anyway.

In the distance now he could see the shimmering wall of the heat waves rising from the clay flatland they wanted to get to. Now they were approaching closer, and it opened to them beyond the heat waves, and they could see once again how

vast it was, a prehistoric lake bed thirty miles long by seventeen miles wide, couched between the two mountain ranges. It
was a flat, beige waste without grass or bush or stone, where a
man might drive a car at a hundred miles an hour with his
hands off the wheel and never hit anything at all. They drove
in silence. The truck stopped bouncing as the tires rolled over
harder ground where there were fewer sage clumps. The waves
of heat were dense before them, nearly touchable. Now the
truck rolled smoothly and they were on the clay lake bed, and
when they had gone a few hundred yards onto it Gay pulled
up and shut off the engine. The air was still in a dead, sunlit silence. When he opened his door he could hear a squeak in the
hinge he had never noticed before. When they walked around
they could hear their shirts rasping against their backs and the
brush of a sleeve against their trousers.

They stood on the clay ground, which was as hard as con-
crete, and turned to look the way they had come. They looked
back toward the mountains at whose feet they had camped
and slept, and scanned their ridges for Guido's plane. It was
too early for him, and they made themselves busy, taking the
gas drum off the truck and setting it a few yards away on the
ground, because they would want the truck bed clear when the
time came to run the horses down. Then they climbed up and
sat inside the tires with their necks against the tire beads and
their legs hanging over.

Perce said, "I sure hope they's five up in there."

"Guido saw five, he said."

"He said he wasn't sure if one wasn't only a colt," Perce
said.

Gay let himself keep silent. He felt he was going to argue
with Perce. He watched Perce through the corners of his eyes,
saw the flat, blond cheeks and the strong, lean neck, and there
was something tricky about Perce now. "How long you think
you'll be stayin' around here, Perce?" he asked.

They were both watching the distant ridges for a sign of the
plane.

"Don't know," Perce said and spat over the side of the truck. "I'm gettin' a little tired of this, though."

"Well, it's better than wages, Perce."

"Hell, yes. Anything's better than wages."

Gay's eyes crinkled. "You're a real misfit, boy."

"That suits me fine," Perce said. They often had this conversation and savored it. "Better than workin' for some goddam cow outfit buckarooin' so somebody else can buy gas for his Cadillac."

"Damn right," Gay said.

"Hell, Gay, you are the most misfitted man I ever saw and you done all right."

"I got no complaints," Gay said.

"I don't want nothin' and I don't want to want nothin'."

"That's the way, boy."

Gay felt closer to him again and he was glad for it. He kept his eyes on the ridges far away. The sun felt good on his shoulders. "I think he's havin' trouble with them sumbitches up in there."

Perce stared out at the ridges. "Ain't two hours yet." Then he turned to Gay. "These mountains must be cleaned out by now, ain't they?"

"Just about," Gay said. "Just a couple small herds left. Can't do much more around here."

"What you goin' to do when you got these cleaned out?"

"Might go north, I think. Supposed to be some big herds in around Thighbone Mountain and that range up in there."

"How far's that?"

"North about a hundred miles. If I can get Guido interested."

Perce smiled. "He don't like movin' around much, does he?"

"He's just misfitted like the rest of us," Gay said. "He don't want nothin'." Then he added, "They wanted him for an airline pilot flyin' up into Montana and back. Good pay too."

"Wouldn't do it, huh?"

"Not Guido," Gay said, grinning. "Might not like some of the passengers, he told them."

Both men laughed, and Perce shook his head in admiration of Guido. Then he said, "They wanted me take over the ridin' academy up home. I thought about that. Two hundred a month and board. Easy work too. You don't hardly have to ride at all. Just stand around and see the customers get satisfied and put them girls off and on."

He fell silent. Gay knew the rest. It was the same story always. It brought him closer to Perce, and it was what he had liked about Perce in the first place. Perce didn't like wages either. He had come on Perce in a bar where the boy was buying drinks for everybody with his rodeo winnings, and his hair still clotted with blood from a bucking horse's kick an hour earlier. Roslyn had offered to get a doctor for him and he had said, "Thank you kindly. But I ain't bad hurt. If you're bad hurt you gonna die and the doctor can't do nothin', and if you ain't bad hurt you get better anyway without no doctor."

Now it suddenly came upon Gay that Perce had known Roslyn before they had met in the bar. He stared at the boy's profile. "Want to come up north with me if I go?" he asked.

Perce thought a moment. "Think I'll stay around here. Not much rodeoin' up north."

"I might find a pilot up there, maybe. And Roslyn drive us up in her car."

Perce turned to him, a little surprised. "Would she go up there?"

"Sure. She's a damn good sport," Gay said. He watched Perce's eyes, which had turned interested and warm.

Perce said, "Well, maybe; except to tell you the truth, Gay, I never feel comfortable takin' these horses for chicken feed."

"Somebody's goin' to take them if we don't."

"I know," Perce said. He turned to watch the far rides again. "Just seems to me they belong up there."

"They ain't doin' nothin' up there but eatin' out good cattle range. The cow outfits shoot them down if they see them."

"I know," Perce said.

"They don't even bother takin' them to slaughter. They just rot up there if the cow outfits get to them."

"I know," Perce said.

There was silence. Neither bug nor lizard nor rabbit moved on the great basin around them, and the sun warmed their necks and their thighs. Gay said, "I'd as soon sell them for riding horses but they ain't big enough, except for a kid. And the freight on them's more than they're worth. You saw them— they ain't nothin' but skinny horses."

"I just don't know if I'd want to see like a hundred of them goin' for chicken feed, though. I don't mind like five or six, but a hundred's a lot of horses. I don't know."

Gay thought. "Well, if it ain't this it's wages. Around here anyway." He was speaking of himself and explaining himself.

"I'd just as soon ride buckin' horses and make out that way, Gay." Perce turned to him. "Although I might go up north with you. I don't know."

"Roslyn wouldn't come out here at first," Gay said, "but soon as she saw what they looked like she stopped complainin' about it. You didn't hear her complainin' about it."

"I ain't complainin', Gay. I just don't know. Seems to me God put them up there and they belong up there. But I'm doin' it and I guess I'd go on doin' it. I don't know."

"Sounds to me like the newspapers. They want their steaks, them people in town, but they don't want castration or branding or cleanin' wild horses off the ranges."

"Hell, man, I castrated more bulls than I got hairs on my head," Perce said.

"I better get the glasses," Gay said and slid out of the tire in which he had been lounging and off the truck. He went to the cab and reached in and brought out a pair of binoculars, blew on the lenses, mounted the truck, and sat on a tire with his elbows resting on his knees. He put the glasses to his eyes and focused them. The mountains came up close with their pocked blue hides. He found the pass through which he believed the plane would come and studied its slopes and scanned the air above it. Anger was still warming him. "God put them up there!" Why, Christ, God put everything everywhere. Did that mean you couldn't eat chickens, for instance, or beef? His dislike for Perce was flowing into him again.

They heard the shotgun off in the sky somewhere and they stopped moving. Gay narrowed his eyes and held the binoculars perfectly still.

"See anything?" Perce asked.

"He's still in the pass, I guess," Gay said.

They sat still, watching the sky over the pass. The moments went by. The sun was making them perspire now, and Gay wiped his wet eyebrows with the back of one hand. They heard the shotgun again from the general sky. Gay spoke without lowering the glasses. "He's probably blasting them out of some corner."

Perce quickly arched out of his tire. "I see him," he said quickly. "I see him glintin', I see the plane."

It angered Gay that Perce had seen the plane first without glasses. In the glasses Gay could see it clearly now. It was flying out of the pass, circling back, and disappearing into the pass again. "He's got them in the pass now. Just goin' back in for them."

"Can you see them?" Perce asked.

"He ain't got them in the clear yet. He just went back in for them."

Now through his glasses he could see moving specks on the ground where the pass opened onto the desert table. "I see them," he said. He counted, moving his lips. "One, two, three, four. Four and a colt."

"We gonna take the colt?" Perce asked.

"Hell, can't take the mare without the colt."

Perce said nothing. Then Gay handed him the glasses. "Take a look."

Gay slid off the truck bed and went forward to the cab and opened its door. His dog lay shivering on the floor under the pedals. He snapped his fingers, and she warily got up and leaped down to the ground and stood there quivering, as she always did when wild horses were coming. He watched her sit and wet the ground, and how she moved with such care and concern and fear, sniffing the ground and moving her head in slow motion and setting her paws down as though the ground had hidden explosives everywhere. He left her there and climbed onto the truck and sat on a tire beside Perce, who was still looking through the glasses.

"He's divin' down on them. God, they sure can run!"

"Let's have a look," Gay said and reached out, and Perce handed him the glasses, saying, "They're comin' on fast."

Gay watched the horses in the glasses. The plane was starting down toward them from the arc of its climb. They swerved as the roaring motor came down over them, lifted their heads, and galloped faster. They had been running now for over an hour and would slow down when the plane had to climb after a dive and the motor's noise grew quieter. As Guido climbed again Gay and Perce heard a shot, distant and harmless, and the shot sped the horses on again as the plane took time to bank and turn. Then, as they slowed, the plane returned over them, diving down over their backs, and their heads shot up again and they galloped until the engine's roar receded over them. The sky was clear and lightly blue, and only the little plane swung back and forth across the desert like the glinting tip of a magic wand, and the horses came on toward the vast stripped clay bed where the truck was parked.

The two men on the truck exchanged the glasses from time to time. Now they sat upright on the tires, waiting for the horses to reach the edge of the lake bed, when Guido would land the plane and they would take off with the truck. And now the horses stopped.

"They see the heat waves," Gay said, looking through the glasses. He could see the horses trotting with raised, alarmed heads along the edge of the barren lake bed, which they feared because the heat waves rose from it like liquid in the air and yet their nostrils did not smell water, and they dared not move ahead onto unknowable territory. The plane dived down on them, and they scattered but would not go forward onto the lake bed from the cooler, sage-dotted desert behind them. Now the plane banked high in the air and circled out behind them over the desert and banked again and came down within yards of the ground and roared in behind them almost at the height of their heads, and as it passed over them, rising, the men on the truck could hear the shotgun. Now the horses leaped forward onto the lake bed, all scattered and heading in different directions, and they were only trotting, exploring the ground under their feet and the strange, superheated air in their nostrils. Gradually, as the plane wound around the sky to dive again, they closed ranks and slowly galloped shoulder to shoulder out onto the borderless lake bed. The colt galloped a length behind with its nose nearly touching the mare's long silky tail.

"That's a big mare," Perce said. His eyes were still dreamy and his face was calm, but his skin had reddened.

"She's a bigger mare than usual up here, ya," Gay said.

Both men watched the little herd now, even as they got to their feet on the truck. There was the big mare, as large as any full-grown horse, and both of them downed their surprise at the sight of her. They knew the mustang herds lived in total isolation and that inbreeding had reduced them to the size of large ponies. The herd swerved now and they saw the stallion. He was smaller than the mare but still larger than any Gay had brought down before. The other two horses were small, the way mustangs ought to be.

The plane was coming down for a landing now. Gay and Perce Howland moved to the forward edge of the truck's bed where a strap of white webbing was strung at hip height between two stanchions stuck into sockets at the corners of the truck. They drew another web strap from one stanchion to the other and stood inside the two. Perce tied the back strap to his stanchion. Then they turned around inside their harnesses and each reached into a tire behind him and drew out a coil of rope whose end hung in a loop. They glanced out on the lake bed and saw Guido taxiing toward them, and they stood waiting for him. He cut the engine twenty yards from the truck and leaped out of the open cockpit before the plane had halted. He lashed the tail of the plane to a rope that was attached to a spike driven into the clay and trotted over to the truck, lifting his goggles off and stuffing them into his torn jacket pocket. Perce and Gay called out laughingly to him, but he seemed hardly to have seen them. His face was puffed with preoccupation. He jumped into the cab of the truck, and the collie dog jumped in after him and sat on the floor, quivering. He started the truck and roared ahead across the flat clay into the watery waves of heat.

They could see the herd standing still in a small clot of dots more than two miles off. The truck rolled smoothly, and in the cab Guido glanced at the speedometer and saw it was past sixty. He had to be careful not to turn over and he dropped back to fifty-five. Gay, on the right front corner of the truck bed, and Perce Howland on the left, pulled their hats down to their eyebrows and hefted the looped ropes, which the wind was threatening to coil and foul in their palms. Guido knew that Gay Langland was a good roper and that Perce was unsure, so he headed for the herd's left in order to come up to them on Gay's side of the truck if he could. This whole method—the truck, the tires, the ropes, and the plane—was Guido's invention, and once again he felt the joy of having thought of it all. He drove with both heavy hands on the wheel and his left foot ready over the brake pedal. He reached for the shift lever to feel if it was going to spring out of gear and into neutral, but it felt tight, and if they did not hit a bump he could rely on it. The herd had started to walk but stopped again now, and the horses were looking at the truck, ears raised, necks stretched up and forward. Guido smiled a little. They looked silly to him standing there, but he knew and pitied them their ignorance.

The wind smashed against the faces of Perce and Gay standing on the truck bed. The brims of their hats flowed up and back from a low point in front, and their faces were dark red. They saw the horses watching their approach at a standstill. And as they roared closer and closer they saw that this herd was beautiful.

Perce Howland turned his head to Gay, who glanced at him at the same time. There had been much rain this spring, and this herd must have found good pasture. They were well rounded and shining. The mare was almost black, and the stallion and the two others were deep brown. The colt was curly-coated and had a gray sheen. The stallion dipped his head suddenly and turned his back on the truck and galloped. The others turned and clattered after him, with the colt running alongside the mare. Guido pressed down on the gas and the truck surged forward, whining. They were a few yards behind the animals now and they could see the bottoms of their hoofs, fresh hoofs that had never been shod. They could see the full manes flying and the thick and long black tails that would hang down to their fetlocks when they were still.

The truck was coming abreast of the mare now, and beside her the others galloped with only a loud ticking noise on the clay. It was a gentle tacking clatter for they were light-footed and unshod. They were slim-legged and wet after running almost two hours in this alarm, but as the truck drew alongside the mare and Gay began twirling his loop above his head the whole herd wheeled away to the right, and Guido jammed the gas peddle down and swung with them, but they kept galloping in a circle, and he did not have the speed to keep abreast of them so he slowed down and fell behind them a few yards until they would straighten out and move ahead again. And they wheeled like circus horses, slower now, for they were at the edge of their strength, and suddenly Guido saw a breadth between the stallion and the two browns and he sped in between, cutting the mare off at the left with her colt. Now the horses stretched, the clatter quickened. Their hind legs flew straight back and their necks stretched low and forward. Gay whirled his loop over his head, and the truck came up alongside the stallion, whose lungs were hoarsely screaming with exhaustion, and Gay flung the noose. It fell on the stallion's head, and with a whipping of the lead Gay made it fall over his neck. The horse swerved away to the right and stretched the rope until the tire was pulled off the truck bed and dragged along the hard clay. The three men watched from the slowing truck as the stallion, with startled eyes, pulled the giant tire for a few yards, then leaped up with his forelegs in the air and came down facing the tire and trying to back away from it. Then he stood still, heaving, his hind legs dancing in an arc from right to left and back again as he shook his head in the remorseless noose.

As soon as he was sure the stallion was secure Guido scanned the lake bed and without stopping turned sharply left toward the mare and the colt, which were trotting idly together by themselves. The two browns were already disappearing toward the north, but Guido knew they would halt soon because they were tired, while the mare might continue to the edge of the lake bed and back into her familiar hills where the truck could not follow. He straightened the truck and jammed down the gas pedal. In a minute he was straight on behind her, and he drew up on her left side because the colt was running on her right. She was very heavy, he saw, and he wondered now if she was a mustang at all. As he drove alongside her his eyes ran across her flanks, seeking out a brand, but she seemed unmarked. Then through his right window he saw the loop flying out and down over her head, and he saw her head fly up, and then she fell back. He turned to the right, braking with his left boot, and he saw her dragging a tire and coming to a halt, with the free colt watching her and trotting very close beside her. Then he headed straight ahead across the flat toward two specks, which rapidly enlarged until they became the two browns, which were at a standstill and watching the oncoming truck. He came in between them, and as they galloped Perce on the left roped one, and Gay roped the other almost at the same time. And Guido leaned his head out of his window and yelled up at Perce, who was on the truck bed on his side. "Good boy!" he hollered, and Perce let himself return an excited grin, although there seemed to be some trouble in his eyes.

Guido made an easy half circle and headed back to the mare and the colt, and in a few minutes he slowed to a halt some twenty yards away and got out of the cab. The dog remained sitting on the floor of the cab, her body shaking all over.

The three men approached the mare. She had never seen a man, and her eyes were wide in fear. Her rib cage stretched and collapsed very rapidly, and there was a trickle of blood coming out of her nostrils. She had a heavy dark brown mane, and her tail nearly touched the ground. The colt with dumb eyes shifted about on its silly bent legs, trying to keep the mare between itself and the men, and the mare kept shifting her rump to shield the colt from them.

They wanted now to move the noose higher up on the mare's neck because it had fallen on her from the rear and was tight around the middle of her neck, where it could choke her if she kept pulling against the weight of the tire. They had learned from previous forays that they could not leave a horse tied that way without the danger of suffocation, and they wanted them alive until they could bring a larger truck from Bowie and load them on it.

Gay was the best roper so Perce and Guido stood by as he twirled a noose over his head, then let it fall open softly, just behind the forefeet of the mare. They waited for a moment, then approached her, and she backed a step. Then Gay pulled sharply on the rope, and her forefeet were tied together. Then with another rope Gay lass'd her hind feet, and she swayed and fell to the ground on her side. Her body swelled and contracted, but she seemed resigned. The colt stretched its nose to her tail and stood there as the men came to the mare and spoke quietly to her, and Guido bent down and opened the noose and slipped it up under her jaw. They inspected her for a brand, but she was clean.

"Never see a horse that size up here," Gay said to Guido.

Guido stood there looking down at the great mare.

Perce said, "Maybe wild horses was all big once," and he looked to Guido for confirmation.

Guido bent and sat on his heels and opened the mare's mouth, and the other two looked in with him. "She's fifteen if she's a day," Gay said, and to Perce he said, "She wouldn't be around much longer anyway."

"Ya, she's old," Perce agreed, and his eyes were filled with thought.

Guido stood up, and the three went back to the truck. Perce hopped up and sat on the truck bed with his legs dangling, and Gay sat in the cab with Guido. They drove across the lake bed to the stallion and stopped, and the three of them walked toward him.

"Ain't a bad-lookin' horse," Perce said.

They stood inspecting the horse for a moment. He was standing still now, heaving for breath and bleeding from the nostrils. His head was down, holding the rope taut, and he was looking at them with his deep brown eyes that were like the lenses of enormous binoculars. Gay got his rope ready in his hand. "He ain't nothin' but a misfit," he said, "except for some kid. You couldn't run cattle with him, and he's too small for a riding horse."

"He is small," Perce conceded. "Got a nice neck, though."

"Oh, they're nice-*lookin'* horses, some of them," Guido said. "What the hell you goin' to do with them, though? Cost more to ship them anywhere than they'd bring."

Gay twirled the loop over his head, and they spread out around the stallion. "They're just old misfit horses, that's all," he said, and he flung the rope behind the stallion's forelegs, and the horse backed a step, and he drew the rope and the noose bit into the horse's lower legs, drawing them together, and the horse swayed but would not fall.

"Take hold," Gay called to Perce, who ran around the horse

and grabbed onto the rope and held it taut. Then Gay went back to the truck, got another rope, returned to the rear of the horse, and looped the hind legs. But the stallion would not fall.

Guido stepped closer to push him over, but the horse swung his head and showed his teeth, and Guido stepped back. "Pull on it!" Guido yelled to Gay and Perce, and they pulled on their ropes to trip the stallion, but he righted himself and stood there bound by the head to the tire and his feet by the two ropes the men held. Then Guido hurried over to Perce and took the rope from him and walked with it toward the rear of the horse and pulled hard. The stallion's forefeet slipped back, and he came down on his knees and his nose struck the clay ground and he snorted as he struck, but he would not topple over and stayed there on his knees as though he were bowing to something, with his nose propping up his head against the ground and his sharp bursts of breath blowing up dust in little clouds under his nostrils.

Now Guido gave the rope back to young Perce Howland, who held it taut, and he came up alongside the stallion's neck and laid his hands on the side of the neck and pushed, and the horse fell over onto his flank and lay there; and, like the mare, when he felt the ground against his body he seemed to let himself out, and for the first time his eye blinked and his breath came now in sighs and no longer fiercely. Guido shifted the noose up under the jaw, and they opened the ropes around the hoofs, and when the horse felt his legs free he first raised his head curiously and then clattered up and stood there looking at them, from one to the other, blood dripping from his nostrils and a stain of deep red on both dusty knees.

For a moment the three men stood watching him to be sure he was tightly noosed around the neck. Only the clacking of the truck's engine sounded on the enormous floor between the mountains, and the wheezing inhale of the horse and his blowing out of air. Then the men moved without hurrying to the truck, and Gay stored his two extra ropes behind the seat of the cab and got behind the wheel with Guido beside him, and Perce climbed onto the back of the truck and lay down facing the sky, his palms under his head.

Gay headed the truck south toward where they knew the plane was, although it was still beyond their vision. Guido was slowly catching his breath, and now he lighted a cigarette, puffed it, and rubbed his left hand into his bare scalp. He sat gazing out the windshield and the side window. "I'm sleepy," he said.

"What you reckon?" Gay asked.

"What you?" Guido said. He had dust in his throat, and his voice sounded high and almost girlish.

"That mare might be six hundred pounds."

"I'd say about that, Gay," Guido agreed.

"About four hundred apiece for the browns and a little more for the stallion."

"That's about the way I figured."

"What's that come to?"

Guido thought. "Nineteen hundred, maybe two thousand," he said.

They fell silent, figuring the money. Two thousand pounds at six cents a pound came to a hundred and twenty dollars. The colt might make it a few dollars more, but not much. Figuring the gas for the plane and the truck, and twelve dollars for their groceries, they came to the figure of a hundred dollars for the three of them. Guido would get forty-five dollars, since he had used his plane, and Gay would get thirty-five including the use of his truck, and Perce Howland, if he agreed, as he undoubtedly would, would have the remaining twenty.

They fell silent after they had said the figures, and Gay drove in thought. Then he said, "We should've watered them the last time. They can pick up a lot of weight if you let them water."

"Yeah, let's be sure to do that," Guido said.

They knew they would as likely as not forget to water the horses before they unloaded them at the dealer's lot in Bowie.

They would be in a hurry to unload and to be free of the horses, and only later, as they were doing now, would they remind themselves that by letting the horses drink their fill they could pick up another fifteen or twenty dollars in added weight. They were not thinking of the money any more, once they had figured it, and if Perce were to object to his smaller share they would both hand him a five- or ten-dollar bill or more if he wanted it.

Gay stopped the truck beside the plane at the edge of the lake bed. The tethered horses were far away now, except for the mare and her colt, which stood in clear view less than half a mile off. Guido opened his door and said to Gay, "See you in town. Let's get the other truck tomorrow morning."

"Perce wants to go over to Largo and sign up for the rodeo tomorrow," Gay said. "Tell ya—we'll go in and get the truck and come back here this afternoon maybe. Maybe we bring them in tonight."

"All right, if you want to. I'll see you boys tomorrow," Guido said, and he got out and stopped for a moment to talk to Perce.

"Perce?" he said. Perce propped himself up on one elbow and looked down at him. He looked very sleepy. Guido smiled. "You sleeping?"

Perce's eyelids almost seemed swollen, and his face was indrawn and troubled. "I was about to," he said.

Guido let the reprimand pass. "We figure about a hundred dollars clear. Twenty all right for you?"

"Ya, twenty's all right," Perce said, blinking heavily. He hardly seemed to be listening.

"See you in town," Guido said and turned and waddled off to the plane, where Gay was already standing with his hands on the propeller blade. Guido got in, and Gay swung the blade down and the engine started immediately. Guido waved to Gay and Perce, who raised one hand slightly from the truck bed. Guido gunned the plane, and it trundled off and into the sky, and the two men on the ground watched as it flew toward the mountains and away.

Gay returned to the truck, and as he started to climb in behind the wheel he looked at Perce, who was still propped up
on one elbow, and he said, "Twenty all right?" And he said
this because he thought Perce looked hurt.

"Heh? Ya, twenty's all right," Perce answered. Then he let
himself down from the truck bed, and Gay got behind the
wheel. Perce stood beside the truck and wet the ground while
Gay waited for him. Then Perce got into the cab, and they
drove off.

The mare and her colt stood between them and the sage
desert toward which they were heading. Perce stared out the
window at the mare, and he saw that she was watching them
apprehensively but not in real alarm, and the colt was lying
upright on the clay, its head nodding slightly as though it
would soon fall asleep. Perce looked long at the colt as they
approached, and he thought about how it waited there beside
the mare, unbound and free to go off, and he said to Gay,
"Ever hear of a colt leave a mare?"

"Not that young a colt," Gay said. "He ain't goin' nowhere." And he glanced to look at Perce.

They passed the mare and colt and left them behind, and
Perce laid his head back and closed his eyes. His tobacco
swelled out his left cheek, and he let it soak there.

Now the truck left the clay lake bed, and it pitched and
rolled on the sage desert. They would return to their camp and
pick up their bedrolls and cooking implements and then drive
to the road, which was almost fifteen miles beyond the camp
across the desert.

"Think I'll go back to Roslyn's tonight," Gay said.

"Okay," Perce said and did not open his eyes.

"We can pick them up in the morning and then take you
down to Largo."

"Okay," Perce said.

Gay thought about Roslyn. She would probably razz them
about all the work they had done for a few dollars, saying they
were too dumb to figure in their labor time and other hidden
expenses. To hear her, sometimes they hadn't made any profit

at all. "Roslyn goin' to feel sorry for the colt," Gay said, "so might as well not mention it."

Perce opened his eyes, and with his head resting on the back of the seat he looked out the window at the mountains. "Hell, she feeds that dog of hers canned dogfood, doesn't she?"

Gay felt closer to Perce again and he smiled. "Sure does."

"Well, what's she think is in the can?"

"She knows what's in the can."

"There's wild horses in the can," Perce said, almost to himself.

They drove in silence for a while. Then Perce said, "That's what beats me."

After a few moments Gay said, "You comin' back to Roslyn's with me or you gonna stay in town?"

"I'd just as soon go back with you."

"Okay," Gay said. He felt good about going into her cabin now. There would be her books on the shelves he had built for her, and they would have some drinks, and Perce would fall asleep on the couch, and they would go into the bedroom together. He liked to come back to her after he had worked, more than when he had only driven her here and there or just stayed around her place. He liked his own money in his pocket. And he tried harder to visualize how it would be with her, and he thought of himself being forty-six soon, and then nearing fifty. She would go back East one day, he knew, maybe this year, maybe next. He wondered again when he would begin turning gray and how he would look with gray hair, and he set his jaw against the picture of himself gray and an old man.

Perce spoke, sitting up in his seat. "I want to phone my mother. Damn, I haven't called her all year." He stared out the window at the mountains. He had the memory of how the colt looked, and he wished it would be gone when they returned in the morning. Then he said, "I got to get to Largo tomorrow and register."

"We'll go," Gay said.

"I could use a good win," he said. He thought of five hundred dollars now, and of the many times he had won five hundred dollars. "You know something, Gay?" he said.

"Huh?"

"I'm never goin' to amount to a damn thing." Then he laughed. He was hungry, and he laughed without restraint for a moment and then laid his head back and closed his eyes.

"I told you that first time I met you, didn't I?" Gay grinned. He felt the mood coming on for some drinks at Roslyn's.

Then Perce spoke. "That colt won't bring two dollars anyway. What you say we just left him there?"

"Why, you know what he'd do?" Gay said. "He'd just follow the truck right into town."

"I guess he would at that," Perce said. He spat a stream of juice out the window.

They reached the camp in twenty minutes and loaded the gasoline drum onto three bedrolls and the aluminum grub box in the truck and drove on toward Bowie. After they had driven for fifteen minutes without speaking, Gay said he wanted to go north very soon for the hundreds of horses that were supposed to be in the mountains there. But Perce Howland had fallen fast asleep beside him. Gay wanted to talk about that expedition because as they neared Bowie he began to visualize Roslyn razzing them again, and it was clear to him that he had somehow failed to settle anything for himself; he had put in three days for thirty-five dollars, and there would be no way to explain it so it made sense, and it would be embarrassing. And yet he knew that it had all been the way it ought to be even if he could never explain it to her or anyone else. He reached out and nudged Perce, who opened his eyes and lolled his head over to face him. "You comin' up to Thighbone with me, ain't you?"

"Okay," Perce said and went back to sleep.

Gay felt more peaceful now that the younger man would not be leaving him. He drove in contentment.

The sun shone hot on the beige plain all day. Neither fly nor bug nor snake ventured out on the waste to molest the four horses tethered there, or the colt. They had run nearly two hours at a gallop, and as the afternoon settled upon them they pawed the hard ground for water, but there was none. Toward evening the wind came up, and they backed into it and faced the mountains from which they had come. From time to time the stallion caught the smell of the pastures up there, and he started to walk toward the vaulted fields in which he had grazed; but the tire bent his neck around, and after a few steps he would turn to face it and leap into the air with his forelegs striking at the sky, and then he would come down and be still again.

With the deep blue darkness the wind blew faster, tossing their manes and flinging their long tails in between their legs. The cold of night raised the colt onto its legs, and it stood close to the mare for warmth. Facing the southern range, five horses blinked under the green glow of the risen moon, and they closed their eyes and slept. The colt settled again on the hard ground and lay under the mare.

In the high hollows of the mountains the grass they had cropped this morning straightened in the darkness. On the lusher swards, which were still damp with the rains of spring, their hoofprints had begun to disappear. When the first pink glow of another morning lit the sky the colt stood up, and as it had always done at dawn it walked waywardly for water. The mare shifted and her bone hoofs ticked the clay. The colt turned its head and returned to her and stood at her side with vacant eye, its nostrils sniffing the warming air.

[1957]

The Misfits [II]

EIGHT

Darkness brightens the neon glare from the bars, and bluish vestigial light still glows along the mountain ridges. Cars are parked tightly against the bar fronts, one of which has been pushed in, its stucco facing hanging agape. The crowd is thinner now and moving at promenade pace. The families are leaving in their cars and trucks. There are many small squads of cowboys moving in and out of the bars, with one girl to a squad. Unknowable conversations are going on in parked cars, between the freights, around unlit corners, between man and man and man and woman, some erupting in a shout and strange condemnations, or laughter and a re-entry into the bars.

Roslyn is cradling her head in her arm in the front seat of the car. Her face is tired from weeping and she is still breathing shakily in the aftermath of a sobbing spell.

Gay calls her name from the window opposite. He has a wryness in his look, knowing she is displeased with him. "Come on, honey, we're gonna have some drinks." The hurt in her face makes him open the door and he sits beside her.

Roslyn: "Is he still unconscious?"

Gay: "Probably, but it ain't noticeable." He turns his head and she follows his gaze through the rear window.

Perce, his head enormously wrapped in white bandage, is heatedly arguing with the rodeo judge behind the car. Guido is standing between them, blinking sleepily.

"He's arguing with the judge about who won the bull ride. You still mad at me?"

Her resentment gives way to relief at seeing Perce alive. Now she turns to Gay. "Why did you hit me?"

"I didn't hit you. You were gettin' in the way and I couldn't carry him, that's all."

"Your face looked different." She stares at him now, a question in her eyes. "You looked like you . . . could've killed me. I . . . know that look."

"Oh, come on, honey. I got a little mad 'cause you were gettin' me all tangled up. Let's have some drinks, come on now."

Roslyn, glancing back at Perce: "He still hasn't seen a doctor?" Gay turns his back to her impatiently. "He might have a concussion! I don't understand anything; a person could be dying and everybody just stands around. Don't you care?"

Gay returns to the seat beside her. With anger in his voice: "I just went in for that boy with a wild bull runnin' loose— what're you talkin' about? I'm damn lucky I'm sittin' here myself, don't you know that?"

"Yes. You did." She suddenly takes his hand, kisses it, and holds it to her cheek. "You did!" She kisses his face. "You're a dear, good man. . . ."

Gay, holding her, wanting her to understand him: "Roslyn, honey . . ."

"It's like you scream and there's nothing coming out of your mouth, and everybody's going around, 'Hello, how are you, what a nice day,' and it's all great—and you're dying!" She struggles to control herself and smiles. "You really felt for him, didn't you?"

Gay shrugs. "I just thought I could get him out. So I did, that's all."

Roslyn, her face showing the striving to locate him and herself: "But if he'd died . . . you'd feel terrible, wouldn't you? I mean, for no reason like that?"

"Honey . . . we all got to go sometime, reason or no reason. Dyin's as natural as livin'; man who's too afraid to die is too

THE MISFITS [II] : 483

afraid to live, far as I've ever seen. So there's nothin' to do but forget it, that's all. Seems to me."

Perce sticks his head into the car. The tape is still on his nose, the bandage like a turban on his head. He is slightly high from the shock. Guido sticks his head in on the other side of the car.

Perce: "Hey, Roslyn! Did you see me?"

"Oh, you were wonderful, Perce! Get in and we'll take you back to—"

"Oh, no, we got to have some fun now!"

Gay: "Sure, come on!"

Roslyn hesitates, then: "Okay. How do you feel?"

"Like a bull kicked me."

Guido opens the door for her. Gay gets out on Perce's side of the car. As she emerges from the car she quietly asks Guido: "Is he really all right?"

"In two weeks he won't remember this—or you either. Why don't you give your sympathy where it's appreciated?"

Roslyn, pointedly but with a warm laugh: "Where's that?"

She walks past him; he follows. They meet Gay and Perce in front of the saloon.

Perce: "In we go!"

Gay has her arm as her escort; Perce is on her other side, his open hand wavering over her back but not touching her: he is recognizing Gay's proprietary rights. Guido walks behind them. They enter the crowded saloon and take seats around a table.

There is a feverish intensity in Perce's speech and in his eyes. As they sit, he calls over to the bartender: "Hey, whisky! For eight people."

He gets into his chair. He is strangely happy, as though he had accomplished something necessary, some duty that has given him certain rights. He laughs, and talks without diffidence to Roslyn now. "Boy, I feel funny! That man give me some kind of injection? Whoo! I see the prettiest stars, Roslyn." He reaches for her hand and holds it. Gay, whose arm is over the back of Roslyn's chair, grins uncomfortably. Roslyn pats Perce's hand and then removes her own. Perce does not notice this, and again takes her hand. "I never seen stars before. You ever see stars, Gay? Damn bull had the whole milky way in that hoof!" Gay laughs. Guido smiles with a private satisfaction. Roslyn is torn between concern for his condition and a desire to celebrate her relief that he is alive. "Say, was that you cryin' in the ambulance? Was that her, Gay?"

"Sure was."

Perce rises from his chair, fervently shaking her hand: "Well, I want to thank you, Roslyn."

A waiter puts two glasses of whisky before each of them, and Perce raises his high.

Perce: "Now! Here's to my buddy, old elderly Gay!"

Roslyn: "Gay's not old!"

Perce: "And here's to old, elderly Pilot. And his five-dollar elderly airplane." They all have glasses raised. "And my friend, Roslyn! We're all buddies, ain't we, Gay?"

Gay grins to dilute the growing seriousness of Perce's meaning. "That's right."

The jukebox explodes with "Charley, My Boy."

Perce: "Then what're you gettin' mad at me for, buddy? Can I dance with her?"

Gay: "Sure! Roslyn, whyn't you dance with Perce?"

Roslyn: "Okay." She gets up and goes onto the dance area with Perce.

Guido: "Nothin' like being young, is there, Gay?"

"That's right. But you know what they say—there's some keeps gettin' younger all the time." He grins at Guido, who turns back to watch the dancers with a faintly skeptical smile. Perce is doing a flat-footed hicky step, and she is trying to fall into it with him. Half-kidding, he nevertheless seems to be caught by an old memory, as he moves with straight-backed dignity.

"My father used to dance like this." Now he twirls her around, and himself starts to circle her; a dizziness comes over him.

"What's the matter!"

"Whoo!"

She catches him as he stumbles. "C'mon, let's see the world." Taking her hand, he goes out a door in the rear of the saloon. She glances back to see Gay turning drunkenly in his chair, and she waves to him as she is pulled out through the back door.

They emerge behind the saloon. Trash, a mound of empty liquor bottles and beer cans, broken cartons, are littered about, but a few yards off the desert stretches away in the moonlight. He looks up at the sky and then turns to her. Wordless, he starts to sit on the ground, taking her hand and drawing her down, too, and they sit side by side on the sprung seat of an abandoned, wheelless car. Now he smiles weakly at her.

"Nobody ever cried for me. Not for a long time, anyway . . ." Full of wordless speech, longing to make love to her and be loved by her, he takes her hand. "Gay's a great fella, ain't he?"

"Yes."

"I want to lie down. Okay?"

"Sure."

He lies in her lap, and suddenly covers his eyes. "Damn that bull!"

She smoothes his forehead. Now he opens his eyes. "Just rest. You don't have to talk."

"I can't place you, floatin' around like this. You belong to Gay?"

"I don't know where I belong."

"Boy, that's me, too. How come you got so much trust in your eyes?"

"Do I?"

"Like you were just born."

"Oh, no!"

"I don't like to see the way they grind women up out here. Although a lot of them don't mind, do they?"

"Some do."

"Did you really cry for me before?"

"Well, you were hurt and I—" She breaks off, seeing the wondrous shake of his head. "Didn't anybody ever cry for you?"

"No stranger. Last April the twelfth, I got kicked so bad I was out all day and all night. I had a girl with me and two good buddies. I haven't seen her or them since."

"They left you alone?"

"Listen . . . let me ask you something . . . I can't talk to anybody, you know?" She waits for him to speak. "I . . . I don't understand how you're supposed to do."

"What do you mean?"

"Well, see, I never floated around till this last year. I ain't like Gay and Pilot, I got a good home. I did have, anyway. And one day my old man . . . we were out back and suddenly, *bam!* Down he went. Some damn fool hunters."

"They killed him?"

"Uh-huh. And . . . she changed."

"Who?"

"My mother. She was always so dignified . . . walked next to him like a saint. And pretty soon this man started comin' around, and she . . . she changed. Three months, they were married. Well, okay, but I told her, I says, 'Mama, you better get a paper from Mr. Brackett because I'm the oldest and Papa wanted me to have the ranch.' And sure enough, the wedding night he turns around and offers me wages. On my own father's place."

"What does *she* say?"

Shaking his head in an unrelieved agony, and with a mystical reaching in his tone: "I don't know; she don't *hear* me. She's all *changed around.* You know what I mean? It's like she don't remember me any more."

She nods, staring.

"What the hell you depend on? Do you know?"

"I don't know. Maybe . . ." She is facing the distant horizon, staring at her life. "Maybe all there really is is what hap-

pens next, just the next thing, and you're not supposed to remember anybody's promises."

"You could count on mine, Roslyn. I think I love you."

"You don't even know me."

"I don't care."

He raises his face to hers, but his eyes are suddenly pain-
racked, and he grips his head. "That damn bull!"

The back door suddenly swings open, throwing the light of
the saloon on them. Gay comes out, walking unsteadily, blinking in the sudden darkness. He calls: "Roslyn?"

"Here we are!" She gets up with Perce.

Gay comes over, shepherding them toward the door. "Come
on, now, I want you to meet my kids."

"Your kids here?"

"They come for the rodeo. I ain't seen them in a year. You
oughta see the welcome they give me, Roslyn! Nearly
knocked me over." They go through the door and up a short
corridor. "She's gonna be nineteen! She got so pretty! Just
happen to be here for the rodeo, the both of them! That
great?"

"Oh, I'm so glad for you, Gay!" They go into the saloon.

Gay, now drawing Roslyn by the hand, and she holding
onto Perce's hand, come up to the crowded bar, where Guido
is standing in a drunken swirl of his own. The air is muddy
with smoke and jazz. Perce is blinking hard, trying to see. Roslyn watches him even as she attends to Gay.

Gay reaches Guido first. "Where are they?"

"Where are who?" Guido turns to him slowly.

"My kids! I told them I'd be back in a minute. You heard
me tell them."

"Went out there." Guido points toward the door to the
street, then looks appraisingly at Roslyn and Perce.

Gay looks hurt and angered, then pushes through the door
and goes out. He looks about at the parked cars and the moving groups of people and the armed deputies, and he yells:
"Gaylord! Gaylord?"

Now Roslyn comes out of the bar, helping Perce. Guido is
with them, carrying a bottle. Their attention is instantly on

Gay, except for Perce, who immediately lays his cheek on the car fender, embracing it.

"Rose-May! Gaylord! Gaylorrrrd?"

Guido comes up beside Gay, a muddled, advice-giving look on his face. Roslyn remains holding onto Perce.

Guido bays: "Gaylord! Here's your father!" He sways, pointing at Gay.

People are beginning to congest around them, some seriously curious, some giggling, some drunk. Roslyn remains with Perce just behind Gay and Guido, watching Gay, tears threatening her eyes.

"Gaylord, where you gone to? I told you I was comin' right back. You come here now!"

A woman, middle-aged, dressed like a farmer's wife, comes up to Gay. "Don't you worry, Mister, you'll probably find them home."

Gay looks at her, at the security emanating from her sympathetic smile. He turns and climbs up onto the hood of the car; he is very drunk, and shaken. He looks over the crowded street from this new elevation. Just below him Roslyn and Guido are looking up into his face, and he seems twice his normal size. Drunks mill around below, the bar lights blink crazily behind him, the armed deputies look on blankly from the doorways, and the jazz cacophony is flying around his ears like lightning. His hat askew, his eyes perplexed, and his need blazing on his face, he roars out: "Gaylord! *I know you hear me!*"

There is now a large crowd around the car, the faces of alien strangers. Gay bangs his fist on the roof of the car. "I know you hear me! Rose-May—you come out now!" He suddenly slips on the hood and rolls off onto the ground, flat on his back. Roslyn screams and runs to him, as the crowd roars with laughter; she quickly lifts up his head and kisses him.

"I'm sure they're looking for you, Gay. They must've thought you'd left." He stares dumbly at her. "Oh, poor Gay, poor Gay!" She hugs his head and rocks him, crouched beside him in the gutter.

NINE

The car is speeding on the dark highway. Guido is driving, the dog asleep beside him. In the back seat Roslyn has one arm around the unconscious Perce, whose legs hang out a window, the other arm around Gay, asleep against her breast. Her eyes are closed.

Suddenly the car bumps up and down, and Guido is trying to bring it back on the highway. For an instant the headlights catch a figure scurrying off the road shoulder. The car swerves back onto the highway. Now a man rises from the roadside, brushes himself off, picks up his bundle, and walks impassively on. It is the Indian.

The ride is smooth again, and Roslyn has opened her eyes. She is drunk and exhausted, a feeling of powerlessness is on her. Guido has a vague look of joy on his face as he drives. She speaks in a helpless monotone, as in a dream: "Aren't you going too fast? Please, huh?"

"Don't worry, kid, I never kill anybody I know."

The speedometer is climbing toward eighty.

"A fellow smashed up my best girl friend. All they found were her gloves. Please, Guido. She was beautiful, with black hair. . . ."

"Say hello to me, Roslyn."

"Hello, Guido. Please, huh?"

His eyes are glazed and oddly relaxed, as though he were happy in some corner of his mind. "We're all blind bombardiers, Roslyn—we kill people we never even saw. I bombed nine cities. I sure must've broken a lot of dishes but I never saw them. Think of all the puppy dogs must've gone up, and mail carriers, eyeglasses . . . Boy! Y'know, droppin' a bomb is like tellin' a lie—makes everything so quiet afterwards. Pretty soon you don't hear anything, don't see anything. Not even your wife. The difference is that I *see* you. You're the first one I ever really *saw*."

"Please, Guido, don't kill us. . . ."

"How do you get to know somebody, kid? I can't make a landing. And I can't get up to God, either. Help me. I never said help me in my life. I don't *know* anybody. Will you give me a little time? Say yes. At least say hello Guido."

She can hear the murderous beating of wind against the car.

"Yes. Hello, Guido."

From over ninety the speedometer begins to descend.

"Hello, Roslyn."

Headlights hit the dark, unfinished house, illuminating the unfinished outside wall and the lumber and building materials lying around on the ground. Now the motor is shut off, but the lights remain on.

No one is moving inside the car. Guido, exhausted, stares at his house. The dog is asleep beside him. Now he opens the door and lumbers out of the car. He opens the rear door and blearily looks in.

Roslyn is sleeping, sitting upright. Perce is still asleep on her lap, his feet out the window; Gay is on the floor. Guido stares at her, full of longing and sorrow for himself. He looks down at Perce, then at Gay, and as though they were unbearably interfering he steps back from the car and walks into the darkness.

Loud hammer blows open Roslyn's eyes; Gay sits up. "Okay, I'll drive, I'll drive."

"We're here, Gay."

"Where?"

She sees something in the headlights through the windshield; carefully she slides from under Perce's head and out the door, and walks unsteadily from the car toward the house, mystified. She walks in the headlight beams; the hammer blows are a few feet away. Awe shows on her face.

Guido is drunkenly hammering a sheathing board to the unfinished wall of the house. It is on crooked, but he gives it a final pat of satisfaction, then goes to the lumber pile and takes off another board, nearly falling with that, and lays it up against the wall, trying to butt it up against the previously nailed board. He hammers, as in a dream, the kind of pleasure and pain that comes of being freed of earthly logic, yet being driven toward some always receding center.

Roslyn comes up to him, not daring to touch him. "Oh, I'm sorry, Guido. Guido? I'm so sorry." He continues dumbly hammering. "Won't you hit your hand, it's so dark? It's dark, Guido, look how dark it is." He hammers on. She almost turns, spreading her arms and looking skyward. "Look, it's all dark!" A sob breaks from her. "Please! Please stop!"

From nearby Gay calls angrily: "What the hell you stompin' the flowers for?"

Roslyn turns to Gay, who comes up to Guido and swings him around by the shoulder and bends to the ground. "You busted all the damn heliotropes!"

Gay is on his hands and knees now, trying to stand up the fallen flowers. Guido is looking down dumbly, the hammer in his hand.

Gay: "Look at that! Look at that, now!" He holds up a torn stem. "What in hell good is that, now?"

Roslyn: "He was trying to fix the house."

Rising unsteadily to his feet, Gay asks menacingly: "What call *he* got to fix the house?"

Roslyn: "Don't! Don't! Please, Gay! He . . . he's just trying to say hello. It's no crime to say hello."

From behind them they hear Perce crying out: "Who's doin' that?"

They turn to see Perce staggering into the headlight beams, trying to free his head and arms from yards of unraveling bandage flowing off his head. He is fighting it off like a clinging spider web, turning around and around to find its source.

"Who's doin' that?"

Roslyn hurries toward him. "Don't! Don't take it off!" She reaches him and tries to unwind his arms.

"Get it off. What's on me?"

"Stop tangling it. It's your bandage."

He stops struggling and looks at the bandage as though for the first time. "What for a bandage?"

Roslyn is starting to laugh despite her concern. A few yards away, Guido is quietly but deeply laughing, glassy-eyed. Gay is beginning to feel the laughter's infectiousness. Feeling a hysteria of laughter coming on, Roslyn tries to wind the bandage on again. "It's for your head."

Perce: "My—" He breaks off as he raises his hands and feels the bandage wrapped around his head. "I have this on all night?" He looks angrily at Guido and Gay, who are roaring now, and to them he says: "Who tied this on me?" He is trying to pull it off his head.

She tries to stop his hands. "The ambulance did it. Don't take it off."

Perce, unwinding and unwinding the bandage: "You leave me at a disadvantage all night? Who put it on? Gay, you . . ." He lunges toward Gay and trips on a board, and the whole pile of lumber topples on him with a great crash. Guido and Gay fall about, dying with hysteria.

Roslyn, between laughter and tears, tries to extricate Perce from the lumber. "Get him up. Gay, come here. Guido! Carry him. Please. He can't help himself." The men come to help her, and still laughing crazily they lift Perce and almost carry him to the door of the house. She goes inside ahead of them.

Looped in their arms, Perce demands: "Who put it on? Leave me at a disadvantage all night?" She and Guido get him through the door of the house. "Where's this? Let me alone. Where is this place?" He lies on a couch as Guido sprawls on his favorite chair, catching his breath.

Roslyn: "This is my house . . . or Guido's." She laughs. "Well, it's a house, anyway."

Perce closes his eyes. Suddenly the house is quiet. She cov-

ers Perce with an Indian blanket, and the touch stirs him to resistance. "No, Ma, don't, don't!" He turns his face away.

Now she stands and sees Gay sitting outside the door on the
step. She goes down to him, starting to wipe the hair out of his
eyes, and he takes her hand. A curious inwardness, a naked
supplication has come into his face.

"Wish you'd met Gaylord, Rose-May. If I had a new kid
now, I'd know just how to be with him, just how to do. I
wasted these kids. I didn't know nothin'."

"Oh, no, I'm sure they love you, Gay. Go to sleep now."

He grasps her hand, preventing her from leaving. "Would
you ever want a kid? With me?"

She pats his hand, starting to turn away. "Let me just turn
the lights off in the car."

He raises up, struggling to get on his feet.

"Whyn't you sleep now . . ."

"I don't wanna sleep now!" He staggers to his feet, swaying
before her. "I asked you a question! Did I ask you to turn the
lights off in the car? What are you runnin' away from all the
time?" With a wide gesture toward windows and walls that
nearly tumbles him: "I never washed the windows for my wife
even. Paint a fireplace! Plant all them damn heliotropes!"

He suddenly goes to the doorway and yells into the house:
"What're they all doin' here? What're you bringin' them
around for?"

"I didn't bring them, they just—"

"Where are you at? I don't know where you're at."

Trying not to offend him and still speak her truth, she embraces him. "I'm here, Gay. I'm with you. But . . . what if
some day you turn around and suddenly you don't like me
any more? Like before, when Perce got hurt, you started to
give me a look. . . . I know that look and it scares me, Gay.
'Cause I couldn't ever stay with a stranger."

"Honey, I got a little mad. That don't mean I didn't like
you. Didn't your papa ever spank you, and then take you up
and give you a big kiss?" She is silent. "He did, didn't he?"

"He was never there long enough. And strangers spank for

keeps." She suddenly presses herself against him and he embraces her. "Oh, love me, Gay! Love me!"

He raises her face and kisses her. She smiles brightly.

Roslyn: "Now we made up, okay?"

Gay: "Yes, okay, okay!" Laughing softly, he hugs her. "You sleep now . . . you're tired. Sleep, darling."

"And tomorrow I'll show you what I can do. You'll see what living is."

She nods in agreement, gently pressing him to the doorway. He goes into the dark house, talking. "We'd make out. I could farm. Or run cattle, maybe. I'm damn good man, Roslyn—best man you'll ever see. Show you tomorrow when we hit those mountains. Ain't many around can keep up with old Gay. You wait and see."

She hears the bed groaning, then silence. She walks unsteadily to the car, reaches in, and pushes the switch. The lights go off. Now she stands erect and looks up at the oblivious moon, a vast sadness stretching her body, a being lost, a woman whose life has forbidden her to forsake her loneliness. She cries out, but softly, to the sky: "Help!"

For a long time she stands there, given to the dreadful clouds crossing the stars, racing to nowhere.

[*1961*]

Fame

Seven hundred and fifty thousand dollars—minus the ten-per-cent commission, that left him six hundred and seventy-five thousand spread over ten years. Coming out of his agent's building onto Madison Avenue, he almost smiled at this slight resentment he felt at having to pay Billy the seventy-five thousand. A gaunt, good-looking woman smiled back at him as she passed; he did not turn, fearing she would stop and begin the conversation that by now was unbearable for him. "I only wanted to tell you that it's really the wisest and funniest play I think I've ever . . ." He kept close to the storefronts as he walked, resolving once again to develop some gracious set of replies to these people who, after all—at least some of them—were sincere. But he knew he would always stand there like an oaf, for some reason ashamed and yet happy.

A rope of pearls lay on black velvet in the window of a jewelry store; he paused. My God, he thought, I could buy that! I could buy the whole window maybe. Even the store! The pearls were suddenly worthless. In the glass he saw his hound's eyes, his round, sad face and narrow beard, his sloping shoulders and wrinkled corduroy lapels; for the King of Broadway, he thought, you still look like a failure. He moved on a few steps, and a hand grasped his forearm with annoying proprietary strength and turned him to an immense chest, a yachtsman's sunburned face with a chic, narrow-brimmed hat on top.

"You wouldn't be Meyer Berkowitz?"

"No. I look like him though."

The man blushed under his tan, looked offended, and walked away.

Meyer Berkowitz approached the corner of Fiftieth Street, feeling the fear of retaliation. What do I want them to do, hate me? On the corner he paused to study his watch. It was only a quarter to six and the dinner was for seven-fifteen. He tried to remember if there was a movie house in the neighborhood. But there wouldn't be time for a whole movie unless he happened to come in at the beginning. Still, he could afford to pay for half a movie. He turned west on Fiftieth. A couple stared at him as he passed. His eye fell on a rack of magazines next to the corner newsstand. The edge of *Look* showed under *Life,* and he wondered again at all the airplanes, kitchen tables, dentists' offices, and trains where people would be staring at his face on the cover. He thought of shaving his beard. But then, he thought, they won't recognize me. He smiled. I am hooked. So be hooked, he muttered and, straightening up, he resolved to admit to the next interloper that he was in fact Meyer Berkowitz and happy to meet his public. On a rising tide of honesty he remembered the years in the Burnside Memorial Chapel, sitting beside the mummified dead, his notebooks spread on the cork floor as he constructed play after play, and the mirror in the men's room where he would look at his morose eyes, wondering when and if they would ever seem as unique as his secret fate kept promising they would someday be. On Fifth Avenue, so clean, gray, and rich, he headed downtown, his hands clasped behind his back. Two blocks west, two blocks to the right of his shoulder, the housemen in two theaters were preparing to turn the lights on over his name; the casts of two plays were at home checking their watches; in all, maybe thirty-five people, including the stage managers and assistants, had been joined together by him, their lives changed and in a sense commanded by his words. And in his heart, in a hollowed-out place, stood a question mark: was it possible to write another play? Thankfully he thought of his wealth again, subtracted ten-per-cent commission from the movie purchase price of *I See You* and divided the remainder over ten years, and angrily swept all the dollars out of his head. A cabdriver slowed down beside him and waved and yelled, "Hey, Meyer!" and the two passengers were leaning forward to see him. The cab was keeping pace with him, so he lifted his left hand a few inches in a cripped wave—like a prizefighter, it occurred to him. An unexplainable disgust pressed him toward a sign overhanging the sidewalk a few yards ahead.

He had a vague recollection of eating in Lee Fong's years ago with Billy, who had been trying unsuccessfully to get him a TV assignment ("Meyer, if you would only follow a plot line   "). It would probably be empty at this hour and it wasn't elegant. He pushed open the bright-red lacquered door and thankfully saw that the bar was empty and sat on a stool. Two girls were alone in the restaurant part, talking over teacups. The bartender took his order without any sign of recognizing him. He settled both arms on the bar, purposefully relaxing. The Scotch and soda arrived. He drank, examining his face, which was segmented by the bottles in front of the mirror. Cleanly and like a soft blow on his shoulder the realization struck him that it was getting harder and harder to remember talking to anyone as he used to last year and all his life before his plays had opened, before he had come on view. Even now in this empty restaurant he was already expecting a stranger's voice behind him, and half wanting it. Crummy. A longing rose up in him to face someone with his mind on something else; someone who would not show that charged, distorted pressure in the eyes which, he knew, meant that they were seeing his printed face superimposed over his real one. Again he watched himself in the mirror behind the bar: Meyer the Morose, Sam Ugly, but a millionaire with plays running in five countries. Setting his drink down, he noticed the soiled frayed cuffs of his once-tan corduroy jacket, and the shirt cuff sticking out with the button off. With a distant feeling of alarm he realized that he was meeting his director and producer and their wives at the Pavillon and that these clothes, to which he had never given any thought, would set him off as a character who went around like a bum when he had two hits running.

Thank God anyway that he had never married! To come home to the old wife with this printed new face—not good. But now, how would he ever know whether a woman was looking at him or "Meyer Berkowitz" in full color on the magazine cover? Strange—in the long Memorial Chapel nights he had envisaged roomfuls of girls pouring over him when his plays succeeded, and now it was almost inconceivable to make a real connection with any woman he knew. He summoned up their faces, and in each he saw calculation, that look of achievement. It was exhausting him, the whole thing. Months had gone by since he had so much as made a note. What he needed was an apartment in Bensonhurst or the upper Bronx somewhere, among people who . . . But they would know him in the Bronx. He sipped his second drink. His stomach was empty and the alcohol went straight to the backs of his eyes, and he felt himself lifted up and hanging restfully by the neck over the bar.

The bartender, a thin man with a narrow mustache and only faint signs of Chinese features, stood before him. "I beggin' you pardon. Excuse me?"

Meyer Berkowitz raised his eyes and before the bartender could speak, he said, "I'm Meyer Berkowitz."

"Ha!" The bartender pointed into his face with a long fingernail. "I know. I recognizin' you! On *Today Show,* right?"

"Right."

The bartender now looked over Meyer's head toward someone behind him and, pointing at Meyer, nodded wildly. Then, for some reason whispering into Meyer's ear, he said, "The boss invite you to havin' something on the house."

Meyer turned around and saw a Chinese with sunglasses on

standing beside the cash register, bowing and gesturing lavishly toward the expanse of the bar. Meyer smiled, nodded with aristocratic graciousness as he had seen people do in movies, turned back to the bartender and ordered another Scotch, and quickly finished the one in his hand. How fine people really were! How they loved their artists! Shit, man, this is the greatest country in the world.

He stirred the gift Scotch, whose ice cubes seemed just a little clearer than the ones he had paid for. How come his refrigerator never made such clear ice cubes? Vaguely he heard people entering the restaurant behind him. With no warning he was suddenly aware that three or four couples were at the bar alongside him and that in the restaurant part the white linen tablecloths were now alive with moving hands, plates, cigars. He held his watch up to his eyes. The undrunk part of his brain read the time. He'd finish this drink and amble over to the Pavillon. If he only had a pin for his shirt cuff . . .

"Excuse me . . ."

He turned on the stool and faced a small man with very fair skin, wearing a gray-checked overcoat and a gray hat and highly polished black shoes. He was a short, round man, and Meyer realized that he himself was the same size and even the same age, just about, and he was not sure suddenly that he could ever again write a play.

The short man had a manner, it was clear, the stance of a certain amount of money. There was money in his pause and the fit of his coat and a certain ineffable condescension in his blue eyes, and Meyer imagined his wife, also short, wrapped in mink, waiting a few feet away in the crowd at the bar, with the same smug look.

After the pause, during which Meyer said nothing, the short man asked, "Are you Meyer Berkowitz?"

"That's right," Meyer said, and the alcohol made him sigh for air.

"You don't remember me?" the short man said, a tiny curl of smile on the left edge of his pink mouth.

Meyer sobered. Nothing in the round face stuck to any part of his memory, and yet he knew he was not all this drunk. "I'm afraid not. Who are you?"

"You don't remember me?" the short man asked with genuine surprise.

"Well, who are you?"

The man glanced off, not so much embarrassed as unused to explaining his identity; but, swallowing his pride, he looked back at Meyer and said, "You don't remember Bernie Gelfand?"

Whatever suspicion Meyer felt was swept away. Clearly he had known this man somewhere, sometime. He felt the debt of the forgetter. "Bernie Gelfand. I'm awfully sorry, but I can't recall where. Where did I know you?"

"I sat next to you in English four years! DeWitt Clinton!"

Meyer's brain had long ago drawn a blind down on all his high-school years. But the name Gelfand did rustle the fallen leaves at the back of his mind. "I remember your name, ya, I think I do."

"Oh, come on, guy, you don't remember Bernie Gelfand with the curly red hair?" With which he raised his gray felt hat to reveal a bald scalp. But no irony showed in his eyes, which were transported back to his famous, blazing hair and to the seat he had had next to Meyer Berkowitz in high school. He put his hat back on again.

"Forgive me," Meyer said, "I have a terrible memory. I remember your name, though."

Gelfand, obviously put out, perhaps even angered but still trying to smile, and certainly full of intense sentimental interest, said, "We were best friends."

Meyer laid a beseeching hand on Gelfand's gray coat sleeve. "I'm not doubting you, I just can't place you for the moment. I mean, I believe you." He laughed.

Gelfand seemed assuaged now, nodded, and said, "You don't look much different, you know? I mean, except for the beard, I'd know you in a minute."

"Yeah, well . . ." Meyer said, but still feeling he had

offended he obediently asked, "What do you do?" preparing for a long tale of success.

Gelfand clearly enjoyed this question, and he lifted his eyebrows to a proud peak. "I'm in shoulder pads," he said.

A laugh began to bubble up in Meyer's stomach; Gelfand's coat was in fact stiffly padded at the shoulders. But in an instant he remembered that there was a shoulder-pad industry, and the importance which Gelfand attached to his profession killed the faintest smile on Meyer's face. "Really," he said with appropriate solemnity.

"Oh, yes. I'm General Manager, head of everything up to the Mississippi."

"Don't say. Well, that's wonderful." Meyer felt great relief. It would have been awful if Gelfand had been a failure—or in charge of New England only. "I'm glad you've done so well."

Gelfand glanced off to one side, letting his achievement sink deeply into Meyer's mind. When he looked again at Meyer he could not quite keep his eyes from the frayed cuffs of the corduroy jacket and the limp shirt cuff hanging out. "What do *you* do?" he asked.

Meyer looked into his drink. Nothing occurred to him. He touched his finger against the mahogany bar and still nothing came to him through his shock. His resentment was clamoring in his head; he recognized it and greeted it. Then he looked directly at Gelfand, who in the pause had grown a look of benevolent pity. "I'm a writer," Meyer said and watched for the publicity-distorted freeze to grip Gelfand's eyeballs.

"That so!" Gelfand said, amused. "What kind of writing you do?"

If I really had any style, Meyer thought, I would shrug and say I write part-time poems after I get home from the post office, and we could leave Bernie to enjoy his dinner. On the other hand, I do not work in the post office, and there must be some way to shake this monkey off and get back to where I can talk to people again as if I were real. "I write plays," he said to Gelfand.

"That so!" Gelfand smiled, his amusement enlarging

toward open condescension. "Anything I would have . . . heard of?"

"Well, as a matter of fact, one of them is down the street."

"Really? On *Broadway?*" Gelfand's face split into its parts; his mouth still kept its smile, but his eyes showed a certain wild alarm. His head, suddenly, was on straighter, his neck drawn back.

"I wrote *I See You,*" Meyer said and tasted slime on his tongue.

Gelfand's mouth opened. His skin reddened.

"And *Mostly Florence.*"

The two smash hits seemed to open before Gelfand's face like bursting flags. His finger lifted toward Meyer's chest. "Are you . . . *Meyer Berkowitz?*" he whispered.

"Yes."

Gelfand held out his hand tentatively. "Well, I'm very happy to meet you," he said with utter formality.

Meyer saw distance locking into place between them, and in the instant wished he could take Gelfand in his arms and wipe out the poor man's metaphysical awe, smother his defeat, and somehow retract this very hateful pleasure which he knew now he could not part with any more. He shook Gelfand's hand and then covered it with his left hand.

"Really," Gelfand went on, withdrawing his hand as though it had already presumed too much, "I . . . I've enjoyed your —excuse me." Meyer's heavy cheeks stirred vaguely toward a smile.

Gelfand closed his coat and quickly turned about and hurried to the little crowd waiting for tables near the red entrance door. He took the arm of a short woman in a mink wrap and turned her toward the door. She seemed surprised as he hurried her out of sight and into the street.

[*1966*]

Fitter's Night

By four in the afternoon it was almost dark in winter, and this January was one of the coldest on record, so that the night shift filing through the turnstiles at the Navy Yard entrance was somber, huddling in zipper jackets and pulling down earflaps, shifting from foot to foot as the Marine guards inspected each tin lunchbox in turn and compared the photographs on identity cards with the squint-eyed, blue-nosed faces that passed through. The former grocery clerks, salesmen, unemployed, students, and the mysteriously incapacitated young men whom the Army and Navy did not want; the elderly skilled machinists come out of retirement, the former truckdrivers, elevator operators, masons, disbarred lawyers, and a few would-be poets, poured off the buses in the blue light of late afternoon and waited their turn at the end of the lines leading to the fresh-faced Marines in the booths, who refused to return their quips and dutifully searched for the bomb and the incendiary pencil under the lettuce-and-tomato sandwiches leaking through the waxed paper, against all reason unscrewing the Thermos bottles to peer in at the coffee. With some ten thousand men arriving for each of the three shifts, the law of averages naturally came into play, and it was inevitable that every few minutes someone would put his Thermos back into his lunchbox and say, "What's Roosevelt got against hot coffee?" and the Marines would blink and wave the joker into the Yard.

To the naval architects, the engineers, the Yard Master and his staff, the New York Naval Shipyard was not hard to define; in fact, it had hardly changed since its beginnings in the early eighteen hundreds. The vast drydocks facing the bay were backed by a maze of crooked and curving streets lined with one-story brick machine shops and storehouses. In dark Victorian offices papers were still speared on sharp steel points and filing cabinets were of dark oak. Ships of war were never exactly the same, whatever anybody said, and the smith was still in a doorway hammering one-of-a-kind iron fittings, the sparks falling against his floor-length leather apron; steel bow-plates were still sighted by eye regardless of the carefully mapped curves of the drawing, and when a man was injured a two-wheel pushcart was sent for to bump him along the cobblestones to the infirmary like a side of beef.

It was sure that Someone knew where everything was, and this faith was adopted by every new man. The shipfitter's helper, the burner, the chipper, the welder; painters, carpenters, riggers, drillers, electricians—hundreds of them might spend the first hour of each shift asking one stranger after another where he was supposed to report or what drydock held the destroyer or carrier he had been working on the night before; and there were not a few who spent entire twelve-hour shifts searching for their particular gangs, but the faith never faltered. Someone must know what was supposed to be happening, if only because damaged ships did limp in under tow from the various oceans and after days, weeks, or sometimes months they did sail out under Brooklyn Bridge, ready once again to fight the enemy. There were naturally a sensitive few who, watching these gallant departures, shook their heads with wonder at the mystery of how these happened to have been repaired, but the vast majority accepted this and even felt that they themselves were somehow responsible. It was like a baseball game with five hundred men playing the outfield at the same time, sweeping in a mob toward the high arching ball, which was caught somewhere in the middle of the crowd, by whom no one knew, except that the game was slowly and quite inconceivably being won.

Tony Calabrese, Shipfitter First Class, was one of that core of men who did know where to report once he came through the turnstile at four in the afternoon. In "real life," as the phrase went, he had been a steamfitter in Brooklyn and was not confused by mobs, Marines looking into his sandwiches, or the endless waiting around that was normal in a shipyard. Once through the turnstile, his lunchbox tucked under his arm again, his cap on crooked, he leaned into the wind with his broken nose, notifying oncoming men to clear the way, snug inside his pile zipper jacket and woolen shirt, putting down his feet on the outside edges like a bear, bandy-legged, low-crotched, a graduate of skyscraper construction, brewery re-pairing, and for eight months the City Department of Water Supply, until it was discovered that he had been sending a substitute on Tuesdays Wednesdays and Fridays while he went to the track and made some money.

Tony had never until a year and a half ago seen a ship up close and had no interest in ships, any more than he had had in the water supply, breweries, or skyscrapers. Work was a curse, a misfortune that a married man had to bear, like his missing front tooth, knocked out in a misunderstanding with a bookie. There was no mystery what the good life was, and he never lived a day without thinking about it, and more and more hopelessly now that he was past forty; it was being like Sinatra, or Luciano, or even one of the neighborhood politi-cians who wore good suits all day and never bent over, kept two apartments, one for the family, the other for the boloney of the moment. He had put his youth into trying for that kind of life and had failed. Driving the bootleggers' trucks over the Canadian border, even a season as Johnny Peaches' bravo and two months collecting for a longshoreman's local, had put him within reach of a spot, a power position from which he might have retired into an office or apartment and worked through telephones and over restaurant tables. But at the last moment something in his make-up had always defeated him, sent him rolling back into the street and a job and a paycheck, where the future was the same never-get-rich routine. He knew he was simply not smart enough. If he were, he wouldn't be working in the Navy Yard.

His face was as round as a frying pan with a hole in it, a comical face now that the nose was flattened, his front tooth gone, and no neck. He had risen to First in a year and a half, partly because the supervisor, old Charley Mudd, liked a good phone number, which Tony could slip him, and also because Tony could read blueprints quickly, weld, chip, burn, and bulldoze a job to its finish when, as happened occasionally, Charley Mudd had to get a ship back into the war. As Shipfitter First, he was often given difficult and complicated jobs and could call on any of the various trades to come in and burn or weld at his command. But he was not impressed by his standing, when Sinatra could open his mouth and make a grand. More important was that his alliance with Charley Mudd gave him jobs below decks in cold weather and above decks when the sky was clear. If indisposed, he could give Charley Mudd the sign and disappear for the night into a dark corner and a good sleep. But most of the time he enjoyed being on the job, particularly when he was asked how to perform one operation or another by "shipfitters" who could not compute a right angle or measure in smaller units than halves. His usual way of beginning his instruction was always the same and was expected by anyone who asked his help. He would unroll the blueprint, point to a line or figure, and say, "Pay 'tention, shithead," in a voice sludged with the bottom of wine bottles and the Italian cigars he inhaled. No one unable to bear this indignity asked him for help, and those who did knew in advance that they would certainly lose whatever pretensions they thought they had.

But there was another side to Tony, which came out during the waits. Before Pearl Harbor there had been some six thousand men employed in the Yard, and there were now close to sixty thousand. Naturally they would sometimes happen to collect in unmanageable numbers in a single compartment, and the repairs, which had to be done in specific stages, made it impossible for most of them to work and for any to leave. So the waits began; maybe the welder could not begin welding until the chipper finished breaking out the old weld, so he waited, with his helper or partner. The burner could not cut steel until the exhaust hose was brought down by his helper, who could not get hold of one until another burner down the corridor was finished with it, so he waited; a driller could not drill until his point was struck into the steel by the fitter, who was forbidden to strike it until the electricians had removed the electric cables on the other side of the bulkhead through which the hole had to be drilled, so they waited; until the only way out was a crap game or Tony "enjoying" everybody by doing imitations or picking out somebody to insult and by going into his grin, which, with the open space in his teeth, collapsed the company in hysteria. After these bouts of entertainment Tony always became depressed, reminded again of his real failing, a lack of stern dignity, leadership, force. Luciano would hardly be clowning around in a cruiser compartment, showing how stupid he could look with a tooth missing.

On this January afternoon, already so dark and the wind biting at his eyes, Tony Calabrese, going down the old streets of the Yard, had decided to work below decks tonight, definitely. Even here in the shelter of the Yard streets the wind was miserable—what would it be like on a main deck open to the bay? Besides, he did not want to tire himself this particular shift when he had a date at half-past four in the morning. He went through his mental checklist: Dora would meet him at Baldy's for breakfast; by six A.M. he would be home to change his clothes and take a shower; coffee with the kids at seven before they went to school, then maybe a nap till nine or half-past, then pick up Dora and make the first show at the Fox at ten; by twelve to Dora's room, bang-bang, and a good sleep till half-past two or three, when he would stop off at home and put on workclothes, and maybe see the kids if they got home early, and into the subway for the Yard. It was a good uncomplicated day in front of him.

Coming out of the end of the street he saw the cold stars over the harbor, a vast sky stretching out over the bay and beyond to the sea. Clusters of headlights coursed over Brooklyn Bridge, the thickening traffic of the homebound who did not know they were passing over the . ard or the war-broken ships. He picked his way around stacks of steel plate and tarpaulin-shrouded gear piled everywhere, and for a moment was caught in the blasting white glare of the arc lamp focused downward from the top of a traveling crane; slowly, foot by foot, it rolled along the tracks, tall as a four-story building on two straddling legs, its one arm thrust out against the stars, dangling a dull glinting steel plate the width of a bus, and led by a fitter hardly taller than its wheels, who was walking backwards between the tracks ahead of it and pointing off to the right in the incandescent whiteness of its one eye. As though intelligent, the crane obediently swiveled its great arm, lowering the swaying plate to a spot pointed at by the fitter, whose face Tony could not make out, shaded as it was by the peak of his cap against the downpouring light of the high white eye. Tony circled wide around the descending plate, trusting no cable or crane operator, and passed into the darkness again toward the cruiser beyond, raised in the drydock, her bow curving high over the roadway on which he walked with his lips pressed together to keep the wind off his teeth. Turning, he moved along her length, head down against the swift river of cold air, welcoming the oncoming clumps of foot-stamping men mounting her along the gangplank—the new shift boarding, the occasional greeting voice still lively in the earliness of the evening. He rocked up the length of the gangplank onto the main deck, with barely a nod passing the young lieutenant in upturned collar who stood hitting his gloved hands together in the tiny temporary guardhouse at the head of the plank. There was the happy smell of burned steel and coffee, the straightforward acridity of the Navy, and the feeling of the hive as he descended a steep stair clogged down its whole length with black welder's cables and four-inch exhaust hoses, the temporary intestine that always followed repair gangs into the patient ships.

His helper, Looey Baldu—where an Italian got a name like Baldu Tony could not understand, unless a Yugoslav had got into the woodpile or they shortened it—Looey was already waiting for him in the passageway, looking twenty-three, dignified and superior, with his high-school education, regulation steel-tipped shoes—which Tony steadfastly refused to wear—and his resolute but defensive greeting.

"Where's Charley Mudd?"

"I didn't see him yet."

"You blind? There he is."

Tony walked around the surprised Baldu and into a compartment where Charley Mudd, sixty, and half asleep, sat on three coils of electric cable, his eyes shut and a clipboard starting to slide out of his opening hands. Tony touched the older man's back and bent to talk softly and put in the fix. Charley nodded, his eyes rolling. Tony gave him a grateful pat and came out into the passageway, which was filling with men trying to pass one another in opposite directions while dragging endless lengths of hose, cable, ladders, and bulky toolboxes, everybody looking for somebody else, so that Tony had to raise his voice to Baldu. He always spoke carefully to the high-school graduate, who never caught on the first time but was a good boy although his wife, he said, was Jewish. Baldu was against race prejudism, whatever the hell that meant, and frowned like a judge when talked to as though some kind of veil hung before his face and nothing came through it loud and clear.

"We gonna watertight hatches C-Deck," Tony said and turned, hands still clenched inside his slit pockets, and walked.

Baldu had had no time to nod and already felt offended, but he followed with peaked eyebrows behind his fitter, keeping close so as not to know the humiliation of being lost again and having to face Tony's scathing ironies implying incessant masturbation.

They descended to C-Deck, a large, open area filled with tiered bunks in which a few sailors lay, some sleeping, others reading or writing letters. Tony was pleased at the nearness of the coffee smell, what with any more than a pound a week almost impossible for civilians to get except at black-market prices. Without looking again at his helper, he unzipped his jacket, stowed his lunchbox on the deck under an empty bunk, took out a blue handkerchief and blew his nose and wiped his teary eyes, removed his cap and scratched his head, and finally sat on his heels and ran his fingers along the slightly raised edge of a hatch opening in the deck, through which could be seen a ladder going down into dimness.

"Let that there cover come to me, Looey."

Baldu, his full brown-paper lunchbag still in his hand, sprang to the heavy hatch cover lying on the deck and with one hand tried to raise it on its hinges. Unwilling to admit that his strength was not enough or that he had made a mistake, he strained with the one hand, and as Tony regarded him with aggravation and lowering lids he got the hatch cover up on one knee, and only then let his lunchbag down onto the deck and with two hands finally raised the cover toward Tony, whose both hands were poised to stop it from falling shut.

"Hold it, hold it right there."

"Hold it open?"

"Well, what the fuck, you gonna hold it closed? Of course open. What's a-matta wichoo?"

Tony ran his fingertips along the rubber gasket that ran around the lip of the cover. Then he took hold of it and let it close over the hatch. Bending down until his cheek pressed the cold deck, he squinted to see how closely gasket met steel. Then he got up, and Looey Baldu stood to face him.

"I'm gonna give you a good job, Looey. Git some chalk, rub it on the gasket, then git your marks on the deck. Where the chalk don't show, build it up with some weld, then git a grinder and tell him smooth it nice till she's nice an' even all around. You understand?"

"Sure, I'll do it."

"Just don't get wounded. That's it for tonight, so take it easy."

Baldu's expression was nearly fierce as he concentrated patriotically on the instructions, and now he nodded sternly and started to step back. Tony grabbed him before he tripped over the hatch cover behind him, then let him go and without further remark fled toward the coffee smell.

It was going to be a pretty good night. Dora, whom he had gotten from Hindu, was a little shorter than he would have liked, but she had beautiful white skin, especially her breasts, and lived alone in a room with good heat no sisters, aunts, mothers, nothing. And both times she had brought home fresh bread from Macy's, where she packed nights. Now all he had to do was keep relaxed through the shift so as not to be sleepy when he met her for breakfast at Baldy's. Picking his way along a passage toward the intensifying coffee smell, he felt joyous, and, seeing a drunken sailor trying to come down a ladder, he put his shoulder under the boy's seat and gently let him down to the deck, then helped him a few yards along the passage until the boy fell into a bunk. Then he lifted his legs onto it, turned him over, opened his pea jacket and shoelaces, and returned to the search for the source of the coffee smell.

He might have known. There was Hindu, standing over an electric brewer tended by two sailors in T-shirts. Hindu was big, but next to him stood a worker who was a head taller, a giant. Tony sauntered over, and Hindu said to the sailors, "This here's a buddy, how about it?"

A dozen lockers stood against the nearby bulkhead, from one of which a sailor took a clean cup and a five-pound bag of sugar. Tony thanked him as he took the full cup and then moved a foot away as Hindu came over.

"Where you?" Hindu asked.

"C-Deck, watertight hatch cover. Where you?"

"I disappeared. They're still settin' up the windbreak on Main Deck."

"Fuck that."

"You know what Washington said when he crossed the Delaware?"

Then both together, "It's fuckin' cold."

They drank coffee. Hindu's skin was so dark he was sometimes taken for an Indian; he made up for it by keeping his thick, wavy hair well combed, his blue beard closely shaved, and his big hands clean.

"I gotta make a phone call," he said quietly, stooping to Tony. "I left her bawlin'. Jesus, I passed him comin' up the stairs."

"Ta hell you stay so long?"

"I coun' help myself." His eyes softened, his mouth worked in pleasurable agony. "She's dri'n' me crazy. We even wen' faw walk."

"You crazy?"

"I coun' help it. If you seen her you drop dead. Byoodiful. I mean it. I'm goin' crazy. I passed him comin' up the stairs, I swear!"

"You'll end up fuckin' a grave, Hindu."

"She touches me, I die. I die, Tony." Hindu shut his eyes and shook his head, memorializing.

Activity behind them turned them about. The big worker, his coffee finished, was pulling on a chain that ran through a set of pulleys hooked to a beam overhead, and a gigantic electric motor was rising up off the deck. Tony, Hindu, and the two sailors watched the massive rigger easily raise the slung motor until it reached the pulleys and could be raised no farther, and three inches yet to go before it could be slid onto a platform suspended from the deck overhead. The rigger drew his gauntlets up tighter, set himself underneath the motor with his hands up under it, and, with knees bent, pushed. The motor rose incredibly until its feet were a fraction above the platform; the rigger pushed and got it hung. Then he came out from under, stood behind it, and shoved it fully onto the platform where it belonged. His face was flushed, and, expanded by the effort, he looked bigger than ever. Slipping off his gauntlets, he looked down to the sailors, who were still sitting on the deck.

"Anybody ever read *Oliver Wiswell?*"

"No."

"You ought to. Gives you a whole new perspective on the American Revolution. You know, there's a school that doesn't think the Revolution was necessary."

Tony was already walking, and Hindu followed slightly behind, asking into his ear, "Maybe I could hang wichoo tonight, Tony. Okay? I ask Cholly, okay?"

"Go ahead."

Hindu patted Tony's back thankfully and hurried up a ladder.

Tony looked at his pocket watch. Five o'clock. He had chopped an hour. It was too early to take a nap. A sense of danger struck him, and he looked ahead up the passage, but there was only a colored worker he did not know fooling with a chipping gun that would not receive its chisel. He turned the other way in time to see a captain and a man in a felt hat and overcoat approaching with blueprints half unrolled in their hands. He caught sight of a chipping-gun air hose, which he followed into a compartment on hands and knees. The two brass went by, and he stood up and walked out of the compartment.

It was turning into one of the slow nights when the clock never moved. The coffee had sharpened him even more, so a nap was out of the question. He moved along passageways at a purposeful pace, up ladders and down, looking for guys he might know, but the ship was not being worked much tonight; why, he did not know and did not care. Probably there was a hurry-up on the two destroyers that had come in last night. One had a bow blasted off, and the other had floated in from the bay listing hard to one side. The poor bastards on the destroyers, with no room to move, and some of those kids seasick in bad weather. The worst was when the British ships came in. Good he wasn't on one of those bastards, with the cockroaches so bad you couldn't sit down, let alone stretch out, and their marines a lot of faggos. That was hard to believe the first time he saw it—like last summer with that British cruiser, the captain packing the deck day and night and the ship in drydock. A real jerked-off Englishman with a monocle and a mustache and a crushed cap, and a little riding crop in his hands clasped behind his back, scowling at everybody and refusing to go off duty even in drydock. And piping whistles blowing every few hours to bring the marines on deck for rifle drill, that bunch of fags screaming through the passageways, goosing each other, and pimples all over their faces. Christ, he hated the English the way they kicked Italy around, sneering. And those stupid officers, in July, walking around in thick blue hairy uniforms, sweating like pigs all over their eyeglasses. You could tell a U.S. ship blindfolded, the smell of coffee and cleanliness, and ice water anywhere you looked. Of course they said the British gunners were better, but who was winning the war, for Christ's sake? Without us they'd have to pack it in and salute the fuckin' Germans. The French had a good ship, that captured *Richelieu,* what paneling in the ward room, like a fuckin' palace, but something was wrong with the guns, they said, and couldn't hit nothin'.

He found himself in the engine room and looked up through the barrel-like darkness, up and up through the belly of the ship. There was, he knew, a cable passage where he could lie down. Somebody he could barely see high above in the darkness was showering sparks from a welding arc spread too far from the steel, but he pulled up his collar and climbed ladders, moved along the catwalks until he came to a low door which he opened, went into a hole lined with electric cables, and lay down with his hands clasped under his head. The welding buzz was all he could hear now. Footsteps would sound on the steel catwalks and give good warning.

Not tired, he closed his eyes to screw the government. Even here in the dark he was making money every minute—every second. With this week's check he would probably have nearly two thousand in his account and a hundred and twenty or so in the account Margaret knew about. Jesus, what a dumb woman! Dumb, dumb, dumb. But a good mother, that's for sure. But why not, with only two kids, what else she got to do? He would never sleep with her again and could barely remember the sight of her body. In fact, for the thousandth time in his life, he realized that he had never seen his wife naked, which was as it should be. You could fill a lake with the tears she had shed these fifteen years—an ocean. Good.

He stoked his anger at his wife, the resentment that held his life together. It was his cause, his agony, and his delight to let his mind go and imagine what she must feel, not being touched for eleven—no, twelve, yes, it was twelve last spring—years. This spring it would be thirteen, then fourteen, then twenty, and into her grave without his hand on her. Never, never would he give in. On the bed, when he did sleep at home, with his back to her, he stretched into good sleep, and sometimes her wordless sobs behind him were like soft rain on the roof that made him snug. She had asked for it. He had warned her at the time. He might look funny, but Tony Cala-brese was not funny for real. To allow himself to break, to put his hand on her ever again, he would have to forgive what she had done to him. And now, lying in the cable passage with his eyes closed, he went over what she had done, and as always happened when he reached for these memories, the darling face of the boloney formed in his darkness, Patty Moran, with genuine red hair, breasts without a crease under them, and lips pink as lipstick. Oh, Jesus! He shook his head in the dark, and where was she now? He did not dare hate his grandfather; the old man was like a storm or an animal that did only what it was supposed to do. He let himself remember what had become for him like a movie whose end he knew and dreaded to see once more, and yet wanted to. It was the only time in his life that had not been random, when each day that had passed in those few months had changed his position and finally sealed him up forever.

From the day he was born, it seemed to him, his mother had kept warning him to watch out for Grampa. If he stole, hit, lied, tore good pants, got in cop trouble, the same promise was made—if Grampa ever came to America he would settle each and every one of Tony's crimes in a daylong, maybe weeklong beating combined with an authoritative spiritual thundering that would straighten out Tony for the rest of his life. For Grampa was gigantic, a sport in the diminutive family, a throwback to some giants of old whose wit and ferocity had made them lords in Calabria, chiefs among the rocks, commanders of fishing boats, capos of the mines. Even his cowed father relied on the absent, never-seen old man for authority and spent every free hour away from work on the BMT tracks, playing checkers with his cronies, rather than chastise his sons. Grampa would come one day and settle them all, straighten them out, and besides, if he did come, he would bring his money. He owned fishing boats, the star of the whole family, a rich man who had made it, astoundingly, without ever leaving Calabria, which meant again that he was wily and merciless, brave and just.

The part that was usually hard to remember was hard to remember again, and Tony opened his eyes in the cable passage until, yes, he remembered. How he had ever gotten mixed up with Margaret in the first place, a mewly girl, big-eyed but otherwise blanketed bodily, bodiless, shy, and frightened. It was because he had just come out of the Tombs, and this time Mama was not to be fooled with. She was a fury now as he walked into the tenement, unwilling to listen to the old promises or to be distracted by all his oaths of innocence and frame-up. And this time fate began to step in, that invisible presence entered Tony's life, the Story; his tight time began when nothing was any longer random, and every day changed what he was and what he had to do.

A letter had arrived that nobody could read. They sat

around the table, Mama and Papa and Aunt Celia from next
door, and Frank and Salvatore, his married cousins. Tony
slowly traced the Italian script, speaking it aloud so that Papa
could mouth the words and penetrate the underlying thought,
which was unbelievable, a marvel that chilled them all.
Grampa had sold his holdings, now that Grandma was dead,
and was sailing for America for a visit, or, if he approved, to
stay the rest of his life.

The cable passage seemed to illuminate with the lightning
flashes of the preparations for the arrival—the house
scrubbed, walls painted, furniture shined, chairs fixed, and the
blackmail begun. Mama, seeing the face of her son and the
hope and avidity in his eyes, sat him down in the kitchen. I am
going to tell Grampa everything what you done, Tony. Everything. Unless you do what I say. You marry Margaret.

Margaret was a year older than Tony. Somehow, he could
not imagine how, now that he knew her, he had come to rest
on her stoop from time to time, mainly when just out of jail,
when momentarily the strain of bargaining for life and a spot
was too much, those moments when, like madness, a vision of
respectability overwhelmed him with a quick longing for the
clean and untroubled existence. She was like a nervous pony
at his approach, and easy to calm. It was the time he was driving booze trucks over the Canadian border for Harry Ox, the
last of the Twenties, and out of jail it was sweet to spend a
half-hour staring at the street with Margaret, like a clam
thrown up by the moiling sea for a moment. He had been in
his first gunfight near Albany and was scared. And this was
the first time he had said he would like to take her to the
movies. In all the years he had known her the thought had
never crossed his mind to make a date. Home that night, he already heard his mother talking about Margaret's family. The
skein was folding over him, and he did not resist. He did not
decide either. He let it come without touching it, let it drape
over him like a net. They were engaged, and nobody had used
the word even, but whenever he saw Margaret she acted as

though she had been waiting for him, as though he had been missing, and he let it happen, walked a certain way with her in the street, touching her elbow with his fingertips, and never took her into the joints, and watched his language. Benign were the smiles in her house the few times he appeared, but he could never stay long for the boredom, the thickness of the plot to strangle his life.

His life was Patty Moran by this time. Once across her threshold over Ox's saloon, everything he saw nearly blinded him. He had started out with her at three o'clock in the morning in the back of Ox's borrowed Buick, her ankle ripping the corded rope off the back of the front seat, and the expanse of her thigh across the space between the back and front seats was painted in cream across his brain forever. He walked around the neighborhood dazed, a wire going from the back of his head to her hard soft belly. She was not even Harry Ox's girl but a disposable one among several, and Tony started out knowing that and each day climbed an agonizing stairway to a vision of her dearness, almost but not quite imagining her marriageable. The thought of other men with her was enough to bring his fist down on a table even if he was sitting alone. His nose had not yet been broken; he was small but quick-looking, sturdy and black-eyed. She finally convinced him there was nobody else, she adored his face, his body, his stolen jokes. And in the same two or three months he was taking Margaret to the movies. He even kissed her now and then. Why? Why! Grampa was coming as soon as he could clear up his affairs, and what had begun with Margaret as a purpose-less yet pleasant pastime had taken on leverage in that it kept Mama pleased and quiet and would guarantee his respectabil-ity in Grampa's eyes—long enough anyway, to get his inherit-ance.

No word of inheritance was written in the old man's letters, but it was first imagined, then somehow confirmed, that Tony would get it. And when he did it was off-to-Buffalo, him and the boloney, maybe even get married someplace where nobody knew her and they'd make out seriously together. And best of all, Mama knew nothing of the boloney. Nowadays she was treating Tony like the head of the house. He had taken a job longshore, was good as gold, and sat home many an evening listening to the tock-tick.

The final letter came. Tony read it alone in the bathroom first and announced that Grampa was coming on the tenth although the letter said the ninth. On the morning of the ninth Tony said he had to get dressed up because, instead of working, he was going to scout around for a good present for Grampa's arrival tomorrow. Congratulated, kissed, waved off, he rounded the block to Ox's and borrowed three hundred dollars and took a cab to the Manhattan pier.

The man in truth was gigantic. Tony's first glimpse was this green suited, oddly young old man, a thick black tie at his throat, a black fedora held by a porter beside him, while down the gangway he himself was carrying on his back a small but heavy trunk. Tony understood at once—the money was in the trunk. On the pier Tony tipped the porter for carrying the furry hat, and kissed his six-foot grandfather once he had set the trunk down. Tony shook his hand and felt the power in it, hard as a banister. The old man took one handle of the trunk and Tony the other, and in the cab Tony made his proposal. Before rushing home, why not let him show New York?

Fine. But first Tony wanted to Americanize the clothes; people would get the wrong impression, seeing such a green immigrant suit and the heavy brogans. Grampa allowed it, standing there ravished by the bills Tony peeled off for the new suit, new shoes, and an American tie. Now they toured the town, sinking deeper and deeper into it as Tony graded the joints from the middle-class ones uptown to his hangouts near Canal Street, until the old man was kissing his grandson two and three times an hour and stood up cheering the Minsky girls who bent over the runway toward his upturned face. Tony, at four in the morning, carried the trunk up the stairs of the tenement on his own back, feeling the dead weight inside;

then back down and carried Grampa on his back and laid him in his own bed and himself on the floor. He had all he could do to keep from rushing over to Patty Moran to tell her he was in like Flynn, the old man loved him like a son, and they might begin by opening a joint together someplace like in Queens. But he kept discipline and slept quickly, his face under the old man's hand hanging over the edge of the mattress.

In the cable passage, staring at the dark, he could not clearly recall his wedding, any more than he had been able to an hour after the ceremony. It was something he was doing and not doing. Grampa had emerged from the bedroom with Tony under his armpit; and, seeing her father, Mama's face lengthened out as though God or the dead had walked in, especially since she had just finished getting dressed up to meet his boat. The shouting and crying and kissing lasted until afternoon, Grampa's pleasure with his manly grandson gathering the complicated force of a new mission in his life, a proof of his own grandeur at being able to hand on a patrimony to a good man of his blood, a man of style besides.

Papa nodded an uncertain assent, one eye glancing toward the trunk, but as evening came Mama, Tony saw, was showing two thoughts in her tiny brown eyes, and after the third meal of the day, with the table cleaned off and the old man blinking drowsily, she laid two open hands on the table, smiled deferentially, and said Tony had been in and out of jails since he was twelve.

Grampa woke up.

Tony was hanging with bootleggers, refused until the last couple of months to hold a regular job, and now he was staying with an Irish whore when he had engaged himself to Margaret, the daughter of a good Calabrian family down the block, a girl as pure as a dove, beautiful, sincere, whose reputation was being mangled every day Tony avoided talk of a marriage date. The girl's brothers were growing restive, her father had gotten the look of blood in his eye. Margaret alone could save Tony from the electric chair, which was waiting for him as sure as God had sent Jesus, for he was a boy who would lie as quickly as spit, the proof being his obvious attempt to hoodwink Grampa with a night on the town before any of the family could get to him with the true facts.

It took twenty minutes to convince Grampa; he had had to stare at Tony for a long time as though through a telescope that would not adjust. Tony downed his fury, defended his life, denied everything, promised everything, brought out the new alarm clock he had bought for the house out of his own money, and at last sat facing Grampa, dying in his chair as the old man leveled his judgment. Tony, you will marry this fine girl or none of my money goes to you. Not the fruit of my labor to a gangster, no, not to a criminal who will die young in the electric chair. Marry the girl and you, definitely, I give you what I have.

First days, then weeks—then was it months?—passed after the wedding, but the money failed to be mentioned again. Tony worked the piers dutifully now, and when he did see Patty Moran it was at odd hours only, on his way toward the shape-up or on days when it rained and deck work was called off. He would duck into the doorway next to Ox's saloon and fly up the stairs and live for half an hour, then home again to wait; he dared not simply confront the old man with the question of his reward, knowing that he was being watched for deficiencies. On Sundays he walked like a husband with Margaret, spent the afternoons with the family, and acted happy. The old man was never again as close and trusting and comradely as on that first night off the boat, but neither was he hostile. He was watching, Tony saw, to make sure.

And Tony would make him sure. The only problem was what to do in his apartment once he was alone with Margaret. He had never really hated her and he had never liked her. It was like being alone with an accident, that was all. He spoke to her rarely and quietly, listened to her gossip about the day's events, and read his newspaper. He did not expect her to suddenly stand up in the movies and run out crying, some two months after the wedding, or to come home from work one spring evening and find Grampa sitting in the living room with Margaret, looking at him silently as he came through the door.

You don't touch your wife?

Tony could not move from the threshold or lie, suddenly. The old man had short, bristly gray hair that stood up like wire, and he was back to his Italian brogans, a kick from which could make a mule inhale. Margaret dared only glance at Tony, but he saw now that the dove had her beak in his belly and was not going to let go.

You think I'm mentally defective, Tony? A man with spit in the corners of his mouth? Cross-eyed? What do you think I ?

The first new demonstration was, again, at the movies. Grampa sat behind them. After a few minutes Margaret turned her head to him and said, He don't put his arm around me, see?

Put your arm around her.

Tony put his arm around her.

Then after a few more minutes she turned to Grampa. He's only touching the seat, see?

Grampa took hold of Tony's hand and laid it on Margaret's shoulder.

Again, one night, Grampa was waiting for him with Margaret. Okay—he was breaking into English now and then by this time—Okay, I'm going to sleep on the couch.

Tony had never slept in bed with her. He was afraid of Grampa because he knew he could never bring himself to raise a hand to him, and he knew that Grampa could knock him around; but it was not the physical harm, it was the sin he had been committing over and over again of trying to con the old man, whose opinion of him was falling every day, until one day, he foresaw, Grampa would pack up and take the trunk back to Calabria and good-by. Grampa was no longer astounded by New York, and he still owned his house in Italy, and Tony visualized that house, ready at all times for occupancy, and he was afraid.

He went into the bedroom with Margaret. She sniveled on the pillow beside him. It was still light outside, the early blue of a spring evening. Tony listened for a sound of Grampa through the closed door, but nothing came through. He reached and found her hip and slid up her nightgown. She was soft, too soft, but she was holding her breath. He stretched his neck and rested his mouth on her shoulder. She was breathing at the top of her chest, near her throat, not daring to lay her hand on him, her face upthrust as though praying. He smoothed her hip waiting for his tension, and nothing was happening to him until, until she began to weep, not withdrawing herself but pressed against him, weeping. His hatred mounted on the disappointed, tattletale sound she was sending into the other room, and suddenly he felt himself hardening and he got to his knees before her, pushed her onto her back and saw her face in the dim light from the window, her eyes shut and spinning out gray teardrops. She opened her eyes then and looked terrified, as though she wanted to call it off and beg his pardon, and he covered her with a baring of his teeth, digging his face into the mattress as though rocks were falling on him from the sky.

"Tony?"

He sat up in the darkness, listening.

"Hey, Tony."

Somebody was half whispering, half calling from outside the cable hole. Tony waited, uncomprehending. Margaret's teardrops were still in his eyes, Grampa was sitting out in the living room. Suddenly he placed the voice. Baldu.

He crawled out onto the catwalk. His helper was dimly lit by a yellow bulb yards away. "Looey?"

Baldu, startled, jerked around, and hurried back to him on the catwalk, emergency in his eyes. "Charley Mudd's lookin' for you."

"Wha' for?"

"I don't know, he's lookin' high and low. You better come."

This was rare. Charley never bothered him once he had given the assignment for the shift. Tony hurried down the circular iron stairway, imagining some invasion of brass, a swarm of braid and overcoated men from the Master's office. Last summer they had suddenly halted work to ask for volunteers to burn an opening in the bow of a cruiser that had been towed in from the Pacific; her forward compartments had been sealed against the water that a torpedo had poured into her, trapping nine sailors inside. Tony had refused to face those floating corpses or the bloody water that would surely come ⌐ushing out.

In the morning he had seen the blood on the sheets, and Grampa was gone.

On B-Deck, scratching his back under his mackinaw and black sweater, Charley Mudd, alarmingly wide awake and alert, was talking to a Protestant with an overcoat on and no hat, a blond engineer he looked like, from some office. Charley reached out to Tony when he came up and held onto him, and even before Charley began to speak Tony knew there was no way out because the Protestant was looking at Tony with a certain relief in his eyes.

"Here he is. Look, Tony, they got some kind of accident on the North River, some destroyer. So grab a gang and take gas and sledges and see what you can do, will you?"

"Wha' kinda accident, Charley?"

"I don't know. The rails for the depth charges got bent. It ain't much, but they gotta go by four to meet a convoy. This man'll take you to the truck. Step on it, get a gang."

"How do I heat iron? Must be zero outside."

"They got a convoy waiting on the river. Do your best, that's all. Take a sledge and plenty of gas. Go ahead."

Tony saw that Charley was performing for the engineer and he could not spoil his relationship. He found Hindu, sent Baldu for his lunch from under the sailor's bunk, and, cursing the Navy, Margaret, winter, and his life, emerged onto the main deck and felt the whip of a wind made of ice. Followed by Hindu, who struggled with a cylinder of acetylene gas held up at the rear end by Baldu, Tony stamped down the gangplank to the open pickup truck at its foot. A sailor was behind the wheel, racing the engine to keep the heater going hot. He sent Hindu and Baldu back for two more cylinders just in case and extra tips for the burner and one more sledge and a crowbar and sat inside the cab, holding his hands, which were not yet cold, under the heater's blast.

"What happened?" he asked the sailor.

"Don't ask me, I'm only driving. I'm stationed right here in the Yard."

Forever covering his tracks, Tony asked how long the driver had been waiting, but it had been only fifteen minutes so Charley could not have been looking for him too long. Hindu got in beside Tony, who ordered Looey Baldu onto the open back, and they drove along the donkey-engine tracks, through the dark streets, and finally out the gate into Brooklyn.

Baldu huddled with his back against the cab, feeling the wind coming through his knitted skating cap and his skin hardening. He could not bear to sit on the icy truck bed, and his knees were cramping as he sat on his heels. But the pride he felt was enough to break the cold, the realization that now at last he was suffering, striking his blow at Mussolini's throat, sharing the freezing cold of the Murmansk run, where our ships were pushing supplies to the Russians through swarms of submarines. He had driven a meat truck until the war broke out. His marriage, which had happened to fall the day after Pearl Harbor was attacked, continued to ache like a mortal sin even though he kept reminding himself that it had been planned before he knew America would enter the war, and yet it had saved him for a while from the draft, and a punctured eardrum had, on his examination, put him out of action altogether.

He had gone into the Yard at a slight cut in pay if figured

on hourly rates, but with a twelve-hour shift and overtime he was ahead. This bothered him, but much less than the atmosphere of confusion in the Yard, for when he really thought back over the five months he had been here he could count on one hand the shifts during which he had exerted himself. Everything was start and stop, go and wait, until he found himself wishing he could dare go to the Yard Master and tell him that something was terribly wrong. The endless standing around and, worse yet, his having to cover up Tony's naps had turned his working time into a continuous frustration that seemed to be doing something strange to his mind. He had never had so much time to do nothing, and the shifts seemed endless and finally illicit when he, along with the others, had always to watch out for supervisors coming by. It was a lot different than rushing from store to store unloading meat and barely finishing the schedule by the end of the day.

It had never seemed possible to him that he would be thinking so much about sex. He respected and almost worshiped his wife Hilda, and yet now that she was in Florida with her mother for two weeks he was strangely running into one stimulation after another. Suddenly Mrs. Curry next door, knowing when he ate breakfast, was taking out her garbage pail at six in the morning with an overcoat on and nothing underneath, and even on very cold mornings stood bent over with the coat open for minutes at a time at the end of the driveway, facing his kitchen window; and every day, every single day now, when he left for work she just happened to be coming out the front door, until he was beginning to wonder if . . . But that was impossible; a fine married woman like her was most likely unaware of what she was doing, especially with her husband in the Army, fighting Fascism. Blowing on his heavy woolen gloves, he was held by the vision of her bending over and thrust it furiously out of his mind, only to fall still, again remembering a dream he had had in which he was coming into his own bedroom and there on the bed lay his cousin Lucy, all naked, and suddenly he fell on her, tripped on the rug, and woke up. Why should Lucy have gone to bed in his room?

But now Brooklyn Bridge was unwinding from the tailgate of the truck, and how beautiful it was, how fine to be speeding along like this on a mission for the country, and everybody, even Tony, springing to action for the sake of the war effort. Baldu had to take off his cap and rub the circulation back into his scalp, and finally, feeling shivers trembling in his chest, he looked around and discovered a tarpaulin folded in a corner and covered himself. He sat under it in the darkness, blowing on his gloves.

Tony ate three spinach sandwiches out of his box, swallowing them a half at a time, like wet green cookies. Hindu had fallen silent, signaled by Tony's edgy look. The fitter was combative, turtled into his shoulders. As they crossed Chambers Street, the tall office and bank buildings they saw were dark, the people who worked in them at home, warm and smart and snug. Anybody out tonight was either a cop or a jerk; the defroster could not keep up with the cold, and the windshield was glazed over except for a few inches down near the air exhaust. Every curse Tony knew was welling up into his mouth. On deck tonight! And probably no place to hide either, on a ship whose captain and crew were aboard. *Margaret!* Her name, hated, infuriating, her sneaky face, her tattletale mouth, swirled through the air in front of him, the mouth of his undoing. For she had made Grampa so suspicious of him that he still refused to open the trunk until he had evidence Margaret was pregnant, and even when she got big and bigger and could barely waddle from one corner of the small living room to the other, he refused, until the baby was actually born. Grampa had not earned his reputation for nothing—stupid men did not get rich in Calabria, or men who felt themselves above revenge.

As the last days approached and the three-room apartment was prepared for the baby, the old man started acting funny, coming over after dinner ostensibly to sit and talk to Margaret but really to see, as the three of them well knew, that Tony stayed at home. Nights, for a month or so now, he had followed Tony from bar to bar, knocking glasses out of his hand and, in Ox's, sweeping a dozen bottles to the floor behind the bar to teach Ox never again to serve his grandson, until Tony had to sneak into places where he had never hung before. But even so the old man's reputation had preceded him until Tony was a pariah in every saloon between Fourteenth Street and Houston. He gave up at last, deciding to go with the hurricane instead of fighting it, and returned from the piers night after night now, to sit in silence while his wife swelled. With about eight or nine days to go, Grampa, one night, failed to show up. The next night he was missing too, and the next.

One night Tony stopped by to see if some new disaster had budded, like the old man's falling ill and dying before he could hand over the money, but Grampa was well enough. It was only his normally hard-faced, suspicious glare that was gone. Now he merely stole glances at Tony and even seemed to have softened toward him, like a man in remorse. Sensing some kind of victory, Tony felt the return of his original filial warmth, for the old man seemed to be huddling against the approach of some kind of holiness, Tony believed, a supernatural and hallowed hour when not only was his first great-grandchild to be born but his life's accomplishment handed down, and the first shadow of his own death seen. The new atmosphere drew Tony back night after night, and now when he would rise to leave, the old man would lay a hand on Tony's arm as though his strength was in the process of passing from him to a difficult but proud descendant. Even Mama and Papa joined in the silence and deep propriety of these partings.

The pickup truck was turning on the riverfront under the West Side Highway; the sailor bent low to see out of the hand-sized clear space at the bottom of the windshield. Now he slowed and rolled down his window to look at the number on a pier they were passing and quickly shut it again. The cab was instantly refrigerated, a plunge in the temperature that made Hindu groan "Mamma mia" and pull his earflaps even lower. The night of the birth had been like this, in January too, and he had tried to take a walk around the hospital block to waste some time and could only get to the corner for the freezing cold. When he returned and walked back into the lobby Mama was running to him and gripping him like a little wrestler, gulping out the double news. It was twins, two boys, both healthy and big, no wonder she had looked so enormous, that poor girl. Tony swam out of the hospital not touching the floor, stroked through the icy wind down Seventh Avenue, and floated up the stairs and found Grampa, and with one look he knew, he knew then, he already knew, for the old man's head seemed to be rolling on a broken neck so frightened was he, so despondent. But Tony held his hand out for the key anyway and kept asking for it until Grampa threw himself on his knees and grasped him around the legs, hawking and coughing and groaning for forgiveness.

The trunk lid opened, Tony saw the brown-paper bundle tied with rope, a package the size of half a mattress and deep as the trunk itself. The rope flew off, the brown paper crackled like splintering wood, and he saw the tied packets—Italian lire, of course, the bills covered with wings, paintings of Mussolini, airplanes, and zeros, fives, tens, colorful and tumbling under his searching hands. He knew, he already knew, he had known since the day he was born, but he ran back into the living room and asked. It had been an honest mistake. In Calabria, ask anybody there, you could buy or could have bought, once, once you could have bought, that is, a few years ago, until this thing happened with money all over the world, even here in America, ask Roosevelt why he is talking about closing the banks. There is some kind of sickness in the money and why should Italy be an exception, a poor country once you leave Rome. Hold onto it, maybe it will go up again. I myself did not know until two weeks ago I went to the bank to change it, ask your mother. I took the whole bundle to the Na-

tional City in good faith with joy in my heart, realizing that all
your sins were the sins of youth, the exuberance of the young
man who grows into a blessing for his parents and grandpar-
ents, making all his ancestors famous with his courage and
manliness. It comes to seventeen hundred and thirty-nine dollars. In dollars that is what it comes to.

I used to make three hundred driving a truck from Toronto
to New York, four days' work, Grampa. Seventeen hundred—
you know what seventeen hundred is? Seventeen hundred is
like if I bought one good suit and a Buick and I wouldn't have
what to buy gas, that's seventeen hundred. Seventeen hundred
is like if I buy a grocery store I be out on my ass the first bad
week. Seventeen hundred is not like you got a right to come to
a man and say go tie that girl around your neck and jump in
the river you gonna come up rich. That's not nowhere near
that kinda money, not a hundred and fifty miles near that
kinda money, and twins you gave me in the bargain. *I GOT
TWO TWINS, GRAMPA!*

The red blood washed down off his vision as the truck
turned left and into the pier, past the lone light bulb and the
night watchman under it listlessly waving a hand and returning to his stove in the shack. Midway down the length of the
piershed one big door was open, and the sailor coasted the
truck up to it and braked to a halt, the springs squeaking in
the cold as the nose dipped.

Tony followed Hindu out and walked past him to the gangplank, which extended into the pier from the destroyer's deck,
and walked up, glancing right and left at the full length of the
ship. Warm lights burned in her midship compartments, and
as he stepped onto the steel deck he concluded that they might
be stupid enough to be in the Navy but not that stupid—they
were all snuggled away inside and nobody was standing watch
on deck. But now he saw his mistake; a sailor with a rifle at his
shoulder, knitted blue cap pulled down over his ears and a
face shield covering his mouth and chin, the high collar of a
stormcoat standing up behind his head, was pacing back and
forth from rail to rail on guard.

Tony walked toward him, but the sailor, who looked straight at him on his starboard turn, continued across the deck toward port as though in an automatic trance. Tony waited for the sailor to turn again and come toward him and then stood directly in his path until the sailor bumped into his zipper and leaped in fright.

"I'm from the Yard. Where's the duty officer?"

The sailor's rifle started tilting off his shoulder, and Tony reached out and pushed it back.

"Is it about me?"

"Hah?"

The sailor lowered his woolen mask. His face was young and wan with staring popeyes. "I'm supposed to go off sea duty. I get seasick. This ship is terrible, I can't hold any food. But now they're telling me I can't get off until we come back again. Are you connected with—"

"I'm from the Navy Yard. There was an accident, right?"

The sailor glanced at Hindu standing a little behind Tony and then at both their costumes and seemed ashamed and worried as he turned away, telling them to wait a minute, and disappeared through a door.

"Wanna look at the rails?" Hindu joked with a carefully shaped mockery of their order, shifting from one foot to the other and leaning down from his height to Tony's ear.

"Fuck the rails. You can't do nuttn in this weather. They crazy? Feel that wind. Chrissake, it'll go right up your asshole an' put ice on your throat. But keep your mouth shut, I talk to this monkey. What a fuckin' nerve!"

Looey Baldu appeared out of the darkness of the pier, carrying the two sledges. "Where do you want these, Tony?"

"Up your ass, Looey. Put 'em back on the truck."

Baldu, astounded, stood there.

"You want a taxi?—move!"

Baldu, uncomprehending, turned and stomped down the gangplank with the sledges.

The door into which the sailor had vanished opened, spilling the temptation of warm yellow light across the deck to

Tony's feet, and a tall man emerged, ducking, and buttoning up his long overcoat. The chief petty officer most likely, or maybe even one of the senior lieutenants, although his gangling walk, like a college boy's, and his pants whipping high on his ankles lowered the estimate to ensign. Approaching, he put up his high collar and pulled down his cap and bent over to greet Tony.

"Oh, fine. I'm very much obliged. I'll show you where it is."

"Wait, wait, just a minute, mister."

The officer came back the two steps he had taken toward the fantail, an expression of polite curiosity on his pink face. A new gust sent his hand to his visor, and he tilted his head toward New Jersey, from where the wind was pounding at them across the black river.

"You know the temperature on this here deck?"

"What? Oh. I haven't been out for a while. It has gotten very cold. Yes."

Hindu had stepped back a deferential foot or so, instinctively according Tony the air of rank that a cleared space gives, and now Baldu returned from the truck and halted beside Hindu.

"Could I ask you a little favor?" Tony said, his fists clenched inside his slit pockets, shoulders hunched, eyes squinting against the wind. "Would you please go inside and tell the captain what kinda temperature you got out here?"

"I'm the captain. Stillwater."

"You the captain." Tony stalled while all his previous estimates whirled around in his head. He glanced down at the deck, momentarily helpless. He had never addressed a commanding officer before; the closest he ever came in the Yard was a severe passing nod to one or two in a corridor from time to time. The fact that this one had come out on deck to talk to him must mean that the repair was vital, and Tony found himself losing the normal truculence in his voice.

"Could I give yiz some advice, Captain?"

"Certainly. What is it?"

"We can't do nuttn in this here weather. You don't want a botch job, do ya? Whyn't you take her into the Yard, we give you a brand new pair rails, and yiz'll be shipshape for duty."

The captain half laughed in surprise at the misunder-standing. "Oh, we couldn't do that. We're joining a convoy at four. Four this morning. I can't delay a convoy."

The easy absoluteness shot fear into Tony's belly. He glanced past the captain's face, groping for a new attack, but the captain was talking again.

"Come, I'll show it to you. Give me that light, Farrow."

The sick Watch handed him the flashlight, and the captain loped off toward the fantail. Tony followed behind. He was trapped. The next time he saw Charley Mudd . . .

The flashlight beam shot out and illuminated the two paral-lel steel rails, extending several feet out over the water from the deck. Two feet in from the end of the portside rail there was a bend.

"Jesus! What happened?"

"We were out there"—the captain flipped up the light toward the river beyond the slip—"and a British ship got a lit-tle too close trying to line himself up."

"Them fuckin' British!" Tony exploded, throwing his voice out toward the river where the Englishman must be. Caught by surprise, the captain laughed, but Tony pulled his hands out of his slit pockets and made a pleading gesture, and his face looked serious. "Why don't somebody tell them to stop fuckin' around or get out of the war!"

The captain, unaccustomed to the type, watched Tony with great expectation and amusement.

"I mean it! They the only ones brings cockroaches into the Navy Yard!"

"Cockroaches? How do—"

"Ax anybody! We get French, Norways, Brazils, but you don't see no cockroaches on them ships. Only the British brings cockroaches."

The captain shook his head with commiseration, tightening

his smile until it disappeared. "Some of their ships have been at sea a long, long time, you know."

Tony felt a small nudge of hope in his heart. "Uh-huh," he muttered, frowning with solicitude for the English. Some unforeseen understanding with the captain seemed to loom; the man was taking him so seriously, bothering to explain why there were cockroaches, allowing himself to be diverted even for ten seconds from the problem of the rail, and, more promising than anything else, he seemed to be deferring to Tony's opinion about the possibility of working at all tonight. And better yet, he was even going into it further.

"Some of those English ships have been fighting steadily ten and twelve months down around the Indian Ocean. A ship will get awfully bad that long at sea without an overhaul. Don't you think?"

Tony put gravity into his face, an awful deliberation, and then spoke generously. "Oh yeah, sure. I was only sayin'. Which I don't blame them, but you can't sit down on their ships."

Another officer and two more sailors had come out on deck and were watching from a distance as Tony talked to the captain, and he slowly realized that they must all have been waiting hours for him and were now wondering what his opinion was going to be.

With a nod toward the bent rail the captain asked, "What do you think? Can you straighten it?"

Tony turned to look out at the damaged rail, but his eyes were not seeing clearly. The pleasure and pride of his familiarity with the captain, his sheer irreplaceability on this deck, were shattering his viewpoint. Striving to knit his wits together, he asked the captain if he could have the flashlight for a minute.

"Oh, certainly," the captain said, handing it to him.

Leaning a little over the edge of the deck, he shone the beam onto the bend of the rail. That pimping, mother-fuckin' Charley Mudd! Look at the chunks of ice in that water—fall in there it's good-by forever. In the skyscrapers at his back men tripled their money every wartime day, butchers were cleaning up with meat so scarce, anybody with a truck in good shape could name his price, and here he stood, God's original patsy, Joe Jerk, without a penny to his name that he hadn't grubbed out by the hour with his two hands.

More than a minute had gone by but he refused to give up until an idea came to him, and he kept the light shining on the bend as though studying how to repair it. There had to be a way out. It was the same old shit—the right idea at the right moment had never come to him because he was a dumb bastard and there was no way around it and never would be.

"What do you think?"

What he thought? He thought that Charley Mudd should be strung up by his balls. Turning back to the captain now, he was confronted with the man's face, close to his in order to hear better in the wind. Could it be getting even colder?

"Lemme show you supm, Captain. Which I'm tryin' my best to help you out but this here thing is a son of a bitch. Excuse me. Look."

He pointed out at the bend in the rail. "I gotta hit that rail —you understand?"

"Yes?"

"But where I'm gonna stand? It sticks out over the water. You need skyhooks for this. Which is not even the whole story. I gotta get that steel good and hot. With this here wind you got blowin' here I don't even know if I can make it hot enough."

"Hmm."

"You understand me? I'm not trying to crap out on ya, but that's the facts."

He watched the captain, who was blinking at the bend, his brows kinked. He was like a kid, innocent. Out in the dark river foghorns barked, testifying to the weather. Tony saw the sag of disappointment in the captain's face, the sadness coming into it. What the hell was the matter with him? He had a perfect excuse not to have to go to sea and maybe get himself sunk. The German subs were all over the coast of Jersey waiting for these convoys, and here the man had a perfect chance to lay down in a hotel for a couple of days. Tony saw that the young man needed precise help, his feet placed on the road out.

"Captain, listen to me. Please. Lemme give you piece of advice."

Expressionless, the captain turned to Tony.

"I sympathize wichoo. But what's the crime if you call in that you can't move tonight? That's not your fault."

"I have a position in the convoy. I'm due."

"I know that, Captain, but lemme explain to you. Cut outa here right now, make for the Yard; we puts up a staging and slap in a new rail by tomorrow noon, maybe even by ten o'clock. And you're set."

"No, no, that's too late. Now see here"—the captain pointed a leather-gloved finger toward the bend—"you needn't true it up exactly. If you could just straighten it enough to let the cans roll off, that would be enough."

"Listen, Captain, I would do anything I could do for you, but . . ." An unbelievable blast of iced wind squeezed Tony's cheeks. The captain steadied himself, tilting his head toward the river again, gripping his visor with one hand and holding his collar tight with the other. Tony had heard him gasp at the new depth of cold. What was the matter with these people? The Navy had a million destroyers—why the hell did they need this one, only this one and on this particular night? "I'm right, ain't I? They can't hold it against you, can they? If you're unfit for duty you're unfit for duty, right? Who's gonna blame you, which another ship rammed you in the dark? You were in a position, weren't you? It was his fault, not yours!"

The captain glanced at him, and in that glance Tony saw the man's disappointment, his judgment of him. He could not help reaching out defensively and touching the captain's arm. "Listen a minute. Please. Looka me, my situation. I know my regulations, Captain; nobody can blame me either. I'm not supposed to work unsafe conditions. I coulda took one look here and called the Yard and I'd be back there by now below decks someplace, because if you can't do it safe you not supposed to. The only way I can swing this, if I could swing it, is I tie myself up in a rope and hang over the side to hit that rail. Nobody would kick one minute if I said I can't do such a thing. You understand me?"

The captain, his eyes tearing in the wind, his face squeezing tight against the blast of air, waited for his point.

"What I mean, I mean that . . ." What did he mean? Standing a few inches from the captain's boyish face, he saw for the first time that there was no blame there. No blame and no command either. The man was simply at a loss, in need. And he saw that there was no question of any official blame for the captain either. Suddenly it was as clear and cold as the air freezing them where they stood—that they were both on a par, they were free.

"I'd be very much obliged if you could do it. I see how tough it is, but I'd be very much obliged if you could."

Tony discovered his glove at his mouth and he was blowing into it to spread heat on his cheeks. The captain had become a small point in his vision. For the first time in his life he had a kind of space around him in which to move freely, the first time, it seemed, that it was entirely up to him with no punishment if he said no, nor even a reward if he said yes. Gain and loss had suddenly collapsed, and what was left standing was a favor asked that would profit nobody. The captain was looking at him, waiting for his answer. He felt shame, not for having hesitated to try, but for a sense of his nakedness. And as he spoke he felt afraid that in fact the repair would turn out to be impossible and he would end by packing up his tools and, unmanned, retreating back to the Yard.

"Man to man, Captain, can I ask you supm?"

"What is it?"

"Which I'm only mentionin' "—he was finding his truculent

tone and it was slowly turning ordinary again with this recollection coming on—"because plenty of times they run to me, 'Tony, quick, the ship's gotta go tonight,' and I bust my balls. And I come back next day and the ship is sittin' there, and even two weeks more it's still sittin', you understand me?"

"The minute you finish I'll be moving out into the river, don't you worry about that."

"What about coffee?" Tony asked, striving to give this madness some air of a transaction.

"Much as you like. I'll tell the men to make some fresh. Just tell the Watch whenever you want it." The captain put out his hand. "Thanks very much."

Tony could barely bring his hand forward. He felt the clasping hand around his own. "I need some rope."

"Right."

He wanted to say something, something to equal the captain's speech of thanks. But it was impossible to admit that anything had changed in him. He said, "I don't guarantee nuttn," and the familiar surliness in his tone reassured him.

The captain nodded and went off into the midship section, followed by the other officer and the two sailors who had been looking on. He would be telling them . . . what? That he had conned the fitter?

Hindu and Looey Baldu were coming toward him. What had he agreed to!

"What's the score?" Hindu grinned, waiting for the delicious details of how Tony had outwitted the shithead captain.

"We straighten it out." Tony started past Hindu, who grabbed his arm.

"We straighten what out?"

"I said we straighten it out." He saw the disbelief in Hindu's eyes, the canny air of total refusal, and he felt anger charging into his veins. "Ax a man for a wood saw and a hammer and if they got a wreckin' bar."

"How the fuck you gonna straighten—"

"Don't break my balls, Hindu, do what I tell you or get

your ass off the ship!" He was amazed at his fury. What the hell was he getting so mad about? He heard Baldu's voice behind him, calling, "I'll get it!" and went to the gangplank and down to the pier, no longer understanding anything except the grave feeling that had found him and was holding onto him, like the feeling of insult, the sense that he could quickly find himself fighting somebody, the looseness of violence. Hindu had better not try to make him look like a jerk.

It took minutes for him to see again within the pier where he walked about in the emptiness, shining the flashlight at random and finding only the bare, corrugated walls. Baldu came hurrying down the hollow-booming gangplank and over to him, carrying the tools. Another idiot. Son of a bitch, what did these guys do with themselves, jerk off instead of learning something, which at least he had done from job to job, not that it meant anything.

The flashlight found a stack of loading trays piled high against the pier wall. Tony climbed up the ten feet to the top tray. "What's this for?" Baldu asked, reaching up to receive it as Tony tipped it over the edge of the stack. He came down without answering and gestured for the wrecking bar. Baldu handed him the saw, blade first, and Tony slapped it away and reached over and picked up the hammer and wrecking bar and set about prying up the boards until the two five-by-five runners underneath were free. "Grab one," he said and proceeded up the gangplank onto the deck.

He measured the distance between the two rails and sawed the runners to fit. It must be near eleven, maybe later, and the cold would be getting worse and worse. He cut two lengths of rope and ordered Baldu to tie the end of one around his chest, tied the other around himself, and then undid Baldu's crazy knot and made a tight one; he lashed both ropes to a frame at the root of the depth-charge rails, leaving enough slack for him and Baldu to creep out onto the rails. He took one end of a wood runner, Baldu took the other, and they laid themselves prone on the rails, then moved together, with the runner held between them, across the open water. He told Baldu to rest his end inside the L of his rail and to hold it from jarring loose and falling into the water, and he wedged his own end against his rail just behind where the bend began. He told Baldu to inch backward onto the deck, and Hindu to hand Baldu one of the sledges. But the sledges were still on the truck. He told them both to go down to the truck and bring the sledges, bring two tanks of gas, bring the burning torch and tips, and don't get wounded.

Baldu ran. Hindu walked, purposely. Tony sat on his heels, studying the rails. The sick Watch paced up and down behind him in a dream. That fuckin' Charley Mudd, up to the ceiling by his balls.

"Hey, seasick," he said over his shoulder as the Watch approached, "see if you can get me a tarp, huh?"

"Tarp?"

"Tarpaulin, tarpaulin. And step on it."

Christ, one was dumber than the other, nobody knew nuttn, everybody's fulla shit with his mouth open. What was the captain saying now, what was he doing? Had he been conned, really? Except, what could the captain get out of it except the risk of his life with all those subs off Jersey? If he had been conned, fuck it, show the bastard. Show him what?

Suddenly, staring at nothing, he no longer knew why he was doing this, if he had ever known. And somebody might fall into the water in the bargain once they started hitting with the sledge.

"Coffee?"

He turned and looked up. The captain was handing him a steaming cup and had two more in his other hand.

"Thanks."

Now Baldu and Hindu were clanking the gas cylinders onto the deck behind them. Tony drank his coffee, inhaling the good steam. The captain gave the two cups to the others.

"Whyn't you get off your feet, Captain? Go ahead, git warmed up."

The captain nodded and went off.

Tony put down his cup. The Watch arrived carrying a folded tarpaulin whose grommets were threaded with quarter-inch rope. Tony told him to put it down on the deck. He let Baldu drink coffee for a minute more, then told him to creep out on his rail and steady the wood runner while he hit its other end with the sledge to wedge it in tight between the two rails. Sliding the sledge ahead of him on his rail, he crept out over the water. At his left, Baldu, tied again, crept out wide-eyed. Tony saw that he was afraid of the water below.

Baldu inched along until he reached the runner and held it in the angle of the L tightly with both hands. Tony stood up carefully on his rail, bent down and picked up the sledge, then edged farther out on the rail to position for a swing. The water in the light held by Hindu was black and littered with floating paper. Tony carefully swung the sledge and hit the runner, and again, and again, and it was tight between the two rails. He told Baldu to back up, and they got the second runner and inched it out with them and wedged it snugly next to the first. Now there would be something to stand on between the two cantilevered rails, although it remained to be seen whether a man could bang the bent rail hard enough with so narrow a perch under him.

He unfolded the tarpaulin and handed one corner to Baldu, took the opposite corner himself, and both inched out over the rails again and tied the tarpaulin on the two runners so that it hung to the windward of the bend and might keep the air blast from cooling the steel. It might not. He backed halfway to the deck and told Hindu to hand him the torch and to grab a sledge and stand on the little bridge he had made and get ready to hit the steel.

"Not me, baby."

"You, you."

"What's the matter with the admiral here?" Hindu asked, indicating Baldu.

"I wanchoo."

"Not me, baby. I don't like heights."

Tony backed off the rail and stood facing Hindu on the deck.

"Don't fuck around, Tony, nobody's payin' me to get out there. I can't even swim good."

He saw the certain knowledge of regulations in Hindu's mocking eyes. His own brows were lifted, his classic narrow-eyed, showdown look was on his face, and never before would he have let a man sneer at him like that without taking up the challenge, but now, strange as it was to him, he felt only contempt for Hindu, who had it in him to hit the beam much harder than the smaller Baldu could and was refusing. It was a long, long time since he had known the feeling of being let down by anyone, as long as it was since he had expected anything of anyone. He turned away from Hindu and beckoned to Baldu, and in the moment it took for Baldu to come to him Tony felt sharply the queerness of his pushing on with this job, which, as Hindu's attitude proved, was fit for suckers and, besides, was most probably impossible to accomplish with the wind cooling the steel as fast as it was heated. He bent over and picked up the slender torch.

"You ever work a torch?"

"Well, not exactly, but . . ."

Tony turned to Hindu, his hand extended. "Gimme the sparkler." From his jacket pocket Hindu took a spring-driven sparker and handed it to Tony, who took it and, noting the minute grin on Hindu's mouth, said, "Fuck you."

"In spades," Hindu said.

Tony squeezed the sparker as he opened the two valves on the torch. The flame appeared and popped out in the wind. He shielded it with his body and sparked again, and the flame held steady. He took Baldu's hand and put the torch into it. "Now follow me and I show you what to do."

Eagerly Baldu nodded, his big black eyes feverish with service. "Right, okay."

Unnerved by Baldu's alacrity, Tony said, "Do everything

slow. Don't move unless you look." And he went to the bent rail and slid the sledge out carefully before him, slowly stretched prone on the rail and inched out over the water. He came to the two runners, from which the tarpaulin hung snapping in the wind, then drew up his legs and sat, and beckoned to Baldu to follow him out.

Baldu, with the torch in his left hand, the wind-bent flame pointed down, laid himself out on the rail and inched toward Tony. But with each thrust forward the torch flame swung up close to his face. "Let the torch hang, Baldu, take slack," Tony called.

Baldu halted, drew in a foot of tubing, and let the torch dangle below him. Now he inched ahead again, and as he neared, Tony held out a hand and pressed it against his head. "Stop."

Baldu stopped.

"Get the torch in your hand."

Baldu drew up the torch and held it. Tony pointed his finger at the bend. "Point the fire here." Baldu turned the torch, whose flame broke apart against the steel. Tony moved Baldu's hand away from the steel an inch or two and now trained it in a circular motion, then let go, and Baldu continued moving the flame. "That's good."

It must be half-past eleven, maybe later. Tony watched the steel. The paint was blackening, little blisters coming up. Not bad. He raised the tarpaulin to shield the flame better. A light yellow glow was starting to show on the steel. Not bad. Gusts were nudging his shoulders. He saw the tears dropping out of Baldu's eyes, and the flame was moving off the rail. He slipped off a glove, reached over, and pressed Baldu's eyelids, clearing the tears out, and the flame returned to its right position. He saw that the Watch was pacing up and down again across the deck behind Hindu, who was standing with the flashlight, grinning.

The yellow glow was deepening. Not bad. An orange hue was beginning to show in the steel. He took Baldu's hand and moved it in wider circles to expand the heated area. He slipped his glove off again and pressed the tears out of Baldu's eyes, then the other glove, and held his hands near the flame to warm them.

The steel was reddening. Stuffing the gloves into his slit pockets, he drew up one foot and set it on the rail, leaned over to the wooden bridge he had built and brought the other foot under him and slowly stood erect. He bent slowly and took the sledge off the rail and came erect again. He spread his legs, one foot resting on the wood runners, the other on the rail, and, shifting in quarter-inch movements, positioned himself to strike. He raised the hammer and swung, not too hard, to see what it did to his stability, and the rail shuddered but his foot remained steady on it. He brought up the sledge, higher this time, and slammed it down and under against the steel, one eye on the bridge, which might jar loose and send him into the water, but it was still wedged between the rails, resting on the flange of the L. Baldu was wrapping his free arm around the rail, and now he had his ankles locked around it too.

Tony raised the sledge and slammed down. The steel rang, and he heard Baldu grunt with the shock coming into his body. He raised the sledge and put his weight into it, and the steel rang and Baldu coughed as though hit in the chest. Tony felt the wind reaching down his back under his collar and icing his sweat. Pneumonia, son of a bitch. He slammed down and across at the rail and let the sledge rest next to his foot. The bend had straightened a little, maybe half an inch or an inch. His arms were pounding with blood, his thighs ached in the awkward, frightened position. He glanced back at Hindu on the deck.

"Not me, baby."

He felt all alone. Baldu didn't count, being some kind of a screwball, stupid anyway, he went around believing something about everything and meanwhile everybody was laughing at him, a clown who didn't even know it, you couldn't count Baldu for anything, except he was all right, lying out there and scared as he was.

He was catching his breath, coughing up the residue of tobacco in the top of his chest. He glanced down and a little behind his shoe at the steel. It was deeply red. He pounded the
steel rail, all alone—and rested again. It had straightened
maybe another half-inch. His breath was coming harder, and
his back had tightened against the impossible perch, the tension of distributing his weight partly behind the hammer and
partly down into his feet, which he dared not move. He was all
alone over the water, the beam of the flashlight dying in the
black air around him.

He rested a third time, spitting out his phlegm. The son of a
bitch was going to straighten out. If he could keep up the
hammering, it would. He dared not let Baldu hammer. Baldu
would surely end in the water—him with his two left feet,
couldn't do nuttn right. Except he wasn't bad with the torch,
and the steel against his clothes must be passing the cold into
his body. He glanced down at Baldu and saw again the fear in
his face with the water looking up at him from below.

He raised the hammer again. Weakness was spreading
along his upper arms. He was having to suck in consciously
and hold his breath with each blow. Charley Mudd seemed a
million miles away. He could barely recall what Dora looked
like. If he did decide to go through with the date he would
only fall asleep in her room. It didn't matter. He let the sledge
rest next to his foot. Now it was becoming a question of being
able to lift it at all. Hindu, to whom he had given a dozen
phone numbers, was far away.

Tony licked his lips and his tongue seemed to touch iron.
His hand on the sledge handle seemed carved forever in a circular grip. The wind in his nose shot numbness into his head
and throat. He lifted the sledge and felt a jerky buckling in his
right knee and stiffened it quickly. This fuckin' iron, this stubborn, idiot iron lay there bent, refusing his demand. Go back
on deck, he thought, and lay down flat for a minute. But with
the steel hot now he would only have to heat it all up again
since he could not pass Baldu, who would also have to back
onto the deck; and, once having stopped, his muscles would

stiffen and make it harder to start again. He swung the hammer, furiously now, throwing his full weight behind it and to
hell with his feet—if he fell off the rope would hold him, and
they had plenty of guys to fish him out.

The rail was straightening although it would still have a little crook in it; but as long as he could spread it far enough
from the other one to let the cans pass through and into the
sea, some fuckin' German was going to get it from this rail,
bammo, and he could see the plates of the sub opening to the
sea and the captain watching the water for a sign of oil coming
up. He rested the sledge again. He felt he was about to weep,
to cry like a baby against his weakness, but he was a son of a
bitch if he would call it off and creep back onto the deck and
have Hindu looking down at him, both of them knowing that
the whole thing had been useless.

He felt all alone; what was Hindu to him?—another guy to
trade girls with and buddy with in the bars, knowing all the
time that when the time came he'd give you the shaft if it was
good for him, like every man Tony had ever known in his life,
and every woman, even Mama, the way she told on him to
Grampa, which if she hadn't he would never have had to
marry Margaret in the first place. He smashed the sledge
down against the steel, recklessly, letting his trunk turn freely
and to hell with falling in.

"That looks good enough!"

For a moment, the sledge raised halfway to his shoulder, he
could not make out where the voice was coming from, like in
a dream, a voice from the air.

"I'm sure that's good enough, fella!"

Carefully turning his upper body, he looked toward the
deck. The captain and two other men and the Watch were facing him.

"I think you've done it. Come back, huh?"

He tried to speak, but his throat caught. Baldu, prone,
looked up at him, and Tony nodded, and Baldu closed the
valves and the flame popped out. Baldu inched backward

along the rail. A sailor reached out from the edge of the deck and grabbed the back of his jacket, holding onto him until he slid safely onto the deck and then helped him to stand.

Out on the rail, the sledge hanging from his hand unfelt, Tony stood motionless, trying to educate his knees to bend so that he could get down on the rail and inch back onto the deck. His head was on crooked, nothing in his body was working right. Slowly, now, he realized that he must not lie down anyway or he would have to slide his body over the part of the rail which was probably still hot enough to scorch him. Experimentally he forced one foot half an inch along the rail but swayed, the forgotten weight of the sledge unbalancing him toward his right side. He looked down at his grasping hand and ordered it to open. The sledge slipped straight down and splashed, disappearing under the black water. The captain and the crewmen and Baldu stood helplessly in a tight group, watching the small man perched with slightly spread arms on the outthrust spine of steel, the rope looping from around his chest to the framework on the deck where it was lashed. Tony looked down at his feet and sidled, inch after inch, toward the deck. Joyfully he felt the grip of a hand on his arm now and let his tension flow out as he stepped off the rail and onto the deck. His knee buckled as he came down on it and he was caught and stood straight. The captain was turning away. Two sailors held him under the arms and walked him for a few steps like a drunk, but the motion eased him and he freed himself. A few yards ahead the captain slowed, and glancing back made a small inviting gesture toward the midships section, and pushed by the wind went through a doorway.

He and Baldu and Hindu drank the coffee and ate the buns. Tony saw the serious smiles of respect in the sailors' faces, and he saw the easy charm with which Hindu traded the jokes with them, and he saw the captain, uncapped now, the blond hair and the way he looked at him with love in his eyes, saying hardly anything but personally filling the cup and standing by and listening to Hindu with no attention but merely politeness. Then Tony stood up, his lips warm again and the ice gone out of his sweat, and they all said good night. As Tony went through the door onto the deck the captain touched him on the shoulder with his hand.

When Hindu and Baldu had loaded the gas tanks onto the truck with the sledges, Tony indicated for Baldu to get into the cab, and the helper climbed in beside the sailor, who was racing the engine. Tony got in and pulled the door shut and through the corners of his eyes saw Hindu standing out there, unsmiling, his brows raised, insulted. "It's only midnight, baby," Tony said, hardly glancing at Hindu, "we got four more hours. Git on the back."

Hindu stood there for twenty seconds, long enough to register his narrow-eyed affront, then climbed onto the open back of the truck.

Outside the pier the sailor braked for a moment, glancing right and left for traffic, and as he turned downtown Tony at the side window saw sailors coming down the gangplank of the destroyer. They were already casting off. The truck sped through the cold and empty streets toward Chambers and Brooklyn Bridge, leaving it all behind. In half an hour the destroyer would be back in its position alongside the cargo ships lined up in the river. The captain would be where he belonged. Stillwater. Captain Stillwater. He knew him. Right now it felt like the captain was the only man in the world he knew.

In the Yard, Tony made the driver take them up to the dry-dock where the cruiser lay on which they had been working. He went aboard with Baldu without waiting for Hindu to get off the back and found Charley Mudd and woke him up, cursing the job he had given him and refusing to listen to Charley's thanks and explanations, and without waiting for permission made his way through the ship to the engine room. Overhead somebody was still welding with the arc too far from the steel, and he raised his collar against the sparks and climbed up to the dark catwalk and found the cable passage and crawled in, spreading himself out on the steel deck. His body felt knotted, rheumatic. His smell was powerful. He went over the solutions he had found for the job and felt good about having thought of taking the runners off the loading tray. That was a damn good idea. And Baldu was all right. He visualized the kink that remained in the rail and regretted it, wishing it had been possible to make it perfectly straight, but it would work. Now the face of the captain emerged behind his closed eyes, the face uncapped as it had been when they were standing around having coffee, the blond hair lit, the collar still raised, and the look in his eyes when he had poured Tony's coffee, his closeness and his fine inability to speak. That lit face hung alone in an endless darkness.

[1966]

In Russia

If an invading army should ever fling itself upon the shores of California and sweep toward Washington, its air force smashing every standing structure, its strategy baffling the defense and overwhelming whole American armies in one massive onslaught which would soon put the capital itself in danger, it is not likely that an American President would have the time or inclination to send out a special team to load onto trucks the contents of William Faulkner's Oxford, Mississippi, house in order to safeguard for the nation the great writer's effects. Nor would this be regarded as a lapse of duty, or the destruction of the property a depredation particularly more meaningful than all the other destruction.

Yet at the height of the chaos during the Nazi invasion, Stalin's men removed Tolstoy's hat and stick, his coats, boots, and chairs, his books, dishes, and desk—the contents of the rambling old wooden home at Yasnaya Polyana—and secreted them all until peace had come. The Germans stormed in and, indeed, barracked soldiers in the house, and leaving it on their retreat accidentally burned part of it down. In a gesture of contempt for the old man's bones, which lay nearby under the tall birch and fir trees, they surrounded his grave with their own dead in this glade where long ago he had sat with his grandchildren, offering a kopek to the one who would *not* think of a white bear.

This tenderness toward the memory of a great artist is ironical in a country which, under all its regimes, never hesitated to censor art and not infrequently exiled recalcitrant artists or even killed them. There is surely an element of travesty in dialectical materialists turning the great mystic's home into a shrine. But there is a certain logic in it too. As I have indicated, the roots of Socialist Realism, the official Soviet credo of all art, are in Yasnaya Polyana.

Socialist Realism, an aesthetic yardstick which frequently is made of rubber and sometimes of oak hard enough to crack any skull, is not a uniquely Russian invention. It demands that a work not merely report life as the writer has seen it, which is mere naturalism and inevitably an escape from the higher truth. That higher truth is made of several parts, chief of which is the superiority of socialism as a civilization, and its inevitable ultimate perfection in Russia and its victory in the world. Thus, a Soviet character who is shiftless, dishonest, with alcoholic tendencies, let us say, and constantly on the lookout for a dishonest ruble, cannot at the same time be a fervent supporter, let alone an official, of the Soviet state. It is not that such people do not exist in all countries and in Russia too, but that they are not typical in Russia. The word *typical* is crucial, and it means that negative characteristics, intellectual confusion or depravity, self-interestedness, careerism, and so on, cannot be ascribed to a socially desirable or socially important person. The higher truth, in short, requires that good be done by good people and evil by evil people. More, typicality means that every art work is at bottom a metaphor of society, however subtly social forces may be disguised in it, so that the outcome or impression of the work must be supportive of socialism as it is practiced in Russia. For a work to conclude differently would have to be a distortion of the truth and therefore bad art. As for art in or about capitalist countries, its metaphor must equal the decadence or anti-human qualities of capitalism; otherwise it is untrue and bad art. Furthermore, the texture of a work, its style and language, must be available to almost everyone. Since art always teaches, whether the artist means to or not, it must teach in favor of humanity, and the cause of humanity is socialism.

Tolstoy spent periods of his life writing essays and tracts to prove that it was depraved self-indulgence rather than art which merely provided sensuous pleasure, enjoyment, or time-wasting amusement. Art must be of use, mainly as a means of opening the eyes of men to the god within them, their inborn goodness. State, church, and other institutions exist only to keep man in ignorance of his real inner self, the more easily to send him into wars for the gain of his masters, or to pit him against his fellow man, the better to seduce him with material wealth and privilege, which kill his soul and enslave him to selfishness.

As a man, Tolstoy tried, sometimes desperately, to shed his own noble privileges—his alienation, one might say—and if his wife had not made it impossible would have published his works without royalty. He stood with the people, down to the lowliest, and art for its own sake was nothing short of sin.

Tolstoy is published in immense editions in Russia. If his religious dedication is an inconvenience in Soviet eyes, it is a small one—he merely reflected truthfully his own historic moment, and his shortcomings are the shortcomings of history; had he lived on into the Socialist era he would no doubt have been a Soviet writer. He is a Soviet writer now, in any case, since some of his writings are still unpublished.

The problem can be seen when it is admitted that in the months and years when Tolstoy was obsessed with teaching and writing educative tracts, his production of fiction fell away. And when his mind was swept with a story and characters and the sensuous spectacle of human beings acting as human beings do, his output of tracts ceased. The fact remains, however, that a Tolstoy shorn of his moral passions would be a mere storyteller.

But it takes a genius of this high order successfully to fuse his moral and social vision with profound compassion for man and his artistic conscience. In lesser hands, the command to teach through art results in neither good teaching nor good art but an art of facsimiles. There is nothing wrong with Socialist Realism as an aesthetic theory, only provided that the artist is indeed a Socialist Realist. If he is not, the theory, especially when it is administered as law and enforced by censorship, is a crippling thing. In a word, Tolstoy would never have stood for it.

The relics of great artists are always misleading. What detritus they leave behind we stare at for meanings and hints of their inner lives when in fact they hardly noticed such things at all. What posterity sees as a life-purpose and design for living, to the artist was makeshift, chaos more often than not. Tolstoy's house is a rambling wooden thing like thousands of other country houses the nobility lived in, but probably none of them with such an austere, workable—one might call it a modern—air. Here is the dining-room table where he tried to shut his ears to his wife's business plans, keep his eyes from his daughters' fancy clothes and the—to him—petty ambitions they signified, and listened like a child to sycophantic compliments of manipulating disciples. Like Pushkin's house, it stands apart from its age in its simplicity. One tries to resist the romance of such a place but in its silence, surrounded by snow and forest, Tolstoy's presence makes itself felt if only because the absence of any splendor speaks of a man at work here, and work in this house meant several masterpieces scrawled onto paper by the gigantic man on the second floor.

Still, he was a fool, like every other man, and caught in a domestic world he had made and could not recognize as his own, striving to slip out of his skin to enter the arena with God, whom he wanted to ask certain questions. Upstairs is his working area, a plain desk and a chair as low as a child's, which brought his eyes close to his paper and obviated the need for spectacles—for he was vain. It is all comfortable but somehow bare, like a prize ring, without the trifles, gewgaws, encumbrances so dear to Victorians. In his stories and novels he is a vast magnifying glass collecting the emanating rays of the Russian people, focusing them to a burning point which scorches their name on the ageless rock. Today it is Socialist Realism they justify by his work, tomorrow it will be something else. He saw life whole and one walks through his hallways believing that one day it will be permitted to see life whole again; somewhere high in the ranks of the powerful there must surely be men who know that for Leo Tolstoy there could be no mediator between a man and truth, not the church and surely not the state, socialist or capitalist, and among the Russian tourists who in summer come by the thousands on buses to walk in hushed silence past the bed he died on and the hat that shaded his eyes from the blazing sun, there are surely some who have received from his work that awareness of an awful, remorseless conscience which tests every work and every boast of man. One leaves Yasnaya Polyana with no worry that Tolstoy has been captured or used for purposes not his own; it is good that they keep his name alive. He is far more powerful than the nets of any program, political or aesthetic, just as the truth is in its survival despite everything. In a strange way it even seems that their strategic idolatry is an expression of their final, unadmitted wish to keep alive the rule by which they may be corrected one day, for the purpose of literature can only be to tell the truth.

[From Chapter IV]

Our last night in Russia, inevitably, brought all the incipient chaos of feelings and unanswered questions to a head. Andrei Voznesensky and his wife, Zoya, good friends of Maya Plisetskaya, prima ballerina of the Bolshoi Ballet, had arranged for us to see her performance. Yevtushenko's wife, Galia, insisted we could not leave the country without seeing a certain painter's work in his apartment far from the center of town. Inge had meanwhile misplaced her passport. A Russian journalist who had broken his back in an Army plane he crashed in Siberia in an attempt to machine-gun a bear had insisted I take home a jar of special honey for my cold and would meet us anywhere. Appointments we had been postponing with three other people now had to be met. And through all these meetings and conversations and gift-giving Inge had to try to get through the telephone system to all the places we had been in the last twenty-four hours to try to locate her passport—a difficulty, when a lot of Russians do not answer their phones unless they have been notified ahead of time as to who is calling.

On top of it all there was a curious mood of uncertainty because a writer friend of the Voznesenskys had just turned up; he had recently come under attack by the Writers' Union, which had gone so far as to publish an article against him in the press. The man some weeks before had gotten so apprehensive that he had gone off to a small town in Siberia to get away from the mutterings against him in Moscow. Now, just back, he was wondering if it had been wise to return. Then again, maybe he should issue some intransigent statement which might rally support for him; on the other hand, *would* others support him? Should he perhaps return again to Siberia? Should he go back to his own Moscow room? On the other hand, maybe he was overreacting altogether, and the whole business was unnerving him more than it should.

Meanwhile we were all moving into the immense crowd pressing into the Bolshoi Theater. To strange eyes it seemed as though the crowd had never before seen a ballet, the eagerness was so intense. We said good-by to the pale, uncertain writer at the stage entrance. He also knew Plisetskaya well and would love to go up to her dressing room and say hello with us, but maybe it was better he did not. We wound our way through the back corridors of the great theater; the public-address-system loudspeakers connected with the auditorium were alive with the powerful rumbling of people excitedly greeting each other as they took their seats out there. We climbed stairs, wound through other corridors, opened doors through sitting rooms, and the Bill of Rights seemed unutterably precious then, the sheer ignobility of hounding the man we had left in the street was a choking, enraging thing. Nothing, no progress could be worth the fear in that writer's face.

A gentleman in frock coat led us into a sitting room to wait until Plisetskaya had dressed. The walls were red velour, the Louis Something furniture covered with white sheeting as though waiting to be unveiled on some occasion of state, the mirror frames gilt, deeply carved—the very flower of the great age of the cataclysmic Czars. Here too the sound of the auditorium could be heard through the speakers, like a sea waiting to be calmed by the holy power of this dancer dressing on the other side of the paneled door. We waited, talked of the decor and its playful silliness, which now, however, seemed so innocent and naïve. Perhaps a Czar had sat here, made to wait a few minutes by some primping ballerina, for it all smelled of Power and therein lay its impressiveness and fatuousness. The frock-coated gentleman, the impresario actually, passed through with a nod to Voznesensky sitting there in his pea jacket and sweater, and opened the paneled door, closing it behind him. In a moment the door opened again—she was ready now.

We filed into Plisetskaya's dressing room. A hall of mirrors. She kissed Andrei. Some time ago he had written one of his best poems about her. They were in league with a spirit that shone in their eyes. She bade us sit down. I had never seen a human being move like this. A racehorse, her muscles swathing the bones. The costume was deceptively casual and peasantlike; in fact, it was an athlete's, like a fighter's gloves, a runner's trunks, and she shifted the waistband of the skirt a quarter-inch as though that infinitesimal adjustment would in a few minutes release her from the pull of earth. She was working now as we talked, turning her feet, ever so slightly stretching her shoulders inside her skin, and the sound of the packed house flowed over her from the loudspeakers, the adoring and menacing sea-rumble of Moscow.

A separate balcony about thirty feet wide hangs over the orchestra of the Bolshoi, in it two high-backed thronelike chairs flanked by lower ones for the noble retainers, the great red drapes framing it all with immense loops and flowings of cloth. The Czar was not in either of the thrones. The stage is very brightly lighted, the faces of the audience await the magic. The curtain lumbers up and *Don Quixote* begins. As a non-fan of classical ballet I decided to sit back in our box just over the footlights and interest myself in the sociology of it all, but as soon as the Knight's soliloquy was over and the girls came on, sociology finished. Each seemed six feet tall, full-bodied, and light as air. What woman could dance more beautifully than these? And Plisetskaya materialized, her body arched forward, it seemed, and her legs and arms shot backward, like a speeding bow freed of the laws of physics. The audience seems to be under her feet, behind her back, over her head, watching every flicker of movement she makes as an infant watches its mother move.

The act is ending. The music stops. She turns to our box, and suddenly I remember that she will be dancing a special cadenza for us. She glances up and begins. The audience knows something unusual is on. A hum, a subdued roar of an oncoming cavalry shudders the house. Wild, noble, unbelievably concentrated inside herself and yet abandoned to a love of air and space, she greets all poets, and perhaps America, with a freed body.

The pleasure of the audience now is like a statement, and the seeming paradox of the Bolshoi is straightened out; there is a mood here different from that in any other place I saw in Russia: the archaism of the house and the classicism of the repertoire are really the forms in which people can simply face beauty, beauty without the measure of utility, cant, or rationalized social significance. Here you are Russian and here you are free, and all the rutted roads, the toilets that don't work, the moralizing posters, all progress and all decay are far, far away as this woman transcends the dialectic and the mortality of thought itself.

We cannot stay for the second act and in Plisetskaya's dressing room we are all, for some reason, kissing each other. And we are off in Galia's little car—from the Bolshoi, as it turns out, to the Bronx, a housing project where her painter friend lives—but it is necessary first to accept the jar of honey from the bear-hunting ex-pilot at the stage door and then to drop Voznesensky at his apartment because he is tired and needs sleep. And where has the pale writer gone to spend the night?

On the way out to the project the passport is suddenly discovered on the floor of the car; how it got there nobody can figure out. The buildings of the project are still under construction. They surround a vast open area which will be a park and is now a playground for bulldozers. A stripe of color across the building fronts is somehow encouraging in the night, a sign of the will to go beyond mere shelter. Galia, efficient as ever, knocks on a door two flights up and is greeted by a bewildered man holding on to his pants and blinking sleep out of his eyes. We flee down and finally stand on the sidewalk resolving to call out the painter's name in hopes he will hear. Modern mass housing must finally cure alcoholism; no drunk could pick out his own building from all the others. At last Galia recalls a house number. There at the head of the stairs is indeed a man awake, the painter, smiling, happy to see us again—for on a previous trip Yevtushenko had taken us here to see him. Now there are improvements, for while his parents still share the apartment he has a permanent girl friend and an additional room. We sit at the bare table surrounded by his immense canvases, drink vodka and brandy, eat salami, olives, potatoes, herring, and bread, and look at his work. He cannot exhibit publicly, but this hardly bothers him any more because he has an underground clientele. His pictures are massive and cryptic explosions of various shades of red and black, strange bloated men move through them cloaked like black-gowned priests surrounded by perfectly edible melons which, however, bleed. He eats, he drinks, he has a quite decent place to live in and an adoring girl and good friends among the poets, the scientists, the intellectuals. Compared to the last time we saw him he seems to have cast off his cares about government disapproval, not because it is no longer serious to him but because he has, perhaps, made his peace with the life he must lead—he will paint what is inside his spirit, and enjoy his food and his girl, and tomorrow will be what tomorrow will be. The perfect idiocy of artistic repression was never so vivid as in that room and in the laughing face of that Russian painter who could hardly bear to waste time by going to sleep at night. His blasting energy is there even in the way he chomps his herring. There is a challenge in this nearly bare room, and a ghastly thought: in the West, where everything in art is allowed, the artists feel unneeded by society, supercargo. Here, the repression is a mark of art's importance, otherwise why would government bother policing it? In which setting is the artist closer to reality?

We fly out. What a relief, like finally getting out of a six-thousand-mile-wide country full of Irishmen. They are, you know, a lot like the Irish when the Irish are just a little bit blasted. You never know what's going to come out of them next. Below, the clouds are closing over the plain of dead armies, the white birches bare, womanlike trees with tender skins, shivering in the snow. Europe soon, and the neon signs brightening the avenue, blazing shop windows full of beautiful things again, plenty. Plenty . . . and the blacks and the students hoisting strange flags on the statues, the magazines announcing revolution in five-color photos, cities on fire beside the green golf course, more bombs dropping on one Vietnam than on the whole earth in World War II, stereophonic sound in the new U.S. cars. Somewhere in Moscow that writer is standing in a hallway, wondering if he dare go home, and the Uzbeks are rebuilding after the earthquake, Yevtushenko is floating down a Siberian river on a raft, Solzhenitsyn's books are passed around in typescript, and in Chicago soon Allen Ginsberg will be humming his "O-o-o-om-m-m-m" to the enraged and astounded cops. The plane's compass steadily hangs on the "W" and thank God. But which way is man? Anywhere?

Possibly we are over Vitebsk now, Smolensk, Minsk, the old invasion path paved with forty million pairs of eyes violently closed; now Poland and Treblinka, Auschwitz, Berlin—the spinning earth should have splashed the sky bloody red by now, but everything is still so innocently blue up here, the dunning of propellers reassures, as though such dutiful precision cannot have come from a species altogether wedded to death. And indeed there are two Chinese across the aisle studying some papers and perfectly at ease, despite the murder in the air between Moscow and Peking. Is there still, beneath the polemics and the threats, an unadmitted commerce of a human kind? Or is there truly no fresh wind in any corner of the sky to blow away the fumes of fear we all breathe now, this terror of each other that will finally murder us all?

As we circle Warsaw, trying for a glimpse through the fog-wetted windows, the cabin so silent and orderly, the thought, for some reason, comes of *The Seagull*. And Chekhov spitting blood in the loneliness of Yalta, and writing those minimal and yet ultimate lines for Nina, the betrayed, suffering girl—". . . to endure. To be able to bear one's cross and have faith. I have faith. I'm not afraid of life." How terrible that seventy years later, seventy years of the most astonishing acquisition of knowledge in man's history, it is so very much harder to speak these lines without fatuousness on this planet.

[From Chapter V]

Lines from California

They meet for purchase or sale
    and to trace their bounds through rosebushes.

There is a catechism. What's your name, what
    do you do, how do you feel, and where you from?

Like people on a perpetual cruise, and the dead
    go overboard into a lawn. It's a deck,
    part of which is always on fire.

Anything inconsequential makes them serious.

Some teach parakeets to climb ladders; they also
    have Malted Milk Specialists.

Tragedy is when you lose your boat.

Life is a preparation for retirement.

The sun is good for business.

Al Jolson left a trust fund which pays
    to floodlight his tomb at night forever;
    even in death a man should have bills.

The second-largest industry is sporting goods.

To succeed as a woman you have to have a car.

California is Christianity plus the conveniences.

Driving from town to town one wonders what will
    happen if neon gas ever runs out; some may
    have to learn to read paint.

When a man admits failure he becomes a pedestrian.

Brotherhood is when two men have the same mother.

Sacrifice is a car sold at a ridiculous price.

Society is when people listen to classical music;
    or a Savings & Loan.

Law is order, Justice a decent return on money.

Progress is anything turning on and off by itself.

Beauty is teeth, deep skin, and the willingness.

Freedom is the right to live among your own kind.

A philosophy is a keen sense of land values
    and the patience to wait.

War is peace waged by other means.

They know they are the Future.

They are exceedingly well armed.

Bibliography

OF WORKS BY ARTHUR MILLER

Plays (*The date in parentheses is of the first production*)

That They May Win (1943), in *The Best One-Act Plays of 1944*, Margaret Mayorga, ed. New York: Dodd, Mead, 1945, pp. 45–59.

The Man Who Had All the Luck (1944), in *Cross-Section*, Edwin Seaver, ed. New York: L. B. Fischer, 1944, pp. 486–552. (This is a pre-production version of the play.)

All My Sons (1947), in *Collected Plays*. New York: Viking, 1957, pp. 57–127.

Death of a Salesman (1949), in *Collected Plays*, pp. 130–222.

An Enemy of the People (1950). New York: Viking, 1951. (Adaptation of Henrik Ibsen's play.)

The Crucible (1953), in *Collected Plays*, pp. 223–330.

A Memory of Two Mondays (1955), in *Collected Plays*, pp. 331–376.

A View from the Bridge (1955). New York: Viking, 1955.

A View from the Bridge (1956). Revised version; in *Collected Plays*, pp. 377–439.

After the Fall (1964). New York: Viking, 1964.

Incident at Vichy (1964). New York: Viking, 1965.

The Price (1968). New York: Viking, 1968.

Radio Plays

The Pussycat and the Expert Plumber Who Was a Man, in *One Hundred Non-Royalty Radio Plays,* William Kozlenko, ed. New York: Greenberg, 1941, pp. 20–30.

William Ireland's Confession, in *One Hundred Non-Royalty Radio Plays,* pp. 512–521.

Grandpa and the Statue, in *Radio Drama in Action,* Erik Barnouw, ed. New York: Farrar and Rinehart, 1945, pp. 267–281.

The Story of Gus, in *Radio's Best Plays,* Joseph Liss, ed. New York: Greenberg, 1947, pp. 303–319.

Fiction and Reportage

Situation Normal. New York: Reynal and Hitchcock, 1944.

Focus. New York: Reynal and Hitchcock, 1945.

The Misfits. New York: Viking, 1961.

I Don't Need You Any More, Stories by Arthur Miller. New York: Viking, 1967.

"Kidnapped," *Saturday Evening Post,* CCXLII (January 25, 1969), 40–42, 78–82.

In Russia. New York: Viking, 1969. (With Inge Morath.)

Articles

"Tragedy and the Common Man," *The New York Times,* February 27, 1949, II, pp. 1, 3.

"Arthur Miller on 'The Nature of Tragedy,'" *The New York Herald Tribune,* March 27, 1949, V, pp. 1, 2.

"Journey to 'The Crucible,'" *The New York Times,* February 8, 1953, II, p. 3.

"University of Michigan," *Holiday,* XIV (December 1953), 68–70, 128–143.

"A Modest Proposal for Pacification of the Public Temper," *Nation,* CLXXIX (July 3, 1954), 5–8.

"The American Theater," *Holiday,* XVII (January 1955), 90–104.

"A Boy Grew in Brooklyn," *Holiday,* XVII (March 1955), 54–55, 117–124.

"On Social Plays," Preface to *A View from the Bridge.* New York: Viking, 1955, pp. 1–15.

Untitled comment, *World Theatre,* IV (Autumn 1955), 40–41.

"The Family in Modern Drama," *The Atlantic Monthly,* CXCVII (April 1956), 35–41.

"Global Dramatist," *The New York Times,* July 21, 1957, II, p. 1.

"The Writer's Position in America," *Coastlines,* II (Autumn, 1957), 38–40.

"The Shadow of the Gods," *Harper's,* CCXVII (August 1958), 35–43.

"Bridge to a Savage World," *Esquire,* L (October 1958), 185–190.

"The Playwright and the Atomic World," *Tulane Drama Review,* V (June 1961), 3–20.

"The Bored and the Violent," *Harper's,* CCXXV (November 1962), 50–56.

"On Recognition," *Michigan Quarterly Review,* II (Autumn 1963), 213–220.

"Lincoln Repertory Theatre—Challenge and Hope," *The New York Times,* January 19, 1964, II, pp. 1, 3.

"Our Guilt for the World's Evil," *The New York Times Magazine,* January 3, 1965, pp. 10–11, 48.

"The Role of P.E.N.," *Saturday Review,* XLIX (June 4, 1966), 16–17.

"It Could Happen Here—And Did," *The New York Times,* April 30, 1967, II, p. 17.

"Arthur Miller Talks," *Michigan Quarterly Review,* VI (Summer, 1967), 153–184.

"Broadway from O'Neill to Now," *The New York Times,* December 21, 1969, pp. 1, 7.

Interviews

Schumach, Murray, "Arthur Miller Grew Up in Brooklyn," *The New York Times,* February 6, 1949, II, pp. 1, 3.

Wolfert, Ira, "Arthur Miller, Playwright in Search of His Identity," *New York Herald Tribune,* January 25, 1953, IV, p. 3.

Griffin, John and Alice, "Arthur Miller Discusses *The Crucible,*" *Theatre Arts,* XXXVII (October 1953), 33–34. (The interview introduces the published play, pp. 35–67)

Samachson, Dorothy and Joseph, in *Let's Meet the Theatre.* New York: Abelard-Schuman, 1954, pp. 15–20.

United States House of Representatives, Committee on Un-American Activities, Investigation of the Unauthorized Use of United States Passports, Part 4, June 21, 1956. Washington: United States Government Printing Office, November, 1956. ("Interview" is not exactly the word for this item.)

Gelb, Philip, "Morality and Modern Drama," *Educational Theatre Journal,* X (October 1958), 190–202.

Allsop, Kenneth, "A Conversation with Arthur Miller," *Encounter,* XIII (July 1959), 58–60.

Brandon, Henry, "The State of the Theatre: A Conversation with Arthur Miller," *Harper's,* CCXXI (November 1960), 63–69.

Gelb, Barbara, "Question: 'Am I My Brother's Keeper?' " *The New York Times,* November 29, 1964, II, pp. 1, 3.

Feron, James, "Miller in London to See 'Crucible,' " *The New York Times,* January 24, 1965, p. 82.

Morley, Sheridan, "Miller on Miller," *Theatre World,* LXI (March 1965), 4, 8.

Gruen, Joseph, "Portrait of the Playwright at Fifty," *New York,* October 24, 1965, pp. 12–13.

Carlisle, Olga, and Styron, Rose, "The Art of the Theatre II: Arthur Miller, an Interview," *Paris Review,* X (Summer 1966), 61–98.

A Bibliography of works about Arthur Miller will be found in the Viking Critical Library editions of *Death of a Salesman,* and *The Crucible,* both volumes edited by Gerald Weales, to whom grateful acknowledgment is made for his substantial contribution to the bibliography printed here.

Reify